Dedicated to myself, because I did this for me.

PROLOGUE

THE FOREST IS DEAD. Bark peels off tree trunks like decaying skin. Branches brittle enough to crack in the wind spiderweb over the full moon. Its broken light barely reaches the forest floor. All is silent, as it should be. Then in the stillness, a sound: an inhalation, sharp and pained. Footsteps follow, the quick one-two of someone running.

It is a girl, sprinting through the forest. Blood blooms from a wound in her thigh. In her wake the air grows cold, the fog chills, and a layer of frost chases her feet. It spreads, faster, until it paves the way before her and her footfalls shatter the crystals. Then, the scent of decay. Her pursuer is closing in.

The girl tries to run faster as she darts beneath the blackened branches of the trees. She cannot; she is confined by her dream, incapable of taking control. Her pursuer is gaining. She hears exhalations of breath, steady despite the pace of the chase. She looks to the moon, bright with the reflected light of the sun, for help, but the moon only laughs. She is slowing, unable to match the preternatural pace of the dark presence. It is heavy, looming.

It is right behind her.

PART I

1

THE DREAM LINGERED as Evie blinked awake.

Plagued by the same dream for as long as she could remember, she used to think it was important. As a child, she scribbled the scene into journal after journal. Later, she read everything by Freud and Jung, trying to find a reason for it all. The forest. The dark presence. The moon. She learned about lucid dreaming and chose totems, triggers, spent countless nights chanting herself to sleep, bought hypnosis tapes to play under her pillow, all in an effort to nudge her conscious mind into the ether of her unconscious.

As she grew up, she saw how silly that was. Dreams were only dreams, not worlds to wade through. She stopped wondering why her unconscious tormented her with the same scene and instead, she wondered why she never dreamed of her mother. She was in there somewhere, Evie knew. A memory lost, a collection of neurons no longer firing, but there, transformable through dreams into a face, a touch, a feeling. But her mother never emerged from the forest. Her voice never sounded over the breath of Evie's pursuer to guide her to safety. Her likeness never appeared over the face of the moon to guard her daughter from above. And so this morning, like every other morning for years, Evie forgot the dream.

It was March in Scotland, marking the end of a long, dark winter and the start of longer, brighter days. On the Summer Solstice, the sun would set at midnight, bathing the Georgian architecture of Edinburgh's New Town in a warm glow all night long. Today, though, the air seeping into Evie's flat was brisk. She dressed in layers and skipped the mirror, knowing her brown curls would be limp, her freckles faded from sunny days spent in the campus library, her blue eyes underlined by dark half-moons from late nights studying. Library bookshelves didn't care what she looked like, though, and her favorite table in the corner between W and X rarely saw other students. One hastily brewed mug of Earl Grey tea later, she was out the door, a tote of art history textbooks weighing her down.

Outside, the cold transformed her breath into crystals and her neighbors walked hunched against the wind. Only Biscuit, the orange cat who belonged to nobody and everybody on William Street, seemed unfazed by the chill. He rubbed against Evie's legs, anticipating the treat she'd been too rushed to remember.

"Sorry, Biscuit." She stooped down to scratch behind his ears, admiring his eyes — one blue, one brown. "Double snacks tomorrow, I promise." Biscuit meowed.

Leaving Biscuit behind, Evie hurried on, past her favorite café, past her William Street neighbors who met her half-wave with a half-smile. They knew her. She knew them. That was enough. After six years in Edinburgh, Evie was comfortable in her neighborhood, which was why, as she waited for the light to change at the Lothian Road crossing, the distinctly uncomfortable feeling of being watched was suddenly apparent.

Accompanying this awareness was the strange sensation of experiencing, more than seeing, the smile of a young boy in her mind. At the same time, she was compelled to stand on her tiptoes to scan the other side of the road. For whom or what, she didn't know, and as soon as she rose, the light changed. The crowd of commuters around her moved en masse. A city bus honked. A group of tourists argued loudly about which way to go. Evie went straight.

At Grassmarket she headed toward Candlemaker's Row, the steep hill that would take her to the University of Edinburgh campus. At the junction, it happened again. The boy's smile, the urge to look, to move, to seek. Without thinking, Evie turned around and went back across Grassmarket, this time to one of the narrow Medieval closes nestled between buildings. She climbed the close's stairs, emerging at the top of the Royal Mile with Edinburgh Castle behind her.

The smile flashed again, accompanied this time by a childish laugh and the twinkle of playful green eyes. Evie was momentarily transported, almost childlike herself, and somewhere in the depths of her memory, the boy's name began to form. She squeezed her eyes shut, desperate to recall more.

A tartan-clad tour guide sidled by her, enveloping her in the group of French students he herded toward the castle. They pushed past, jostling her, and the boy's eyes closed. His laugh flitted away on the wind. His smile vanished, leaving Evie feeling confused and ridiculous. She shook her head and then her shoulders and then her whole upper body to exorcise whatever had prompted her behavior, then set her sights back on campus, heading down the Royal Mile toward World's End Pub. Nothing befell her for the rest of the walk.

She tried not to dwell on the odd experience, but part of her buzzed with excitement at the notion it could have been a memory. This would be remarkable, as Evie could not recall anything from the first years of her life. That time was a void, utterly empty, like the nothingness of nothing from which the Big Bang had sprung. All lives were like that, Evie supposed, but they emerged from nothing at birth. They didn't exist and then they did, starting at zero. Evie felt that she had appeared at four years old, having simply skipped years one through three. This always troubled her, but never seemed to concern anyone else.

"There's nothing to remember," her father often said. Then, taking a sip from the mug that never left his hand, "Only things to forget."

This non-answer used to infuriate Evie, though she quickly learned not to expect anything useful from Richard Lennon. Instead, she went to her school counselor in middle school, who was equally unhelpful.

"I don't think it's unusual," she said gently. "Most people don't remember their early childhood." Noting Evie's frustration at this explanation, she added, "But I'm not a psychologist."

So, Evie found a psychologist.

"Don't tell me it's normal," she pleaded. "It's not that I simply can't remember things. It's as if I didn't *exist*." It only took a few sessions — three, to be exact, the amount that Evie could pay for with money she'd pilfered from her father over the years — for the psychologist to reach a conclusion.

"Our caregivers explain our world to us in our formative years," he said. "But you never knew your mother. Your father is emotionally absent. No one told you your own story." He shrugged sympathetically. "Learn to accept it."

But Evie couldn't just accept that she would never read the first chapter in the book of her life. That chapter might tell her what happened to her mother. It might explain why her father refused to speak of her. And now, she suspected it might reveal who the boyish smile and green eyes belonged to.

As she walked through Old Town, Evie strained to remember something more from those blank early years. As usual, nothing emerged but her earliest memory at four years old in which she stood on an enormous leather chair in her father's study, reaching for a shelf too high for her little arms.

"What are you doing, Evie?" Her father had rushed into the study. Gentle hands guided her safely back to the floor.

"I want my book. The black book with the gold tree."

At this, the paternal protection vanished. "We have no such book, Evie," her father said. "Who told you that we did?"

She'd plopped into the chair, its leather worn and soft on the seat and arms. Pulling her knees close to her chest, she said, pouting, "My mother."

"That book doesn't exist. Do you understand me?"

"It does. It's mine."

"Listen to me." He knelt before her. "Forget the book. Forget her."

Her. It was the only way Richard ever referred to Evie's mother. As a child, she begged and pleaded for him to give her a name, as a teenager she screamed and swore. The outcome was always the same, which was nothing, not even a birth certificate bearing her mother's name. It was, conveniently, lost, as was knowledge of the actual day of Evie's birth —

each December, Richard wished his daughter a happy birthday on a different day.

Evie didn't care about her birthday. She cared about her mother, but with no information from the only person who could provide it, she was left to speculate. On good days, Evie believed her mother was alive, forced away by circumstances beyond her control. On bad days, Evie believed her mother was dead.

Regardless, that vague memory of the book with a golden tree told her nothing. She wasn't even sure the book was real; she'd searched her father's study when she was older, tearing through his eclectic collection of books on mythology, the witches of Salem and Triora, cathedral architecture, stone circles, Hieronymus Bosch, and more. She never found the book she'd wanted so desperately as a child. Eventually, the idea of it disappeared into the void, along with her real birthday and her mother.

A church bell tolled nearby, pulling Evie back to the present and reminding her of the time. She hurried across George Square to the campus library. Whatever the reason for her odd behavior that morning, it had cost her a precious twenty minutes to work on her dissertation, *Who was Christ? One man's face across centuries*, before attending a lecture led by her mentor, Professor Atkinson.

She nodded to the young woman manning the desk in the library, making a beeline for it when the woman waved her over.

"That new book you wanted has been returned," she told Evie. "I haven't put it away yet. I figured I'd see you today." She pulled *Hieronymus Bosch: The Paintings - Complete Edition* from a caddy behind her.

"You figured right," Evie said, smiling. "I'll sign it out. Thank you."

With the Bosch book under her arm, Evie settled into her predictably empty table between W and X. Her dissertation had nothing to do with Hieronymus Bosch; it was purely personal interest that kept her checking the library for any new books on the Flemish Renaissance painter. His otherworldly creatures and alienesque landscapes stood out among the typical religious themes that ruled so many artists' paintings from the Renaissance, which intrigued Evie. That, and she felt a deeply personal connection to his work — like he wanted to tell the world something through his paintings, and Evie was the only one willing to listen. She knew how that sounded, but the feeling had stuck with her ever since she first saw an image of Bosch's *Garden of Earthly Delights* triptych in one of her father's books as a child.

Hieronymus Bosch: The Paintings — Complete Edition was new to the University of Edinburgh library as of a few weeks ago, but when Evie went to retrieve it after a weekend trip to the Highlands, it had already been checked out. She lifted the cover now, curious to see which of her peers had snagged it before her. She didn't recognize the name on the slip card, written in elegant, looping cursive: *Charlie Rutherford.*

The boy in his entirety flashed before her: the smile, the eyes, the laugh, a shock of copper blonde hair, small hands holding a sphere of sparkling light, there and gone like the flashbulb of an old camera.

Except this time, he didn't disappear. The flashbulb produced a photograph, crisp and clear. Evie could envision the boy like he was next to her, her sole companion at the table between W and X. Like she had known him once and could recall him fondly.

Like he was a memory.

2

CHARLIE WAS five when he looked out the window and saw a weary Adena Callidora trudging up the moonstone path to his family's home with a girl in one arm and a book in the other. He shouted for his parents, then trailed them into the courtyard where his father swiped an arm through the affrim to open the gate outside. Hidden behind a column, Charlie watched the Arbiter of Callidora collapse before his parents.

Someone dangerous was coming for her, Adena said. Desperate to ensure safety for her daughter and the book, she begged Liam and Juliette Rutherford to deliver both to the girl's father. It struck Charlie that a book could be as important as a child, held just as tightly, handed over with just as much reticence. But handed over they were, along with very specific, very unusual instructions on how to reach the girl's father.

Adena left. Nobody saw her again.

The girl was frightened, not only of being in an unfamiliar place with unfamiliar people, but of whatever had prompted her mother's behavior, which she couldn't articulate. Juliette comforted her as best she could, pattering down the hall when the girl cried at night, pulling starlight from the sky. And when the girl cried so quietly that only

Charlie heard, it was he who ran to her, his little hands summoning starlight into a comforting orb. Though, he wasn't very good at that yet.

Only the book calmed the girl, but she wouldn't, or couldn't, explain what lay beneath the black cover emblazoned with a golden tree. Nobody could figure it out, in fact. The language inside was indecipherable, all swirling loops and symbols, and Adena had provided no context outside its importance as a family heirloom. Still, Charlie pretended to read from it, making up stories as he turned the gold-tinged pages until the girl fell asleep and his starlight orb died out.

But a solitary glimmer remained in the darkness; a thread, thin and silver, unfurling in the space between Charlie on the floor and the girl on the bed. He blinked and it vanished, now as invisible as the millions of others that wove the world.

One day the girl was gone, too. Charlie's parents told their children to forget about her; she was safe, somewhere only they knew existed. They told them to forget about the book; someone dangerous wanted it and it should never be mentioned again. And they told them to forget about Adena, to pretend that the powerful Callidora Arbiter, descendant of an Original, had never appeared with her secrets.

Charlie, Marcus, and Serena didn't forget, not at first. They stayed up at night, whispering that the girl had been taken to a land beyond the sea. They hounded their mother, peppering her with questions that she answered with sighs. They snuck into their father's study, searching for clues that didn't exist. They marveled over the strange symbols that Charlie, obsessed with what he'd named the Tree Book, had copied down from memory.

Eventually, time transformed childlike wonder into something else. Marcus became unimaginative and obedient, more concerned with pleasing their father than solving childhood mysteries. Serena fell wholeheartedly into her empathic abilities, shifting concern from the girl in her past to the people in her present. Only Charlie continued to obsess. Where had the girl gone? What was in her book? Most importantly, was she safe?

In his teenage years, Charlie channeled his fixation on the girl into a fixation on history. He read every book in the Benclair Archives, skimming for a whisper of the Tree Book. He sought the State's oldest citizens, seeking answers in local legends. He showed the handwritten symbols to linguists, desperate for someone to recognize them. These endeavors told him two things. First, that his parents were right. It seemed nobody but the Rutherfords knew about Adena Callidora's secrets.

Second, that studying history was an unacceptable pursuit in his father's eyes. Liam Rutherford expected both his sons to exhibit an unwavering desire to succeed him as Arbiter one day at the expense of their own dreams. Naturally charismatic and competitive, inclined toward politics, law, and Alicrat, Marcus fell in line. Unwilling to walk the path his father laid, Charlie did not. Instead, after completing his Third Libellum of compulsory study, and tired of wondering about the girl's safety, he forged his own.

Telling nobody of his plans, Charlie traveled to Ulla, crossed the Empty Fields, and stood before the Eternal Tree. It was the Invernal Sun Day, after all, and hadn't Adena explained the journey was only possible on Sun Days? He remembered the exact instructions he'd overheard while hiding in the courtyard so many years ago. He knew his parents had followed those instructions and returned, bewildered.

Still, he didn't believe it until the light took him.

He emerged in a place he would later learn was called Rosslyn Chapel, where he came face to face with an eccentrically dressed man. Entirely nonplussed with the sudden materialization of a person before him, the man introduced himself as Professor Atkinson, peered at Charlie with one eyebrow raised, and asked, "Are you a Rutherford, by chance?"

As he escorted Charlie to the library of his nearby Rosslyn Castle residence, Professor Atkinson explained his tradition of waiting inside the Chapel on what he called the Solstices and Equinoxes. "I consider it my duty," he said, "to welcome visitors and guide them on this side. Though besides you, it's only been your parents and that frightened young girl, years ago." He swung open a door as he spoke.

Charlie gasped. Before him, in floor-to-ceiling shelving stuffed with books, was a whole new world of history to explore. He was momentarily speechless, but then the professor's words hit. He whirled around, eyes wide. "She's here?" he asked. "She's safe?"

"Here in Edinburgh, entirely safe," the professor said. He crossed the library to climb a ladder that leaned against one of the walls. At the top, he groped around the highest shelf. "And thriving in her studies, I might add!"

"She remembers nothing?"

"Nothing," Professor Atkinson confirmed, descending the ladder with a book. He handed it to Charlie. "Here you are, then. Your parents asked me to keep this safe. I assume you've come to take it back?"

Astounded, Charlie paged through the Tree Book. When he didn't respond, Professor Atkinson added, quietly, "Have you come to take *her* back?"

Charlie looked up. He hadn't thought that far. Just finding her was a fantasy, something to dream about with the understanding it may never happen. Of course he longed to see her, to hug her, to know if she felt that silver thread of connection. Part of him longed to bring her back, too, but he desired more deeply to keep her safe. There was only one way to ensure that.

"She should stay here," Charlie told the professor. "The danger Adena feared might still be out there, looking for her. Looking for this, perhaps." He turned another page of the Tree Book, brow furrowed. The language was no less confounding now than it was when he was a child. "I don't suppose you can read it?"

"I'm afraid I never learned Alterra Lingua," Professor Atkinson said. Smiling at Charlie's surprise, he added, "Her father told me what it's called. That's all he knew about it. Strangely, though, there's another book in this world written in the same script."

This excited Charlie, but the professor was quick to squash any hope. "Our Voynich Manuscript may be more widely known here than your Tree Book is at home, but I'm afraid it's no better understood," he said. "Centuries of scholars have failed to translate it."

Still, Charlie was eager to announce this information to his family upon his return on the next Sun Day — the Spring Equinox, according to the professor. Their awe at his bravery would outweigh any lingering anger at his wordless departure, and they, like him, would jump at the chance to finally decode the Tree Book's secrets! So he hoped, naively. Though Juliette softened upon hearing the girl was safe, Liam could not abide Charlie's disobedience and swiftly cut him out from Arbiter consideration.

So it was, in a way, a success.

Charlie turned to his siblings for admiration, but they, too, disappointed him. Marcus refused to display the respect Charlie thought the discovery deserved. Serena just smiled, accepting the incredible information and claiming that she sometimes dreamed about people from a different vibrational plane. What Charlie described must be, simply, that.

Whatever or wherever it was, Liam forbade Charlie to return. And so, he returned on the very next Sun Day to stay longer, and again, staying longer. Professor Atkinson funded Charlie's travel throughout the area known as Europe, securing him seats in interesting lectures at prestigious universities, and Charlie acquired knowledge equivalent to multiple degrees. And somehow, as the years passed, he refrained from seeking her out.

At first, he avoided Edinburgh entirely. But the invisible string between them felt like it was contracting, luring him toward her in a way that was becoming impossible to ignore. To satiate this, he started venturing to the National Galleries or the University's library when the professor informed him that she was out of the city. He'd glance at a painting, grab a book, then spend the rest of the day straining his Alicrat across Edinburgh, hoping to sense her lingering energy.

That angst aside, Charlie was content with his double life. His prolonged absences from Benclair only made Juliette that much happier to have him home. His siblings became satisfyingly curious after all, listening raptly to tales of airplanes and computers over bottles of vocat at the Golden Pec. Only Liam maintained his status quo, upholding a silence that lasted until Charlie's most recent visit home.

"Tensions are rising in Maliter," he told Charlie, standing before the window in his tower study, hands clasped behind his back, gazing out at The Fern. Strange, Charlie thought, for his father to broach a discussion on politics with him. Stranger still after the years of silence.

"It's only a matter of time before they make their move elsewhere," Liam said. "Iristell, perhaps. Teraur." He spun around. "Benclair."

Dread slinked down Charlie's neck. He was aware of the issues in

Maliter, the persistent rise of a vicious cult that abused Alicrat and went against every foundational rule of the Normalex. Aware, yet far removed.

Liam continued. "Their rise began after Adena's disappearance. I've suspected for years, but now I'm certain. It was they who hunted her. Nobody else would be delusional enough. They wanted that book, which means it contains something they need, which means it contains something we need to know."

"I'll translate it," Charlie said immediately. "Somehow. I can ask —"

"What you can do, Charles, is bring her back. She might remember something useful if she comes home."

The dread crept, cold and heavy, across Charlie's shoulders, down his back. "Father, she'll be in danger here."

"Only our family knows she exists."

"She doesn't know *we* exist! She won't believe —"

"Make her believe." Placing his hands on the table, Liam leaned forward. "I should have asked for this years ago, before it was so urgent, but I..." Incapable of admitting to his petulant behavior, he just cleared his throat "Marcus doesn't know the destination like you do. Your mother won't dare make the journey again, and I'm needed here. You need to do this. Can you do this, Charles?"

Charlie would look back and see how expertly his father framed the demand. But in that moment, he only heard that he was needed for his knowledge. He only saw the worry that darkened his father's eyes, tightened his lips, erasing his typical Arbiter haughtiness. He only understood that it needed to be done.

On the Winter Solstice at midnight, Charlie emerged in the dark dampness of Rosslyn Chapel. Professor Atkinson stood to offer his usual warm greeting. Then he met Charlie's eyes, and his demeanor went as cold as the Chapel's air.

"You've come to take her back." Not a question, this time. Lacking any loyalty to Liam Rutherford, the professor did not appreciate Charlie's change of heart. "Just what is it you plan to do?" he demanded. "Push her through the portal?"

"I won't force her," Charlie said calmly. "I'll show her the Tree

Book. I'll tell her about Adena. If she wants to return, Professor, who are we to stop her?"

Eventually Professor Atkinson conceded, begrudgingly, on the condition that he broker their first meeting. "After her Art of Manuscripts class," he said. "Not only is she entirely at ease in my lectures, we have a session on the Voynich Manuscript in March, a week before the Spring Equinox. Fitting, I daresay."

This gave Charlie two months to plan his approach. He would let her speak first, giving her a chance to remember him — or not. It gave him two months to practice his speech. He would be measured, believable. And it gave him two months to ruminate, to weigh the safety of his home and family against the safety of the person he wanted to protect most.

Edinburgh was hectic on that brisk March morning, full of visitors craning for a picture of the castle and the locals who pushed past them. They all thrummed the same, dull note, and Charlie plodded heavily amongst them. So depressing was their energy that when he sensed her, it was unmistakable. Profound. Her energy was a vibrant chord, one note as foreign as the people around him, the other as familiar as the hills of Benclair. It pulsed through that ever-present thread between them, straight into Charlie, and before he could stop himself, he traced it. She was across the street, waiting for the light to change.

But now was not the time.

He forced himself away, onto King's Stables Road and toward Grassmarket, where he darted up one of the narrow staircases that spat him out at the base of Castle Hill. There, he paused to calibrate his Alicrat, searching for her without looking, intending to confirm she'd moved away from him. Instead, he found her again, now at the top of the same stairs he'd taken. The energy between them intensified, an incessant buzz, unbelievably strong after two decades.

Unable to stop himself, Charlie looked.

Long curls the color of coffee beans danced around her face, kicked up by the constant breeze at the top of Castle Hill, framing her like

Botticelli's Venus. Clear blue eyes looked around, just as bright and curious as they'd been as a child. Her face was delicate, with whispers of Adena, though she had a beauty all her own. She was remarkable.

Charlie relished the sight of her for an indeterminable moment before she was rendered invisible by a passing tour group. When he could see her again, her brows were knitted with confusion. She shook herself vigorously, then pivoted on her heel, setting off with purpose. He watched her disappear down the Royal Mile until she was a dot in the crowd, until, just like when they were children, she was gone.

3

AFTER PUTTING the final touches on her dissertation, Evie slipped into a full lecture hall where Professor Atkinson was already addressing the class. He winked, letting her know he'd seen her slink into the room.

Six years ago, it was the professor who had swept into the lecture hall late — Introduction to Renaissance Art, then — all Harris Tweed and contrasting Liberty prints, grinning widely. "What is art?" he'd asked, eyebrows raised over his tortoiseshell glasses. Then, without waiting for a response, "Art is a window into humanity's collective heart. Oh, you can read books to learn about history, but only through art can you *feel* history."

That was enough for Evie. She was hooked, not only on the subject, but on Professor Atkinson's perspective. Over the next six years of lectures, papers, visits to the National Gallery, and eventually, invitations to his Rosslyn Castle library to parse through his collection of historic books, he'd gone from a favorite professor of Evie's to a trusted mentor in her field of study.

He stood before the class now, brimming with excitement, and clapped the lecture hall to attention as Evie settled in. "Today, we bid farewell to our study of the Lindisfarne Gospels," he announced, "and begin a new topic: the Voynich Manuscript."

Evie sat forward in her seat. As with Bosch, she was fascinated by the Voynich Manuscript. Though unlike with Bosch, she couldn't articulate what drove her interest. Her father had no books that referenced it. The academic lore accompanying the manuscript was certainly alluring, but there was something more, almost instinctual, that had Evie borderline obsessed with the mysterious book.

Professor Atkinson dimmed the lights. An image of an open book was projected onto the screen. On the first page was a drawing of an unusual plant: a primary stalk with six leaves branched into two secondary stalks, each bearing a flowering head reminiscent of a blue sunflower. Unrecognizable, uninterpreted text was scrawled at the top and also covered most of the other page.

"The Voynich Manuscript," Professor Atkinson said. "Technically speaking, it is an illustrated, handwritten codex on vellum. But as any scholar will tell you, it is almost certainly much more than that. The problem is, we do not know *what* it is."

A new slide appeared, then another, and another, dozens of slides displaying floral imagery in quick succession. "One hundred and twelve folios displaying botanical images. Most of them unidentified," the professor said. Pages of crudely drawn stars and Zodiac images replaced the flowers. "Twenty-one folios containing astronomical drawings, including depictions of Zodiac constellations."

Pages of bizarre circular diagrams came next. "Thirteen cosmological folios, including this one," he said. He paused on a slide showing a large parchment that, when folded, fit within the confines of the book, but when unfolded, created a page six times larger than the others. Drawn upon it were nine orbs: eight around the periphery and a bigger one in the middle. This oversized page was Evie's favorite. It was no more perplexing than the rest of the book, but always made her feel like she was on the verge of a major discovery when she looked at it.

Professor Atkinson completed the summary with drawings of roots, leaves, and apothecary jars, followed by twenty-two pages full of text, uninterrupted by any imagery. At this, the entire class leaned back in their seats, stupefied.

"The manuscript's language, which contains approximately 35,000 words with no discernible etymology, is unknown," the professor said.

He stepped away from the podium to pace the length of the lecture hall, indicating the start of the dramatics he was famous for on campus. "Who wrote such a thing? Who devised this unusual language, and for what purpose?"

Another slide appeared, but it wasn't of the Voynich Manuscript. Rather, the images shown looked like someone's attempts to copy the manuscript's language and style of drawing. "This is the work of Giovanni Fontana, a 15th century Italian engineer," the professor said. "Oddly similar, no? Does this indicate authorship, or inspiration? We may never know, as the first *confirmed* mention of the manuscript comes two centuries after Fontana's life. In 1639..."

As he continued, the slides returned to images from the Voynich Manuscript, shifting between astronomical curiosities and odd plants. Eventually, the very first image filled the screen once more.

Seraphille, commonly known as the sun plant.

Evie whirled around. She'd heard *sera-fill* clearly, as if it had been spoken directly in her ear, but the students behind her were rapt with attention toward the professor. Confused, she turned back to the plant on the page. She stared hard at it, trying to summon the voice again. It had sounded so familiar... It didn't return. The screen flipped to a new image. Those, too, were silent.

She replayed the voice in her head for the rest of the lecture. Had she seen the plant before? The imagery in the Voynich Manuscript was not exactly drawn well, so it was hard to say what a lifelike version might look like. Had she simply heard the word once and it happened to resurface, unrelated to the image on the page? No, she knew now, just as surely as she knew that Bosch was a Flemish Renaissance painter, that the plant in the Voynich Manuscript was indeed a seraphille. Then there was the voice itself. Something — one of those dormant neurons that refused to inform her dreams, maybe — told Evie it was her mother's voice.

"...which brings us to the early 20th century," Professor Atkinson was saying, "when Wilfrid Voynich came into possession of the manuscript, giving it the name we know today. It now sits in Yale University's Beinecke Library, where it continues to confound academics. And that is time!" He grinned at the collective disappointed groan, promising the class they would revisit the manuscript next week.

Evie slowly gathered her books as the lecture hall emptied around her. Only when the door closed behind the last student did she notice Professor Atkinson beckoning her forward.

"Is everything alright, Evie?" he asked, frowning as she joined him at the podium. "I noticed you drifting as I spoke of the manuscript's provenance. I know you've been looking forward to this lecture. Was it not compelling?"

"It was," Evie said. "I just...I have a strange question, professor."

Hearing her tone, Professor Atkinson straightened up. "I actually have a rather strange question for you, too." He paused, seeming to consider something. "Why don't you go first?"

Feeling silly, Evie said, "Do you know what a seraphille is?"

It was as if she spoke them into existence. A forest of them exploded into her mind, towering over her like trees, sunlight passing through their wide, blue petals. There was something else, too...a hand clutching hers, flowing blonde curls, the glint of a blue eye... The eye blinked, and it was green. The seraphilles disappeared, but there was the boy again, his entire face this time, youthful and full and smiling.

Just like the flashes that morning, a compulsion followed. Something had risen Evie onto her tiptoes at the Lothian Road crossing, pulled her across Grassmarket to Castle Hill, and now, something compelled her to turn around.

At the top of the lecture hall stairs stood a man, tall and well-dressed in a tweed jacket, with reddish blonde hair. He started down the stairs eagerly, then slowed, composing himself, seeming to force a calmer demeanor.

Evie glanced at Professor Atkinson. He'd not said a word, but was clearly unperturbed by the stranger. Instead, he was looking at Evie with an expression she couldn't quite place. His eyes welled with tears yet crinkled at the corners from his smile. Not quite happy, not quite sad, he seemed somehow moved by the stranger, anticipating Evie's reaction.

The man stopped before her. There were those eyes again, a patch-work of green underscored by faint smile lines that hadn't been there when he was a boy. The youthful fullness of his face had settled into an attractive angularity, too, but there was no mistaking him.

Still, Evie's whisper was a half statement, half question. "I know you?"

The lecture hall, already quiet, stilled entirely for one long blink of an eye, one drawn out intake of breath, one last, lingering moment before another world collided into Evie's.

"My name is Charlie Rutherford," the man said. He spoke with measured confidence. "It's wonderful to see you again, Evie."

4

THE TAXI TAKING Evie to Rosslyn Castle slowed in the Bruntsfield traffic. Stone façades crept past in the setting sun; cafés closing for the day and bars opening for the night. Students trudged home after a long week of study and parents hurried out of Waitrose doors, their arms heavy with groceries, children trailing behind. A little girl held out a hand to her mother, who smiled and scooped her into her free arm. Evie turned away from the window. The taxi sped up.

The driver dropped her off near Rosslyn Castle's gatehouse and politely refused her money — Professor Atkinson had prepaid the fare. The *crunch* of gravel under the tires faded as he backed out, leaving Evie alone beneath the portico, where she remained for a long minute.

Rosslyn Castle lay ahead, its pink stone darkened by the dampness of a Scottish evening. Smoke curled from the chimney, lights were on in the foyer and the sitting room. It looked as it always did, except now, there were secrets inside. Maybe they were within Charlie, who'd claimed he had something to show Evie in the professor's library. Maybe they'd been in the castle all along, sitting on a shelf too high to reach or trapped beneath a floorboard like her memories.

Charlie opened the front door before she had a chance to knock.

"I'm glad you decided to come," he said, taking her coat and hanging it in an adjacent closet.

"You seem rather comfortable here," Evie noted.

"Professor Atkinson graciously allows me to stay here when I visit Edinburgh."

"Visit from where, exactly?"

Charlie smiled slightly. "I'll get to that."

"Charles and I are old acquaintances," Professor Atkinson said unhelpfully, entering the foyer from the sitting room. He greeted Evie with substantially less pomp than she was accustomed to, then took her hand in his and gave it a grandfatherly pat. "I won't be accompanying you into the library, Evie," he said. "You shall find me in the sitting room when you are done, where I promise to answer all your questions. Though, I suspect you will only have one."

He nodded to Charlie, then gave Evie the same look she'd noted in the lecture hall, a sort of resigned, sorrowful smile. Unease clenching her stomach, she followed Charlie to the library.

There, her unease was momentarily forgotten as she breathed in the familiar scent of history: parchment, leather, and dust. The Rosslyn Castle books had been bought, gifted, or otherwise curated by Professor Atkinson and his St. Clair ancestors for centuries, as evidenced by the titles; John Locke's *On the Reasonableness of Christianity* sat next to a tattered spine bearing the name *Nostradamus*. Others had no titles at all, holding poetry or musings from various unknown authors. Evie had parsed through them all at some point. If whatever Charlie wanted to show her was in the library, it was unlikely she'd not already seen it.

She was silent as he climbed up a ladder, reaching for something on the top shelf. She was silent as he descended the ladder with a book. She was silent as he closed his eyes before her, readying himself. He placed the book on a small table between them and her unease returned tenfold.

The book was thick, slightly taller and wider than a standard sheet of paper, its cover made of soft, black leather. A large tree was embossed in gold on the front. Spanning the bottom were twisted roots from which a trunk and branches grew. Toward the top, the branches cradled a sphere filled with clouds and heavenly rays of light. The rest of the branches curled around the spine and onto the back. There was no title, no author's name, no indication as to what lay inside.

Evie knew two things immediately. The book was ancient, impossibly so, and the book was hers. But it was an old knowing, buried under years of being told to forget, and it emerged in a slow, hazy way.

Without taking his eyes off Evie, Charlie leaned over and carefully lifted the cover like it was an entity that did not want to be disturbed.

Evie gasped. The text inside was written with the same symbols as those in the Voynich Manuscript, perhaps even by the same hand. There were no drawings, though, only words, arranged into distinct paragraphs like stanzas. Charlie turned a page. The gold branches from the cover spilled inside onto the new page, twining around the stanzas. Another page turned, this time by Evie's hand, and another, and another, until she was swiping through with a sudden lack of restraint or regard for its old age. She flipped through every page until she closed the back cover, turned to Charlie, and announced, "This book is mine."

Her words shifted something in the fabric of the library. There was no obvious noise or disturbance, yet the room filled with a profound energy, impossible to comprehend, impossible to ignore. On instinct, she clutched the book to her chest like she was late to class and needed to sprint across campus. The book seemed to clutch back, memories wrapping around her like arms, pulling her into her own past.

Glowing orbs of light illuminate the golden tree and a cascade of blonde curls as gentle hands tuck Evie into bed. Pages of the book flutter in the breeze as Evie sits cross-legged in a forest of seraphilles. The green-eyed boy earnestly reads an invented fairytale from the confounding language. Those same green eyes well with tears as Evie is carried away.

Visually, the memories were nothing more than snippets of scenes, but the emotions that came with them were strong and undeniable. The feeling of being loved wove into Evie — strange, for she couldn't claim to have truly felt it before. But it was there, vestiges of love clinging to the pages, spiraling into her, along with a deep, emotional certainty about the man standing before her now.

"Are you okay?" Charlie was leaning over the table, peering at her.

Evie set the book down and threw her arms around him. She repeated his name, muffled into his shoulder. He hugged back tightly, exhaling relief into her hair. "That was more of the reunion I was hoping for," he whispered, then pulled away, smiling widely.

Overcome with the broken memories, Evie explained, with some difficulty, what she'd experienced. "This book is mine," she repeated, shaking her head. She stared at it, wary, then looked back to Charlie. "And you... How do I know you? You..." She faltered, trying to put the abstract experience into words. "You cared about me," she finally said.

Reddening, Charlie looked down. So quietly Evie barely heard it, he said, "I never stopped."

Heat rose in Evie's cheeks, too. Clearing her throat, she picked up the book again and opened it to a random page. The symbols inside were like puzzle pieces strewn about the floor, albeit, pieces she'd seen before. "This is the same language that the Voynich Manuscript is written in."

"It's called Alterra Lingua."

Evie glanced up. "High earth language?" she said, translating what sounded like Latin. "But the Voynich language has no Latin root. Scholars agree on that."

"You're right," Charlie said slowly. "The language itself has no Latin root. Alterra Lingua is the Latin name given to an even older language."

Evie raised her eyebrows. "Older than Latin? How do you know this, but the entire academic world doesn't?"

The library was silent for a beat before Charlie said, "A language older than Latin, yes." He paused again. "Your world doesn't know about Alterra Lingua, because it was spoken by the Original rulers of another world."

More silence.

"Another world," Evie repeated flatly.

The snippets of memories she'd seen from the book whispered support for Charlie's bizarre claim, but they were new and timid in her mind, and they cowered against the complete impossibility of what she'd just heard.

Noting her skepticism, Charlie continued hurriedly, but with conviction. "I'm from that world, Evie. So are you. We knew each other there, as children."

The impossibility grew bolder, laughing as it strode down the corridors of her mind, shoving her new memories aside.

"Your mother was a citizen of that world," Charlie said softly, placing his hands on Evie's shoulders. "She was a beloved Arbiter, the ruler of a powerful State, one of the last of an ancient bloodline. Her name was Adena Callidora."

At the mention of her mother, the impossibility in Evie's mind halted its advance.

"When you were three years old," Charlie said, "your mother delivered you and the book — the Tree Book — to my parents, claiming that you were in danger. She begged them to bring you to this world, to your father. They obliged, not really believing her claims until they followed her instructions and ended up in Rosslyn Chapel. Shortly after, your mother disappeared."

Disappeared. Not died.

Hope swept in, armoring her newfound memories. Together, they vanquished the impossibility of what Charlie claimed and settled into a certainty so strong it left no room for disbelief. She picked up the book again, tears welling in her eyes. She paged through it frantically, snapped it shut, turned it over, turned it around, trying to prompt another flurry of memories, one that would reveal her mother's face.

"My father told me to forget about this book," Evie said. "To forget about *her*. But it was here, and she was there, all this time..."

A tear fell onto the cover, then another, and another. They glided over the indents created by the embossed gold, flowing through the maze of branches, down the trunk, pooling in the roots. Watching this, a singular thought took form in Evie's mind, its own roots drilling into her very being, twisting around her heart, making clear it was there to stay.

She looked up at Charlie, staring hard at him, her eyes determined behind the sheen of tears. "Take me there."

Charlie exhaled obvious relief for the second time. Still grasping Evie's shoulders, he squeezed them, taking his time to respond. "I want you to understand," he finally said, "the odds that your mother is alive are slim."

"I understand."

"There's something else you need to know," he continued. "Evie, Adena was frantic. Paranoid about a danger so terrible, it prompted her to give you up. It's...they're..."

He trailed off, flustered. Evie just watched him, waiting for him to collect himself and resume. "There's a dangerous cult in my world," he started again. "We believe they wanted the Tree Book. It's likely that whatever happened to your mother was at their hand."

"Why would they want the book? What's in it?"

"That's the problem. Nobody speaks Alterra Lingua anymore, so we can't read it. But we hope you have memories that will help us figure it out. Because Evie, we *need* to figure it out."

Evie nodded fervently. "I'm sure I'll remember something once I'm there."

Charlie wasn't done. "The world you were born in is incredible, filled with things I can't wait to show you. Remind you of, rather." He smiled, but quickly turned serious again. "There's another side of it that's dangerous. Decrepit. Pure evil, if I'm being completely honest. That side wants something that belongs to you, and that makes it more dangerous for you than anybody. I need to know you understand what you'll be returning to."

"I see," Evie said, not seeing at all.

It wasn't that she didn't believe Charlie. She simply had no recollection of the cult he spoke of, no residual fear from hearing tales of them as a child. She was protected by the naivety of learning about dangers without having experienced them, which only bolstered her armor. She heard Charlie's words, but their meaning didn't penetrate.

Still, she pursed her lips in contemplation, the same façade she used to put on as an undergraduate in her non-art history seminars during which nothing compelling was discussed. She looked thoughtful for a decent amount of time, then took a deep breath, appearing to decide in that moment what she had already decided minutes ago.

"I understand," she said. "Take me back, Charlie."

5

PROFESSOR ATKINSON'S ST. Clair relatives stared at Evie from their antique frames on the dark paneling of the sitting room's walls. The professor's painted likeness was the only one bearing an open-mouthed grin. The professor next to her on the couch, however, looked more somber than his 16th-century ancestors.

Charlie was making tea in the adjacent kitchen. Over the crackling of the fireplace, Evie could hear the *clink* of cups and saucers, the whistle of the kettle as it came to a boil. It lulled her into a comfortable trance as she waited for an answer to her question. Professor Atkinson had been right. She'd had only one.

"Why didn't I tell you?" he repeated quietly. Sighing deeply, his eyes darted from portrait to portrait. "The St. Clair legacy. You may think all they left me was this magnificent castle and that glorious church up the street, but what they *really* left me was a mystery. Clues and curiosities, hidden within the castle, carved into the Chapel, all of which pointed me toward a great and remarkable truth."

"The other world," Evie said.

"As I'm sure you've surmised, Rosslyn Chapel, among many other mysterious sites in this world, is a doorway to the other. I learned this on the Autumnal Equinox twenty-two years ago when Liam and Juliette Rutherford appeared in the Chapel out of thin air, a girl in their arms."

Evie turned to face her mentor, shocked. "You knew me when I was a child?"

"Not only that," the professor said, meeting her gaze. His was ashamed. "I knew your father. It was I who bridged the ocean between the Rutherfords and the man Adena beseeched them to find."

The last six years spiraled before Evie as fragments of her relationship with Professor Atkinson fell into place within a much larger picture. There was the way he had taken her under his wing as an undergraduate. The fact that he never asked about her family as they'd grown closer, despite regaling her with centuries of St. Clair history. And there were those odd moments in his lectures during which he would speculate, seemingly at random, outside the confines of accepted academia.

He'd purport that the stone circles of Europe sat upon invisible Ley Lines, which supposedly demarcated paths of unusual energy around the world. He'd theorize that Hieronymus Bosch's bewildering beasts were not merely the result of a remarkable imagination, but a rendering of another reality. He'd end lectures on cathedral architecture with tangential musings about sacred geometry and its ability to "open divine doors." These, and other instances, always ended with a variation of the same theoretical question posed to Evie's class: "Is there a world beyond our own? Somewhere the ancients and artists of our past knew of, that we do not?"

Now, like Ley Lines circling her head, everything connected.

"You dotted your lectures with clues to see if I'd bite," she said. "To see if my father had told me anything." She inhaled deeply, fighting a burgeoning anger. "Clearly, neither of you ever planned to."

"We wanted to protect you," Professor Atkinson said, his voice uncharacteristically meek.

"How did you meet him?" Evie asked, more forcefully than she'd intended.

"It was four years before I met you," Professor Atkinson said slowly, looking as though he'd rather talk about anything else. "I was on Orkney Island, researching its magnificent Temple of the Sun under suspicions it was a portal to the other world. As if to confirm this, your father materialized within the stones at the stroke of midnight." He looked at Evie pointedly. "He was coming home."

"He's been there?" And then, shaking her head, "Of course. How else would he have met my mother?" Leaning back, she sank into the couch, overwhelmed with the onslaught of information over the last hour.

"Your father's story is his to tell," Professor Atkinson said. "Evie, I do not underestimate the betrayal you must be feeling right now, but please understand. Your father experienced terrible, dangerous things in that world. The same horrors likely hounded your mother. Whatever would become of their daughter if she were to return?"

He took off his glasses to dab his eyes. Looking at him now, Evie had to wonder how many of his smile lines were carved by worry instead, or whether his dramatics masked anxiety during his lectures, fear that she'd linger after class to reveal that she agreed, that there *was* another world, that she was going to return to it.

Trying to sound reassuring, she said, "Charlie said only his family knows I exist."

Professor Atkinson let out a quiet scoff. "The Rutherfords can't be certain of that. And whether the darkness there is aware of you or not, they are most certainly aware of your book. I do not —" his voice caught. "I do not dare to think what might happen if they discover it is within their grasp once more."

It should have hit harder, but the professor's warning had even less of an effect than Charlie's. No cult, nor otherworldly horror, could be as bad, Evie thought, as spending the rest of her life knowing she could have found her mother, but never tried.

As if reading her mind, Professor Atkinson said, "Charlie is right. I know that. It's not our place to stand in your way, and you..." His eyes grew misty again. "You deserve to know the truth. But I would be remiss if I did not ask you to reconsider. You can study the book here, you know. In safety."

"You know I can't do that, Professor," Evie said. "The book is here. She's not."

"No," he said. There was that sad smile again. "She's not."

By the time the last log in the fireplace turned to ash and Charlie joined them with tea, Evie's anger with the professor had subsided. She forgave him, the way one might forgive a grandparent for an out-of-touch comment. His remorse was clear, and she understood why he'd chosen not to reveal the truth.

Revealing the truth, after all, had been someone else's responsibility.

Evie's childhood home looked exactly as it had the day she'd left for university. Books strewn everywhere, stacks of paper gathering dust, empty liquor bottles on the kitchen counter, the grandfather clock in the corner *tick, tick, ticking* away what was surely its millionth *tick* since she'd sat down.

She'd stormed in straight from the airport, unannounced. Everything Charlie had told her spilled out, along with her memories from the Tree Book and Professor Atkinson's confession. She'd expected denial, stonewalling. The relief on her father's face had surprised her.

She'd apologized, gathered herself, and now she sat across the dining table from him, waiting for him to speak. When she couldn't take the silence any longer, she cleared her throat and asked, "How did you get there?"

Her father stared at her for one more silent minute, looking as though he couldn't believe he was about to reveal what he'd spent so many years hiding, then finally said, "Stonehenge. It's a clock, you know, but on the Solstices and Equinoxes, it becomes a door. Some people can walk through. Most can't. I could."

"How, exactly?"

Richard shrugged. "One moment I was laying there, looking at the stars. The next I was elsewhere, in a place without time. We're so attuned to time. When it's gone, you know."

Tick, tick, tick.

"And how did you meet Adena?"

He visibly winced at her name and took a gulp from the coffee mug that was not filled with coffee. "Met her after everything."

"What was everything?" Evie pushed.

"Maliter. Verstin."

"Who was Verstin?"

"Con man. Fewer morals than teeth, that man. Picked me up when I came through. Saved me, I guess, then roped me into his dealings."

Evie scoffed. "That's what was so bad? Cons?"

Richard went to the kitchen, straight for the bottle of vodka on the counter. He paused before it, then filled the mug with tap water instead.

"Your mother," he said, sitting back down. He looked up at the ceiling for a long time, as if the ability to speak about her was somewhere up there, then divulged, in one breath, "After everything, I ended up in Callidora. Heaven to Maliter's hell, the most beautiful place I'd ever seen. I met your mother there, when I was working in Perdita's bakery. Perdita was ancient. A hollow. No Alicrat, lit fires with sticks. It's probably why she took to me. We were alike. I baked her bread." He nodded proudly.

The excitement at this memory seemed to strengthen him. He leaned forward enthusiastically. "I delivered it, too, usually to families in town. Perdita went to Callidora Castle herself most days, but one day, she sent me instead. Adena noticed me, and we just..."

"What was she like?"

Richard's eyes went misty. "So beautiful. So clever. Altruistic. She secured me a cottage in the Olubil Hills of Callidoralta, brought me a little orange kitten as a companion. She knew I was an outsider, struggling. She knew what that was like, the way her father kept her sequestered. She was destined to become Arbiter, and those duties prevented her from living freely. But she was curious, and I — I was an object in her cabinet of curiosities. Her window to the world. Worlds. I couldn't give her much, but I could give her that."

Alicrat. Olubil Hills. Arbiters. Fragments of a place Evie did not understand. She felt like she'd been dropped into an advanced class on a topic she knew nothing about, an exam looming in the form of her journey there.

"She already knew about this world," Richard said, frowning. "She knew a lot of things, and I don't know how. Maybe they were in that damned book. She showed it to me once. I asked what was in it, what that weird language said. I'll never forget what she said. 'It's Alterra Lingua. The language of secrets.'"

Richard quieted, then leaned forward, eyes narrow. "I'll tell you what wasn't a secret, though: how much her father, Clement, hated me. He saw me as a threat — to Adena and to the Callidora secrets. It killed him to have me near either."

"So you left her?"

Richard became defensive. "I had no choice! One of Clement's oafs showed up one day to take me to the castle. Brought me straight up to Clement's study, where he cut to it. He said if I didn't leave Adena, she would never be Arbiter. He would appoint her sister, Naveena, instead." He looked down at his hands. "So I left."

There was a beat of silence during which the same thought struck Evie and her father at the same time.

"I didn't know she was pregnant," he blurted, before she could ask.

"And if you had known?" An alternate reality materialized before Evie: a mother, a less troubled father, a life in another world. But the fantasy was blurry, as if the universe knew it wasn't actually possible. More silence, longer this time, confirmed that.

"Your mother was meant for so much more than me," Richard said eventually. "I played my part in her life, offering a reprieve from the secrets that burdened her family. She played her part in mine, saving —" His voice cracked. "Saving me from myself. Staying would have served me, but ruined her."

Evie looked at her father, properly, for the first time in years. At a glance, he was unkempt, permanently exhausted, ghosts dulling his brown irises. But she could imagine him charmingly disheveled in his twenties, exhausted only because he'd socialized too late the night before, his eyes clear and bright, having not yet seen whatever terrible things they would eventually see. She envisioned a young man full of adventure and possibility, willing to love, willing to sacrifice. Whatever he'd endured in the other world had defeated him almost wholly.

"Why do any of it?" she asked. Her voice rose with each word, pushed up by an unwelcome lump in her throat. "Why didn't you just come home? Avoided everything?"

Richard gave her a chastising look. "We're dealing with something greater than either of us can comprehend, Evie," he said. "There's no guidebook, no bureau of tourism. The doors open four times a year, and God only knows where all the doors are. Stonehenge dropped me in the middle of nowhere in Maliter. No landmarks. Nothing to guide me back — not that I'd have dared set foot there again after my escape. Once I'd settled in Callidora...well, I didn't want to leave. I had a home. I'd found love. For all the horrors of that world, there is splendor in equal measure."

"What horrors?" Evie asked again. "Why can't you tell me what happened to you in Maliter?"

He glared at her, frustrated with her persistence. "We're all evil, you know. For some, it's a curiosity left untouched. For others, it's actively relished, honed. For most of us, it's just a capacity. Something to draw upon for self-preservation. I drew upon my evil in Maliter. That's all you need to know."

His chair scraped against the floor as he stood. He went to the kitchen again, forgoing the tap water this time, and downed the slug of vodka he poured. "Callidora was a dream," he said from the kitchen. "Maliter was a nightmare. I lost part of myself in both. Whatever's left just wants to forget."

"You're welcome to forget," Evie said, following him into the kitchen. "But what about me? You kept the truth of my existence from me! And my mother! Why not at least tell me about her?"

He turned away from her. "You'd hate me if you knew."

"I hate you because I didn't know!"

Evie gasped at her own words, escaped from her lips before she could stop them. "I'm sorry," she said immediately. The lump in her throat tightened. She took a step toward her father to hug him, but even the thought was foreign, and she paused an awkward distance away. "I didn't mean that," she said quietly.

There were a thousand other things to say, a thousand other ways her father's choices had affected her. Part of her wanted to list them all, unrelenting, battering him with the consequences. But he was already so beaten, Evie thought. Tears welled in her eyes. What good would more punishment do either of them? There was, then, only one more thing to say.

"I'm going back."

Richard snapped to attention. "Have you heard nothing I've said?"

"You haven't really said much. Besides, I'll be with the Rutherfords. They kept me safe once. They can do it again. I'm going to find her."

"There's nothing to find," he said. "I told you, the Callidoras kept secrets. Those secrets caught up with your mother. And you're one of them, Evie. The darkness will want to know what you know. It will want *you*. Please don't go." Tears spilled from his eyes. "Please," he repeated desperately, again and again.

Packed into that little word was more care than Evie had felt from her father in her lifetime. It chinked the armor that had deflected Charlie's warning and the professor's worries, allowing an iota of fear to creep in.

"What happened to you?" she whispered.

He shook his head.

That was it, then. Evie gave her father's shoulder a squeeze and left before she could change her mind.

6

DARK CLOUDS BLANKETED the skies above Rosslyn Chapel on the afternoon of the Spring Equinox, hanging so low they could have kissed the buttresses. Evie, Charlie, and Professor Atkinson sat inside, chilled and anxious, having been waiting all day for the door to the other world to open.

Charlie had explained that on the Solstices, when the shortest and longest days of the year aligned in both worlds, the portals activated like clockwork in the final moments of sunlight. The Equinoxes, though, being the midpoints between the Solstices, were neither shorter nor longer than any other day. The portal could open at any time. And so, they waited.

After handing in her dissertation early and finding someone to sublet her flat, Evie had packed up her belongings for storage at Rosslyn Castle. Charlie had told her to bring nothing and to wear the most neutral attire she had, assuring her she would get a suitable wardrobe once they settled in. Shivering, she pulled her baggy sweater, purchased last fall from a John Lewis clearance rack, closer around her body.

"It won't be as chilly in Benclair," Charlie promised, putting an arm around Evie to warm her. He'd traded his modern attire for something Evie could only describe as vaguely historic: tight, tapered pants, a loose, tunic-style top, a wool sweater draped over his shoulders, and soft leather boots. A leather satchel completed his otherworldly look, inside which he'd packed some food for the journey and the Tree Book.

Growing more anxious by the minute, Evie rose from her place in the pews between Charlie and the professor to look at the Chapel's multitude of carvings for the umpteenth time. They never ceased to fascinate her; so used to dissecting Christian themes in Medieval and Renaissance art, she loved the contradiction of Rosslyn's pagan carvings. They were even more interesting now that Professor Atkinson claimed the Chapel held clues about another world.

"There are rumors, in fact, that an ancient, megalithic site once stood upon Rosslyn soil," he'd added earlier that morning. "I believe my ancestors meant to honor something greater than the Christian God when they built the Chapel."

"Because of the carvings?" Evie asked.

"And its orientation, Evie, its orientation!" He'd walked the circumference of the Chapel, pointing at certain stained-glass windows as he spoke. "The Chapel is positioned to observe the Solstices and Equinoxes perfectly from within."

"Strange for Christians to honor the sun like that," she'd said.

"Strange for Christians to honor the wrong son."

Evie circled the Chapel now, pondering the purpose and meaning behind each carving. Among the Pagan imagery were some homages to Christianity, like the inverted Lucifer tumbling into the darkness of hell after being banished from heaven. But they were outnumbered by their secular counterparts, some of which were rather confounding, others, a clear reference to fertility, nature, and mortality.

She paused before the famous Apprentice Pillar, one of her favorite carvings. The Tree of Life encircled the height of the pillar, flourishing despite the dragons etched into its base. In Christianity and Judaism, the tree represented the source of eternal, infinite life in God's paradise, outside the confines of time and space. But the sulking dragons, gnawing at the tree's roots, intent on destroying the source of life, came from Norse mythology.

Then there were the Green Man carvings — human faces with vegetation sprouting from their nostrils, mouths, and eyes — on which Evie had written her undergraduate thesis. Throughout the Chapel, vines of stone wove through the chubby faces of Cherubic youth, out the eyes of weathered elders, and into the crevices of long dead skulls.

"Representative of humanity's relationship with nature, right?"

Evie jumped at Charlie's voice. She hadn't heard him join her to examine the Chapel's most famous Green Man.

"That's what most historians believe," Evie said. "Nature, or fertility. I took a different approach for my thesis."

Charlie smiled at her. "Of course you did."

She questioned, "Why vary the faces by age? And look here, at the vines." She pointed. "See how they're connected? I think the vines represent the relentless march of time to which we will all succumb. Once we die, time will carry on without us. Young, middle-aged, old, it doesn't matter. Time will pass, as it does." She looked lost for a moment. "I heard that once, somewhere. I can't remember where."

"Also," Charlie said conspiratorially, pointing at one particularly disgruntled looking face, "if it was about the unity of mankind and the natural world, why does he look so angry about it?"

Evie laughed, a genuine, easy laughter that made her feel like she'd known Charlie her entire life. Twenty-two forgotten years aside, she supposed she had.

Watching them from the pews, Professor Atkinson remarked, "I wonder what marvelous works of art await you on the other side, Evie. Oh, to be in your position, on the verge of an incredible experience!"

Evie crossed the Chapel with Charlie to join the professor once more. "You're welcome to come with us, Professor."

"Alas, even if I wanted to, I cannot," Professor Atkinson said, giving her a forlorn look. "Once upon a time, I wanted nothing more than to make the journey. I used to stand on the precise flagstone," he pointed to a stone at the top of the aisle, "from which various Rutherfords have appeared and disappeared before my eyes. On Solstices at midnight, on Equinoxes for hours, much to the dismay of Chapel docents, I have stood there, waiting. To no avail." He sighed heavily. "This is to say, I believe the portals can sense when the right traveler is in their midst."

"How could it know?" Evie asked, then immediately remembered her father's words.

We're dealing with something greater than either of us can comprehend.

"I cannot say," the professor said. "Written in the stars that shine in the shared heavens of the worlds, perhaps?"

This triggered a jolt of panic in Evie. Would the portal open for her at all? Could it sense that up until a few days ago, she was a non-believer of the supernatural? Maybe the other world didn't want her back. Maybe she would step into a blank expanse, void of the vines of time that wove through the Green Man, and remain, floating aimlessly between realms.

It was as if this burgeoning fear set it all in motion.

First came a low hum, a strange frequency of two discordant tones. Then came the light, bursting through the windows with unfathomable brilliance, pure white despite passing through colorful stained glass. Last was the pulse, similar to the buzz of energy Evie had experienced in the castle's library, but even more overpowering. It was not a noise like the hum, nor could she see it like the light. She could only feel it, waves of it pushing through her body, imploring her to move toward it, into it, as if she had no choice.

Charlie rose, glancing at Professor Atkinson. Clearly oblivious to the hum, the light, and the sensation, the professor stood too, holding his arms out to Evie. She embraced him, clinging not only to her mentor, but to an entire world, for one more moment.

"Be safe, dear girl," he whispered, and released her.

The hum crescendoed, its notes becoming harmonious as the worlds connected in some invisible way. Evie moved to take Charlie's hand, but he'd already found hers. Calm and protective, he guided Evie to the top of the aisle.

There, the hum was no longer a hum, but an otherworldly, euphonious sound that seemed to resonate beyond Evie's ears and straight to her core. The light had also changed; it was so bright now, Evie couldn't keep her eyes open. It didn't matter — they'd reached the top of the aisle.

Thinking only of her mother, Evie took one more step.

7

THE SPACE WAS UTTERLY STILL with no discernible edges or boundaries. Evie had no sense of whether she'd just arrived or had been there forever. She felt weightless, certain she was floating, but when she took a tentative step, her foot hit something invisibly solid. She took another step. Nothing told her she was moving forward other than instinct. She called out to Charlie, but her voice fell flat, muted as soon as his name left her lips.

She was alone.

As soon as she understood this, a glimmering human form emerged before her, though whether mere feet or a hundred miles away, she couldn't tell. She watched it develop arms, a head, cascading curls of light, chatoyant in the shape of a person. She watched it for a thousand years, or was it only a second? She was drawn to it, inexplicably, feeling neither danger nor excitement, just instinct.

A force catapulted her forward. Evie landed face down on grass. Time returned and she understood immediately how ephemeral the whole experience had been; the blink of an eye, if that. She remained in the grass for a few seconds, its blades soft upon her cheek, before slowly coming to her feet.

She stood in an emerald ocean. A blue sky stretched above her, hued faintly with lavender. The only brightness she could see now was the sun, low on the horizon, though she could not feel its warmth. She was shaded by the long arm of a massive tree, its trunk the size of a small house, its peeling bark tinged with gold. Innumerable, weatherworn branches spidered out in fractals, their leaves flashing greens and golds.

Charlie stood beneath the tree, eclipsed by its size. "The Eternal Tree," he said, placing a hand on its trunk. "It's said to be the first living thing brought forth by the energies of creation. As long as it lives, so does our world...or so the legend goes." He shrugged. "It's why there's nothing around us for miles. The Empty Fields are empty by law to protect the tree."

Joining Charlie by the tree, Evie placed a tentative palm next to his. The lowest branches swayed gently, curving toward her in an arboreal embrace, yet the air was still. Gasping, she pulled her hand away.

Charlie smiled. "It's pretty perceptive, for a tree. Welcome to Benclair, by the way." He touched Evie's arm lightly, resting his hand near her elbow. "Are you alright? The journey wasn't too much?"

"There was —" She stopped herself. The glimmering form she'd seen in the space between worlds felt personal, somehow. Unique to her. "Nothing. There was nothing. It happened so fast. I'm completely fine."

Charlie smiled again, wider this time, obviously relieved. "I just need to reassemble my traveling cache — I keep a change of clothes and currency for both worlds inside it, just in case — then we can set out."

He took a few deliberate steps away from Evie, held out his hands, and moved his fingers as if playing an invisible piano. Thin, almost imperceptible bits of light twined toward them from all directions, curving through the air in delicate arcs. They converged on the grass beneath Charlie's hands where, incredibly, a small wooden box bearing a copper clasp materialized.

"Lesson one about this world," Charlie said, his casual tone a stark contrast to Evie's wide eyes, "is that magenu here have an ability called Alicrat. It allows us to sense and manipulate the threads of energy that weave everything around us."

So *that* was Alicrat, Evie thought, feeling, for the first time, a sense of camaraderie with her father as she wondered what he'd thought when he first witnessed the astonishing act. Hesitantly, she knelt before the box and touched it, not quite believing it was real. "So you just...what? Summoned it?"

"I rewove it. When I'm away, I keep it absconded by unweaving the threads that build it and tossing them about. It disappears, or at least, it seems to. Really, it's just dismantled."

Evie nodded slowly, trying to visualize what Charlie was saying. She looked around the Empty Fields. There was nothing to see besides the Eternal Tree and grass. She squinted, straining to picture the millions of threads that wove the branches, the leaves, the velvet blades of grass. This felt less possible than visualizing atoms without a powerful electron microscope.

"Can't other...what's the word you said before?" she asked. "Magicians?"

Charlie grinned playfully. "Magenu. It's how we refer to ourselves here. Magenu is the plural. Magena and mageno are the female and male singular, respectively."

Evie continued to nod, filing everything away like she would need to recount it later. "Can't other magenu find your box and reweave it themselves?" she asked.

Charlie undid the clasp and opened the box. He pulled out a pouch jingling with coins and some small bundles tied with string. "If someone was looking for it, sure. But it's normal here for threads to be out of place. Alicrations are performed all the time. We don't pick upon commonplace manipulations unless we're actively seeking something."

"Like how you might not smell everything that crosses your path unless it's particularly strong or unusual?" Evie ventured.

"Yes! It's exactly like that with Alicrat." Excited by her understanding, Charlie continued, "If you truly wanted to keep something hidden, you'd need to weave its threads deep into other energies. That's called vanesco." Pocketing the pouch and bundles, he stood up. "It's more difficult than absconding, not to mention illegal. It was feared people would use it for sinister purposes. Hiding a body, for one."

Unable to envision the dismantled energy of a body braided into the energy of its surroundings, but trying to keep up, Evie said, "Surely it could have positive uses?"

Charlie shook his head grimly. "Better safe than sorry. That mindset wrote half the laws in our Normalex. The register of common law," he added. "There are commonplace alicrations needed to survive or make life easier. Then there are alicrations that push the boundaries of what's natural, even moral. Those are banned."

Belongings secured, Charlie moved his hands back over the box in another strange pattern. Ribbons of light were visible only for an instant as he flung them around the Empty Fields, rendering the box absconded. Evie stared at the spot where it had sat. Her rational, academic brain was moving excruciatingly slowly, struggling to catch up to her new reality. The concept of Alicrat made sense, on some theoretical level, but to see it in action was almost too remarkable to grasp.

She stood, looking into the distance. "How empty are these Empty Fields?"

"Empty enough that we should start walking." Charlie glanced at the sun. "We could partume, but it's not my greatest skill and it might be...a bit much for you. We'll cover a few miles on foot, and camp tonight. We'll reach Ulla tomorrow morning, then Orefo, then The Fern. That's home," he added.

Charlie seemed eager to utilize those miles to get to know Evie. It had to be strange for him, she realized, to have been reunited with someone he'd remembered every day for the last twenty-two years. He seemed deeply curious about her, genuinely and endearingly so, and she found herself wanting to catch him up on her life. Not that there was much to share, from her perspective — she spoke of her father, of the home she'd found in Edinburgh, and of her love for art, especially Hieronymus Bosch.

All the while, Evie ran her fingers through the grass, closed her eyes, inhaled deeply, did everything she could think of to heighten her senses in an effort to see the world the way Charlie did. The world remained exactly the same. "How is it done?" she asked, tossing a handful of grass away. It swirled to the ground in a kaleidoscope of jade and emerald. "How do you do Alicrat?"

"Well, to start," Charlie said, "it's not like magic. You don't do Alicrat. You *have* Alicrat."

"That's what he meant," Evie murmured to herself. Then, to Charlie, "My father mentioned a woman with no Alicrat. He said he was like her. I must be, too. Hollow."

He shook his head. "I don't think so, actually. True, there are some people here, the hollows, with no innate alicrative ability, but I don't think you're one of them. This is only a theory, mind you, but I think people in the Other World — what my family calls the world you were raised in — *do* have Alicrat. They just don't know it."

"I think we'd know," Evie said, wiggling her fingers around in the air, mimicking Charlie, "if we could do what you do."

Charlie smiled. "Not necessarily. Here, we grow up knowing that our world is woven with threads, seeing others manipulate those threads, *believing* that we can, too. It's not the same in the Other World. From the time I've spent there, I don't think most people could even fathom the notion of Alicrat, let alone truly believe it's possible."

"Science is our Alicrat," Evie said, seeing what Charlie meant. "If I saw someone do what you did with your box, I'd assume they were using technology."

"Or you'd call them a witch and burn them at the stake." Charlie paused, contemplating something. "I think if you believe in it, though, you'll find your Alicrat."

"That sounds a little simplistic."

"Maybe, but don't forget, your mother was a magena. Which means," Charlie waved his hands around the expanse of the Empty Fields, "*this* is your home. True, your energy is a chord, a note from each world. But the dominant tone comes from here."

"My energy," Evie repeated. "Threads weave people?"

"Of course," Charlie said matter-of-factly. "Threads weave everything, tangible and intangible. That includes emotions."

"When I held the Tree Book, I felt my mother's love," Evie said, understanding. "And your...concern, like I was feeling it for the first time."

"Emotional threads," Charlie said, nodding. "They're strong, and they linger. They weave themselves into important objects to linger even longer."

"Incredible," Evie whispered. Then, exhaling sharply, asked, "I believe you. I believe in Alicrat. Why am I not sensing any threads?"

"Alicrat is a bit mysterious," Charlie said. "It doesn't just appear for you. You have to *find* it first. Even here, that takes some magenu longer than others. Our entire First Libellum of study — three years — is dedicated to this. You've been here an hour." Charlie squeezed her shoulder reassuringly. "You'll have lessons in The Fern with my old teacher, Pembroke. One thing at a time."

Five miles later, when the sun had dipped below the horizon and the stars had blinked to life over the relentlessly unchanging Empty Fields, Charlie decided they should make camp. "I'll get us some water," he said.

Evie looked around. She saw no nearby lake, heard no rushing stream. This didn't seem to trouble Charlie, who started swiping his arms through the air in a half-moon shape. After several sweeping motions, two curves of water materialized, arcing to follow his arms.

"Aquenum," he explained. "Technically, the alicration manipulates hydrogen and oxygen particles to merge into water." He concentrated, nudging the two arcs into a single sphere of liquid. "At least, I think that's what it does. The scientific explanation of the Other World still confuses me."

He waited as Evie leaned forward to sip from the airborne orb, pleased with her astonishment, then pushed it aside. It remained hovering, waiting obediently.

"How will we camp, Houdini?" Evie asked.

Charlie produced the bundles of fabric he'd pocketed earlier. "This is our tent and blankets, minuted. The threads are compacted."

He untied the twine and the bundles twitched, their condensed energy anxious to expand. In one swift movement, he yanked his hand over the parcels, flinging the collection of energy outward. It sailed through the air, materializing into a canvas tent before hitting the ground. He repeated the same motion with the other bundles. They floated down gently, having resized into large, feather-filled blankets.

"One more. Lustris," Charlie said. He moved his hands again, in a way Evie was finding less strange and more beautiful with each alicration, until a sphere of gently pulsating light bobbed before her.

"I've seen this before," she whispered, glancing at Charlie.

"Starlight. When I was a child..." She danced her fingers around the orb, mesmerized.

Illuminated by their piece of the universe, they settled into the tent. The feathers inside the blankets were alicrated to move, keeping the space between Evie's body and the ground plush while maintaining warmth. Wishing her pleasant dreams, Charlie pierced the starlight orb with a finger like a child poking a bubble of soap. Stars rained down, blinking out one by one until it was dark, and for the first time in a long time, Evie slept without dreaming.

8

THE NEXT MORNING, after another lengthy trek, a small village encircled by a stone wall and shrouded with weeping willow-like trees finally came into view. "Ulla," Charlie said. "The oldest town in Benclair. Young magenu in small towns usually move to The Fern after their Libellums, but most Ulla residents remain for life. They consider themselves protectors of the Eternal Tree."

"Protecting it from what?" Evie asked.

"Nothing, but newcomers are watched by a silent guard, just in case."

"That's welcoming."

"Don't worry. You'll be with me," Charlie said, putting an arm around Evie's shoulders.

He did this often, Evie noted, and she didn't mind at all. It felt comfortable, but she couldn't yet tell if it was a friendly comfortability or something more. Charlie was handsome, his looks not unlike the few men she'd dated in Edinburgh, and there was a natural chemistry. From her side, at least. His gestures toward her felt caring and protective, but measured, not like attempts to pursue.

At the wall, Charlie placed his palm against the stones. "Ulla has an old security system," he explained, "put in place before the States of the Northlands existed. Back then, only energy from Ulla's citizens summoned the door. Magenu from other villages weren't recognized."

As he spoke, wood radiated from his hand, overtaking the stone and culminating in a door carved with the Eternal Tree. "Today, magenu from the whole of Benclair are accepted. And their guests," he added, pushing the door open. "After you."

Evie stepped onto a quiet street paved with pearly stone in a herring-bone pattern. It was moonstone, according to Charlie, and it also covered the roofs of the buildings lining the street. Vines with lavender buds hung from their rafters, echoing the hues of their pastel façades, perhaps once vibrant before being muted by centuries of sun.

They followed the moonstone street toward the town center, Charlie relishing Evie's excitement as she paused every few steps to examine another charming shop front. She exclaimed before Old Ernst's Bakery, an entirely pink affair with loaves of bread piled behind the windows. At Nesbitt Butchers, she gawked at the sausage links hanging in the window like tinsel, preserved with a cooling alicration Charlie called frigidium. They stopped inside Ulla Wine & Vocat so that she could try some of the syrupy local spirit, of which she had a second and third glass. And at Benclair Dairy, she marveled at the white cow hovering in the window, which was actually milk, suspended in the same way Charlie had suspended their orb of water, though much more artis-tically.

People milled about in the street, popping into shops or pausing to chat. The men were dressed like Charlie in tight trousers, leather shoes, and loose tunics or sweaters. The women wore a feminized version of this or dresses, both of which were incredibly flattering. Unusually inse-cure, Evie fussed with her baggy sweater and linen pants as they walked. It was the women's hairstyles she coveted the most, though. Compli-cated braids and weaves cascaded down backs or piled locks atop heads, no doubt easier to accomplish with the assistance of Alicrat.

Most people were dressed in shades of neutrals, which Charlie explained came from an old tradition by which only ruling families of the Northlands were permitted to don the bright State colors. "Benclair is green, Teraur is gold, Iristell is plum, Maliter is crimson, Callidora is blue." He glanced at Evie, considering something. "Darker than your eyes, though. If your eyes are the blue of a summer sky, Callidora's blue is the deepest ocean." Cheeks reddening, he continued hurriedly, "Anyway, those rules are no longer in place, but most citizens still dress neutrally —"

"Ah!" Evie exclaimed, stumbling forward. Charlie grabbed her arm, steadying her. She'd tripped to avoid stepping on a fuzzy mass, which was now bouncing around her feet.

"Hoppy!" A little boy darted in front of her, bending to scoop up his rabbit. "Sorry," he said, grimacing. "He just appeared yesterday. We're still learning."

"Quite alright," Charlie said.

Clutching his rabbit, the boy ran off. It was then that Evie noticed the menagerie of creatures — rabbits, cats, dogs, deer, falcons, and more — interspersed among the Ulla residents.

"They're familiars," Charlie explained. "Animals summoned by a magenu's emotions, bonded for life. They usually appear for the first time after a particularly emotional experience in childhood, then come and go after that."

This delighted Evie as much as it saddened her; like Alicrat, she had to wonder if familiars were just another part of this world she might not be able to experience.

At the crowded village square, an enormous water orb hovered over a moonstone basin, rotating slowly as people filled jars and pitchers. "Can't they alicrate their own water?" Evie asked.

"Of course," Charlie said, "but it's impolite to do so in public spaces. Imagine dozens of discarded, half-drunken orbs hovering around! Are you hungry?"

Taking Evie's hand, Charlie steered her through the people and into a pub across the way. Inside, a long wooden table ran down the center with benches on each side, filled with people digging into bowls of stew. The establishment's lone worker, a handsome man around Charlie's age, was stationed at a bar at the other end.

"Welcome to the Village Kitchen," he called out. Then, glancing up, "Rutherford?" He left the bar to approach the pair, shaking his head in disbelief.

Charlie greeted him with a handshake that morphed into a masculine embrace. "Kellan, how does it find you?"

"Very well! You've been traveling again?" Kellan faced Evie. "And who is this?"

"Evie," she said, offering her hand. "Pleasure."

"All mine," Kellan said, grinning. "Tell me, where did my friend sneak off to this time? The Midlands? The Meridan Isle? He's rather secretive, if you didn't know."

"And I'll tell you my secrets someday, Kellan, if you can convince me to drink more than a glass of your homemade vocat. For now, they stay here." Charlie tapped his head.

Kellan rolled his eyes in mock indignation. "I'm convinced he knows more than he lets on," he told Evie.

"About what?"

"About everything! Maybe you'll get more out of him than I have." His tone made Charlie's cheeks redden again. Kellan clapped him on the back and laughed, pulling him into another hug. "Ah, it's great to see you."

"Same, friend," Charlie said. "Say, Evie and I need a couple horses to ride to Orefo. We'll leave them at the Starsen."

"They'll be ready within the hour," Kellan said. "Now, sit! We've a hearty stew today."

Horses procured after generous portions of stew, Evie and Charlie left Ulla behind on a route that was, thankfully, far more interesting than the Empty Fields. It wove through a forest dense with trees, moss draping from their branches like curtains. Charlie held the moss aside for Evie to pass through, smiling wider each time.

"What is it?" she asked, looking around.

"Nothing," Charlie said. Then, outright grinning, "You'll see."

After some time, the trees transformed. Their trunks were green, not brown, and enormous leaves jutted out from their sides, not from branches. Flowering heads erupted at their tops with colorful petals on some, while on others, bulbous heads dangled like Christmas ornaments weighing down an evergreen branch. Others still had no flowers; trunks merely grew into tapered, curling tips like a beanstalk.

They weren't trees at all, Evie realized. They were utterly gigantic flowers. Recognizing their details, she pulled her horse to a stop. "The Voynich Manuscript!" she cried. "These are the plants from the drawings!"

"Florens Arbor," Charlie said, stopping his horse next to Evie's. His eyes twinkled as he took in her excitement. "The genus to which your seraphilles belong."

"Are there seraphilles here?"

"Not here, but beyond The Fern, there's a whole forest of them. The Silvana Seraphilles."

Evie laughed in disbelief and closed her eyes, letting a ray of sun warm her face. "This is unbelievable," she said, spreading her arms wide. "My whole academic career, I've returned time and time again to the Voynich Manuscript. Something just drew me to it. Now I know." She opened her eyes. "I've been looking at a scrapbook of my home. Though," her brow crinkled, "it begs the question: if the drawings of plants are florens, how does everything else depicted correspond to this world?"

Charlie shrugged apologetically. "I've studied the manuscript a great deal myself. Aside from the plants, I've not been able to connect the other images."

To Evie's joy, the path kept them among the florens until the sun sank low in the sky. Charlie steered them out of the forest then, toward Orefo's walls, which also recognized his Benclair citizen touch.

Orefo's buildings were more brightly pigmented, a reflection of its livelier social scene. All around the town square were numerous pubs, crowded with mingling locals drinking ale and vocat. A mageno walked the perimeter of the square, lighting posts with flames conjured from a pouch of kindling hanging from his waist.

The quiet side street Evie and Charlie turned onto was already bright with the alicrated posts. They hitched their horses outside the Starsen Inn, a tall brick building with massive stained-glass windows running the entire height of its façade. The foyer was equally grand, boasting a dark blue ceiling dotted with innumerable golden stars. They blinked to life as Evie waited for Charlie to collect their keys, growing brighter as the sky outside grew darker.

Upstairs, in her own room, Evie collapsed into bed. It was plush with the same alicration that had kept the previous night's blankets cloud-like, and the ceiling above her twinkled with the same alicrated stars as the foyer. She drifted off, imagining the invisible threads of the universe stretching from the stars in the sky, light years away, all the way to the pinpricks on the Starsen ceilings. When the last one finally brightened to life, Evie fell asleep.

The *tap, tap, tap* of gentle rain pattered outside. It was early, well before Evie and Charlie had agreed to meet. She couldn't fall back asleep. Her mind wandered to the events of yesterday: the glimmering form in the portal, the Eternal Tree, Alicrat, florens. Despite traveling alongside the florens for hours yesterday afternoon, Evie wanted more.

Restless, she dressed and left the Starsen Inn. The horses were gone — moved to a stable, presumably — so she walked through Orefo instead. The town reminded her of the small English villages she visited in the summers between terms at Edinburgh. She'd wander the streets as the city came to life with bakers pushing trays of bread into ovens, baristas grinding beans to caffeinate commuters, maintenance men sweeping the streets so that they could be dirtied again. It had often rained during those walks, which always felt romantic to Evie.

She ended up on the opposite side of town where, just beyond the wall, she saw the edge of the floren forest. Bordering the florens where she approached was a bush bearing raspberries. She grabbed a few and popped them into her mouth. They were plumper and sweeter than any raspberry in the Other World. Actually, was it even a raspberry? It was too sweet, too juicy. Delicious. She reached for more.

A vine shot out from the bush and coiled itself tightly around her wrist. She yanked her arm back, burning her skin beneath the vine. It didn't relinquish its grip. Instead, it pulled harder, playing tug of war. Another vine emerged and coiled around her abdomen, dragging her into the density of the bush. She screamed for help, loud and clear. She screamed again, but her second cry was weak. When she screamed a third time, no sound came out.

The bush reeled her in further. Her legs went limp, though the grip of the vines kept her upright. Smaller tendrils crept up the back of her head, snaking into her hair, down her forehead, obscuring her eyes, pushing their way into her mouth, scratching her throat. With her last lucid thought, she noted the irony. The grinning, plant-infested face of Rosslyn Chapel's Green Man, was her.

9

"EVIE?" Charlie called for the third time. He knocked again. "Are you there?"

She wasn't — his Alicrat sensed nothing but inanimate objects on the other side of the door — but his time in the Other World had acclimated him to things like asking someone to confirm their presence instead of just sensing it.

He inventoried the rest of the threads in the Starsen Inn. Everything was woven as expected, nothing out of place, torn, or otherwise damaged. This did little to quell his worry. Outside the Starsen he honed his Alicrat again, but he was too unsettled to properly audit the threads around him. Instead, he ran through Orefo, up and down streets, calling Evie's name. At the north wall he pushed the door open and paused, overwhelmed.

All of Benclair sprawled before him, vast and green. If she'd left, she could be anywhere — halfway to The Fern, heading back to the Eternal Tree, lost in the florens. Charlie squinted at the edge of the forest. Was that...?

He sprinted to the florens, heart racing. This side of the forest was lined with virdisemp, a deadly plant able to mimic any fruit or flower necessary to lure its prey. Locals knew to avoid it, but Evie could have been fooled. Charlie yelled for her as he reached the bushes, though he knew it was no use. The plant's toxins would have muted her by now.

Sure enough, amongst the writhing green was a patch of cream; one linen leg of Evie's pants. Both her hands were free, too, but rendered useless by her pinned forearms. Part of her face was visible — a cheek and one eye that darted nervously, not noticing Charlie.

"Curse the moon," Charlie whispered. He focused his Alicrat on the vines, sensed their threads, and hastily severed them with a manipulation. Vines tore, but they weren't the ones wrapped around Evie. Stressed and harried, his Alicrat was imprecise. Charlie thought back to the days he spent deep in the Benclair Archives rather than perfecting practical alicrations with the rest of his Libellum class. "Curse the moon!" he yelled, meaning, of course, himself.

Frantic, he dove toward the virdisemp to tear at its vines manually, but one of them lashed at him with a painful slap to his wrist. He tried again, but the lengths of vine not occupied with Evie played defense, preventing him from getting close.

An authoritative voice bellowed behind him. "Move!"

Charlie stepped aside just in time to avoid the unicorn that skidded to a stop before the virdisemp. It tore into the bush with vicious precision, using its horn to slice through the vines that bound Evie. Her arms were freed, then her leg. The smaller tendrils obscuring her face retreated. The largest vine around her stomach went slack and she fell forward, collapsing onto her knees. Charlie helped her away from the bush, barely registering the orange cat that stalked around the unicorn's legs, hissing and clawing at the now dead remnants of virdisemp. Nor did he notice his brother, at least, not until Marcus kneeled next to him.

"Good thing I had Nica with me," he said, peering at Evie. "Is she okay?"

"I'm okay," Evie whispered, wincing. "Sore throat. Bruised. I feel like I was hit by a car."

Marcus looked confused.

"Can you stand?" Charlie asked. He rose slowly with Evie, steadying her as she came to her feet. Once upright he examined her, gently pushing the hair off her face, feeling around tenderly for broken bones.

She was definitely bruised — her forearms already bore purple welts — but was otherwise alright. Still, Charlie didn't take his eyes off her.

Marcus, having also stood, cleared his throat and dipped into a low bow before Evie. "Lovely to see you again, Evie. Remember me?" he said, lifting his head to wink at her. To Charlie's dismay, Evie laughed despite her sore throat, thanked him, and offered her hand for a chivalrous kiss.

"I don't, but thank you for..." She gestured at the eviscerated virdisemp behind her.

"It was all Nica," Marcus said, patting the unicorn. "I was just in the right place at the right time."

Only then did Evie seem to notice that Nica was not a horse, but a horse with a horn. Mouth agape, she circled the unicorn, tilting her head this way and that, as if perhaps, she was hallucinating the fairytale creature. Nica snorted softly, tipping her nose toward Evie. Tentatively, she touched Nica's nose, then patted it, then stepped closer to run a hand over her glossy mane.

"She was just a foal when you were with us," Marcus said, "but I think she remembers you. Of course," he leaned closer to Evie, "how could anyone forget?"

"Shall we be off, then?" Charlie said crisply. "Let's get you onto Nica, Evie."

She stepped into his interlaced fingers, grimacing in obvious discomfort. The orange cat followed, bounding from Charlie's hands up her leg and into her lap. Now noticing the cat for the first time, Evie exclaimed, even more bewildered by it than she'd been by Nica.

"Biscuit? How did you get here from Edinburgh?" She held the cat close to her face, interrogating it. "It's him, look." She turned Biscuit toward Marcus and Charlie, as if they would recognize him from William Street, Edinburgh, Other World. "One blue eye, one brown. Just like Biscuit."

Marcus shrugged. "He must be your familiar."

"Manifested in the Other World, though?" Charlie pondered.

"You said familiars usually appear in childhood," Evie said. "I only met Biscuit when I moved to Edinburgh. Did he follow us through the portal?"

Biscuit just meowed placidly, unconcerned with his own logistics. He settled into a donut shape in Evie's lap, and with that, the trio, the unicorn, and the cat set off to cover the last few miles to The Fern.

———

Charlie's hometown lay at the base of the hill they crested a few hours later. Lost in his thoughts, he'd not realized how close they were until Evie shouted from up ahead.

"It looks like the Emerald City!"

"Emerald City?" Marcus asked.

His ignorance was astounding.

"From the Wizard of Oz, a story from the Other World," Charlie said, jogging to catch up. He'd deliberately fallen behind to sulk, annoyed at Marcus' heroic appearance, more annoyed that Evie seemed to like him, and most annoyed by knowing he couldn't have saved her without his brother. "Dorothy travels to the Emerald City and discovers its wizard is not the all-powerful entity he was made out to be," he added, joining them.

"Very interesting," Marcus muttered.

Evie wasn't wrong. The Fern was a multifaceted quilt of green, named for the lush vegetation that crept through its streets and covered stone buildings in the form of moss, actual ferns, and vines — the non-deadly kind.

"We'll take the tunnels," Marcus declared as they approached the walls. "You know how news travels. If we go through town, Mother will know Evie's back before we reach the gates." Kneeling, he held his palms over the grass. Just as Ulla and Orefo's doors had materialized at Charlie's touch, so too did a trapdoor become visible beneath Marcus' hands.

"It's an old escape route," Charlie told Evie, "from when sieges on the castle were regular occurrences. They haven't been used for centuries, though. Not since the Northlands Wars."

"Speak for yourself," Marcus said, heaving the trapdoor open. "How do you think I snuck home after nights out?" Winking at Evie, he lowered himself into the opening.

Charlie helped Evie down, then gestured for Nica to carry on and meet them at the castle. Biscuit leapt off the unicorn and shimmied up Charlie's leg, wrapping himself around his neck like a stole.

The tunnels were wide, tiled with moonstone on the ground and walls, and dimly lit thanks to beams from the alicrated sunlight Marcus had brought. They walked until the tunnel gave way to stairs and then they climbed, up the hundreds of steps equivalent to ascending the hill upon which the castle sat. At the top, Charlie pushed past Marcus to force the trapdoor open.

"Evie, come next," he called back, and exited, unwilling to miss her reaction as she emerged.

Above ground, behind Charlie, rose an intimidating iron gate aglitter with faint security alicrations. Behind the gate was the start of the pine forest that carpeted the hillside down to The Fern's edge. A moonstone-paved path curved its way through the trees, past the gate, all the way up to the castle, where Adena Callidora had once stood with her daughter and the Tree Book.

Evie came out from the tunnel, helped up by Charlie. "Is it familiar?" he asked, his voice low, head bent, the question just between them.

Thousands of years old, the castle was an enormous square structure of ivy-covered stone, five stories high, with arcading across the façade that provided glimpses of the interior courtyard. In addition to numerous small towers, a wide drum tower protruded from the northern wall with the Benclair flag and the top of a tree bursting through its roof. A memorable feature, surely.

Before Evie could answer, though, Marcus joined them and made a show of alicrating the glimmering gates open to allow Nica through. Biscuit leapt from Charlie's shoulders back onto the unicorn as she trotted by, heading for the stables.

Without waiting for Charlie and Evie, Marcus strode into the courtyard, bounded up the grand staircase that allowed access to the five stories of the castle, and started down a corridor on the fifth floor. Charlie remained alongside Evie, slowing on the stairs as she smoothed out her sweater and combed through her hair for remnants of virdisemp leaves.

"What a terrible first impression I'm going to make," she muttered.

"May I?" Pulling her to stop at the top of the stairs, Charlie carefully rubbed a bit of dirt off her cheek. "You look perfect," he whispered.

"Are you two coming?" Marcus called, now standing outside the doors to Liam's study at the end of the corridor. As soon as Evie and Charlie caught up, he swung them open with a pompous air and marched inside.

Liam's tower study was a mix of the homely and the official, filled with books on law, finance, and economics, and one painting of his children, hung over the fireplace. In the center of the room was the top part of the tree that grew straight through every level of the castle and emerged through the study's roof. At a table under the tree sat Liam and Juliette in what appeared to be strained silence, Liam poring over Benclair reports, Juliette gazing at the painting of her children.

Using a branch of the tree, Marcus swung himself toward his parents, landing at their chairs. "Mother, Father! How does it find you?"

Liam and Juliette stood; Juliette to embrace Marcus, Liam to clap him on the back. "Successful trip, son?" he asked.

"More than. Look who I brought back!" The words were out of Marcus' mouth before Charlie had a chance to make his and Evie's presence known.

Juliette turned first and rushed over as soon as she saw Evie, the silky skirts of her dress sweeping behind. "Oh, my," she managed. "Oh, Evie!" Pulling Evie into her arms, she caught Charlie's eyes and mouthed, "Thank you."

"Well done, son," Liam said.

Charlie looked at his father, but he was smiling at Marcus, who, arms crossed over his chest, watched Evie and nodded with satisfaction. An old, familiar frustration, awakened in Charlie after the virdisemp encounter, heated up. But his father was approaching Evie now, all Arbiter authority, so Charlie swallowed his irritation.

Towering over six feet tall, only the flecks of white in his hair and beard belying his age, Liam Rutherford cut an imposing figure. He came to a stop before Evie, waited for three uncomfortable seconds of silence during which it was clear she was not to speak first, then addressed her.

"Evangeline Callidora."

She tilted her head.

"Ah. I don't suppose you went by that name in the Other World, did you? Evie, then. Welcome to Rutherford Castle." A bit of the smile he reserved for visitors to the castle curled his lips.

"Welcome *back*," Juliette said, gracefully side-stepping in front of Liam, "to your home." Her gaze moved across Evie's hair and attire as she spoke, her nose crinkling ever so slightly. "Come. I'll show you to your quarters. Illis will draw you a bath. We shall get you a fresh wardrobe tomorrow, of course, but until then, some of Serena's clothes should fit. Do you remember Serena? We'll visit her tomorrow..." Chattering about inconsequential things, Juliette led Evie out of the study.

Charlie moved to follow, but Liam called him back, gesturing for him and Marcus to join him at the table. Reluctantly seated, Charlie listened as Marcus rattled off a report. He'd gone to Maliter, where their contact — they had a contact in Maliter? — had filled him in on the latest. "It's as we feared," Marcus said. "Tenebris usurped the Arbitership from Eliot. It was he who set Eliot Castle alight, then demanded loyalty from Eliot's Mensmen and village Maiors. Those who refused..." Marcus quieted, uncharacteristically unnerved.

"Out with it, son."

"He killed them. With an obscurity. There was no more dissent after that."

Charlie leaned forward. "Do you mean Adrian Tenebris? Isn't he —"

"The leader of the Obscures? Yes," Liam said.

"I didn't see him," Marcus said, "but I heard plenty. He has a dark charisma that appeals to far too many citizens. He's tripled the cult's membership, practically normalizing them! It's the decent citizens who are underground now. I'm surprised I made it home."

Liam stroked his beard, ignoring Marcus' last comment. "Things continue to move faster than we anticipate."

"What about the other States?" Charlie asked.

"They are aware," Liam said tactfully. "Whether they'll stand with us or cower is another question."

"Well, we know not to expect much from Naveena," Marcus said under his breath.

Liam leaned forward, palms on the table. "Which brings us to Evie. What does she know?"

"Nothing yet," Charlie said. "But it's early."

"It's late," Liam corrected. "I won't risk acting until we have something to leverage, but we must ensure it does not become *too* late. Get to work on the book. I don't need to remind you how important this is, Charles."

"No," Charlie said. "You don't."

Liam rose, indicating the conversation was over. He moved to leave the study, listing off a number of to-dos pertaining to State business as Marcus trailed behind. Alone, Charlie laid his head in his hands. Home again, in the place he'd already scoured from top to bottom for clues about the Tree Book, he was reminded how impossible a task lay before him and Evie. Impossible, yet imperative. He slammed his palms on the table.

A sudden urgency befell him, like a stopwatch from the Other World had settled into his mind permanently, counting down an unknown amount of time before an unknown catastrophe. Charlie pulled the Tree Book out of his satchel, opened it to a random page, and stared, for the millionth time in his life, at the baffling symbols.

10

THERE ARE *no stars in the sky. There is no pursuer in the forest. There is nothing.*

Exhausted from running, Evie falls to her knees, the wound in her thigh still painful and bleeding. A twig snaps — somebody is there after all. She whirls around, eyes searching, but sees nothing in the darkness, senses no life among the trees.

Another snap.

"Who's there?" Evie calls.

A voice laughs, softly at first, then louder. Taunting peals reverberate off the trees.

"You know me, Evie."

Cold breath whooshes over her ear. Still, she sees no one. She crouches, but the icy breath finds her again.

"Time and time again, you wake and forget me. But I am always with you. Every night. Look up, and there I am."

Evie rises slowly, wincing as the cut on her thigh protests.

"I've been with you since before you were born."

Evie starts to run again. The bodiless voice comes from all sides; behind her, before her, in past lives, and in her next life. She wills herself to wake up. She cannot.

"You can help me."

"I will never help you!" The response is instinctual, and she shouts it with all her might.

"You say that now." The voice remains alongside her. "There is much you do not yet know."

Evie trips and falls, pulls herself up, and carries on. The edge of the forest is visible ahead. The voice laughs again, a horrible, decapitated laugh. It laughs until Evie wakes up.

11

SOFT, lavender dawn bloomed above the tops of the trees outside Evie's window. She watched it usher the sun back into the sky, watched it drench the leaves in light, watched it melt into the crisp blue of an early Benclair morning.

The tower room she'd slept in was larger than her entire William Street flat. Despite its size, it was decorated simply; a curved bed nestled into the arc of the rounded wall, a smattering of rugs in shades of green lay haphazardly on the stone floor, and a sizable wardrobe sat in the corner. The one dramatic element was the spiral staircase that disappeared into the wood beamed ceiling, seeming to go nowhere.

Yesterday evening, Juliette had fawned over Evie all the way to her room, her joy matched only by the housekeeper, Illis. Busy filling the wardrobe with Serena's old clothes when Evie and Juliette entered the room, Illis had shrieked when she saw Evie and smothered her in a maternal embrace.

"Draw her a bath please, Illis. Use those sumptuous oils from Iristell," Juliette said. Then, to Evie, "She will bring a tray for dinner, then you should rest. You've had quite the journey, dear." She looked at Evie for a long moment, her eyes welling with tears for the second time that evening. "I see her in you," she whispered. She placed a hand against

Evie's cheek but drew it back quickly, seeming to think the gesture too much, and left the room.

Illis scooted Evie into the moonstone laden washroom like she was still a child. Too tired to protest or feel self-conscious, Evie stripped away her dirty traveling clothes and stepped into the water, which had been alicrated to the perfect temperature.

Illis shrieked again. "In the name of the sun!"

"What? Oh — my bruises." Evie grimaced, taking in the purple lashes twining around her body.

Illis tutted, shaking her head. "You'll see the medice tomorrow. Seely can mend anything. In you go, now, in you go."

Clean, dressed in a sleeping gown, and overcome by the sudden presence of not one, but two motherly figures in her life where there'd previously been none, Evie had slept immediately and deeply. Now, watching the morning sky change colors from the bed, it could have all been a dream. Though, one she could remember.

Serena's clothes in the wardrobe consisted of predictably neutral trousers, shirts, and a few dresses. Evie found her John Lewis sweater, too, freshly laundered — Illis must have returned it after she was asleep — though her pants, torn from the virdisemp, were likely discarded. She chose a pair of Serena's trousers to wear with her sweater, then stepped out in search of breakfast. She immediately tripped over Charlie, asleep by the door, Tree Book on his chest.

The book fell to the floor as he shot upright, rubbing his eyes, embarrassed. "I thought I should be here when you woke," he said. "Newcomers often get lost trying to find their way around."

Evie picked up the Tree Book. "Trying to crack the code?" she asked, handing it back to him.

He let out an exasperated sigh, then glanced beyond Evie, his eyes darting toward her room's ceiling. "Mother didn't show you?" he asked, pulling her back inside and up the spiral staircase.

At the top, he pushed up against the ceiling. Evie followed him through the ensuing passage into another level of the tower, this one twice as high as the bedroom below. A ring of glass ran around the perimeter at the very top, letting in the late morning sun; its beams criss-crossed over each other and down to the floor in a patchwork of light, setting particles of dust aglitter. The room's furnishings included a sizable table and several comfortable chairs. As for the walls, except for the window and the catwalk installed halfway up, they were shelves of books.

"These are all mine," Charlie said, running a hand along the books nearest Evie. "Collected over years, across worlds. I thought you might enjoy them, so I moved them here for you."

Struck by his thoughtfulness, Evie didn't know what to say. She turned toward a bookshelf to hide the blush creeping into her cheeks.

"I remember how excited I was when I was introduced to a whole new world of knowledge," Charlie explained hastily. "I didn't mean to be presumptuous, of course. If it's too much, I can —"

"Charlie, it's incredible," she said earnestly, and gave his hand a quick squeeze.

She did a lap around the level beneath the catwalk, noting history, speculative nonfiction, and classics of the Other World: *The History of the Ancient World; Fingerprints of the Gods; A Tale of Two Cities; The Lion, the Witch, and the Wardrobe.* So many others. And from this world: *First Libellum Alicrations,* as well as *Second* and *Third; A Lengthy History of Arbiter Lines; Essential Oils: How Essential are They?* and children's books, like the adorably named *Felix and the Florens.*

Charlie slid the Tree Book into an empty space on a shelf. "We'll do our research here," he said, his previous exasperation returning. "If we find anything to research, that is. Come, I'll give you a tour of the castle."

Evie's room lay at the end of a long corridor which eventually opened to the grand staircase. "We're on the fifth floor," Charlie said as they descended. "Father's study is up here, along with mine and Marcus' rooms in the Eastern Wing."

On the fourth floor was Liam and Juliette's room, the main library, and guest quarters. The third floor, mostly empty, housed the live-in staff's quarters. "These days," Charlie said, "it's just Illis, our groundskeepers Beinelton and Codes, our stablehand Leon, and our chef, Plum."

Benclair business took place on the second floor, though the many meeting rooms were empty at the moment. "It will be busy later,"

Charlie said. "Maiors and Mensmen are always coming and going. Don't let it faze you."

In the courtyard, Evie was immediately distracted by a hovering disc the size of a round banquet table, its edges slightly curved up, emitting a pulsing green hue. She'd not noticed it yesterday, nervous as she was to meet Liam and Juliette.

"It's an affrim," Charlie explained. "Our version of technology. When a visitor is at the gates outside, the security alicrations there relay their energy pattern to the affrim. The gates open for approved magenu. An alarm is raised for unknown or blacklisted energies."

"Seems complicated," Evie said, running her hand through the green glow.

"No more than a computer," Charlie said. "Though, not many magenu have the skills required to create these kinds of things. There's spectrum when it comes to alicrative talents beyond your basic, everyday tasks."

They poked their heads into some of the other rooms accessible from the courtyard: the ballroom, the dining room, and Evie's favorite, the sitting room. An enormous white couch with bulbous pockets of alicrated fluff, reminiscent of a cumulonimbus cloud, dominated the space. Coupled with the blue silk-covered walls, stepping into the room was like stepping into the sky.

Hanging on the walls were portraits of the Rutherford children. Most were of Marcus: Marcus on a unicorn in an official Benclair uniform; Marcus with a bow and arrow slung over his shoulder, holding a medal; Marcus as a child in a virtuous pose at a piano, among others. There were also numerous portraits of a girl, airy and ethereal with long blond hair and a dreamy look in her eyes. Serena, Evie assumed. And then there was Charlie, boyish and shy in three portraits with his Libellums and nothing more.

One more painting, not a family portrait, hung over the fireplace. Evie was certain she'd never seen it before, yet she recognized the work of Hieronymus Bosch immediately. "What is that doing here?" She spun around to confront a grinning Charlie. "How — did you *steal* it?"

"Certainly not," Charlie said, holding up his hands and suppressing a laugh. "It's been hanging here my entire life. I didn't realize what it was — rather, who'd painted it — until I went to the Other World and saw an eerily similar painting in Spain's Museo del Prado."

"The *Garden of Earthly Delights*," Evie said. "Bosch's most famous triptych."

"I became obsessed. Not only with Bosch, but with finding out how one of his paintings ended up here."

"And?" Evie said eagerly.

"I have no idea." Charlie shrugged an apology. He removed the painting from the wall with a retrieval alicration he called venen — a swipe of his arm, to Evie — and leaned it carefully against the back of the couch. "Take a look," he said. "Tell me what you see."

A naked woman lay entangled in limbs, gazing up at an Adonis-Devil hybrid. Envious figures looked on from a distance, whispering behind their hands. One maniacal onlooker crept along the periphery, brandishing a knife. Others watched indifferently, unfazed by his clear intent to slash and kill. A lone figure in the corner, painted mid-step like he was about to walk out of the frame, glanced back at it all with sadness.

Head cocked, Evie pointed at the naked woman. "Indicative of Lust, perhaps?" Familiar with Bosch's allegorical style, the rest quickly fell into place. "Envy, Anger. Pride and Sloth!" She gripped Charlie's arm. "This must be the missing central panel of the *Seven Deadly Sins* triptych! This belongs between *An Allegory of Intemperance* and *Ship of Fools*, which depict Gluttony, and *Death and the Miser*, which depicts Greed. Those are on display in New Haven, Washington D.C., and Paris, but the central panel has been lost forever."

"Not so lost, after all," Charlie said, alicrating the painting back onto the wall. "More mysteries."

In the kitchen, he performed an alicration over what looked like a stove with no knobs. "Ignidium," he said, setting a pot of oatmeal on the metal grate over the flames that had jumped to life. Breakfast cooking, he joined Evie at the table to explain, with some reticence, what Marcus' trip to Maliter had uncovered. "Maybe it was ignorant of me, but I didn't think anything so dire as a usurpation would happen while I was away. Neither did Father."

"So, the cult believed to have hunted my mother for the Tree Book,"

Evie said slowly, "openly rules Maliter?" The chill she should have felt in Rosslyn Castle or in her father's apartment finally ran down her spine, though the notion of being even remotely connected to something so apparently consequential was still more unbelievable than not.

Charlie grimaced, noting her reaction. He clearly disliked revealing the worst parts of his world to her, but continued. "They're called Alicrat Obscura; interchangeably the Obscures or the AO. Adrian Tenebris is their leader."

"Might I guess," Evie said, "that they use those unnatural and immoral alicrations? The ones that are banned?"

"Abuse is more accurate. Though," Charlie said, "they weren't always evil. The Obscures began as many things do: with curiosity. In the earliest days of our world, new alicrations were discovered through innocent experimentation. Some of those first manipulations were deemed unnatural and banned in the Normalex."

"Define unnatural," Evie said. "Everything I've seen so far is unnatural."

"True," Charlie said. "Things like attempting to make oneself invisible or tampering with the intricate weave of time. Innocent experiments, driven by curiosity, but still, things the Originals of our world claimed should be controlled."

"I see nothing good has come of controlling humanity here, either," Evie said wryly.

Charlie shook his head. "Some magenu continued pushing the boundaries, experimenting with Alicrat to harm or kill. Laws followed to ban these obscurities, too, and the offending magenu were punished. That just pushed them underground, where they remained for centuries, little more than Maliteran legend. Only recently has the cult emerged, slowly infiltrating the Maliteran government, normalizing obscurities in the streets. Preparing, I suppose, for Adrian Tenebris to step forward."

Charlie paused to check the oatmeal and returned to the table with two bowls of steaming oats, a dish of sugar, and a pot of cream. "Given what they're capable of," he said, spooning sugar over his oats, "my father won't take action until we know if the Tree Book's contents will give us an advantage."

"What about Naveena?" Evie asked, shrugging. "Adena's sister. My father mentioned her. Maybe she can read the Alterra Lingua." It seemed utterly obvious to her, but as soon as she asked the question, she realized there must be a very good reason the Callidora Arbiter couldn't help.

The look Charlie gave her confirmed this. "Naveena is unreachable. A recluse. She's completely withdrawn from Northlands culture, pulling Callidora away with her."

"Maybe she's still in mourning."

"It doesn't matter. Of all the States, Callidora should be the last to weaken." Charlie finished his oatmeal in four huge bites and pushed the bowl away. He placed his palms on the table, looking serious. "I've mentioned the Originals a few times."

Evie nodded. "I was going to ask about them."

"They founded the Northlands States," Charlie said. "For thousands of years, the seat of Arbiter passed to Original descendants of Benclair, Teraur, Iristell, Maliter, and Callidora. Eventually, the Original bloodlines died out and new Arbiters were voted in. That's how the current ruling families in Teraur, Iristell, and Benclair came to be. Maliter, too, before Tenebris."

"But not Callidora," Evie said. "I'm the descendant of an Original?" She looked down at herself, as if this realization might change her very being.

"Original blood is a powerful claim," he continued. "It means something to Northlandans. Naveena could use that claim to stand up to the Obscures. To save Maliter. Instead, she's silent. Has been for over a decade, ignoring my father and the other Arbiters. It's no use trying to contact her."

Evie stood. "Then ask someone else."

Charlie ran a hand through his hair. "I've already tried everyone in Benclair. Besides, our records don't go back farther than the Northlands Wars, when our earliest archives were destroyed."

"Someone in Callidora," Evie said, leaning forward, palms on the table.

Charlie shook his head. "I just told you, Evie."

"Not Naveena. Someone else. If Alterra Lingua was the language of the Originals, and the Callidora line is the only one left that can trace its roots to the Originals, there must be *someone* in Callidora who can read the Tree Book."

Charlie rose too, his face alight with the hope of a new angle. He was about to respond when Juliette walked in, dressed like the day was a party, another luscious skirt trailing behind her.

"Evie, there you are!" Taking her by the shoulders, she promptly steered her out of the kitchen. "Come. I'm taking you to The Fern."

12

WALKING alongside Juliette down the path from Rutherford Castle to The Fern, twisting through the dense pine forest, Evie tried to remember something. Anything. Being carried through the same trees by a frightened Adena? Darting amongst the trunks with a young Charlie or Marcus? As ever, memories refused to surface. Perhaps the day's events in town would uncover something.

"Have I been to The Fern before?" Evie asked.

Juliette assured her she had not. "You stayed in the castle," she said. "Your mother wanted you protected."

"From the Obscures," Evie said, somewhat absentmindedly, trying to keep track of her own past.

At mention of the Obscures, Juliette scoffed. "They're nothing more than a silly little cult," she said dismissively. "People on the fringes. Best they congregate in the cesspool of Maliter than lurk in the civilized States." She nodded curtly.

Evie decided she'd stick to Charlie for political information. "Juliette, what exactly did my mother tell you when she left me here?"

Juliette stared straight ahead. "Not enough. I didn't even know you existed. Even today, we Rutherfords are the only people who know who you are."

"Illis knew me."

"Illis knows you are the child we took in two decades ago. She does not know you are the daughter of Adena Callidora. You are a secret."

"You'd think Adena would have been happy to share that the Original bloodline would continue," Evie mused.

"I can only guess that your paternal heritage caused some consternation," Juliette said delicately. "Especially to Clement, who assumed Adena would marry Callidoran nobility. Not an outsider of the State. Certainly not an outsider of this world. If he even knew where Richard came from, that is. So many secrets in that family," she added. "I was your mother's best friend, Evie. I thought I knew her better than anybody. In fact, I knew barely a thread of her."

Evie fell silent, perturbed by Juliette's use of the past tense. True, Charlie had warned her of the unlikeliness that Adena was still alive. True, twenty-two years had passed with no trace of her. Yet Evie had assumed this world — or the Rutherfords, at least — still had hope that their revered, Original Arbiter was alive.

The forest opened at the base of the hill, revealing the outskirts of The Fern, even more lush and green up close. Moss covered the cobblestones, trees lined the streets, ivy crawled in the spaces between it all. Had she not caught sight of a brick here and there, Evie would have thought the buildings themselves were made of plants. She thought the greenery would engender a calm environment, but in contrast to the tranquility of Ulla and the frivolity of Orefo, the town was distinctly business-like.

Residents of The Fern seemed perpetually harried, darting from establishment to establishment like they were late for an endless string of meetings. Unicorns were tied outside buildings with rope or hasty alicrations, some of which didn't catch, though the unicorns waited obediently anyway. A myriad of familiars appeared out of nowhere, summoned by the stress of their magenu to traipse alongside them or perch on their shoulders as they conducted their business.

All the while, thin ribbons of light swirled and looped around Evie as the world's energies were twisted, tied, and otherwise manipulated for various purposes. Not everything was accomplished by alicrations, though. Turning a corner, Evie narrowly dodged a small creature zipping through the air, clinging to envelopes more than twice its size. Another one came flying after the first and grabbed at the envelopes, managing to pilfer a few before flitting away.

"Menaces," Juliette said, swatting the air. "Work has slowed for the pixies, what with the development of loquers. With fewer messages to deliver, they're becoming competitive." Noting Evie's confusion, she explained further.

"Loquers carry the threads of one's voice to a designated target. They're quick and easy, but can be intercepted with keen Alicrat. You should still use pixies," she leaned closer to Evie, "for secrets. Do not loquer anything you wouldn't want others to hear. Ah! Here we are."

They'd arrived at Timpson's Tailors, their first destination of the day. Juliette had made clear that securing Evie a suitable wardrobe was of the utmost importance. Evie had agreed, though Juliette seemed more motivated by fashion than practicality.

The tailor's shop was dimly lit, with rolls of fabric shoved deep into shelves and spools of thread — real, visible thread — piled in the corners. A short man, stubbled and gruff, rose from the table where he'd been seated, counting buttons. "Jules! Come to see the new fabrics?" He spoke with the gravelly timbre of a smoker. Confirming this, he pulled a twig about the length and thickness of a pencil from his pocket and lit the end with a snap of his fingers. "How does it find you?"

"Very well," Juliette said. "This is Evie, a friend of the family."

Timpson held the smoldering twig her way. "Semp?"

Evie declined. He took a long drag.

"Evie's belongings were lost on the journey here," Juliette said, waving wisps of earth-scented smoke away. "We shall need to outfit her with a full collection." She rattled off an order: trousers, various shirts, sweaters, dresses, shoes, a variety of coats, and a lingerie shop's worth of undergarments. "And something lovely for the Congregation," she added, turning to Evie. "The annual gathering of the Northlands States. Benclair is hosting this year." She beamed with pride.

"Colors?" Timpson asked. "Fabrics?"

"Everything," Juliette said. "Linen and cotton for the warmer days of the Second, but don't skimp on the cashmere and silk, naturally."

"Naturally. Arms up," Timpson said, and proceeded to take Evie's measurements by circling her body, his hands held a few inches away from her, without a tape measure.

"I'll be needing a Congregation gown as well," Juliette said as he worked. "Something grand. Use the green silk from the Orenisles, won't you? That rare, expensive one you procured last quarter? You have my measurements, of course."

With Evie's taken and the lengthy order recorded, Timpson declared everything would be ready in two weeks. "Payment upon delivery?" he asked.

"We'll settle it now," Juliette said. "You know how Liam can be with what he considers a frivolous purchase. What he expects the girl to wear, I do not know." She pulled a coin pouch from the voluminous skirts of her dress. "Four thousand pecs, I assume?"

"Four thousand nine hundred," Timpson confirmed.

Evie had no understanding of the local currency, but five thousand pecs sounded like a substantial sum. Once outside, she assured Juliette she would pay her back, though she hadn't the slightest idea as to how she would acquire any money.

"Don't be silly," Juliette waved her away. "True, Timpson is more expensive than most. True, his garments arrive with the slight scent of semps, which Illis must alicrate out." She wrinkled her nose. "But I assure you, no other tailor in town has his connections for fine fabrics. Besides," she patted Evie's shoulder, "you're family, and we're Rutherfords."

They continued through The Fern, now along quiet, residential streets, away from the business center of town, until they reached the apothecary.

"Seely is our family medice," Juliette said, pulling aside the vines that dangled over the apothecary's front door. "She mends everything to befall our family."

She raised a fist to knock but the door swung open before she had the chance, revealing a woman in a linen smock and no shoes. Her hair frizzed out in all directions, leaves and twigs interspersed in the tangles. Evie couldn't tell if they were placed there deliberately or if the woman had just woken from a nap in the forest.

"Illis told me you would come!" Seely proclaimed, smiling.

"Evie encountered a virdisemp yesterday," Juliette said, pushing back Evie's sweater sleeve to prove it. "She requires mending."

Eyes wide, Seely made a tiny, comical hop backward. "A tincture for the toxins, then!" she said, singsong. "A tincture for the toxins and a poultice for the bruising!"

Inside the apothecary, she flitted about, filling her arms with dozens of the bottles and jars that lined her shelves. Tiny bottles of oils and larger jars of powders piled up on the worktable, along with trays of stones, a bowl of dried insects — though Evie was certain she saw one wriggling — and long vials of multicolored light that vibrated so aggressively, they had to be secured to the table to prevent them rolling off. Ingredients gathered, Seely got to work combining drops of this and essences of that together.

Evie crept closer to watch, curious. "May I ask what you're doing?"

"Is it not clear?" Seely stopped to look at her concoction. "I am harnessing the botanical properties of nature to create a healing blend."

"Oh. Of course," Evie said. "I'm not from here. We do it a bit differently at home."

Seely's laugh sounded like a songbird's chirp. "No matter where you come from, the essence of nature powers life." She continued grinding and pouring and mixing until she had a small bottle of liquid and a poultice the size of a golf ball, wrapped in muslin and tied with twine.

"Soak with the poultice in the bath," she said, placing the ball in Evie's hand. "Ensure the water is like a cup of tea to the touch. And drink this." She handed Evie the bottle. "Half tonight. Half tomorrow. Leave no drop!"

Evie nodded solemnly. "Thank you, Seely."

Once outside, well past the apothecary and enroute to their next stop, Evie asked Juliette if the remedy would actually work.

"Why wouldn't it?" Juliette frowned. "Oh. Charlie told me healing is quite different in your world. He claimed to have taken a man-made pill for an ailment. Nature provides the same results, you know."

"What about alicrations? Are they used to mend, too?"

"Certainly. Fusing bones, cooling fevers."

"And deadlier diseases? Cancer?"

"Whatever is cancer? Oh, it's the boys! Milo, Nim!"

They'd reached the yard outside Serena's home, where two straw-berry-blonde heads bobbed about in the tall grass. Evie recognized Serena sitting nearby, a bohemian beauty in a flowing dress with a long, blonde braid. Next to her sat a plain, slender man — Finneas, Juliette provided, Serena's husband. They made a lovely family, Evie thought, the Joneses of this world with whom everybody else on the street surely strove to keep up with, a picture that she, perhaps, could have been part of were it not for her mother's secrets.

The boys saw their grandmother approaching and shrieked, running to greet her. Serena glanced up, meeting Evie's eyes, and like a sudden pain, it came to her. Piercing. Terrifying. A memory.

13

IT WAS DARK, but not black. The Silvana Seraphilles at night was a deep, navy blue, and besides the eclipsing florens surrounding her, Evie was alone.

Where was her mother? She called out, frightened.

"I'm here, Evie." Her mother's voice was so weary. She sat against the base of a floren. "Go back to sleep."

"The ground is too hard. Can't you make it soft?"

"Remember what I said?"

"We need to be careful."

"Exactly. We can't do anything that can be traced. No alicrations." Adena nestled a blanket tighter around Evie. "It's an adventure, remember? It will make you stronger. You may not always be able to manipulate the world to suit your needs, after all."

Evie pouted herself back to sleep and woke again with the sun, its golden rays bursting through the gaps in the floren canopy. Blue seraphille petals wafted in the morning breeze, swirling their sweet scent. Nearby, her mother struggled to fit the blanket into their bag alongside a week's worth of food and necessities.

"Make it small," Evie demanded.

Adena replied with uncharacteristic impatience. "How many times must I tell you? No alicrations. Hold this."

She pulled out a book that was lodged inside the bag and handed it to Evie. It was her book with the golden tree, her prized possession. Even at three, she understood it was important. A few days before they'd left, her mother and grandfather had presented the book to Evie, their faces serious, voices stern.

"This book was mine," her mother had explained. "Before that it was Grandfather's. Before that it was his father's, and his father's mother's, and so on until so long ago you couldn't even count the years with all your fingers and my fingers!"

"What about Grandfather's fingers?" Evie had asked.

Smiling through his beard, Clement had wiggled his fingers. "Still not enough! The book is yours now, Evangeline. Keep it safe. Do you understand?"

Clutching her book in the forest of seraphilles, Evie watched her mother finally readjust the bag. She added the book, tied everything shut, and they set out for another day of walking. It was boring and tiring and Evie didn't understand why they'd left Grandfather and the castle in the first place. Her mother had offered no explanation, only that it was "time to go." That had been days ago.

"Do you know what these florens are called, Evie?" Adena asked, gesturing. Evie shook her head. "They are seraphilles, commonly known as the sun plant. Seraphilles are one of the oldest plants in the world. Isn't that amazing? People believe they go back to the beginning."

"The beginning of what?"

"Time, of course."

Adena stopped then, tense and alert. Abruptly, she scooped Evie up and then they were running, seraphille stalks blurring together into a solid green haze, until, as suddenly as she'd taken off, Adena halted.

"Don't look, Evie!"

Evie should have listened. Instead, she watched a man materialize before them, completely bald with dark, nearly black eyes. His skin seemed soft, sculpted out of clay, as if he weren't quite real.

Adena acted swiftly. Shifting Evie to one arm, she thrust her free hand into the air, slicing downward at a diagonal. A gash appeared on the man's chest, but he barely flinched, barely bled. Snarling, he gestured wildly. Black tendrils swirled about, darkly manipulated energy that curled toward Adena.

Adena slid Evie to the ground and swiped through the air again. A *crack* sounded, then a *whoosh* as a seraphille hurtled to the ground. Pulled by Adena's alicration, it fell faster than the man could anticipate. Evie squeezed her eyes shut just before the heavy stalk met his body.

The soft mass of her mother draped over Evie, heaving with exhaustion, and stayed there for a long time. When Adena finally lifted her daughter off the forest floor, all was still. Again, she told Evie not to look. Again, Evie disobeyed.

The crushing weight of the seraphille had severed the man. On one side of the stalk his legs were splayed, tendons and muscle exposed. On the other side, guts spilled from his open abdomen, a puddle of blood spreading beneath it all. Evie's eyes, childish and naive, met the man's, their darkness frozen in shock. He blinked.

Desperate to forget his face, Evie looked to her mother instead. She memorized her every feature, from the arch of her brow to the determined line of her lips, but also the fear in her eyes. To see her mother afraid was more terrifying than anything. Something charged forth to protect Evie, locking away the memory, including her mother's face, for the next twenty-two years.

"I've always said Serena looks a bit like Adena," Juliette said quietly. "It's no wonder the sight of her affected you so."

Evie, Juliette, and Serena sat in Serena's kitchen, watching Milo and Nim mimic Finneas' alicrative hand movements as he warmed a pot of tea. Finneas was one of Liam's Mensmen, the trusted advisors to whom Arbiters delegated State business to, along with Marcus, a man named Oleander, and some others. It was his role as Serena's husband, though, that meant he knew who Evie was and where she came from.

"You're starting to feel better," Serena assessed, accurately, though Evie hadn't realized it until Serena said so. In response to her surprise, Serena added, as casually as people in the Other World mentioned they were a Capricorn, "I'm an empath. I'm more attuned to emotional energy than the average magenu." With this, her constant, distant gaze made more sense.

Fineness delivered everyone's tea. Placing his hands on his wife's shoulders, he said, "It's a heavy burden, the feelings of the world, but Serena carries it beautifully."

Evie smiled, having warmed to Finneas immediately. He possessed a gentle demeanor with an undercurrent of unshakeable loyalty, as much a Rutherford as Marcus or Charlie.

Still observing Evie, Serena continued to announce her feelings like a weather report. "Your energy is strong. Singular," she said, pursing her lips. "You are so determined, aren't you?"

"Of course," Evie said, setting down her cup of tea. "I'm going to find my mother."

Nobody said anything. Finneas stirred his tea. Juliette glanced out the window. Only Serena maintained eye contact with Evie, nodding slowly. "I do not doubt you will do everything in your power to understand Adena's fate," she said carefully. She leaned forward, squinting at Evie as if she'd become blurry. "There's more in that determination, though."

"Perseverance?" Evie guessed, slightly uncomfortable.

"Hm." Serena continued to nod, but fell silent, apparently not ready to reveal whatever else she sensed.

"Who was the man in my memory?" Evie asked the table. "Was he an Obscure?"

"If he was, it only shows how deluded those people are," Juliette said, another derisive response to the mention of the cult. "Chasing an Arbiter, thinking he could best her? Evie, I told you. The Obscures are nothing."

Finneas met Evie's eyes, indicating he did not agree.

"Charlie is coming," Serena announced. "He's quite excited."

There was a rap at the door, followed by the sound of it opening and footsteps hurrying into the kitchen.

"Evie," Charlie said, out of breath. He tousled Milo and Nim's hair, grinning as they clung to his legs. "There you are. Come — we're going to meet Pembroke."

"Alicrat lessons already, Charlie?" Juliette said. "She's only just arrived. Surely, she's exhausted." She yawned daintily on Evie's behalf. "Let her rest and enjoy the castle."

"She's not a tourist, Mother."

"It's alright, Juliette," Evie said, standing. Then, facing Charlie, "Let's meet Pembroke."

The revered Alicrat instructor's cottage was a short stroll from Finneas and Serena's. "He's a bit odd," Charlie said as they walked, "but absolutely brilliant. He's trained generations of The Fern in his two hundred years."

"Two hundred years?" Evie exclaimed.

"Well, one hundred and eighty or so. Magenu live longer than humans in the Other World," Charlie said. "I suspect it has something to do with our relationship with the world's energies. Anyway, Pembroke's methods are strange, but reliable. Trust him."

Pembroke's cottage, a small, whitewashed stone structure, was the only home in The Fern not crawling with greenery. Just like at Seely's apothecary, the door opened before anyone had the chance to knock. Unlike at Seely's apothecary, there was no one waiting on the other side.

"He probably sensed us a mile away," Charlie whispered, but added, more loudly, "Pembroke? It's Charlie Rutherford."

"Well done, you're you," a voice called back. "Come in."

The single-roomed cottage, also whitewashed inside, contained two wooden chairs. Sitting cross-legged in one of them was the man Evie took to be Pembroke, dressed in loose trousers and a tunic, each the same toasted almond shade of his skin, which looked as though he'd spent the entirety of his one-hundred-and-eighty-or-so years directly under the sun. Bare feet matched his bare head. Wrinkles etched their way around his eyes and lips, but his face held a sort of vitality Evie had the sense would never fade.

Marcus was seated in the other chair, legs splayed casually, arms crossed.

"What are you doing here, Marcus?" Charlie asked.

He rose, smiling lazily. "Father sent me to arrange lessons for Evie."

"I was already planning to do so. Obviously."

"Just following orders, brother." Marcus turned his attention to

Evie and dipped into a low bow, winking as his head popped up. "Hello again, Evie."

"Surely there are more pressing tasks he can send his favorite Mensmen to accomplish," Charlie muttered.

The brothers broke into a childish argument. Unsure as of yet what to make of their relationship — and her place in it — Evie left them to approach Pembroke on her own. He'd not moved from his cross-legged perch on the chair, but had closed his eyes.

"Sit," he said. "Ignore them. Their negative energies will generate adverse vibrations for you." Eyes still closed, he frowned. "I said sit."

Evie flopped obediently onto the vacated chair.

"Align your vibrations with mine."

"How do I do that?"

"You align your vibrations with mine."

"Yes, but how —"

"You align —"

"Okay! Okay." Evie closed her eyes. Taking her own interpretation of Pembroke's words, she tried to relax into the meditative state yogis of the Other World always preached about.

"You are not aligned," Pembroke said, tutting. Evie opened her eyes to catch him shaking his head. "Disastrous vibrations."

"Go on, then," Marcus was saying. He made a mock grand gesture toward Pembroke, whose eyes opened on cue.

Charlie stepped in front of his brother. "Pembroke, may I introduce Evie?"

"We have met. Vague Northlandan energies splattered with mud. Tragic." Pembroke turned to Evie. "Who are you?"

"Evie?" Evie said, as if she was no longer sure. "Charlie just introduced me."

"I asked who you are, not what you are called." He stared expectantly.

Evie glanced at Charlie and Marcus, who were each suppressing smiles — Marcus' amused, Charlie's, apologetic.

"Well," Evie tried again, "I was raised...elsewhere. Maybe that accounts for the mud."

Pembroke addressed the brothers. "What am I to do with her?"

"She needs lessons, Pembroke," Charlie said.

"I do not accept pointless endeavors."

"We wouldn't ask if it wasn't important."

"Yet you will ask even if it is impossible."

"It's an order," Marcus said sharply. "Liam is requesting it. Apologies, Pembroke," he added, less authoritatively. "But you can't really refuse."

Pembroke frowned. "I promise no results. She is shrouded. I sense a glimmer of possibility, but it may be a glimmer of nothing. Nothing often masquerades as possibilities, after all. She is —"

"She is sitting right here!" Evie said. She only felt ashamed when she saw Charlie's face, eyes wide. Marcus, on the other hand, stifled an appreciative laugh.

"With respect, Mr. Pembroke, I don't care what you can or can't sense," Evie said, more calmly. "You don't seem to be sensing my capacity to learn, or the fact that I *want* to learn."

"Excellent!" Pembroke said. "Step one is done. Step two is due. We shall convene at the schoolhouse tomorrow. Goodbye." He closed his eyes again, a clear dismissal.

"That went well!" Marcus said brightly, once outside. He clapped Evie on the back. "I think he likes you."

Laughing, she rolled her eyes. "He thinks I'm covered in mud."

"Nah, he just wanted to get you to ask for the lessons yourself."

"I told you he was odd," Charlie said as they headed together toward the castle. "The best thing you can do with Pembroke is react genuinely, which is what you did. He doesn't believe in placations."

Marcus threw an arm around Charlie. "You should have seen us when we were boys, Evie. I don't know how Pembroke managed to teach us anything! We spent most of our lessons trying to alicrate each other's pants off before we'd even learned to summon it."

"He always said we had to release our negativity before we'd find our Alicrat," Charlie said. "Though, I'm not sure of the merit of that now. I do plenty of alicrations when I'm annoyed." He glared at Marcus out of the corner of his eye.

Later, as Evie and Charlie sat on the cloud couch trading theories about the Rutherford Bosch, she asked him a question that had been on her mind since the virdisemp. "What is it with you and Marcus?"

"What do you mean?" Charlie said defensively, clearly knowing full well what she meant. He let out a resigned sigh. "He's so arrogant. You see it, don't you? How could he not be — he's always been Father's favorite. Better at archery, interested in politics..." His stared at the portraits of Marcus on the wall. "I've always been the dark moon of this family. The black sheep," he added, glancing at Evie.

"Surely you're respected for your own pursuits, Charlie."

He shook his head. "You wouldn't understand. You didn't grow up with him."

Evie wasn't sure if 'him' referred to Marcus or their father. Either way, she let it be.

14

"WHO CAN TELL me the first law of Alicrat? Relph?"

A poised six-year-old stood. "Energy cannot be created or destroyed, only manipulated," he recited.

"And the second law?" the teacher asked.

Relph, again. "The amount of energy required to manipulate threads is equivalent to the scale of the task."

"Close, Relph. You're correct that manipulating fewer threads usually requires less energy from the mageno or magena, while manipulating more threads requires more energy. Does anyone know what else affects the amount of energy required to perform an alicration?"

"If the threads are alive!" Relph called out. "Manipulating the threads of a living thing requires even *more* energy." Grinning, he sat back down, pleased to have remembered before his classmates.

"Exactly," the teacher said. "The threads that weave a living being are more challenging to alicrate than those of an inanimate object. Why might this be?"

No one, not even Relph, ventured a guess.

"Well, naturally, the threads that create living things *want* to stay woven, don't they? That's the essence of life, isn't it? So, it takes more energy to alter them. Now, what is the third law of Alicrat?"

Silence, and then Relph. "Everything begins with the same threads of energy!"

"Well done. From rocks and trees to you and me, everything started with the same threads of energy. How they're woven is what makes all of the different things in our world."

"But how did the very first threads decide what to be?" a girl asked.

"Well, nobody was there in the beginning, so nobody really knows."

"There must have been a person in the beginning," the girl said, matter-of-factly. "A person who wove things."

This was too much for Relph. "You're silly!" he cried. "If a person created everything, who created the person?"

Listening outside the schoolhouse window as she waited for Pembroke, Evie felt a twinge of sympathy for Relph. Not only did she share his sentiments on the notion of a creator, she was feeling like a bit of a know-it-all, too. Having studied the laws of Alicrat last night from Charlie's First Libellum book in her library, she wanted to shout the answers out loud with Relph.

"Shall we?" Pembroke's voice startled her. She turned around to catch him walking past without so much as a momentary pause or glance toward her.

"How does it find you?" she said, striding to catch up. She was trying to use the common Northlands greeting more often, though it still felt awkward.

"Tired, with aching bones."

"Did you sleep poorly?"

"I am one hundred and eighty-one years old."

"Right," Evie said. "Where are we going?"

"To the forest."

"What's there?"

"Trees."

Evie held her tongue for the rest of the walk.

Lessons were to take place in a forest clearing outside The Fern. Pembroke marched into the clearing, spun around with Professor Atkinson-like dramatics, and regarded Evie intensely. "I trust you were listening during the children's lesson," he said.

"Yes. I also studied on my own."

"Ah! Then you understand Alicrat."

"In theory."

"Have you balanced your energies?" Pembroke pushed Evie's shoulder, hard. She stumbled back, barely catching herself. Pembroke tutted. "You are not balanced."

Clueless, Evie closed her eyes and tried, like the day before, to find some semblance of a meditative state. She also grounded her feet, and when Pembroke shoved her again, she stayed put.

"Fine, for now," he said. "How do you feel?"

"Good," Evie said, opening her eyes to find Pembroke's weathered face a scant inch from her own.

"No. Not how do you feel. How do you feel?"

"I'm apprehensive, but..." She paused, trying to understand Pembroke's language. "Ah. Okay. Well, music moves me. An amazing soundtrack — er, symphony of sound — evokes strong emotions."

Pembroke nodded. "And?"

"Actually touching something, of course —"

Pembroke held up a hand, silencing Evie. He pulled a minuted parcel from his pocket and, with a flourish, resized it into a length of fabric that he proceeded to wrap around her head, obscuring her vision.

"Excuse me, but what exactly — hey!" Evie's hands jerked behind her back, clasped together by something invisible. Pembroke had alicrated them, she surmised. She was, effectively, helpless.

"Find the flower," came his muted voice.

Evie couldn't see a flower. She couldn't reach out to feel for one. She couldn't even smell her way toward anything. The purpose of the exercise didn't elude her; clearly, she was meant to summon her sixth sense to find the flower's energy. Relph's voice came to her: *Everything begins with the same threads of energy.* How, then, did one distinguish between a flower and a rock? She tried, for over an hour, to figure that out.

Eventually, Pembroke released her. She glared at him as soon as she could see again. "I'm not sure you understand, Mr. Pembroke," she said. "When I said I wasn't raised here, I meant it. Not just Benclair or the Northlands, but..." she stopped herself, wary. "My father was a hollow. He had no Alicrat and resented those who did. It was forbidden in our household."

Pembroke said nothing.

"I need instructions."

"You declared your desire to learn," he said placidly. "Did you lie?"

"No, but —"

"Do you believe you can?"

"I don't know," Evie admitted. "I hope that I can. But I can't believe something without some sort of proof."

"You have witnessed no Alicrat?"

"I have. What I mean is..." Like Serena, Pembroke was speaking to parts of Evie she didn't fully understand. "I have no proof I can do this."

"What is belief?" Pembroke asked.

"A conviction."

"And?"

Evie shrugged, exhaling loudly.

"I believe my energy will carry on to what comes next when my physical body dies," Pembroke said. "I am not dead. I have no proof. Yet I believe."

"Belief is conviction in the absence of proof."

"Quite. Therefore, you cannot excuse your low confidence with a lack of proof. Therefore, I do not accept your former statement. Children understand this concept. Shall I enroll you in the First Libellum course with the youths?" Pembroke tilted his head to the side, smiling, and began to skip about, childlike himself.

Evie pushed, ignoring his antics. "I can't summon belief from nothing."

"You don't *summon* belief." Indignant, he stopped skipping. "It is there or it is not."

"And if it's not there?"

"Then you do not belong here in the first place." He looked at her as if he didn't just mean in the forest, trying to learn Alicrat. "So? Is it there? Is it not?"

"I don't know."

Pembroke started to walk away.

"Mr. Pembroke, wait!" Evie hurried to catch up. "I still want to try. Where are you going?"

"Home. I am tired of explaining something so simple." Still, when they reached The Fern's wall, Pembroke declared they would meet the following morning for another lesson, then ignored Evie's goodbye as he whistled his way down the street.

Sulking, ready to put the morning's nonsense behind her, she started toward the moonstone path leading to Rutherford Castle.

"Oi! Wait up!"

Behind her was Marcus, smiling in his easy, charismatic manner. It was so different from Charlie's, which, although genuine and warm, always felt politely restrained to Evie. The brothers' looks in general were indicative of their differences, she thought. Side by side, it was obvious they were related, each good-looking with attractive eyes and Liam's strong jaw. But where Charlie's face appeared to be the product of a thoughtful sculptor, each chip made with careful consideration, Marcus' features looked, by comparison, like they had been chiseled with swift determination and confidence, giving mistakes like his slightly crooked front tooth an endearing effect.

"How does it find you?" Marcus asked, reaching Evie. He pushed a swath of brown hair off his forehead. "Or, what do you say? What's above?"

"What's up?" Evie corrected him. She smiled, then scowled as they started up the pearly moonstones in step. "Nothing. I just spent a couple senseless hours wrapped in fabric, literally and figuratively."

"Ah, the old flower lesson."

"In the Other World, lessons come with instructions."

"It's not really the kind of thing you can instruct," Marcus said unhelpfully. "Look, haven't you ever sensed something you couldn't explain? Felt something in here or in here?" He lightly tapped Evie's head and the top of her sternum. "It's probably happened, but you've ignored it because you were never taught it meant something."

She thought of that morning in Edinburgh and the abstract sensation she now understood had been spurned by Charlie's presence nearby. "I guess. Maybe," she said. "It's hard to articulate."

Hearing her frustration, Marcus gave her a sympathetic look. "You're not used to explaining it, that's all. I mean, you can describe my good looks because you can rate these smoldering eyes against those of average men." He grinned. "But you've nothing with which to compare the feeling of Alicrat."

Evie rolled her eyes, but had to smile back at him.

"All I'm saying is, your senses are stronger than you think," Marcus said, giving her shoulder a comforting squeeze.

This made Evie think of something else, something she'd not considered could be significant until now. She told Marcus as much. "It's probably nothing, though," she added hastily.

"Stop discrediting yourself. What is it?"

"In the Other World, I study art," she started slowly. "It's a timeless form of expression, a way to connect to our forebears as if there weren't hundreds of years separating us. Well, sometimes, it's almost like...like I know the artist," she blurted. "One in particular. Hieronymus Bosch. Of course, I don't know him; he's been dead for centuries. But sometimes it's like he speaks to me — just me — through his art. Not always. But when it happens, it's profound."

Marcus stared ahead, looking reflective.

"It's silly. Just daydreaming, really."

"Hey," he said, and stopped walking. "Don't do that, remember?" He smiled, a softer version of the cheeky grin from before. "Why would you keep that to yourself?"

"I guess you're right. I never recognized it for what it was. Besides," Evie laughed, "who would I have told? In the Other World, people who speak to the dead are crazy."

Marcus hesitated, then said, "Well, I'm one to talk. I've felt the same way you do with art, but with music. I haven't told a soul." A shyness Evie wouldn't have guessed he possessed crept into his words.

"Piano?"

"Ah, you saw the paintings in the sitting room." They started walking again, Marcus growing more animated as he spoke. "My great uncle Llewelyn gave us all lessons as children. I fell in love immediately, not only with playing piano, but with what I felt when I did."

"Which was?"

"The composer's emotions." He looked contemplative, then said, "It's like the emotional detritus of history tries to cling to objects — a painting, a book, a piece of music. It doesn't want to get swept up in time, lost to the ages. It tugs at us in the present, wanting us to remember the past."

"You should talk to Charlie about this," Evie said. "I think he would appreciate your perspective."

Marcus let out a sardonic laugh. "Doubtful. Charlie thinks I'm a replica of Father, waiting to become Arbiter. Nothing more."

They'd reached the castle gates, their alicrated protection shimmering in the late afternoon sun as it assessed their energy. Facing Marcus, Evie asked, "Is he wrong?"

He glanced past her. The sun glinted off his irises, revealing the deep, golden flecks that contributed to their hazel color. Evie thought again of the brothers' sculptor, now handing over the completed busts to a painter who gave Charlie green eyes — the color of safety, a solid hue, no surprises — then splattered Marcus' eyes with whatever colors were left. Caramels and tawny browns and the remaining green — bold, unpredictable.

Those eyes were back on Evie. Marcus grinned, suave and confident once more. "I'll be Arbiter whether I want to or not," he said, shrugging away the question. "Hey, before I forget, how are your virdisemp injuries?"

Evie winced at the mention, though Seely's remedies had healed most of the bruising surprisingly quickly. She rolled up her shirtsleeve to show this. Marcus grasped her forearm, pulling her a step nearer to him in the process, and gently ran his other hand down its length.

"Much better," he said softly.

In that precise moment, Evie became acutely aware of an electric fog that hung between her and Marcus, thick with possibility, crackling with lightning that would strike if she allowed it. She wondered for a split second if this was Alicrat, wondered in the next second if Marcus felt it, too, and knew another second later that he did. Unlike Charlie, there was nothing controlled or measured in his touch. If there was, he would have lowered her arm already. He still held it, his thumb pressing into the soft underside of her wrist, his eyes watching her for any sign of rebuke.

The castle's gates swung open, breaking the moment, the affrim inside having received their energies to alert whoever was nearby that they were coming. As it happened, that was Illis, who was still not over Evie's return. She greeted her with as much excitement as she had on the first day, then pointed her toward the stairs, informing her that Charlie was waiting for her in the library.

Evie took her time walking to her room, waiting for that fog of possibility to dissipate. But as she climbed the spiral staircase to the library, remnants of mist clung to her like dew on a blade of grass. Alicrat or not, whatever she'd felt, she could not unfeel.

15

CHARLIE BALANCED on the highest rung of the tallest ladder on the catwalk level of the library, his head in the rafters of a turret where excess books were stacked precariously, bursting with anticipation to share his discovery with Evie.

"Charlie?" Her voice sounded from far below.

"Evie!" He descended from the ladder and leaned over the railing of the catwalk. Then, without warning, he flung himself over the edge and came barreling down. Evie's shock had barely registered on her face when he slowed, floated through the last two meters of air, and touched down lightly.

"Tardevol," he said. "Manipulating the threads of gravity to slow a fall."

"A simple alicration, I'm sure," Evie said, waving a hand. "I'll learn right after I find the flower."

Oblivious to her annoyance, Charlie beckoned her to the table in the middle of the library, which was covered with books and loose pages of hastily scrawled notes. One of the books was a compilation of Hieronymus Bosch's works. Another was the Tree Book. The next wasn't a book at all, but the Rutherford Bosch painting.

Charlie took a deep breath, excitement lighting his eyes. "I was considering," he said, "what kind of person in Callidora might know Alterra Lingua. My first thought was a Mensmen. One Mensmen is always responsible for keeping records — Maiorial elections, Normalex violations, things like that. One such Mensmen, current or retired, might also know Alterra Lingua. Then I thought, no." He raised a finger, though Evie hadn't interrupted.

"If the information in the Tree Book is so important, the Callidoras would not have entrusted the ability to decode the book's contents to someone obvious. The Callidoras themselves are the most obvious. A Mensmen would be, too. Either one of them understanding Alterra Lingua would be like keeping a key right next to a locked door you want no one to enter. Do you see?"

"I guess so," Evie said. Her fingers traced the frame of the Rutherford Bosch absentmindedly. "Charlie, what's your theory? I would be so grateful for someone to just explain things outright to me today."

"An inconspicuous advisor, Evie!" Charlie said. "I think the key to the locked door, the Alterra Lingua interpreter helping generations of Callidoras decode the Tree Book, is a *nobody*. So, if you don't keep the key with the door, it stands to reason that this person would not be someone enmeshed in Callidora politics."

"Someone far removed from the Callidora family," Evie said, nodding. The nod turned into a shake of her head. "This person could be literally anywhere."

"Far removed on paper, yes. Maybe not geographically. In fact, I believe this person is, and always has been, in Callidora."

Evie pursed her lips. Charlie could tell she thought he was grasping at straws. "Look here!" he said hurriedly. He pointed to a cluster of florens painted in the periphery of the Rutherford Bosch. "Do you see these deep red starburst petals? These are a species of floren called callindros."

"Indigenous to Callidora, I assume?"

"Not only that. Callindros cannot grow anywhere else. The Rutherford Bosch is indisputably set in Callidora."

Evie lit up. "Bosch must have visited Callidora!"

Charlie grinned, a professor relieved to have finally engaged his reluctant student, then shifted gears again. "Stick with me, now," he said. "What does the viewer see when the left and right panels of the *Seven Deadly Sins* triptych are closed? When the broken pieces from the Other World — *Ship of Fools, Allegory of Intemperance, Death and the Miser* — are folded over the missing central panel, our Rutherford Bosch?"

"The cover of that triptych is called *The Pedlar*," Evie said. "According to art historians, the Pedlar is an allegorical figure who actively chooses destitution and refuses all possessions, lest he fall into the sinful traps of humanity. A fitting cover for a triptych representing mankind's greatest sins."

"The Pedlar," Charlie confirmed, pointing to an image in the Bosch book.

The man depicted in the image was haggard, painted mid-step, with one leg bent and ready to carry him onward toward the metaphorical Ox — a symbol of Christ — waiting by the gate. The other leg paused behind him, his body turned three-quarters, his gaze fixed on what he would be leaving behind: a tavern of drunken patrons. The Pedlar was on the cusp of leaving a life of frivolity and sin to take up the righteous path of Christ.

"Now, look here." Charlie pointed again, this time at a figure on the Rutherford Bosch. "The Pedlar."

Evie nudged him aside to get closer to the painting, peering at the lower right-hand corner. She'd noted it before; the man painted as if about to step out of the frame. Now, she saw he held the same pose, carried the same burden upon his back, displayed the same wrought glance back at humanity's sins as the Pedlar.

"So," Charlie said, "we have the Pedlar depicted on both the cover and the central panel of a triptych which, because it also depicts callindros, is set in Callidora."

Evie squinted at the two Pedlars, one painted, one printed. "Okay," she said eventually. "So what?"

Charlie grew serious, nearing the climax of his theory. "I believe the Pedlar is the Alterra Lingua advisor to the Callidoras."

Straightening up, Evie regarded Charlie with a skeptical tilt to her head. He barreled on. "I believe the pack on his back is a metaphorical burden. He looks at humanity with longing, wishing he could unload that burden and live like everybody else. He cannot. He must continue on his path, wherever it may lead, and he must carry that burden no matter what."

"And the burden is?"

"Knowledge of Alterra Lingua. Knowledge that enables him to interpret the Tree Book's secrets for the Callidoras."

Exhaling heavily, Evie flopped into a chair.

Charlie sat in the chair next to her. Leaning over, he said, "We need to track down the Pedlar."

"Come on, Charlie. A man painted five hundred years ago?"

"An impoverished man who would never set foot in Callidora Castle," Charlie continued, ignoring her tone. "An insignificant man who would not be looked at twice by the Obscures as the key to the Tree Book. An unassuming man who you'd never guess was privy to the secrets of the Northland's most powerful family." He took her hand, imploring her to see his logic. "At least, that's who I would use as the key to my deepest secrets."

Capitulating slightly, she said, "It's an interesting theory. But why do you assume Bosch knew this secret keeper in the first place? Why do you think he had any knowledge of the Tree Book at all? The Pedlar is probably just a man he saw in Callidora."

Finally, the question he was waiting for. Charlie grinned. "I knew you would ask that." Referring to the Bosch book once more, he flipped to a bookmarked page displaying the famous *Garden of Earthly Delights* triptych, showing how the left and right panels folded over the bright blues, greens, and pinks of the central panel. The resulting cover, *Creation of the World*, displayed an earthly sphere in the grey monotones of grisaille.

Evie was so focused on examining the *Creation of the World* that she didn't immediately notice Charlie pushing the Tree Book closer. He didn't speak as her gaze shifted to the golden tree, as her eyes traced the tree from its trunk to its branches, and finally, to the earthly sphere they cradled. One in gold, one in grisaille, otherwise, the very same sphere.

"Hieronymus Bosch knew about the Tree Book," Charlie said. "Its golden cover inspired his *Creation of the World*."

Evie gasped, her eyes darting between the two books before her. She leaned forward, one palm on the Tree Book's golden sphere, textured and aged, one palm on the Bosch book's greyscale print, glossy and smooth. "Maybe..." she whispered. "Maybe Bosch didn't just know the secret keeper. Maybe he *was* the secret keeper. The Pedlar could be a self-portrait!"

Now animated and engaged, Evie continued to speculate out loud. Smiling, Charlie leaned back in his chair, watching her; the way her eyes brightened as she recounted his theory, the sharp intakes of breath that preceded each new idea, the slight parting of her lips when she paused, thinking. She was simply incredible, he thought — physically beautiful, yes, but also energetically so. He sensed it in the unique weave that made her *her*, felt it in the gentle thrum of the silver thread that was now a near-constant presence between them.

Since seeing her again on Castle Hill, Charlie had not allowed himself to even think of Evie this way, let alone sense her energy so intimately, let alone act on the way it made him feel. Someday, he would. It was a thrilling thought, one that made him want to clear the table of the Pedlar and Bosch with a swipe of his arm so that he could focus instead on Evie, study Evie, *learn* Evie, with no great mysteries casting shadows over their path forward!

Charlie reeled himself back. There was too much to accomplish, not only for Liam and the safety of the Northlands, but for Evie. Part of her was contained within the Tree Book, and she deserved to be whole. Charlie wanted her whole.

And so, he averted his gaze from Evie and instead, stared at the iterations of spheres and Pedlars before him, vestiges of one world painted from another. Next to him, Evie was focused on the Pedlar, as if waiting for the painted man to step out of the Rutherford Bosch's frame, lift the Tree Book's cover, and recite her family's secrets out loud.

He did not, and by the time the stars and the moon sent the sun home, Charlie's excitement over his breakthrough had spoiled to worry. He worried they would never find the Pedlar. He worried they would never decode the Tree Book. He worried Evie would never be whole.

16

Weeks passed, and in those weeks, Evie settled into a routine.

Her wardrobe from Timpson arrived and she tore into the packages with more enthusiasm than she'd expected. Thanks to the alicrations woven into the cloth, everything fit her perfectly. She now had a collection of practical trousers, shirts, and shoes, plus a slew of dresses and more fashionable garments Juliette had insisted on. With help from Serena, Evie also mastered some simpler woven hairstyles. Sporting a five-stranded braid and her new clothes, she finally looked like a Northlands citizen — sans Alicrat.

She woke with the sun each day to roam the castle grounds, starting with the stables, where Nica lived with another unicorn, Shu. She met Leon, the quiet stable hand with flowing grey hair that rivaled the unicorn's manes, and the only hollow employed at Rutherford Castle. He showed her where Biscuit had taken up residence in Nica's pen; it seemed the cat had grown used to the attention garnered by sticking around on William Street rather than appearing at the whim of Evie's emotions.

After visiting the stables, Evie circled behind the castle, where she had a view of the lake that shone purple in the early lavender light.

Often, she'd spot Charlie and Marcus there, lifting rocks or swimming laps in the lake, racing and roughhousing like children until they doubled over in laughter. Evie would watch them like a hidden sociologist, trying to reconcile that brotherly camaraderie with the far more typical interactions she witnessed.

By the time she returned to the castle, the staff's daily activities were underway. There was a sizable orchard and garden on the property, and Evie often lingered nearby to watch the groundskeepers, Beinelton and Codes. They worked their way methodically through the produce, pulling weeds and picking fresh fruit by hand. Watching Beinelton strain to reach a juicy appleberry dangling from a particularly high branch one morning, Evie asked why they didn't use Alicrat.

"Who's to say?" Beinelton said, snatching the appleberry. Then, triumphantly, "It's more rewarding to do this kind of work manually, no?" He handed the fruit to Evie. "Besides, manipulating living things is so very draining. You'd be surprised at how stubborn the threads of a weed can be."

Not fully understanding, but having always done that sort of work manually, Evie agreed. And so, in an environment where nobody questioned her lack of Alicrat, she helped the groundskeepers. She was tasked with weeding the rows of stellans, a plant that looked like dried dandelions, but stood as tall as Marcus with heads the size of a globe. Their multicolored fluff was carefully trimmed by Beinelton and Codes on orders from Juliette, who was keen to cover the entirety of the ballroom with them for the upcoming Northlands Congregation.

When she tired of weeding, Evie took pallets of produce back to the kitchen for Plum, who always seemed stressed. She whipped up Evie's oatmeal each morning in the time it took her to say hello, slid it down the length of the table, then glanced at her every few minutes to see if she was finished before whisking the empty bowl away with the last spoonful still raised to her mouth.

"She's not always like this," Illis said one evening while delivering Evie's laundered clothes. Evie had offered to do her own washing, but Illis had shooed her away as if any labor on her part was out of the question. Well enough, as the household chores, including laundry, were done with alicrations. "We all become a bit crazed when Benclair hosts the Northlands Congregation," she said.

"Is it that important?" Evie asked, putting some trousers in the wardrobe.

"Hardly." Illis chuckled. "But don't tell Juliette that! It's a party, nothing more. A chance for Arbiters, Maiors, Mensmen, and their families to enjoy the music and food of the hosting State. Juliette puts far too much pressure on herself to impress the guests. All people need is a vocat and they'll be happy."

Juliette did not share that sentiment. She was up earlier than Evie most mornings, flitting about the castle, taking measurements and miming the positions of decorations with a trio of planners from The Fern. They caught the sound threads of her voice as she spewed ideas, saving them to reference later, and rolled their eyes when her back was turned.

Catching Evie one morning on her way to meet Pembroke, Juliette asked, "Have you decided?"

Evie paused in the courtyard. "Decided?"

"Your dress!" Juliette looked exasperated. "Serena has chosen a periwinkle monstrosity. She claims it is *comfortable*. You'll chose a jewel tone, won't you?"

"I haven't —"

"Not green, though the deep green of the esmardo gem would compliment you. But I'll be in green. My gown from Timpson should arrive any day...oh, you'll just *die* over the luscious silk I've chosen, Evie! Perhaps burgundy for you?"

Evie agreed, unsure whether she had a burgundy dress.

Pleased, Juliette returned to her serious consideration of which room the affrim should be moved to, if at all. "It's only, not many can boast an affrim of such size," she mused to herself. "Perhaps we keep it out to be admired?"

The planners cast Evie a jealous look as she slipped out the door.

Every day Evie met Pembroke at the wall. Every day they walked to the clearing. Every day he spoke in convoluted riddles, and every day Evie found herself unable to predict if he would answer her questions or insult her. Nor could she predict how long she would stand in the clearing, shrouded, before being released. One day, Evie broke.

"Maybe I'm just not meant to find my Alicrat," she said, yanking the shroud off. "Maybe I'm a hollow. Maybe I'm predisposed to obscurities and my mind doesn't want to let them out."

"That tirade was most unbecoming," Pembroke said. "And obscurities are not a predisposition. They are part of us all. Rogue magenu chose to act as they do."

It was the most straightforward he'd been with Evie, and she wanted more. Frustration forgotten, she said, "Obscurities aren't a special skill, then?"

Pembroke began walking away without warning, as usual, but continued to speak. "Anyone with the desire to perform an obscurity may do so."

Evie ran to catch up. "Charlie told me that the AO cult began innocently," she ventured, "with curious magenu looking to expand the possibilities of manipulations."

"Indeed. Most found those curiosities satisfied with dabbling. Most understood there were lines that should not be crossed. Those who harbored a desire to harm stepped up to the line and over it."

Still walking, he picked up a small twig. "We were once one," he said, then snapped the twig into uneven halves. He tossed the larger piece to Evie. "Everyday magenu. Flawed, but inherently good." He stopped walking, held up the shorter piece, and dropped his voice to a whisper. "A dangerous minority."

Pembroke stared at Evie for a long time as if trying to work out which part of the twig she belonged to. "We shall walk in silence now," he finally said, concluding the first and last time he ever spoke to her with such clarity.

Wandering The Fern helped Evie clear her mind after Alicrat lessons. The Obscures didn't exist in the town's enchanted, mossy streets. She didn't need Alicrat to admire the displays in shop windows. One shop in particular — a bespoke watchmaker's shop called Teller's Time — became her favorite.

She'd first noticed it due to the familiar Green Man motifs carved on the lintel. Just like those in Rosslyn Chapel, their grinning faces were overrun with the vines of time, though in The Fern, the vines that wove into the mouths and nostrils were real. It was curious that such a distinct artistic theme existed in both worlds, and Evie often which world's artist had journeyed through a portal, bringing their artistic visions with them.

Green Man aside, it was Teller's wares in the window that kept her coming back. Some of his handcrafted watches marked time traditionally, looking no different than a timepiece from the Other World. Others had the added functionality of days, quarters, and the upcoming hundred years. Some didn't reference time at all, displaying the position of stars in the sky instead. Evie's favorite contained the whole of the universe within its tiny face, all sparkling galaxies and swirling nebulas.

Sometimes she caught Teller's attention when he looked up from tinkering. He'd smile and wave, a twinkle in his eye suggesting he knew something she'd very much like to know.

Inevitably, after these meanderings, Evie would run into Marcus finishing up business in The Fern or returning from a neighboring town, and together, they would walk the moonstone path home. Perhaps also inevitably, she found herself moving more slowly through the pines, deliberately drawing her time with him.

Marcus could be conceited, pompous, and often stepped over the line that bordered confidence and arrogance. But he also possessed an attractive wit and curiosity that kept Evie teetering on a line herself — one separating simmering interest with unadulterated captivation.

She found herself humoring his curiosity, or perhaps, trying to impress him, with shocking descriptions of the Other World: cars, roller coasters, computers, diseases, television. She'd often talk them all the way back to the castle without Marcus getting a word in edgewise, which he didn't seem to mind. He listened attentively, gasped satisfyingly, and laughed at all the right moments. Often, their conversations turned to Evie's past and its connection to the Obscures. Marcus had strong opinions and was not afraid to share them with her, a welcome change from Charlie's carefully delivered updates.

"Of course you're in danger," he'd say. "They may not know you exist, but that doesn't mean they can't figure it out." Or "As you know, Father doesn't care if you're happy here or not. He just wants you to decode that book," or "You'd best find your Alicrat soon if you ever want to travel outside Benclair." He was more forthright than Charlie in other ways, too. "You know," he would always add, his fingers grazing hers as they walked, "I care about you, Evie."

Inevitably, this made Evie think of that night in the Rosslyn Castle library, when Charlie's care for her — decades-old and undeniably strong — wove back into her. She *knew* Charlie cared about her, yet she could not imagine him declaring it now, and certainly not with Marcus' confidence. The pang accompanying this understanding always surprised her.

Not wanting to dwell on that feeling, she'd turn the conversation onto Marcus. "Aren't you also in danger?" she asked during one such discussion. "Surely, being Liam's right-hand Mensmen isn't the safest job. He sent you to Maliter, after all."

Marcus placed a hand over his heart. "Your concern touches me so." He was playing, but when she didn't respond in jest, he became serious. "We all have jobs to do. I can't very well walk away from mine, can I?"

"What if you could? Would you?"

"Probably."

These moments hinted at what might lie beneath Marcus' good looks and confidence, and Evie wanted more. Predictably, he would bounce back with a sly grin or comment before she could dig much deeper. In the afternoon before the Northlands Congregation, it came in the form of a raised eyebrow and an outstretched hand.

"Are you ready to dance tonight?" he asked as they entered the castle. "Surely Charlie has taught you the Tripudio." Aghast when she said no, he pulled her through the courtyard and into the ballroom.

The stellans, so carefully pruned by Beinelton and Codes, had been placed around the perimeter of the room in a repeating expression of the rainbow. Thick vines draped across the ceiling, meeting in the center like a whimsical circus tent. The rest of the room was empty, save for a piano, which Marcus sat down at and began to play.

The ballroom filled with arpeggios, working their way up octaves in elaborate variations before winding back down. A melody emerged in the treble, a haunting tune that tricked Evie into believing it was mournful before erupting into a major resolution. Marcus swayed over the keys, eyes closed, fingers moving as if he were alicrating the song into existence, and at that moment, Evie saw what he would have liked to do were he not his father's favorite son.

The song morphed into a lighthearted, folksy tune that could have been playing in a Bavarian beer hall instead of Benclair. Marcus bounded through a few bars then stopped, wove his hands through the air, and joined Evie in the center of the room. The music continued to play around them, its threads prevented from fading.

"Tripudio is a group dance," he said, moving to the beat, "so don't worry about being perfect." He hopped from foot to foot, jumping twice or three times before switching to the other. Evie mimicked him reluctantly. "Good! Next, you'll clasp hands with the person in front of you, then..." Marcus pulled her close, chest to chest.

Pressed against him, Evie became intensely aware of his physicality: the strength of his arms, the cadence of his breath, the heat of his body in the moment he held her. He smelled of pine, ink, and the indescribable scent of another, and she resisted the urge to inhale deeply.

He pushed her away and swung her to the left, all while continuing the hopping pattern they'd started with. They carried on until Evie was performing the dance on autopilot, making mistakes only when she laughed too hard. Each time Marcus pulled her in, he held her for a second longer, a scant bit tighter, his head dipping lower, until finally, their foreheads touched.

They stopped dancing. The music quieted, replaced by Marcus' breathing. There was that urge to inhale deeply, uncontrollable this time. There was his hand, moving lower on her back. There was that fog again, and now, Evie wanted it to envelop her, wanted the lightning to strike...

"Evie?"

She turned. Charlie stood at the entrance to the ballroom, arms crossed, palpably angry. She took a quick step away from Marcus. He pulled her back.

Charlie's voice was flat. "Mother is looking for you. She wants to arrange your hair."

"Of course. Thanks for the lesson, Marcus."

"Anytime," Marcus said. "I do more than dance, you know." With a wink, he released her.

Evie hurried out of the ballroom and up the stairs. The brothers' voices followed, along with the scent of pine and the rapid beat of her heart.

17

Rutherford Castle was abuzz with energy. Decorative alicrations lit up the towers, exploding at the top in bursts of Benclair green. Nica and Shu stood outside to greet visitors, lowering their heads for the children who rushed forward to pet them. Even Biscuit made an appearance, sometimes finding a welcoming shoulder to perch on, sometimes finding a swift hand. Ivy hung over the castle entrance, a curtain through which guests left Benclair behind and entered the enchanted forest that Juliette's vision — and a flurry of workers from The Fern — had created.

Inside, clusters of transplanted florens rose past the five stories, their expansive petals creating a canopy beneath which spheres of sunset bled lavender and golden hues. Most impressively, an aquenum alicration pulled water from the lake through a window on the fifth floor. It cascaded down the staircase like a waterfall, pooled at its base, then rushed back to the top via the handrails. Milo and Nim stood around the small pool, marveling at the fish Leon had brought in for the occasion.

Evie watched Liam and Juliette greet the steady flow of magenu — rather, she watched Liam nod curtly at fellow Statesmen while Juliette bore the labor of actually making guests feel welcome. She smiled at the women and complimented their gowns, danced expertly between flirtation and flattery with their husbands, and fawned over the children who threatened to spill, splash, or otherwise wreak havoc on the world she'd so carefully crafted within the castle.

As the courtyard filled, Evie started to notice minor differences in the affects of each State. Benclair citizens seemed politely restrained compared to the open joviality of Teraur guests and the passionate dramatics of Iristell magenu. Callidora and Maliter were notably absent, though she couldn't help but imagine her fellow Callidorans would command a quiet power over the Congregation. When she envisioned Maliter, she saw only blank faces, dead eyes, lost souls.

Wanting to find Charlie, Evie gathered the weight of her dress to peruse the courtyard. To Juliette's joy, she *did* have a burgundy gown, one with intricate pleats that made it twice as heavy as something simpler would have been. She passed Serena, who looked ethereal and, certainly, comfortable, in her periwinkle dress. She chatted to visitors with airy confidence alongside Finneas, who, with Marcus, wore trousers and a sharply cut jacket in dark green velvet.

This attire helped Evie identify the other Benclair Mensmen, who were dressed identically. Having finally located Charlie, she stood next to him as he named them one by one. "Eilif of Manitolla," he said, indicating toward a slender woman wearing a more feminine cut of the Mensmen suit. "Sharp as a knife. If my family weren't in power, my pecs would be on her to lead Benclair."

He pointed to two men, heads cocked in serious admiration of the affrim that pulsed with a steady, safe green, registering and recognizing the multitude of energies on Rutherford property. "Caym of Norrisson and Lamino of Lochend. Neither as smart as Eilif, but Marcus claims they're persuasive pontificators. And the last..."

One more green-clad Mensmen approached Charlie and Evie and, despite being shorter than Charlie, pulled him into a hug that lifted him clear off the ground.

"Ole!" Charlie laughed, squirming. "How does it find you, mate?"

"You know me. Great as ever!" He turned to Evie, a gregarious smile touching blue eyes a shade darker than hers, and bowed deeply. "Oleander of Orefo, at your service."

"Charmed, I'm sure," Evie said, smiling herself. Oleander's energy was infectious.

Charlie pulled Evie closer to him. "This is Evie, Ole. A family friend."

"Oi, Charlie!' Marcus called from a few meters away. "Help me with these vocats."

Charlie gave Evie's waist a parting squeeze and joined his brother, who was pouring bright purple vocat into glasses. A curious task, as orbs of ale, wine, and vocat already hovered around, allowing for bottomless refills provided one retained their glass.

Leaning toward Evie, voice low, Oleander said, "I know who you are."

Evie whipped her head around.

"It's okay," he said, hands raised. "Liam and Marcus told me everything yesterday. They wanted extra eyes on you tonight, just to be safe." He nodded seriously, but quickly broke into a grin, whispering in earnest, "I can't believe I'm meeting someone from another *world*!"

Evie relaxed, feeling nothing but affable protection from Oleander. They chatted about nothing in particular — Oleander clearly trying very hard not to ask about the Other *World!* — until Charlie returned with Marcus and a round of vocats.

"Enjoy," Marcus said, handing a glass to Evie. His arm froze. He stared at her unabashedly, as if seeing her for the first time, taking in her cinched form with blatant interest. Blushing and aware of Charlie's eyes on them both, Evie stuck her nose into the glass of vocat. The scent was unfamiliar, a cross between blackberries and bitter chocolate.

"Leideberries," Charlie said. "The leide plant only grows in northern Benclair and produces berries once every ten years. Leide products are rare —"

"— and expensive," Marcus finished. "Hence why it's not floating around with your average cherry and plum vocats. Can't imagine how Mother convinced Father to splurge on six bottles."

"Cheers!" Evie lifted her glass. Charlie joined, leaving Marcus and Oleander looking confused.

"Soli," Charlie clarified, and all four glasses clinked.

Evie nearly spat out her gulp.

"Yeah, it's not great." Marcus conceded, grimacing as he swallowed.

"Bleh!" She thrust her empty glass back at him. "I'm good now, thanks."

He chuckled. "Oh, you will be!"

"Leideberries are quite potent," Charlie explained. "The vocat induces a mild euphoria, but the pure berries are downright addictive. Just one dulls pain, physical or emotional. Not that I would know from experience," he added hastily, glancing at Oleander.

Oleander smiled guiltily. "Mum still has that bottle of dried leideberries! You remember trying one, don't you, Marcus?"

Marcus laughed. "I remember Charlie threatening to tell Mother."

Charlie, Marcus, and Oleander began recounting childhood memories, moments together that Evie could have been, but wasn't, present for. Despite the jovial environment, she felt that familiar pang of regret, wondering what she'd missed out on by growing up in the wrong world.

"I'm going to help Serena with the boys," she lied, interrupting the reverie. "I'll find you later."

"Okay," Marcus and Charlie said in unison. Her words had landed somewhere between the two of them, and she walked away before she could decide for whom they were actually meant.

Slipping through a cluster of stellans, she stepped into the sitting room, where the thrum of the Congregation was considerably muted. She was not alone. Juliette lay sprawled across the cloud couch with a hand over her eyes. Upon hearing Evie, she sprang upright to smooth her unwrinkled gown. Its train took up an entire side of the couch. Evie sat in one of the armchairs across from her.

"I am merely taking a repose," Juliette said before Evie could ask, gesturing at the courtyard. "It is dreadfully exhausting, carrying the conversation for two." Her brow furrowed.

"Liam not the sociable type?"

Juliette smiled wryly. "He is distracted with Northlands issues, I suppose...not that he would deign to tell me anything of importance. And it is my role, after all, as lady of the castle..." She spoke more to herself than Evie, rubbing her forehead. "Whatever are you doing away from the excitement?"

"Also needed a repose," Evie muttered.

Juliette regarded her, sadness clouding her features. "I met your mother at a Congregation, you know." She smiled wistfully. "My first. Adena was the only person to make me feel welcome."

"Were you not —"

"I was a commoner," Juliette said bitterly. "A mere serving girl at the Golden Pec, dreaming of a better life, when a young Liam Rutherford walked in. Everyone around me saw Benclair's next Arbiter. I saw an opportunity."

Evie couldn't hide her shock. Not only did Juliette's candor surprise her, she couldn't believe the woman seated across from her, who looked every bit a queen as Elizabeth, had grown up outside castle walls.

"I became the woman I needed to be," Juliette continued softly, "for Liam, at least. The wives and women of other States weren't so quick to believe my charade. But to your mother, it didn't matter. She welcomed me with open arms."

Evie felt an involuntary sense of pride for the woman she had only a tenuous understanding of. She leaned forward, wanting to hear more.

"With Adena, I could be myself," Juliette said. "We drank brown ale instead of sipping cherry vocat. We spoke about topics most *unbecoming* to ladies in our positions." She outright grinned and a very different Juliette from the one Evie knew emerged momentarily.

"You were like Richard," Evie mused. Juliette looked horrified. "I think Adena had a thing for outcasts. You and my father were her windows to the rest of the worlds because she knew she would never have a door."

Juliette softened, nodding. "Perhaps you're right."

"There you are, Evie!" Oleander's face peeked into the sitting room. "Time to dance. You too, Juliette!"

Starlight orbs hovered amongst the vines in the ballroom, creating a dim glow ideal for drunken dancing and illuminating countless iridescent sparkles on the floor. "Sopul dust," Juliette informed Evie as they crossed the ballroom, arm in arm. "Rather exotic. I had it imported from the Orenisles. Don't tell Liam." She giggled like a schoolgirl.

Evie drifted away from Juliette and Oleander, drawn to a trio of magenu in one corner of the ballroom. A board hovered before two of them, which they struck with a metal rod. The ensuing notes began with the wooden *ding* of a xylophone, then carried on with the vibrato of strings, which the third mageno wove into a song that was cast throughout the ballroom. Evie would have watched the musicians all night, mesmerized, if Charlie hadn't pulled her away to begin the Tripudio.

Evie shot Marcus a grin, grateful for his foresight a few hours earlier, and slipped into the line of women that was forming, each with a corresponding man across from them. Both lines swayed back and forth in unison, arms clasped around each other's waists as the melody started, and then, to Evie's surprise, they started to sing.

"The rolling hills of Benclair, I sing to thee! I thank you for the sun, the moon, the stars, and the trees. The gentle land of Benclair, I sing to thee! Of all the worthy Northlands States, it's here I long to be."

The citizens of Teraur and Iristell shouted their own names in place of Benclair, resulting in congenial laughter, only the most stoic voices holding it together for the next verse.

"As I went roaming o'er the land, I traveled far and wide. But elsewhere in the great sun's world, I could not abide. I yearn for thee! I sing to thee!"

Juliette and Serena's hands slipped away from Evie's waist to thrust into the air.

"Benclair! Benclair!"

Another verse began and then it was all repeated, so Evie joined in the second round. The leideberry vocat had settled into her system and she felt one sip short of the euphoric haze Charlie had described. He smiled lazily at her, swaying next to his brother and looking, for the first time since Evie had met him in Edinburgh, completely relaxed.

The music transitioned into the lively tune Marcus had played earlier. Evie hoped alongside Juliette and Serena, discovering quickly that doubling over in laughter was actually an essential part of the dance. They jumped left and right, barely in sync but hardly caring. The men were no better. Oleander had no rhythm at all, and Finneas barely maintained his composure as he watched his friend hop off beat. Charlie and Marcus were clearly the best of anyone at the Tripudio; their crisp steps were in perfect sync, and for once, they weren't trying to outdo each other. Even Liam appeared to be having a good time, hopping between his Mensmen Caym and Lamino.

Oleander reached out to grab Evie's hands, grinning widely and yelling over the music. "Best not to form your opinion of me based on this dance!"

Evie laughed. "Me, either!" They pulled themselves together, broke apart, and Evie swung to the left.

"Fancy seeing you here," Marcus quipped. He pulled her in sharply, taking advantage of their brief proximity to press his lips against her cheek before she veered down the line again.

"Having fun?" Charlie asked. Cheek burning, room blurring, Evie could only smile.

She shifted down the line, facing mageno after mageno, all of whom were predictably intoxicated on vocat. Liam even flashed a grin before sending her away. The music grew faster, magenu from Benclair, Teraur and Iristell blended into one, and then she was before Oleander, Marcus, and Charlie once more. She stood face to face with them, shoulder to shoulder with Serena and Juliette, tears of laughter rendering them all unable to dance and none of them caring.

The world around Evie became something she never could have imagined, filled with people she could not fathom losing. A heady joy emerged that had nothing to do with the leideberry vocat, and Evie sank into the bliss. Even though she knew it wasn't true, even though she knew she would feel differently come morning, she let herself pretend, for the rest of the night, that she could be happy never knowing what happened to her mother.

18

As the frivolity of the Northlands Congregation wore off, life returned to normal. Evie resumed her morning strolls around the castle, pointless Alicrat lessons with Pembroke, post-lesson walks with Marcus, and long sessions in the library with Charlie. They'd made no further progress on the Pedlar.

Evie understood the importance of translating the Tree Book for the sake of the Northlands, but she was starting to wonder if it was really the best hope of discovering what happened to her mother. The problem was, short of going to Callidora, she didn't know where else to look.

Marcus was game to speculate about Adena's fate, but Evie knew he assumed her dead, just as Liam did. Juliette was forthcoming with memories, but they involved drinking brown ale and ranking attractive Northlands Mensmen with the former Callidora Arbiter. Evie stewed on the possibilities alone until one day, as she meandered The Fern after another flowerless lesson with Pembroke, an alternative theory came from an unlikely source.

"Care for a pearsnip puff?"

Evie pulled herself away from Teller's watches to find Oleander behind her. "Parsnip?'

"Pearsnip. The Golden Pec makes the best puffs."

They secured a table outside The Golden Pec, wobbly on the mossy cobblestones, which Oleander fixed with an alicration. Puffs ordered, he sat back in his chair, smiling at Evie. "It's just incredible you're from..." he glanced around, "...you know."

Returning his smile, Evie noted, "You were quick to accept the concept of another world."

Oleander shrugged. "I grew up believing anything is possible, thanks to my Mum. She's got all sorts of strange beliefs about magenu falling out of time, disappearing without a trace...she has one about your mother, actually."

The pearsnip puffs arrived and Oleander made a point of Evie trying one before he continued. She bit into the fruit-filled pastry with enthusiasm, delighted by the starchy sweetness of the insides. She took a second bite, nodding at Oleander.

"Good, right?" he said, pleased with her reaction. Then, with absolutely no build-up, "My mum's theory is that Adena was displaced."

"Displaced?"

"It's when your own energies are pushed out of the world's frequencies. It doesn't have to be extreme, just enough to land you on a different vibrational plane."

"Charlie never mentioned this."

"It's not exactly an accepted concept," Oleander said. "More of an old hollow's tale. But I think it happened to my Da. He fancied himself an explorer, see. He'd leave for days, partuming around the Northlands, until the Northlands became too small. He started traveling further, to other lands. Not unheard of, but rare. He went to the Midlands, the East Expanse, the Iceisles. How he reached these places, I don't know. It's hard enough to locate threads from a place you've never been to, let alone fold them accurately enough to land somewhere safe."

Evie wiped puff crumbs from her lips, shaking her head. "I don't follow."

"Ah, I take it you haven't had the pleasure of partuming yet."

"That, Charlie mentioned," Evie said, recalling their trek through the Empty Fields, "but never explained."

"Partuming allows us to travel over great distances by locating the

117

threads extending to our desired destination, folding them, and... creating a doorway?" Oleander chuckled. "I can do it, I just can't describe it."

"Like a wormhole," Evie said, nodding. "A shortcut."

"Sure," Oleander said, also nodding. "Anyway, Da left to explore the Vastlands and never came back. The Vastlands are far across the sea, a dangerous partume even if he'd found the right threads. He's probably floating around in limbo, unable to detangle the threads of a place he's never known in order to land."

It sounded horrible to Evie, but Oleander appeared blasé. "Something similar could have happened to your mother. Something that put her in limbo."

"Sure," Evie said, her turn to nod without understanding.

Yet Oleander's theory kept her up that night as she imagined her mother trapped in an unknown realm. Unable to sleep, she padded up the spiral staircase to the library, which, without electricity nor starlight orbs, was dark. She patted her way to the table where Charlie had thoughtfully left a cluster of candles and a matchbook from Edinburgh's Scotch Malt Whisky Society.

Mindful of the literal walls of books surrounding her, Evie lit the candles, illuminating the Rutherford Bosch. She pulled it closer, then pulled it upright so that she was face-to-face with it.

"Are you there?" she whispered, remembering Marcus' words.

It's like the emotional detritus of history gets swept up in time... It tugs at us in the present, wanting us to remember the past.

She brought her face closer to the painting, so close her nose was almost touching the Adonis-Devil hybrid in the center. There was nothing. No understanding of Bosch's intent when he'd painted the sinful scene, no fleeting explanation for the presence of the Pedlar in the corner.

Frustrated, Evie laid it back on the table with more force than she'd intended. She cringed, fearing she'd cracked the old wood it was painted upon. She raised it again to check the back. No cracks. But there was something: a piece of paper, yellow with age, one corner lodged into a divot in the wood. She tugged at it carefully, jostling it this way and that until it came loose. She slid one of the candles closer, held the paper beneath it, and read the small, tight cursive.

At first, the skies were black and the earth was bare. But soon, the sisters began to weave wonderful things with the threads of the Ortus. The sun, the moon, the stars. The mountains, the oceans, the grass. The florens, the flowers, the trees. This was The First Sfyre, and it was beautiful. They gifted this world to their children who maintained harmony with the land, helped by their Higher Knowledge which the sisters had bestowed upon them. These children were the magenu, and they

It ended abruptly. Evie envisioned the author being called away unexpectedly, never to return. She turned the paper over.

"Oh my God," she whispered.

Charlie's room was just as Evie imagined it would be: neat. A tartan blanket from the Edinburgh Woolen Mill was folded precisely over an armchair, his boots were lined up perfectly against the wall, and the desk was covered in tidy stacks of paper.

He'd not answered her early morning knocks. Assuming he was exercising at the lake with Marcus, she'd let herself in to wait. She sat patiently in an armchair for a while, until curiosity took over, drawing her to examine the stacks of paper on the desk. One contained college-ruled notebooks filled with lecture notes, and another, crisp A4 pages with twelve-point Times New Roman detailing a religious studies thesis. The last pile, all old paper with rough edges, was topped by a makeshift notebook. *Charlie Rutherford* was written proudly across the cover. Evie opened it to a random page.

58th of the Fourth, 11,1995

I cannot find the Tree Book anywhere! Mother says it is lost. She doesn't understand. I wanted to learn what was inside! And she said Evie had to go back, but she will not tell me where. I fear she is gone forever.

Underneath were Charlie's attempts at replicating Alterra Lingua from the Tree Book. Evie flipped through the notebook, finding the rest of the pages filled with the symbols, carefully approximated by his childish hand. He had even drawn the branches from the cover of the Tree Book that continued onto the pages with solitary stanzas.

Why are these alone? he'd scrawled.

Hearing footsteps down the hall, Evie put the notebook back and returned to the armchair as the door opened. Charlie had indeed been exercising at the lake, as evidenced by his lack of shirt and wet hair.

"Name of the sun!" he said, taken aback. "What are you doing in here, Evie?"

She stood, trying not to stare at his bare torso, which was decidedly more fit than she'd assumed. "I couldn't wait. Have you seen this before?" She handed him the paper from the back of the Rutherford Bosch. He took it with one hand as the other absentmindedly alicrated dampness from his hair and chest.

"It sounds like a creation myth," he said, clearly unsure what to make of it. "Which is strange, because we don't exactly have those here." He handed the paper back to Evie.

"That's what I thought," she said, trailing him as he went to his wardrobe, picked a shirt, and pulled it on. "I mean, no religion, right? I've noticed. The First Libellum teacher told the children that the threads of this world simply fell into place naturally. So why does this reference a world — the First Sfyre — being gifted to the magenu by a higher power? What's the Ortus?"

"I don't know," Charlie said, grabbing the paper to look again.

"Well, turn it over."

On the other side, faint but visible, was a sketch of a sphere containing trees and clouds. The outline of two women hovered above it. It would have been unremarkable, had Evie and Charlie not seen almost the exact image before.

"*Creation of the World*," Charlie whispered.

It was nearly identical to the grisaille painting on the cover of the *Garden of Earthly Delights* triptych, except rougher, like a quick sketch to get an idea out of one's head. The only difference was that the singular, male God in the final Bosch painting was, on the paper in Charlie's hand, two women.

"There's an inscription," Charlie said, looking closer. He read haltingly. "For they spoke and it was done. For they commanded and they were created."

"Psalms 33:9 and 148:5," Evie said. "It's written on *Creation of the World* too, but there, the pronouns are 'he,' referring to God. Here it's 'they,' referring, I guess, to these two women. Who are they?"

"Who indeed? And look here. More text. Barely legible."

"What?" Evie took the paper back from Charlie. She'd not noticed anything else in the dim library, but in Charlie's room, bright with the morning sun, she saw it. "As told by...Mel...Chomp...Dito?"

Charlie peered over her shoulder. "Melcholm," he said definitively. "It's a common first name here. There's a surname too, which I've not heard, but I'm pretty sure it says Perdito. *As told by Melcholm Perdito.* Have you heard of him?"

"I've not heard of any Melcholm Perdito," Evie said slowly. "But Perdita, I have. My father worked in her bakery in Callidoralta. I suppose it's not quite the same name, though."

"It is." Charlie stared at her, dumbfounded. "Though not common now, older family names were often gendered with vowels, similar to the structure of the Other World's Romance languages. A Perdito and Perdita are likely related." He said this calmly, but excitement brightened his eyes.

"My father said she was ancient, but maybe she's still alive. Maybe she's still in Callidora. Let's go and find her bakery!"

Evie wanted Charlie to pick her up and swing her around in celebration of a desperately needed breakthrough, to kiss her and tell her how brilliant she was. Instead, he began soberly pacing, running a hand through his hair.

"Let us consider our assumptions," he said. "We assume Bosch visited Callidora. We assume he not only saw the Tree Book, but that it inspired his *Creation of the World* painting. Now, with that same sphere as a rough sketch upon a page with a creation myth referencing an actual Sfyre, credited to one Melcholm Perdito, we can assume..."

He came to a stop in front of Evie, seeming unable to articulate the conclusion.

Evie said it for him. "We can assume the Callidora's secret keeper, their Alterra Lingua advisor, was Melcholm Perdito. The whole Perdito family, probably. Perdita would be the most contemporary."

Breaking into a grin, Charlie took her by the shoulders and pulled her a half-step closer, then all the way, bringing his forehead to touch hers. He lowered his voice. "We must find Perdita."

"Then let's go to Callidoralta," Evie repeated, pulling away. "Let's find her bakery!"

"Callidoralta is enormous, Evie. There's probably dozens of bakeries there." He stroked his chin. "We'd be better off starting with the State archives to find records of Melcholm or Perdita. But with the unknowns there…" He shook his head. "It could be dangerous, and you still don't have Alicrat. We should wait."

They left Charlie's room together, Charlie to update Liam in his study, Evie to return to her room — begrudgingly. This was the breakthrough they'd been waiting for, a real lead on someone who might speak Alterra Lingua, and Charlie wanted to wait? She'd been patient through the hours under Pembroke's shroud, the hours poring over books in the library. Now, finally armed with something actionable, Charlie wanted to —

"There you are!" Marcus said.

Lost in her thoughts, she'd run, quite literally, into Marcus. It appeared he'd also been exercising at the lake, as he was also lacking a shirt.

"I've been looking for you. Come with me? I need to get dressed. Unless…" He leaned against the banister, arms crossed, eyebrow raised.

Suppressing a grin, Evie waved him along.

Marcus' room was much messier than Charlie's and smelled, now familiarly, of pine and ink. There were obvious signs of his role as a Mensmen, but it was also cozy, lived in, and bore evidence of the Marcus Evie had come to know. A piano in one corner held piles of well-loved music, including handwritten sheets he'd composed himself. A collection of bows and quivers of arrows hung on a wall, along with a slew of awards from competitions.

Flopping onto a couch, Marcus said, "I've had a revelation."

Evie sat next to him. "I thought you needed to get dressed."

He flipped the usual bit of hair off his forehead. "I figured I'd have a better chance of convincing you like this."

"Of what?"

"It has to do with your memory from the Silvana Seraphilles. I can't believe I didn't think of it before." He paused, waiting for Evie to guess or beg. She didn't give him the satisfaction. Smirking, Marcus leaned forward, elbows on his knees, and said, "Let's go there. All this sitting around, hoping something will come to you, waiting for Charlie to decode that book...it's pointless. Let's see if being in the forest conjures more memories."

The notion was more than intriguing. "Will we partume?"

Marcus leaned back onto the couch, looking impressed. "You're learning fast, aren't you?" He stroked his chin thoughtfully. "No, we'll take Nica and Shu, spend the night. Someone could track a partume. Someone could follow and ruin our fun."

Unsure if he meant Liam or Charlie, Evie said, "I suppose we'll need your father's approval."

"Let's just do it. Let's leave at dawn and not tell anyone." Marcus gazed at the wall of archery medals, whether with resentment or pride, Evie couldn't tell. "So," he said after a moment, "what do you say? Ready to — what's the word? *Ditch* a few of Pembroke's lessons?" He winked, back to his usual self.

Charlie proposed waiting. Marcus proposed action.

Evie was more than ready.

19

HEAD BENT, face hidden by the hood of an oversized cloak, Blair moved quickly through Talus. The tattered thing was far too big for her, a discarded rag from Stin, but it was better than nothing. She preferred the visual protection of larger clothing anyway, though the cloak would be of no help should she encounter danger on her commute. In Talus, that was certain.

It was early morning, and the sun should have been drenching the town in gold. Blair remembered when that used to happen, barely. A childhood memory, one of the few she allowed herself to recall fondly, involved feeling the sun's warmth on her bare skin. Early childhood was the last time she could remember being truly carefree, unaware of the problems around her. Now, she was lucky to have a few minutes during the day to let her guard down, and the sun remained hidden behind impenetrable grey clouds.

Talus had been a dark town even before the sun retreated, for its streets and buildings were built of charcoal-colored stones. This made the end of one building and the beginning of the next nearly indiscernible and, with the clouds, created the illusion that Talus was a cave. The stones were hewn from the nearby quarry and cobbled together with mortar to create the lopsided buildings that were in a seemingly constant state of disrepair. Only the homes of the wealthy were made with alicrations anymore, because only the wealthy could afford magenu labor. These days, the wealthy were predominantly Obscures.

The rest of Talus — the rest of Maliter, really — relied on the cheap manual labor of the hollows who were lured the Northlands' most wretched State by the promise of paid work that did not require Alicrat. Though they made up a scant fraction of Talus' million citizens, the hollows comprised almost the whole of the quarry's workforce. But Stin worked in the quarry, too, so Blair knew the hollows were prisoners, not citizens, and the work they did was unpaid. Toiling for a pittance along-side the hollows and Stin were a few dozen other magenu, desperate enough to take on the dangerous job. Death seemed to visit the quarry even more than he did the streets of Talus, after all, which was to say, often.

The building where Blair worked was also made of dark stone, but it was a grand building, recently erected in the name of the Alicrat Obscura cult, and so it was constructed of quality, polished obsidian. Mortar wasn't needed; blocks of the glinting stone were fit together seamlessly with binding alicrations that would take hundreds of magenu hundreds of years to undo. The Domus, as it was called, was named for the large, domed roof that capped the Atrium at the center of the struc-ture. The roof was made of glass. Blair liked to stand beneath it and watch the clouds.

The Domus was an unusual structure, and not only because of its fine obsidian stone and unique architecture. It was also the only building in all of the Northlands in which the Arbiter, Mensmen, and Maiors conducted their business that was not the ancestral home of the Arbiter. That particular tradition used to be honored in Maliter — the Mensmen and Maiors had convened in Eliot Castle for centuries — but no longer.

Last year, an expanse of homes in Talus were demolished without warning, their residents still inside, so that construction of the Domus could begin. It was said the bodies of the casualties were buried beneath the liquid obsidian that was poured to form the ground floors. Towns-people flocked to the building site anyway to admire the gleaming stone and enormous panels of glass. Nobody knew what the building was for until it was too late. Eliot Castle burned to the ground after that, the flames so bright they woke Blair from her sleep miles away and tricked her into thinking the sun had shown its face again. It hadn't been the sun, of course. Adrian Tenebris declared himself Arbiter the next day and moved into the Domus.

The danger in Talus multiplied after Adrian took the Arbitership, though to ever call Blair's hometown 'safe' was laughable. When the children in other States learned how to sense the world's beautiful threads with their Alicrat, Blair was taught to sense bad intentions. As other children learned to alicrate spheres of water, Blair was taught to weave her surroundings into a shield against sudden attacks. While other children ran together in the schoolyard, Blair ran from Obscures.

She learned to sense when she was near a shade maker, an Obscure who might snatch her off the street and kill her for the sole purpose of practicing reanimation. The resulting shades weren't dangerous, only deeply depressing. They floated through town, mobilized by energy that did not belong to them. Not quite transparent, not quite opaque, they left a chill in their wake that took hours to dissipate.

Blair was also taught to look out for changelings, a quickly growing subculture of the AO. Changelings contorted their own threads to become something different, often horrifying. They were difficult to identify by sight alone — they could look like almost anything — but few were skilled enough to become a perfect replica of their subject. Most appeared as something or someone damaged. A dog with a bent tail. A man, ordinary until he opened his eyes to reveal empty sockets. Blair had mistaken true magenu for changelings more than once, but as Stin always said, better to offend a disfigured person than trust a changeling.

The biggest lesson of Blair's childhood was to keep her Alicrat on alert at all times. It had always been dangerous to walk the streets with one's guard down, but ever since the Obscures started showing their faces without shame, it was downright treacherous. Nothing stopped an Obscure from manipulating at random. Nothing stopped an innocent passerby from being the unfortunate recipient of a new obscurity.

Blair could not recall in her lifetime any real regulations of obscurities, but she knew the AO used to operate underground. When they started to emerge, she remembered thinking that surely, they would be stopped. Surely, it would be easier for the Enforcers to police disobedience when it happened out in the open. She wasn't alone. So many people she'd known in those years had assumed the same, but it soon became clear the Enforcers couldn't, or wouldn't, hold the AO accountable. And rather than face the truth before them, citizens closed their eyes and made excuses.

But no one I know is an Obscure, they said, as if that meant no Obscures existed outside their circles.

They're just a silly little cult! they insisted, as if that wasn't how all dangerous entities began; a gathering of the few, the fringe, the maligned.

The time when that notion didn't strike Blair as absolutely naive was now as distant as the last time the sun kissed her skin. Nobody stood up to the AO. Everybody learned to keep quiet and look out for themselves. Now, it was a nice little rhyme that children recited: *In Maliter, you'll never thrive, but with vigilance, you might survive.*

Also distant was the last time Blair allowed herself to feel something about anything. Of course she grieved, she resented, she despised, but she kept it all buried, rarely allowing herself the luxury of emotional freedom. Instead, she masked every feeling with a credible impassivity. This allowed her to convince roaming Obscures she was one of them, which spared her from having to torture innocents with obscurities to prove herself. This was the biggest fear of the remaining Norms — that they would encounter a band of Obscures who would demand a show of loyalty.

Blair was thirteen the first time she was accosted by the AO. A pack of Obscures demanded she abscond the bones from the body of an unsuspecting Norm. An impossible task for a child, even if it weren't so gruesome. Yet Blair found something within herself, disturbingly easily, which allowed her to bend the weave of the Obscures' blackened bones until they believed she was one of them.

Now, when Obscures passed her in the street, they didn't question her loyalty. Only yesterday a teenage boy, assuming Blair was one of his own thanks to the dark energy she projected, flashed her a conspiratorial smile before taunting a nearby Norm. The woman was forced to summon and kill her own familiar, a beautiful grey deer, by a boy young enough to be her son.

Her ability to exude convincing darkness often disgusted Blair. There was something wrong with her, she thought, to have such easy access to something so despicable. Then she would wonder what had happened to the woman who killed her familiar — part of herself, really — and she was grateful for the protection her inner demons offered. Besides, Blair's icy façade did more than convince the AO she was one of them. It also froze the pain engendered by all she had witnessed, preventing it from overtaking her. There were many ways to die, after all. Sorrow could kill you, too.

As she grew up, Blair learned that most Obscures were just cowards who found easy protection beneath something larger than themselves for the small price of identifying with its doctrine. Others, of course, were bullies, and some were truly evil, born with insatiable, morbid curiosities that they pursued as their moon-given right. Blair only feared the evil Obscures. The others, she pitied. To survive, though, she respected them all.

Collectively, they created an entity with such power that it did demand respect. It was to be feared. Blair knew this, and she accepted it, begrudgingly. But beneath her mask, dark as the floors of the Domus, burned a rage brighter than any sun. Blair accepted the Obscures, for now. She also planned to do something about them.

20

FASTER, *faster, Evie tells herself. Once more step and she is out of the forest.*

She takes that step and she falls straight off a precipice that was not there before. She falls until she no longer feels it in the pit of her stomach, until the airborne sensation is expected. Why has she not landed? Why have her bones not shattered on impact with the ground?

Because she is dreaming.

And if she is dreaming, she is not really falling.

Evie is back on solid ground, standing in a vast, empty field under a starry, but moonless, sky. Stars move toward each other, collide, and light up the heavens with double the brightness before breaking apart again. This happens over and over, twin constellations converging and separating. But where is the moon?

"You do understand why you can see them, don't you?"

Her pursuer is behind her. Evie tenses, ready to flee.

No, she reminds herself. It is a dream. It cannot hurt you.

"Ah, you've caught on." The voice is not taunting, not angry, not anything. It is just a voice.

Evie turns to face her pursuer, but there is little to face. The outline of a hooded figure, perhaps, but it's too dark to tell. Though the stars shine, they alone cannot illuminate the night. They need the moon.

"You see no stars in the daylight, do you?" the figure muses. "The sun denies them, believing herself to be the most important entity in the sky. Entire days of the year are devoted to the sun's glory, and for what?"

Evie doesn't know.

"Even at night, the sun makes herself known, shining on the moon, allowing it to be seen. And the moon must suffer further embarrassment, forced to wax and wane, allowed to be seen in her entirety for such a short time before shrinking to a sliver once more. Why the ritualistic humiliation?"

Evie scans the sky again.

"The moon left," the figure says, sounding bored. "It's gone to wherever it goes when it wants to escape the sun. In the Somund, at least. Where it can explore. You still haven't answered my question."

"Because it is dark," Evie says.

"Indeed. You can see the stars because it is dark. One needs darkness to appreciate the light. Both are necessary, working in harmony. The sun thinks she doesn't need the darkness. She is wrong."

An icy edge has returned to the voice. Evie decides she wants to wake up.

"Not so fast. We've only just become properly acquainted, haven't we?"

Evie squints, trying again to see who she is speaking to. There could be an army behind the shadowy figure. There could be nothing.

"I told you," the figure says, "I have been looking for you for a long, long time. It has been difficult, especially after what she did to me. She didn't believe me, but look! Darkness every night. Just as I said. It is natural. Necessary. And it is my darkness, not hers, yet she controls the moon and orchestrates the stars and sends Dawn to usher her back to her throne each morning! But as she has performed this ritual without me, I have had time. Time to think. To understand. To find you, Evie."

Evie speaks without thinking. "I have nothing to do with this."

"You have everything to do with it. Where do you think we are right now?"

Evie scans her surroundings. In the distance, something rises from the *ground, enormous and ancient, reflections of starlight upon its leaves. Evie knows where they are.*

"I don't know."

"Liar." Suddenly, the figure is very clearly standing inches away from Evie's position. "This is your dream, not mine. Where are we?"

Evie remembers how the breeze blew across the grass when she first arrived in this place, the countless shades of green dancing against each other at her feet. That same breeze passes through her dream and catches the edge of the figure's hood, lifting it. The stars continue to swing around each other above, merging and separating. Stars collide and the concentrated light hits the figure's face beneath its lifted hood.

But there is no face to be seen, only the deep, empty craters of the dark side of the moon.

21

"Woohoo!" Marcus cried, blazing past Evie on the black unicorn, Shu.

Evie nudged Nica to keep the pace. Her hair whipped in the wind and the cloak she'd worn to keep off the early morning's chill billowed behind her as she pulled up alongside Marcus.

They'd left a loquer in the courtyard explaining to anyone who passed through it that they'd return in two days' time. Evie had considered telling Charlie where she was going, then decided he could hear it from the loquer, like everyone else. She tried not to dwell on what felt like a small betrayal, lest she consider *why* it felt like a small betrayal.

The Silvana Seraphilles lay to the west of The Fern, where the snow caps of distant mountains glinted against the rising sun as dawn's lavender gave way to the morning's blue. Once the world around them was bathed in light, Marcus slowed Shu to a trot. Evie followed suit.

"We've got a ways to go," he said. "If we want to get there and back in two days, we'll need to pick up the pace."

"I have enough riding experience," Evie said, readying herself for a more punishing gallop.

Marcus looked apologetic. "What do you know about unicorns, Evie?"

"Only what my world's mythology believes. Their blood is said to have healing properties."

"That much is true, but there's something else. Something your world doesn't seem to have figured out. Unicorns are fast." Marcus leaned forward on Shu and gripped her horn. "Hold on tight, like this. Brace yourself firmly with your legs. Nica will take care of the rest."

By fast, Marcus meant impossibly fast.

Evie barely had time to register Nica's readying whinny before the unicorn took off. She had even less time to register anything around her as they traveled; trees and florens appeared for blink-and-you'll-miss-them moments, entire lengths of villages were reduced to snapshots. They traveled like this for over an hour, the world reduced to an inconceivable blur, until Nica finally slowed in tandem with Shu.

The unicorns' preternatural pace had brought them clear across Benclair. Though still surrounded by hills, these were steeper and more plentiful than those in the eastern territory. The previously distant mountains were much closer, too, but still lay well beyond a vast expanse of blue valley below. Only it wasn't a blue valley, Evie realized. It was the Silvana Seraphilles as seen from above, its blue-petaled florens rippling in the breeze like waves in an azure ocean.

Not taking her eyes off the seraphilles, Evie dismounted from Nica. "My God," she whispered, surprised by the lump in her throat. Maybe it was the fact that the forest was the last place she could remember having been with her mother, or the only place from her childhood she could remember at all. Whatever the reason, she blinked back tears as she stepped forward, fixated on the seraphilles.

Through blurry eyes, she noticed something, barely, upon the seraphille heads. She wiped her eyes, trying to see more clearly. Noticing this, Marcus reached out, grabbed hold of nothing, and pulled his hands back, bringing a quartet of seraphille heads with them.

They were magnified images, semi-opaque, like holograms, hovering before Evie in miniature. An amplio like the one he'd just performed, Marcus explained, was a difficult alicration, requiring one to grab hold of specific threads and to pull them in together. "I might have dropped a few along the way," he said, "so it's a bit fuzzy. But you get the idea."

The resulting image was clear enough for Evie to see what sat atop the amplioed seraphilles: birds, four of them, unlike any birds of the Other World she could recall seeing. The first was large, tan, and covered with small black dots. The second resembled an owl, but below its beak protruded two feathers, like a handlebar mustache. The third was crow-like but huge, sporting a long tail. The fourth was a sad-looking creature with a short beak and beady eyes, and though the least interesting of them all visually, was also the most familiar.

While Evie examined the birds, Marcus stepped away from her to assess their path down to the forest, rendering him visible through the amplioed seraphilles like an underlaid image. He bent to adjust his boots, and in that exact moment, his torso lined up with the last bird's beak. The beak opened, creating the illusion the bird was swallowing Marcus whole.

"Bosch!" Evie cried. That sad creature was identical to a bird from the *Garden of Earthly Delights*, the one seated on a chair in the Hell panel, swallowing a man. They were all Bosch birds, in fact, which delighted Evie.

"Your artist, right?" Marcus said, returning to her position.

"Oddly enough, he's one of yours, too. You know that painting above the sitting room fireplace? He painted that."

Evie filled Marcus in on what she and Charlie had been researching. A grudging respect overcame what was initial resistance in Marcus' eyes, and though he didn't admit it, it was plain he could see the value of Charlie's effort. More surprising, he added to it.

"I know where that painting came from," he said as he performed a reverse amplio to return the seraphilles. "Your great grandfather, Erskine of Callidora, gave it to my great uncle Llewelyn."

Of everything she'd seen, learned, and experienced, *this* stunned Evie. "My ancestor knew Bosch?"

Marcus tilted his head toward the seraphilles. "Let's walk."

They began their descent of the hill leading into the forest. Soft grass soon gave way to wilder terrain, and as they carefully stepped around rocks, thistles, and a few rogue virdisemp bushes, Marcus told his story.

"Llewelyn was the family rebel," he said. "His father, Maxwell, wanted him to become Arbiter, but Llewelyn's passion was music. He left Benclair to travel the Northlands and make a name for himself as a composer."

"That's where you get your talent," Evie said.

"I'm nothing compared to Llewelyn," Marcus said with uncharacteristic modesty. "He was commissioned by Erskine to compose a symphony in celebration of the peace following the Northlands Wars. In an effort to rebuild friendship between States, Erskine started the tradition of the Northlands Congregation with Llewelyn's music as its anthem. Erskine appreciated the power of the arts, and he and Llewelyn became close friends. So rare here, that kind of understanding," he added wistfully.

"Before Llewelyn returned to Benclair, Erskine told him to take whatever he wanted from the Callidora collections — your ancestors were avid collectors of art and oddities of all sorts — as a parting gift. He took that painting."

"Excellent choice," Evie said.

"Not for Erskine," Marcus said. "Apparently, he was reluctant to give that particular piece up. He told Llewelyn it had been in the family for generations."

"I wonder how my family first acquired it."

Without realizing it, Marcus completed the circle. "Llewelyn told me that, too. A couple hundred years earlier, an artist had wandered into Callidoralta. He rented a room above a local bakery and spent all day inside, drawing and painting. At the end of the day, he'd toss his work out the window. It became a sort of ritual, I guess, and townspeople flocked to the bakery to collect these images."

"That had to be Bosch!" Evie cried.

"Well, Bosch, I suppose, disappeared one day, leaving behind one painting. The baker auctioned it off and Isabil Callidora, the Arbiter back then, bought it for 600 pecs."

A genuine Bosch for less than a full wardrobe of new clothes, Evie thought.

"It stayed with the Callidoras until Erskine let Llewelyn take it, but he made Llewelyn promise that the Rutherfords would never sell it and that they would return it to any of Erskine's descendants who wanted it back. Father offered it to Naveena years ago, before she'd gone full recluse, but she said it was ugly and told us to keep it." Marcus glanced at Evie, eyebrow raised. "Technically, it's yours."

Evie stopped in her tracks and rescinded her former thought. *This* was actually the most impossible, wonderful, stunning scenario; all she had to do was ask, and she would own a Bosch painting. The elements of the dismantled *Seven Deadly Sins* triptych would reside in the Yale Museum of Art, the National Gallery of Art, the Louvre, and whatever flat she ended up in back in Edinburgh. She imagined the graduate student dinner parties she would throw, telling her peers, "That? Yes, it's a genuine Bosch. Just something my family picked up from an other-worldly bakery."

"Do you want it?" Marcus moved closer to her. "Or anything else from me?" He winked. Evie shoved him playfully.

"Really though," she said as they resumed their walk, "this is incredible! I wonder why Charlie didn't know his own great uncle procured the painting?"

Marcus laughed joylessly. "He could have asked me about it, but then again, the sun would sooner die. Father doesn't know, either. I heard all this from Llewelyn himself." He laughed again, considerably more joyfully now, recalling something. "After piano lessons, he used to tell me all about —"

Evie and Marcus ran into Nica and Shu, who had come to a halt. Marcus tried urging Shu on, but she snorted a definitive no, her glossy mane swinging as she shook her head. They'd reached the bottom of the hill, near the edge of the seraphilles, and the unicorns refused to go any further.

Marcus peered into the forest. "Something is wrong," he said quietly. "I don't know what's in there. It's hard to tell without getting closer." He turned to Evie to say, bluntly, "It could be dangerous, but it's your decision. If you want, we'll go home."

Evie peered into the forest too, but she saw nothing threatening, sensed nothing malicious, between the looming seraphille stalks. Instead, she saw Charlie, his eyes pained and serious, in the Rosslyn Castle library, struggling to articulate the dangers of his world. She saw her father, lost and broken and begging for her to forget, to stay. She saw her mother and the fear behind eyes that looked so much like her own as she'd carried Evie out of the seraphilles, toward safety.

Come back, said Charlie.

Stay, said her father.

Don't look, said her mother.

Ignoring them all, Evie turned to Marcus. He was watching her, more concerned than she was used to seeing him, but still solid and strong. "I didn't come here to wait for a book to translate itself," she said. "I have to go in there."

Marcus nodded slowly. "Then we'll go in."

Setting her gaze on the seraphilles, Evie marched on.

22

THE AIR in the forest was faintly blue, textured by spirals of mist rising from the soil. Animals growled and grunted, Bosch's birds screeched and chittered. Marcus kept an arm around Evie, both of them wary, moving in silence. Glimpses of the sun between the dense stalks were their only indication as to how long they'd been walking.

And then Evie saw him. So too had Marcus, for he thrust an arm out, preventing her from moving closer. The mageno Adena had killed years ago lay before them, each half of his torso drained of blood, his viscera splayed and encrusted. Birds had plucked his clothes to shreds, yet his visible skin was completely intact with no signs of decay, no evidence that animals had feasted upon it. The fallen seraphille hadn't rotted, either. Its stalk was just as green, just as alive as the rooted florens around it.

"How is he not decayed?" Evie managed.

As she spoke, the mageno's eyes blinked once, twice, excruciatingly slowly. A shallow breath escaped through cracked lips. He was not decayed, and he was not dead.

Marcus approached the severed torso. Kneeling alongside it, he carefully held his hands above it. He pivoted to the fallen seraphille and placed his hands directly on the stalk. When he rose, he said, plainly, "Your mother performed an obscurity."

"She wouldn't," Evie said reactively, struggling to reconcile her limited knowledge of obscurities with her limited knowledge of her mother. Obscurities were evil. Her mother was not.

"Evie, there's an obscurity over this man, binding him to the seraphille. It's preventing him from dying. Barely."

"I don't understand," Evie said. "Charlie said only the worst magenu use obscurities."

"Charlie coddles you," Marcus muttered. He steered her to a floren log, away from the mageno, where they sat side by side.

"He wants to protect me," Evie deflected. "Anyway, that's hardly coddling. Pembroke said the same thing."

"Pembroke wants you to protect yourself," Marcus said, "with Alicrat. Charlie curates information so you'll *need* him to protect you. It's different."

Stiffening, Evie looked away.

"Look," Marcus said, "My brother can't keep you safe from everything. Neither can I, as much as I may want to." He took her hand, pulling gently for her to face him again. "I understand that. I'm not sure Charlie does."

"Can we stop talking about him?" Evie said.

"Let's talk reality, then," Marcus said, sighing heavily. "We have a contact who works at the Domus, the Obscures' hub in Maliter. One of the interesting things she told us is that the cult has a security alicration called a floccin to track their important members. It's linked to every living Obscure of importance." He glanced at the halved mageno. "When one dies, their energy disappears from the floccin. An unexpected disappearance of energy is cause for alarm."

Evie understood immediately. "If he'd died, they'd have sent someone to finish the job."

Softly, Marcus said, "Adena did what she had to do to survive. So too may all of us, eventually."

The magenu huffed out another breath and worked his face into a pitiful, but disturbing sneer.

"He's listening to us," Evie whispered. She looked away, horrified. "We can't keep him like this, Marcus."

"It's cruel, I know," he said. "But it's been effective for over two decades."

"Exactly. Surely they're not still monitoring his energy."

Marcus shook his head. "We should leave him."

Evie forced herself to look at the Obscure. Perhaps he deserved this kind of suffering, she thought, watching the florens around him receive the gift of death, his last breath never his last. Then again, it didn't matter what he deserved. It mattered what she could live with.

"He'll haunt me forever, Marcus."

Marcus pushed the unruly bit of hair off his forehead and rose from the floren log. "Okay," he said, exhaling. "Stay back, will you? I'm going to try to untie the alicration."

Standing over the mageno, he got to work, his fingers moving with slow uncertainty. But soon the felled seraphille log started to wither, seeming to melt away as it decomposed into earth. With the removal of the threads that bound his life to the seraphille's, the man's halves decayed until they, too, were soil.

Just like that, he was released. Evie wondered vaguely where he'd gone — to this world's hell? To the Other World's? Perhaps the two shared a fiery eternity.

A twig snapped with the weight of a step.

Immediately, Marcus pulled a minuted parcel from his pocket and tossed it into the air. He caught the resized bow with one hand and slung his quiver of arrows over his shoulder with the other. Evie stood motionless at his side, barely breathing, and in the indeterminate moment before chaos broke, she became inexplicably aligned.

The forest had grown darker, yet she saw its life, its essence, its *threads* in full color. The greens thrummed, the blues pulsed, the browns hummed. The seraphilles' energy was innocent, unaware of the danger brewing beneath them. Next to her, Marcus' adrenaline pumped through her like they shared a heart. Whoever had snapped the twig, though hidden from view by a seraphille stalk, emanated a terrifying calm. All of these energies exploded around Evie in a chaotic weave and she saw the elaborate tapestry of the world.

In the next instant, she understood how complicated it all was. There were too many threads, woven too tightly, too intricately...how could she understand one, let alone millions, to twist, tie, manipulate?

With that, the glimmer of alicrative understanding vanished.

A black-clad figure stepped out from behind the stalk. It was a woman, her face uncanny, like she'd contoured her features with alicrations. Her hand snatched something out of the air — Marcus had shot an arrow. She hurled it back at him like a javelin, which he narrowly dodged.

Spotting Evie, she reached out her hand and grasped air. Before Evie could react, she was pulled out of her cloak and dragged across the forest floor. Twigs tore through her shirt, cut up her back, and then she lay at the magena's feet, staring up at her unsettling face. The magena yanked her up by her hair and snaked her left arm around Evie's neck. Her other hand hovered over Evie's chest, poised as though ready to stab, yet she held no knife, no weapon of any kind.

She didn't need one, Evie remembered in a detached way. She was an Obscure, and Evie felt more hollow than ever.

The magena told Marcus to drop his bow. He did. "Hold up your hands," she said. "If I catch the slightest hint of alicrative movement, I will stop her heart."

Marcus' eyes darted to the hand hovering over Evie's chest. He obeyed, but also took a step forward. "I'm Marcus Rutherford, son of Liam Rutherford, Arbiter of Benclair," he said, a slight cockiness edging his voice. "You're trespassing and you're threatening my friend with an obscurity."

The woman didn't flinch. "You shot an arrow at me."

"We'd come across a dead body. I assumed you had something to do with it."

The magena jerked her head toward the spot where the halved mageno had lain. She chuckled in Evie's ear, a deceivingly normal sound that did not at all prepare her for what was said next. "That was Adena Callidora's doing, not mine."

Evie tensed — the whole forest seemed to tense.

"And so what?" The magena dropped her voice. "We killed her in the end."

Marcus caught Evie's eyes, shaking his head. She didn't know what he meant until she realized her elbow was thrusting itself with all the force she could muster into the woman's stomach, who buckled in surprise at the manual attack. Evie wrangled herself free and ran behind a particularly thick seraphille stalk. Her contribution had been meager, but it was enough to let Marcus rearm and land an arrow in the woman's thigh.

"Arrows won't cut it, boy," she said, pulling it out of her flesh. "Try it my way, won't you?" Grinning, she spread her arms wide in a come-at-me stance.

Temptation darkened Marcus' face, different from the concentration Evie observed in magenu when normal alicrations were performed. It was a consuming, furious focus that frightened, but also intrigued and attracted her — to Marcus, and to the concept of a dark manipulation.

Marcus sliced his arms through the air with bellicose. Slits appeared in the fabric of the magena's shirt. Small nicks sliced her face and chest, too, yet she remained utterly motionless, save for an amused sort of smile, until Marcus stilled, spent from his efforts.

"Pathetic." She wiped a red drop from her cheek, sneering. "Did you mean to do *this*?" She slashed the air as Marcus had, but where his movements had been forced and aggressive, hers were delicate, almost lazy, like she was conducting a waltz.

Marcus screamed, a horrified wail of both pain and disbelief. His clothing darkened to a wet crimson and he cried out again, worse, for Evie could hear the defeat. Still, she remained useless behind the seraphille, infuriated by the Obscure's casual ease, reeling from the confirmation that her mother was dead, watching Marcus writhe as his flesh was flayed — yet completely, utterly frozen.

Another scream, but not from Marcus. It was the Obscure, yelling and stumbling as a creature the size of a large dog and covered in reptilian scales gnawed through her ankle. Another animal, orange as the setting sun, wrapped itself around the magena's head and dug its claws into her eyes. She fell to the ground and the reptile-dog pounced onto her chest, gnawing into the softness of her throat. Pinned, hemorrhaging, the woman raised her intact arm toward Evie. She moved her fingers in an attempted alicration, but could not complete it. Her arm fell. Her eyes closed. Her chest stilled.

Evie ran to Marcus, who had also collapsed, but was still breathing. Blood flowed from lacerations on his face, his arms, his fingertips... surely everywhere else, for his pants and shirt were saturated. Though, unlike his attempted obscurity, which had sliced the magena's clothing but barely scratched her body, his garments were completely intact. Such had been her skill that she'd chosen what to slice and what to spare — flesh or fabric.

Evie's cloak lay in a heap next to him. She tore it into strips with her teeth. Lifting his shirt carefully, she set about trying to staunch the flow of blood from the worst of the gashes, which exposed tissue and muscle. He cried out through clenched teeth, chest heaving.

"I'm s-sorry, Marcus," she said. She longed to comfort him, to lay a healing hand on his chest, but there was no unwounded skin. She could only apologize pitifully.

"Summon..." Marcus said. His breath was ragged, his words forced. He lolled his head to the side, eyes closed. "Unicorns."

Not knowing how else to accomplish that, Evie lifted her head and yelled into the night for Nica and Shu. She yelled until her voice was hoarse, scanning between seraphille stalks all the while for signs of another Obscure. With each passing minute, though, it seemed clear the dead magena hadn't been important enough to be monitored on the floccin. Nobody, Obscure nor unicorn, came.

Leaves crunched behind Evie; the reptile-dog was making its way toward them, Biscuit perched atop its back, licking blood off his paws. Evie vaguely recognized the creature from another Bosch painting, but her former elation at seeing his painted beasts in the flesh now felt shamefully silly.

"Bowie," Marcus whispered, opening his eyes a fraction. "Well done."

Sniffing Marcus carefully, Bowie began gently licking his deeper wounds. Biscuit, meanwhile, had hopped off Bowie's back to circle Evie, purring. She picked him up and inhaled deeply. He smelled of coffee from the café on William Street, hay from the stables, and blood.

"My familiar," Marcus said, trying, and failing, to raise an arm to pet

Bowie. He started to tell Evie how they'd first found each other, but she shushed him, unable to bear how clearly painful it was for him to speak.

"You'll tell me later," she whispered, pulling his head into her lap. Comforted by the animals, they waited like that, Marcus drifting off, Evie continuing to staunch his wounds.

At last, Nica and Shu skidded to a stop behind them, whinnying their relief. Seeming to register Marcus' state, Shu circled him, stamping her hooves. Nica, in response, placed her horn against Shu's neck and pushed, creating a small incision. Shu lowered herself down, allowing Marcus to run a finger along the injury. Once coated in blood, he brought it to his lips.

Almost immediately, color returned to his face and his breathing became less forced, though far from steady. The thinnest of his cuts vanished. Most of them stopped bleeding, and after another drop of Shu's blood, some even crusted over. "I think that's the best we can do," he said. His voice was quiet, but an underlying strength had returned. "We need to leave."

Evie helped Marcus onto Shu, then climbed onto Nica, their familiars leaping up after them to settle into their laps. The unicorns trotted out of the Silvana Seraphilles, clambered back up the hill, then resumed a slightly calmer version of their former preternatural gallop, understanding the urgency, but also the poor condition, of their humans.

Away from the forest, comprehension that her mother was truly dead hit Evie. She swerved the thought, letting it blur into the dark of the Benclair night. She did the same with the realization that Marcus could have died because of her. She would let these thoughts solidify later. She would feel grief and shame later. For now, she let everything melt into a heavy, black haze, willing it to seep into the sky and disappear, as they rode home.

23

WHEN HE COULDN'T SLEEP, Charlie wandered through the castle. In the dead of night, there were no Mensmen pushing past him, no disappointed father frowning at him, no strutting brother acting as though he were already Arbiter. Charlie felt most at home in Rutherford Castle at night, when it was just himself and thousands of years of history.

From an open window, he pulled a bit of starlight into a sphere to light his way down the corridor. Portraits of his ancestors peered at him along the way: his grandfather Issac in full Arbiter regalia; Issac's brother Llewelyn smiling behind a piano; their father Maxwell, the stern man from whom Charlie got the copper in his hair; Maxwell's mother Luisal, one of Benclair's most beloved Arbiters.

Then there was Liam, painted in his prime before the stress of Northlands politics and familial disappointments bent his shoulders. In another portrait of Liam, Juliette stood behind him, satisfied and entitled. They were surrounded by their adult children: Marcus, handsome and confident, Serena, with her placid, probing stare, and Charlie, bearing a forced grin. The portrait had been done the day before he first went to the Other World.

In the courtyard he tossed the sphere back into the sky, the stars overhead providing sufficient light. Amidst the distant chirping of insects and the rustle of wind, he heard the low hum of the affrim. A reminder that no unknown energies were near, it was a soothing sound. Charlie needed soothing.

It wasn't as if he'd been oblivious over the past few weeks. He'd seen the stolen glances here, the lingering touches there. He'd tried to ignore it until he couldn't any longer and instead, resorted to grim acceptance that Marcus and Evie were...friendly. Of course, he worried there was something more. Of course, he wished she wasn't with his brother now, alone, wherever they'd gone. And of course, he had to admit that if anyone besides himself could keep Evie safe, it was Marcus.

As his thoughts raced, a faint image materialized above the affrim's disc. It became more vivid as the visitors grew closer, but there was still a blurriness to it, which, he soon understood, was due to the fact that the figures were traveling at a ferocious pace on horseback.

It was Evie and Marcus, not on horses, but on unicorns, galloping up the path at an incredible speed. Evie looked exhausted, and Marcus...! Charlie rolled his eyes, his efforts to view his brother magnanimously quickly evaporating. Marcus was slumped over Shu's neck, barely gripping her horn. A clownish display of his riding prowess.

Then he saw the blood.

He flung an arm through the affrim to open the gate. He shouted for help, his loquered cries summoning Liam, Juliette, and Illis. He threw another loquer to The Fern for Seely and pulled open the courtyard doors just in time for the unicorns to thunder in.

As soon as they were stationary, Evie slid off Nica and into Charlie's waiting arms. He held her tightly, hands splayed wide to protect as much of her as he possibly could. She felt stiff in his arms. He recognized Bowie nearby — he hadn't seen his brother's familiar since he was a child — with Biscuit on his back. They observed the scene and their magenu carefully, not quite ready to leave them.

Liam pulled Marcus off Shu. Held upright, Marcus' head rolled to the side. His eyes opened a fraction. "Ah," he managed. "The hero's welcome I always deserved."

Seely arrived in the courtyard then, having partumed immediately from The Fern. "What in the name of the sun?" she cried, taking in the scene. "Get him inside!"

Liam and Juliette led Marcus to the dining room where Illis had set up a makeshift surgery. They laid him on the table and Seely got to work immediately. She ran a finger down the length of his torso, splicing his bloodstained clothes down the middle and pulling them off, undressing him down to his undergarment. "Normally I'd buy you a vocat first, Seely..." Marcus muttered, which she ignored.

Charlie looked on, horrified. Every inch of his brother's body bore cuts crusted with dried blood, masking what was surely ghostly skin beneath. Shu's blood had healed the lesser wounds, but they still left fresh, pink scars. Juliette whimpered and even Liam appeared affected; he held the back of his hand to his mouth, unblinking.

Only Seely was unfazed. "I can fix this. It is a matter of cleaning the wounds, stimulating blood replenishment, and binding the skin," she said as she administered drops of oil into the cuts. Marcus winced.

"But what of the scars?" Juliette cried. "Oh, they're all over his face!"

"If I work quickly, he will be fine," Seely said. "How did this happen? Certainly not a knife?"

"We were ambushed by an Obscure in the Silvana Seraphilles," Evie said. The room fell into collective silence; even Seely paused working for a moment, but quickly resumed her ministrations. "She threatened to kill me. Then she went after Marcus..." Evie trailed off, her glance toward Marcus not unnoticed by Charlie.

"She attacked me," Marcus said, looking up at the ceiling.

Oh, no. Charlie knew that upward glance, Marcus' tell, though he hadn't seen it since they were teenagers.

"Without cause?" Liam asked.

"Since when do Obscures need cause?" Marcus snapped. Despite his condition, he lifted his head and looked right at his father. "She *provoked* me."

Liam flung the dining room doors open with a messy manipulation, knocking chairs over in the process, and demanded that Illis, Seely, and Juliette leave.

"I must mend this large cut," Seely said, focusing on the deepest wound across Marcus' abdomen. "He will be left with a terrible scar if I don't bind the skin now."

"Later," Liam barked. Marcus winced again, though Seely had not applied any more oil to his injuries.

With a withering stare, Seely reluctantly followed Illis and an equally reluctant, but obedient, Juliette out. The door shut quietly.

Liam lowered his face over Marcus'. Charlie stiffened, readying himself for his father's anger. But it wasn't anger that tinged Liam's words, it was angst. "*Why* in the name of the sun would you do such a thing?" he said.

"Would you rather us dead?" Evie blurted. Charlie grasped her arm to quiet her, but she was enraged. "He had to do something! You weren't there. You don't understand!"

Liam whirled around. "I understand that you did nothing to assist during this ordeal. Dare I ask how your lessons are going with Pembroke? And you." He turned back to Marcus, no longer concerned, just immensely disappointed. "What an idiotic stunt, trying to best an Obscure. We aren't ready for what you may have started tonight."

Flinching, Marcus closed his eyes.

It was all too familiar, Charlie thought. The exasperation, the shame. He didn't like seeing it, even if it was, for once, directed at his brother.

"Tell me the rest," Liam demanded.

Evie complied, hurrying through the arrival of the familiars and the magena's death. Charlie's heart ached as she spoke, horrified at what she'd endured, what she'd witnessed. He moved to comfort her, but stopped, for in the next moment, something changed. Evie's face, previously frantic, became impassive. Her eyes narrowed, her jaw set. She'd gone cold.

"The Obscures killed my mother," she said flatly. "The magena admitted it."

"At last," Liam said after a moment of silence. "Confirmation of the obvious."

"Father, please," Charlie said softly. He put an arm around Evie, then, though it was clear that wasn't what she needed. He didn't know what she needed.

"There's still one thing I don't understand," Liam continued. "How did this magena come to find you in the first place?"

"It all happened so fast, Father," Marcus said. "I don't really —"

"It was my fault," Evie said. She told the beginning of the story in grim detail; the half-dead mageno, her mother's obscurity. "It was my idea to free him," she said. Her eyes remained fixed, unflinchingly, on Liam.

"You stupid girl."

Charlie inhaled sharply. Another of his father's tones he knew well — incredulity, which usually preceded an eruption.

"I made a mistake," Evie said, "but it wasn't asking Marcus to undo the alicration. My mistake was not being prepared. Not being ready..." she looked at Marcus, eyes roving over his injured body. "Not being ready to fight." She lifted her chin a fraction. "I can't change it, Liam. All I can do now is make sure nobody else is put in danger because I'm unprepared. It will never happen again."

Liam considered Evie for a long moment. She considered him right back, projecting a steely exterior Charlie did not entirely recognize. Finally, his father broke the stare and bellowed for Seely, who burst back into the room, clearly having been poised and ready on the other side of the door the entire time. Immediately, she resumed tending to Marcus.

Juliette rushed back to his side, too, but Illis pulled her away gently. "Let her work," she said. "He will be fine. There's not a thing that could happen that Seely can't fix, Juliette. Not a thing."

"It's time we make progress," Liam said.

Charlie, Finneas, and Oleander sat at the table in Liam's tower study the next day. Liam stood over them, hands on the table, his statement directed at Charlie.

"We've made progress," Charlie said.

"A dead artist, the man he painted, and a baker. Where does that get us?"

Charlie sighed heavily.

"Exactly." Liam moved to stand at the window he was so fond of. Mulling something over, he gazed out at The Fern. Charlie crossed his arms and looked away, avoiding meeting his friends' sympathetic grimaces.

"I've not wanted it to come to this, given the unknowns," Liam finally said, turning back around to address the table. "Callidora. It's time."

Finneas and Oleander straightened up, ready to receive orders. Charlie sank further in his chair, but didn't protest. He'd known this was coming. It was one thing he and his father agreed on: visiting Callidora was the next logical step in translating the Tree Book. What they didn't agree on was whether Evie needed to participate.

"Shall I send a loquer?" Finneas asked with a slight mocking tone.

Liam's lips curled. "Not if we want to waste more time. No, we won't send a loquer. We won't ask permission. You'll just go."

Oleander glanced nervously at Finneas. "With respect, that's not exactly the way of things."

"For Statesmen, no. But for commoners traveling State to State?" Liam shrugged. "Magenu partume across borders all the time. It's entering the towns that requires further approval."

"Approval from the walls," Finneas said, understanding immediately. "Validating one's citizen status." He looked at Charlie. "Is she capable?"

Charlie was already shaking his head. "It doesn't matter if she's capable. It matters if she's safe. What if someone recognizes her? We don't know the situation in Callidora. What Arbiter has ever gone dark for a decade? Something terrible could be happening there." He stood, not angry, exactly, but urgent, sensing how quickly the whole situation was spiraling out of his control. *He* needed to go to Callidora. Not Evie. Yet he knew it was impossible that he, nor anyone, could enter the Callidoralta walls sans State approval, without her.

"You're right," Liam said. "We don't know the state of things, but it's time we find out." Decision made, he turned to Finneas and Oleander. "You two, Charlie, and Evie. Marcus won't be ready to make the journey."

Charlie exclaimed, "How soon do you expect —"

"Tomorrow," Liam said curtly. "Charles, there is a dead Obscure on Benclair land. We are running out of time to gain our advantage. If it even is an advantage!" he added, his tone betraying uncharacteristic desperation.

"We'll keep her safe," Finneas said calmly, looking at Charlie.

"Absolutely, mate," chimed Oleander.

Charlie sat back down, defeated.

"Though I must ask, Liam," Finneas said, looking thoughtful, "how we plan to enter the castle. Given Naveena's lack of communication for so long, we'd be prudent in assuming the worst. She could be dead. Or alive, but unwilling to grant us entry."

Liam smiled. "Evie will be able to help with that, too." He described the specifics of Callidora Castle to Finneas and Oleander, who hadn't the pleasure of formerly visiting, as their Mensmen careers had started when Naveena was already reclusive.

As his father spoke, Charlie's thoughts drifted to Evie. He'd seen something new in her last night; an edge in her eyes, a hardening of her energy. He'd not had the chance to talk with her alone since she'd returned from the seraphilles, but he desperately needed to. Perhaps there was merit to his thought, perhaps it was just anxiety, but Charlie feared, deeply, that with her mother confirmed dead, Evie might slip away. Finding Adena was the reason she'd agreed to come back, after all. What good would translating the Tree Book do her if it just led her to a corpse?

"How long will it take to find what you're looking for, Charlie?" Finneas asked, pulling his attention back.

"I don't know," he admitted. "We need information about a specific family, but part of our theory is that this family is deliberately difficult to track. It could take a day. It could take weeks."

"You'll have a day," Liam said. "Once Finneas and Oleander recon the castle, you'll leave. We can't risk anybody discovering Evie's identity. Not until we know who can be trusted in that State."

The four men fell silent, meeting each other's eyes with unsettled brevity. It was unusual for any of them to act on such little information, such empty planning, but everyone understood the need. Nobody had said it, but nobody needed to. After last night, Charlie knew they were running out of time.

24

Evie had never been one to scrutinize her looks, but there she stood, staring into the moonstone-framed mirror in her bathroom. She used to have a softness, a naivety that filled her out, padding against the dark truths her father and Professor Atkinson had kept from her for so long. That was gone now, sliced away in the forest by the Obscure and abandoned in a puddle of Marcus' blood, right alongside her hope.

Now, she looked sharper. Colder. She wouldn't go so far as to say ruthless, yet she felt certain it was in her somewhere, stoking the fire that had ignited in her belly overnight. She didn't recognize herself. She didn't care.

Dressed in black pants, black boots, and a black henley shirt — a bit on the nose, Evie thought wryly — she stepped out of her room and into the corridor where she was met, once again, by a waiting Charlie. This time he was stood there, arm raised, ready to knock.

"Evie," he said, dropping his arm. "We're going to Callidora tomorrow." He said this with obvious concern.

"Good," Evie said, moving to walk past.

"Good?" Charlie repeated. He stepped in front of her. "Don't you remember what I said in the library? We don't know what's happening there. It could be dangerous." Then, noting her lack of apprehension, "You still don't have Alicrat."

"I'm aware of that," Evie said cooly. "But I will by tonight." She stared at him, emotionless.

"Evie," Charlie said softly. "Evie, please." Hands on her shoulders, he closed the gap between them. She stiffened, knowing his imploring had less to do with visiting Callidora and more to do with confronting her mother's murder.

She looked away, lips trembling. She pressed them together, not ready to face the onslaught of emotions climbing up her throat.

"She's dead. The Obscures aren't, but they should be. We still need to decode the Tree Book, don't we? So, I'll be ready for Callidora," she said, avoiding Charlie's eyes. She grabbed his hands, squeezing them briefly as she removed them from her shoulders. "Don't worry."

With that, she stepped past him. She marched down the corridor, down the stairs, through the courtyard, through the gates as they opened to let her through, down the moonstone path, through The Fern, and straight through Pembroke's front door, which also opened as she approached.

She found the Alicrat teacher exactly as she had the last time she'd been in his home: sitting cross-legged on a wooden chair, trance-like. His eyes blinked open as she came to a stop before him.

"Something is different," he said immediately.

"I'm ready," Evie said.

Pembroke stood. "Yes," he said. "You are."

Beneath Pembroke's shroud in the clearing, Evie focused, willing herself into the state she'd fallen into before everything had erupted in the seraphilles. Surely, she thought, the knowledge she was in danger had prompted her sixth sense to emerge. Something within her must have known that only with Alicrat did she have any hope of defending herself. An instinct must have kicked in.

She returned to that moment in her mind, that brief understanding of the world's weave, but immediately knew it wasn't enough. She was not in the seraphilles. She was in the clearing with Pembroke, safe beneath the shroud.

She went back further, to the snap of the twig that had warned her and Marcus something was amiss. He'd sprung into action, readying his bow and arrow to protect them both. That, she realized, was it. It wasn't just knowing that she was in danger — it was knowing that *they* were in danger. Her Alicrat had emerged to protect Marcus, too.

Shame warmed Evie's face beneath the fabric as she internalized the fact that she could have acted, but chose not to. The clarity had been there, waiting to be utilized, but so quickly after had come the confusion, the intimidation, the fear. She'd chosen not to act — a subconscious choice — but a choice nonetheless, and that choice had consequences.

She relived those consequences in the clearing, hearing Marcus' anguished cries as the magena slashed and sliced. Marcus became Charlie, and Charlie wailed as a faceless Obscure dove into his mind with plundering obscurities to steal his knowledge. Charlie dissolved into Serena, bent over Milo and Nim to protect them. Serena became Juliette, dead and decaying over her own children. Juliette became Adena, also dead, though despite the magena's confession, Evie could not picture that reality. Instead, she saw her mother's body floating in an unknown, unreachable realm.

A new fear solidified: the fear of losing those she loved. The scene in the Silvana Seraphilles flashed through her mind again, unbidden, like someone else had pressed play and Evie was forced to watch with her head strapped to a chair and her eyelids peeled back. There was the magena's face, her features drawn with evil. There was Marcus' body, blood flowing fast from his wounds. Then the scene rewound; Marcus rose, whole, the magena retreated, the twig unsnapped, and again, the world exploded in breathtaking clarity. Evie pressed pause.

In the forest clearing, her Alicrat returned, a brilliant combination of her five senses stitched together with an irrefutable, inherent knowing. She sensed Pembroke first, emanating one million confounding things at once, but one of them was very clear: belief in Evie. A thread of faith connected them, so thin it was scarcely visible, but it existed. Everything else followed. She understood the towering trees, the blanket of moss, the curling ferns, the static rocks, each buzzing insect, every writhing worm, the soil beneath her, the sky above her. The tapestry of existence was indeed intricate and confusing, but this time, that made it all the more beautiful.

Evie focused on a grey thread before her for no reason other than it hung heavily beneath the others. She reached out to grasp it; it was hard and cold, though she knew she was only grasping at air. Part of the grey thread hovered out in the open, woven with the green of the moss and the brown of the topsoil. The rest of it was buried deeply beneath other threads, like the bulk of an iceberg underwater. She tugged on it. It was too heavy to manipulate.

No. The physical stone it wove was too heavy. The thread was just energy.

Evie tugged again, displacing moss and soil threads in the process, then dropped the stone's thread in surprise at her success. The fabric was pulled from her head. Her Alicrat diminished, now competing with her other senses. Pembroke stood before her, jubilant.

"It is free!" He burst into a round of applause, literally circling Evie while clapping, then grabbed her hand and pulled her to where an inconspicuous rock jutted out from the ground. A groove about a foot long was etched into the soil behind its current position, creating a misshapen hole where the bulk used to hide.

"I did that," Evie said, dumbfounded, then again, "I did that!"

"Step Three, it is free!" Pembroke shook her vigorously by the shoulders. "Well done, dear girl, well done! I knew you could do it!"

A weight rose off her shoulders like a bird taking flight. Immediately, a much heavier creature descended. "I need to learn alicrations, now. Defensive manipulations. Where do we start?"

"Not so fast. You have skipped Step Two."

"I found my Alicrat, Pembroke. You said it yourself."

"No, no." Pembroke clicked his tongue. "Step One is done. Step Two is due. You did not find the flower."

The damned flower.

Was it hidden by an alicration? Was that the test? Or maybe it was absconded, like Charlie's box by the Eternal Tree, and she needed to piece it back together. She hadn't sensed anything like a flower, though.

155

Trees and moss, soil and stone, animals and insects, yes, but no flowers. Not only had she not sensed a flower, she'd never even seen one on her daily walks to the clearing, nor on the path through the pines to Rutherford Castle. Eyes could be deceived, of course. Evie didn't think Alicrat could.

"There is no flower," she said.

"Step Two is true!" Pembroke squealed. "Step Three it's free! Step Four, you'll soar, or proceed no more."

"What does that mean?" Evie asked, then realized, with surprising pleasure, she understood her teacher better than she thought. "Alicrat abilities vary by magenu," she mused. "Just because I've found it doesn't mean I can use it well."

"There is a spectrum of skill, to say the least," Pembroke confirmed. "Brother Charles epitomizes practiced skill. Brother Marcus epitomizes natural skill. We know not yet which you contain," he said pointedly. "Let us discover."

It took Evie a few minutes to find the solid alicrative state she'd been in before. The sights, sounds, and smells of the forest proved to be distracting and she actually longed for the shroud. But there was no summoning to be done anymore, no need to imagine the torture of her adopted family to help her Alicrat emerge. It was readily accessible, and she managed to nudge it into a position from which it could be stronger than her other five senses.

"Good, good. Soon, it will hum constantly alongside your other senses, and you will not need to focus so intently each time," Pembroke said. "Now, find the water in the air."

Aquenum. Evie searched the space before her, pushing threads aside to locate the essence of water. She sensed, more than saw, what she needed: bits of energy that had clearly existed in other states — solid and liquid, she would have said in the Other World. Here, she simply perceived small variations in the energy. Once she knew what she was looking for, it was everywhere.

"Manipulate their form," Pembroke said. "Gently. If you are too fast, you will produce —"

"Heat," Evie finished. "It needs to be cooled, doesn't it? To condense into liquid."

"What is condense but sheer nonsense? Evoke their evolution."

With those predictably vague directions, Evie found her arms mimicking what Charlie had done in the Empty Fields. Bits of gas moved through the air toward each other, guided by the gentle ministrations of her hands and the energy of her intention. She pulled them in from above and below, from left and right, and they glinted like crystal as sunlight struck their semi-transparent shells. As they collided, liquid threads began to rebuild until she had two, then four, then an exponential number that soon became a visible collection of water.

Something else emerged too, and it was pulling her water down. Gravity. It grasped at the water, coaxing it toward the earth. The blob began to fall, slowly at first, then all together it splashed at Evie's feet. She dropped her arms in frustration.

"Alas, it takes most magenu days," Pembroke said, in what Evie took as attempted reassurance.

"When they're children," she retorted. "I should be able to do a simple task."

"Your mindless reaction to failure is most unbecoming," Pembroke said. "Try again."

Evie did, four more times, and her water fell to the ground each time. Pembroke offered no advice, of course, preferring instead to merely observe her struggles. On her fifth try, she impulsively tore the gravity threads pulling at the water. They collapsed into the ground, obeying her manipulation. The water remained airborne.

"A bit harsh," Pembroke said. "I will overlook it as you are inexperienced, but know that I will not tolerate disrespect for energies. Gravity will obey if you ask it kindly. And remember," he added seriously, "hovering orbs and slowing one's fall with tardevol are the only instances in which the Normalex permits magenu to interact with gravity. Please do not attempt something so foolish as flying."

Evie spent the rest of the day in the clearing with Pembroke, playing with the energies around her. She wasn't entirely sure at any point quite what she was doing, but on some level, it all made sense. Charlie had been right; despite growing up in the Other World, she had as much Alicrat as any magena. Not only that, it seemed she erred on the side of Marcus' natural skill, as Pembroke had put it. She was finding the basic tasks before her relatively simple, achieving most after only a few attempts.

She sent threads of water into a frenzied dance, resulting in a boiling sphere. She sensed ripe fruit somewhere nearby, found the threads of sweet pearsnips, and broke the threads connecting them to the tree. She pulled them toward her clumsily, hitting Pembroke in the face with a pearsnip in the process. He presented her with a twig bearing a solitary leaf, and Evie focused on detangling the threads for an hour before it was fully absconded. After another hour, she had collected them all to reweave the twig in its entirety, though the leaf ended up in the wrong position.

Clouds darkened the sky as she worked. By late afternoon, they broke open. Mimicking Pembroke's gestures — after he'd shocked Evie by repeating them a scant bit slower for her benefit — she managed to create a protective barrier around herself that repelled the rain. As with everything else she'd done, it wasn't perfect, but it was far more than she'd expected of herself after a single day.

"The sun has bid us farewell," Pembroke announced. "We shall retire."

"Just a bit more," Evie protested. "We can practice in the castle."

"I am tired. You forget, I am rather aged." Pembroke made to walk out of the forest. This time, Evie let him go.

Exhausted, she unwove her umbrella alicration. She laid on the ground, letting fat raindrops hit her face, one after another, mixing with the tears she finally allowed to fall. She lay there until the rain soaked her clothes, soaked into her skin, reinvigorating her for what lay ahead. What that was, exactly, she did not know. She only knew that this time, she would be ready.

It wasn't hope, for hope could be killed, left for dead on forest floors. It wasn't a fact, either, as she had very little proof. But what was conviction in absence of proof, Pembroke would ask?

It was belief.

PART II

25

HANDS ON EVIE'S SHOULDERS, Marcus gazed into her eyes. "Trust me," he said. "It will be like nothing you've ever felt before."

They stared at each other for a long moment.

"Oh, for the sun's sake!" Throwing his arms up, Charlie crossed the courtyard to where they, along with Oleander, stood.

Everyone was readying to depart for Callidora, sans Marcus, much to his chagrin. Thanks to Seely's ministrations, most of his wounds had healed, though the worst cut across his ribs remained raw and another deep gash on his thigh caused him pain when he walked. His face bore a few thin scars, too, visible when the sun hit them at the right angle. He claimed he was fit for the journey, but Liam wouldn't allow it.

"What? It's true," Marcus told Charlie. "The first time I partumed, I almost passed out from the shock. Evie should know what to expect."

"He's not wrong," said Oleander, stifling a laugh. "The last thing you want while partuming is to be unconscious. Makes landing so difficult."

"Evie will not actually be partuming," Charlie pointed out.

"She'll still be traveling over one hundred miles in the span of a few seconds," Marcus said, releasing her shoulders.

Oleander interjected before Charlie could retort. "All you need to worry about, Evie, is linking arms and enjoying the ride. Finneas will do the actual partuming."

On cue, Finneas and Serena joined the group in the courtyard. Serena's brow furrowed as she approached Marcus. "Your despondency is so very draining," she told him. "Can't you cheer up, just a thread?"

Marcus glowered at his sister, but straightened up in an attempt to appear unaffected by missing out on the journey.

"We'd best be off," Finneas said. "We've quite the day ahead of us, and that's assuming it unfolds according to plan."

The plan, insofar as they had one, involved partuming as close to Callidoralta as Finneas could get them and entering the city walls with Evie's touch. Liam believed her Callidora energy would grant them access to Callidora Castle, too, which had a different type of security alicration than Rutherford Castle's affrim. Provided this all went well, Oleander and Finneas would search for Naveena, and Evie and Charlie would scour the archives for mention of Melcholm or Perdita.

"And if we're accosted by Obscures?" Evie had asked, only half joking.

"The whole of the Northlands will be accosted by Obscures if we don't act," Liam had said. "And I will not act without —"

"— knowing what's in the Tree Book," Charlie had huffed, still clearly displeased with his father's insistence that Evie accompany the group. Evie, conversely, was thrilled.

"Right, then. Let's line up," Finneas said, giving Serena a farewell kiss.

Everyone linked arms; Evie and Finneas in the middle, Charlie and Oleander on either side. Finneas held his hands in front of him, eyes closed, concentrating. Evie focused alongside him, urging her Alicrat to see past the millions of threads in the immediate vicinity to find those that extended beyond. How to identify which ones reached Callidora, she had no idea.

Finneas counted them down. On three, Evie lifted her right foot. For a frozen instant, the courtyard of Rutherford Castle stilled as the world beyond stretched like taffy. An inch into her foot's descent in tandem with the others, Evie caught Marcus' wave and then, without warning, they slingshotted away.

Riding Nica was like walking compared to the unfathomable speed at which Finneas' partume carried the group across Benclair. The threads in Evie's peripheral vision blurred into an endless tunnel of brilliantly colored, but unidentifiable, world, while straight ahead, a mass of green and grey erupted into focus as hills and jagged, snowcapped mountains. In the blink of an eye — or not, as it passed so quickly there was no time to blink — they'd arrived. The creamy stones of the castle courtyard were gone, replaced by cool air smelling of seraphilles and resin.

Evie lowered her leg to complete the single step it took to reach Callidora from Benclair, stumbling as her foot hit solid ground. "Well done!" Oleander said, holding her up. "Not much to it, right?"

"There is if you're the one doing the partuming." Finneas, spent from pulling four adults over a hundred miles, now busied himself replacing threads.

They stood among the same hills that comprised the Benclair landscape, which continued ahead for a fair stretch before transforming into the mountains Evie had admired from the Silvana Seraphilles. Lakes dotted the valleys between the hills, hugged by the vibrant blues and reds of seraphille and callindro clusters.

As Evie took in the landscape around her, Charlie came to stand at her side, his hand grazing her back. He leaned over to whisper in her ear. "Beautiful, isn't it? Welcome home, Evie."

She wasn't prepared for the elation his words unlocked. The sights and smells of Callidora did not summon memories — she'd not expected them to — yet she knew, deeply, that she was home. She was where she belonged.

Until she remembered that she couldn't belong, not yet. In the previous night's briefing with Liam, everyone had agreed she would have to lie about who she was to anyone who asked. The need wasn't lost on her, but she did find it darkly ironic that, upon finally returning home, she could not be herself.

Finneas questioned her as they approached the Callidoralta walls. "What brings you to the Northlands?"

"I'm a historian seeking information on Iceisles-Northlands relations," Evie recited. "I started my research in Benclair, where Charlie, a fellow historian, was kind enough to assist with my work."

Finneas nodded, deeming this acceptable, though Evie felt it was as cobbled together as the rest of their plan. There was no time to dwell on it, though.

Absurdly tall and dense, clearly having been reinforced many times over the years, Callidoralta's walls resonated an ancient energy. Drawn to it, Evie placed her hands against the stone as the others looked on anxiously. Something jolted from the wall to her palms, then from her palms outward.

"Yes," a voice said. "Place your hands just like that."

Evie didn't have to ask or wonder. The voice was her mother's. Adena stood next to her at the wall, a child at her side, both of them dull and hazy, not quite solid. Evie would have cried out, thinking she was seeing a ghost, if not for the presence of the child — her three-year-old self.

"Thousands of years ago," Adena told the child, adjusting her little hands, "your great, great, many times great grandmother built these walls. She placed an understanding inside so that they would always recognize her children."

A door appeared before the child, as it did before Evie, towering over them in both instances. Golden rivets formed a large sun with wide-reaching rays and the initials *C.C.* in the center. Before the child, the rivets gleamed. In front of Evie, they were tarnished and dull. She pushed the door open, and the living memory faded.

Though the rivets were tarnished, Callidoralta shimmered inside the walls. Multilevel structures with decorative carvings, terraced balconies, and roofs shingled in silver lined the streets, their brilliance more akin to diamonds than to the pearly sheen of Benclair's moonstone. Evie was reminded of Haussmann's Paris with its uniform architecture and wide boulevards, but instead of Haussmann's creamy *Pierre de taille*, Callidoralta's edifices bore varying shades of blue, from the azure of seraphilles to the navy of the sea.

Hills circled the town, rising tall around the walls, offering another layer of protection. Homes had been built into the hillside, too; up its length, little chimneys poked out of the ground like candles on a birthday cake.

"The Olubil Hills," Charlie told her, pointing.

"That's where my father lived!" Evie exclaimed, grabbing Charlie's arm. She craned her neck, wondering which home had been Richard's.

As she did, an inexplicable sensation overcame her. She *knew*. Not which door lodged in the hillside had belonged to her father, but that she had stood in the very same spot in the street before, wondering the very same thing about his home.

"A memory?" Charlie asked when she tried to describe it.

"Not quite." Evie rubbed her forehead. "A feeling."

"It makes sense," Charlie said. "You were born here. Surely things feel familiar."

"No, it was more like...I've been here before as *me*." She gestured down her body. "As an adult. Like *déjà vu*."

"Vidisti," Charlie provided for the others.

"Or, perhaps, videbo?" Finneas said.

"Archaic terms for 'already did' and 'someday will do,'" Charlie explained. "They originated back when magenu believed in things like oracles and prophecies."

"Hey," Oleander chimed in, "don't forget, my Mum still does."

Whether vidisti, videbo, or something else, the sensation lingered over Evie until the group turned onto the main street of Callidoralta, when it vanished, leaving her questioning its existence in the first place.

The city center was a bustling metropolis, far busier than The Fern and filled with wealthy-looking magenu. Fine fabrics Juliette would covet, more luxurious than the natural weaves favored by Benclairans, draped over men's shoulders. The women wore jewelry — mined from Teraur, Oleander noted — not unseen in Benclair, but uncommon. There were apothecaries and bookstores and the usual shops, and all of them, even the simplest grocer, boasted elegant marble façades, enhancing the inescapable sense of luxury drenching the Callidoralta air.

"*Where is Naveena?*"

Evie stopped in her tracks. The voice was not any of her companions', yet it had sounded directly into her ear, like someone walking beside her had spoken. "Who said —"

"*Who is running our State?*" The voice continued, unbidden, over Evie's confusion. "*These questions are worth asking. Callidorans deserve the truth. Join Veritas Callidora on the 66th of the Second at sundown to learn more.*"

Swatting at her ear, Evie recited what she'd heard to the group.

"You ran into a loquer," Charlie said.

"An interesting one," Finneas said. "It doesn't seem to have been meant for anyone specific. This Veritas Callidora entity appears to be recruiting for their cause."

"Liam should join," Oleander joked.

"66th of the Second, is that soon?" Evie said. "We should go. Maybe we'd get some answers."

"We should not," Finneas said, glancing around. "Our objective is to enter the castle, find Naveena, and get you into the archives. If we're successful, we'll get those answers from Naveena herself."

But their list of questions only grew as signs of political dissent and mistrust among the citizens became more alarming further into Callidoralta. Flyers in shop windows bore ominous messages: *Speak up! Keep obscurities OUT of Callidora!* and then, *If you sense something, say something. Help our Enforcers keep Callidora safe.* Charlie intercepted another public loquer, a woman's pleading voice informing citizens: "*It's been ten years since Toddin disappeared. Have you seen my husband?*"

At the city's edge, they encountered an Enforcer, standing at an intersection that forked toward a lower neighborhood of Callidoralta. "Going to Basso?" he asked as the group approached.

Finneas cleared his throat. "Not planning on it."

The Enforcer nodded curtly. "Good. More reports of obscurities last night. Best stay away."

"Thanks for the information," Finneas said neutrally, motioning the group on.

Callidora Castle lay just beyond the city via a path that swung around the base of the Olubil Hills. A lake came into view as they rounded the bend, tucked into the valley between the hills and the more jagged foot of the opposing mountains. In the middle was a lone isle, and upon it sat Evie's utterly decadent childhood home.

Towers of blue-grey stone erupted from every side of the enormous structure, building upon each other like fractals, some spawning four or five more upon themselves, all capped with shining crestings. The windows were balconied by glinting fences that looked to be carved of crystal, and pearly moonstone blocks punctuated the corners. It was straight out of a fairytale, Evie thought. Looking at it, she became convinced that a cohort of Medieval European stonemasons had come through a portal, been inspired by Callidora Castle, and returned home to build the likes of Neuschwanstein or Hohenzollern Castles.

The Other World's European castles had something Callidora's did not, though: a way inside.

"You're up again, Evie," Oleander said, sounding, despite her success at the walls, apprehensive. She hardly heard him anyway. She was already approaching the lake.

Vaguely aware she was not moving entirely of her own volition, Evie paused at the water's edge. Glass-like, it was utterly still. She stared at herself in its reflective surface, knowing instinctively that all she had to do was stare at the castle instead, allowing it to read her Callidora energy, and a walkway would weave itself over the lake.

"Can't we take the secret way?"

The hazy child's reflection appeared in the water alongside hers, holding Adena's hand. Evie faintly recalled protesting having to cross the lake path, faintly recalled the water frightening her.

"The secret way was not built for everyday use," Adena said. "It's meant only for emergencies. Do you remember how to reach it?"

Evie hadn't, not for twenty-two years, but as the child began to recite, the rhyme came to her easily. "Surrounded by faces of ancestors past, remember that this one will always outlast. It looks like a painting and feels like one too, but a Callidora will know what's true."

Adena nodded along, joining in for the last line. "Find the threads that will keep you safe and follow them through to the secret place."

Mother and daughter faded again, leaving the adult Evie alone on the lakeshore. She took a deep breath, readying herself for whatever awaited her inside the castle. She was about to lift her head when her reflection distorted, graced by ripples. She looked up — the walkway was already emerging.

"Well done!" Charlie called from behind her.

Evie whirled around, worry lifting her brows. "I didn't do it," she said, hurrying back to the group. "I didn't —"

Shock registered on her friends' faces. She glanced back at the castle. A man was making his way down the path, his black boots clipping squarely onto each narrow stone as they became visible over the water. He wore the navy Callidora dress uniform, though it looked like a costume on his thin frame.

Crossing the last few stones, the man stepped ashore. He paused before the group, smoothed his greasy hair, and smiled artificially. "Welcome to Callidora Castle. I am Sillen Rancell. Who are all of you?"

26

"WE WERE NOT EXPECTING VISITORS," Sillen said, now addressing the group in the castle's sumptuous foyer. "But far be it from us Callidorans to turn away guests. Especially an esteemed Benclairan historian," he added, smirking at Charlie.

In their halting introductions made on the lakeshore, Charlie had claimed to be an academic nobody, boring Sillen with a nervous speech about his deep interest in historic Northlands-Iceisles relations. Evie had confidently recited her cover story, and Finneas and Oleander had introduced themselves as mere companions, not Mensmen, so as not to arouse suspicion that Benclair had come snooping. With that, Sillen had reluctantly escorted them across the lake path and inside the castle, stating that nothing would please him more than to share Callidora's rich history with academics. His derisive tone did not match his words.

He made to leave the foyer. "The archives lay in the belly of the castle. Follow me."

"We'll wait for you here," Finneas called, remaining put with Oleander.

Pausing, Sillen turned to look at Finneas. Incredulity tightened his features. Seeming to realize this, he quickly plastered on another smile. "Certainly," he said. Then, chuckling, "Don't stray."

Through hall after hall filled with riches that Evie couldn't help but think were hers, she and Charlie followed Sillen. Sculptures and artwork, ancient weaponry manipulated to jab and slice, and furniture too decorative to sit upon were only the start of the vast Callidora collections. Cages lined the walls in one corridor, inside which colorful birds fluttered among exotic plants. Another was overflowing with tottering stacks of plates, bowls, and cups against the walls. The next, to Evie's amazement was filled with her family.

"The Hall of Portraits," Sillen intoned. "Centuries of Callidora Arbiters, Mensmen, so on..." He waved a hand flippantly.

Evie couldn't very well pause to search for Adena or Clement, but she was still struck by some of the faces she passed. A man with long hair and deep-set eyes resigned to some sad, unknown fate — Christian Callidora, according to the plaque — looked familiar, until she realized she had merely studied similar faces for her dissertation on the depiction of Jesus Christ over the centuries. Further down she passed Erskine, patron to Marcus' beloved Llewelyn, all bright eyes and unruly curls. She caught a glimpse of Isabil, too, a golden-haired beauty with something mischievous behind her eyes. Yet when they left the hall, only Christian's two-thousand-year-old sadness remained with Evie.

They descended flights of marble staircases as wide as the lake's stones had been narrow until they were on the lowest level of the castle. It was musty and damp, the precise opposite of desirable conditions for preserving precious history. Sillen moved through the underground labyrinth like a snake, slithering on smooth marble no longer, but on gravel and rocks.

Clink. Clink. Clink.

The sound of rock hitting rock sounded from somewhere beyond their position. "Vermin," Sillen informed them, stopping abruptly before a door blackened with mold.

He pushed it open, lobbed an orb of light inside, then stepped it into a tiny, dank room filled to the brim with documents and antiquities. Shelves were crammed with books, stacks of paper lined the walls, and everything was rendered inaccessible by towering piles of folios. In the corners, paintings, vases, and small pieces of furniture deemed unacceptable for public display appeared to have been abandoned carelessly. Rolls of yellowing parchment were shoved into every remaining nook.

Evie brushed a layer of dust off a worktable. "It's a bit...small, isn't it?"

Sillen let out a sound of disgust. He made his way to the other side of the room by turning sideways to slip through towers of paper. "This is merely the spillover room," he said, "where the Callidoras housed their unwanted garbage." He performed an alicration and a shelf swung open. "Here is the rest."

He nudged the orb of light over the first dozen meters of an aisle a scant meter in width, but so long its end was not visible. On both sides were shelves bearing annuals, each one dark leather with a year painted on the spine in gold. It was what Evie had expected of Callidora's archives and more, but the vastness made her heart sink. They would need centuries to read everything, one for each housed there.

"Splendid!" Charlie said brightly. "Thank you greatly, Sillen."

"Thank you!" Evie said, even brighter.

They stood there for an uncomfortable minute, all three of them grinning on the outside, seething within, until Sillen recalled the orb and handed it to Charlie.

"I shall leave you to it," he said.

The ancient door creaked shut behind him.

<hr />

Alone with Charlie in the small spillover room, Evie pushed her way through a collection of antique chairs toward the most recent aisle of records to retrieve another annual. They'd decided to start with the castle's expenditure logs, looking for invoices from bakeries, and had worked through twenty-odd years of records with no success. Crouching close to the shelf, she tugged out another heavy tome, brought it back to the table and, with a frustrated sigh, started fluttering through the pages.

"Wait!" Charlie stuck a finger out, holding a place on a page. Thinking he'd caught a glimpse of the Perdito name, Evie flipped back excitedly. But it was a page titled *BIRTHS*, and Charlie was not pointing to a Perdito name.

"*Lennon, Evangeline,*" Evie read. "*Born 82nd of the Fourth, 11,991.*" She straightened up, mystified to see in writing what she knew logically to be true, but had struggled to believe her entire life. "I exist, Charlie." She chuckled to herself. "I didn't just appear at four years old."

"What?"

"Never mind." She stared at her name, smiling at the proof of those lost, yet-to-be remembered years of her life. "I guess I really am a secret. I'm recorded in the history of my homeland as a Lennon, not a Callidora." Then, cocking her head, "What's with the date?"

"We divide our years into quarters, so that's December 21st, 11,991," Charlie said. "The Winter Sun Day."

"I mean the year. It's absurd!"

"No Jesus." Charlie shrugged. "No B.C., no A.D. We simply count from the beginning. The beginning of magenu recording history, at least — almost twelve thousand years ago."

Evie glanced at the miles of annuals in the other room. "Do you think the archives go back that far?"

They crawled over artifacts toward the shelf Sillen had pushed open and, with the orb of light, started down the endless aisle.

They walked for minutes, deeper into the State's history yet nowhere near the end. The further they went, the colder and heavier the air around them grew, as if it protested being used after an eternity in solitude. In the stillness, a flicker of gold flashed.

"Did you see that?" Evie whispered.

They walked on and there it was again — not gold, but a cascade of blonde hair gleaming in the glow of the orb. It was the hazy Adena again. The child at her knees pouted, tugging at her mother's skirts. Evie felt a ghostly brush of velvet between her fingers.

Adena led the child past thousands more years of Callidora history, followed by Evie, followed by Charlie, and when she stopped, they all stood before the very first shelf of annuals nestled against a crumbling stone wall.

"This," Adena said, pointing at the top shelf, "is the beginning of the knowledge." The child nodded without understanding. Evie knew it didn't matter. Her mother was not speaking to the little girl, but to the woman she would one day be.

A less-than-sturdy ladder leaned against the wall. Evie shuffled it into position and climbed, tentatively placing her weight onto each rung, toward the top shelf. Charlie protested beneath her, but when she didn't stop, he moved into place at the base of the ladder, holding it steady as Evie reached the highest rung.

The books on the top of the shelf were crudely bound compared to the more recent annuals at the beginning of the aisle. Their leather was deteriorated, revealing wood beneath, and mold occupied the crevices. Evie looked to the right. There were thousands of annuals leading back to the start of the aisle. She looked to the left. There was a single, book-sized space — empty — and then the wall. The first book in the series of thousands was gone. Sitting in its place was a folded square of paper, covered in cobwebs, yellow with age.

Evie took the second book off the shelf and, balancing precariously on the ladder, lifted the cover. Carefully, she turned page after page of names and dates, births and deaths, starting, remarkably, with *Year 1*. What, then, did the missing book contain? She placed the old annual back on the shelf, grabbed the folded paper from the empty space, then slowly lowered herself down to where her mother, the child, and Charlie waited.

Crouching next to the child, Adena spoke with urgency. "These books contain our history," she said. "Our births and deaths. Our greatest achievements and worst failures. The growth of our industries, establishment of our guilds, the development of new alicrations... The Callidora story is all here. There is one book, though, that contains much more. There is one book, Evie, that contains the story of everything."

This captured the child's attention. "Everything?"

"Long ago, that story lived up here." Adena tapped her head. "Magenu once passed the tale of their origins from generation to generation. But over time, the story was forgotten. It became a legend, and then a lie, and then lost, as did the language in which it was told."

"How did they write a story they forgot?" the child said, tilting her head in a miniature of the same look Evie sometimes challenged Professor Atkinson with during his lectures.

Adena smiled. "Twelve thousand years ago, a woman appeared on the shores of our lake. She spoke the ancient language of the Originals and she held the story of our creation in her head. She wrote that story in a special book, bound between wood gifted from the Eternal Tree."

The child had lost interest again. "I don't care," she said.

"You will care someday," Adena said.

She stared past the child's shoulders, into the darkness of the archives, seeming to lock eyes with the adult daughter she wouldn't live to meet. The threads of her unraveled until a solitary, golden hair remained. It drifted to the floor, vanishing on contact with the present.

"Evie?" Charlie whispered. "Are you with me?"

She spun to face him, eyes welling with tears. "I saw my mother. I've *been* seeing her...she was at the lake, too, and the walls..." She shook her head, the weight of it finally landing, the realization that these blurry, living memories would be the closest she would ever get Adena.

Wordlessly, Charlie held her. Evie sank into him and they stood there for a long minute, still as the ancient history surrounding them. How long had the annuals waited, Evie wondered, to be touched again? To be opened? She longed to carve out a place for herself on the shelf and join them, waiting for the hazy version of her mother to reappear. She would wait forever.

Slowly, Charlie pulled away. He wiped a tear from Evie's cheek — comforting, but with an underlying indication that they needed to move on, that they had work to do.

Clearing her throat, Evie wiped her other cheek. "My mother said the first book in this entire collection contains knowledge of the creation," she told Charlie. "Written in Alterra Lingua."

"The Tree Book?"

"Whatever it is, it's missing. It's not up there. This paper was in its place." Brushing away its cobwebs, she unfolded the paper. They bent over it, heads touching, to read the six-hundred-year-old confession it held, scrawled in a rough precursor to the common Florentine dialect of the fifteenth century.

Mi dispiace. Era troppo interessante. Non potevo resistire. Isabil, per favore, perdonami? Giovanni.

"I'm sorry. It was too interesting. I couldn't resist. Forgive me, Isabil. Giovanni," Evie translated.

Something darted through the hallways of her mind. Not a lost memory, but a recollection from her not-so-distant past in the Other World: Professor Atkinson, regaling her class with legends of the Voynich Manuscript, sharing oddly similar drawings from the Italian engineer Giovanni Fontana.

"Does this indicate authorship, or inspiration?" he'd asked. Inspiration, Evie decided, imagining Giovanni Fontana tumbling through a portal, winding up in Callidora, somehow laying eyes on that curious book of creation, and bringing it home to the Other World.

"Charlie," she said slowly, "did Professor Atkinson ever talk to you about —"

"Giovanni Fontana," Charlie said excitedly, already on the same page. "All the time. And the Voynich Manuscript *is* written in Alterra Lingua, after all. If we're right, that means..."

"The Voynich Manuscript contains the creation story of this world," Evie finished softly. "Oh, if Professor Atkinson could see this." Sighing, she folded Fontana's note and pocketed it. "It's all very interesting — astounding, really — but it sheds no light on the Tree Book."

"Perhaps we should change tactics," Charlie said, looking up and down at all the annuals surrounding them. "Let's search for Bosch's Perdito instead of Richard's Perdita."

"Where would we even begin?" Evie groaned.

"Callidora Arbiters are collectors, aren't they?" Charlie lit up, inspired. "What's one thing we know used to reside in one of their collections?"

"The Rutherford Bosch," Evie said. She'd told Charlie about Marcus' insight during their walk to Callidoralta. The flash of jealousy in his eyes had been brief, replaced by what Evie took to be surprise that his brother was useful, or perhaps, regret for not considering that he could be.

Charlie snapped his fingers. "Isabil bought it for 600 pecs from the bakery. Clearly, Arbiters didn't record every loaf of bread purchased, but surely, they'd have recorded the acquisition of an expensive painting."

They raced back up the aisle, locating annuals from Isabil's reign near the door to the spillover room. Grabbing as many as they could carry, they hauled them back to the worktable to peruse.

Two annuals in, Charlie yelped, pointing a dusty, ink-stained finger at an entry in a debit column: *52nd of the Third, 11,488. 600 pecs to M. Perdito for purchase of painting (The Sins of Man, H.M. Boshe) Remit payment by pixie to World's End.*

"World's End?" Evie whispered, gripping Charlie's arm. "Where is that?"

"We'll figure it out later," Charlie said, then shocked Evie by tearing the page from the annual with only the slightest wince at maiming a historical text. "Let's find Finneas and Oleander and get out of here."

Back outside the archives, they set about returning to the main level of the castle. "We came from there," Evie said, pointing. Charlie indicated the opposite way, but the noises they'd heard before sounded again from the hall Evie wanted to take.

"That way," she said, her certainty burgeoned by a faint glow that shone ahead. Thinking it must be the staircase that would take them out of the lower level, Evie moved toward it, trailed by a skeptical Charlie.

The *clinking* grew louder and faster as they walked, building to a steady staccato. "It wasn't like this before," Charlie called from behind Evie, sounding worried. "And we didn't walk this long."

Evie agreed but continued, their goal of returning upstairs suddenly unimportant. She sped up, toward the noise and the light, toward the unknown, moved again by another indescribable compulsion. Charlie fell further behind, the light's radius grew larger, and the noise quickened again. She jogged to match its beat, further into the bowels of the castle.

The noise stopped abruptly. So did Evie, gravel skittering around her feet. She couldn't go further; the weave of an alicration obstructed her path. Behind the imperceptible blockade was an orb, pulsing dimly, but not hovering. It sat on the ground, like it had tired of floating.

A rock clattered, tossed aside by someone unseen. A shape formed in the glow of the orb, a hunched mass emerging from the shadows.

Had she been watching a movie in the Other World, Evie would have braced herself for a jump scare. But there in the depths of her castle, she just stood, waiting.

"Is it you?" The voice, rough as the gravel at Evie's feet, croaked each word slowly.

Evie stepped closer to the alicrated barrier. "Show yourself," she said.

The figure stepped into the orb's radius. It was a woman, her gown threadbare, her golden curls gone gray and hanging in limp clumps down her back. Her face was gaunt, just skin over skull. Blue eyes matched Evie's, though hers were eerily vacant. She looked broken in every sense of the word, a woman who'd lost everything except her life.

"Have you come to hear my confession?" she hissed. "Have you come to absolve me of my sins, sister?"

27

"NAVEENA?" Evie whispered.

Her heart thudded in her ears. This had to be her, a shadow crippled by sorrow and years underground, mistaking her niece for her dead sister.

"Naveena, it's me. Evie. Evangeline." There was no recognition in her aunt's eyes. "Adena's daughter."

At this, Naveena's head snapped up, alert. "Adena did not have a daughter." She peered at Evie through the alicration, bewildered, and repeated, barely a whisper, "Adena did not have a daughter."

Evie didn't respond. Her Alicrat thrummed, trying to read the weave of the invisible prison, trying harder to read her aunt's energy. She struggled to find the baseline comprehension of a person afforded by Alicrat, akin to what the Other World would call a gut instinct, in Naveena. She struggled to find anything within herself, either; she was not elated, nor relieved, to be reunited with her mother's kin. She was only wary.

Gravel crunched behind Evie. Charlie, having rushed to catch up, was approaching, out of breath. She flattened her hand at her back, indicating for him to stay quiet.

"How long have you been here, Naveena?" she asked softly.

Naveena's head ticked back, incredulous. "Nearly forever," she said. She took a step closer to Evie, leaving mere inches and one complex alicration between them. "Have you come to rescue me? Have you overthrown them?"

"Sillen?" Evie asked. "Is he an Obscure?"

Naveena shuddered at his name. "And Grilt, the traitor. He was Clement's Mensmen, and Adena's. Mine, for a short while. But he never belonged to any of us."

"Where is everyone else?"

Naveena laughed, the sound unnatural as it reverberated into the depths of the castle.

Unnerved, Evie looked to Charlie to gauge his assessment, but he was focused on the alicrated web before them. Brow furrowed, his fingers moved rapidly in what Evie presumed was an attempt to free Naveena.

"We're going to get you out of here," she decided, glancing back down the corridor for any sign of Sillen. "You can tell us everything from the safety of Benclair."

"This manipulation is incredibly intricate," Charlie whispered, more to himself than Evie, eyes narrowing. "It's woven with threads from all over of the castle, pulled here and intertwined. I can undo them, but I'm not sure I can put them all back where they belong."

"They'll sense your ministrations," Naveena said, singsong.

Evie tensed; was she mocking them? She tried again to get a sense of Naveena's energy, but still couldn't. Was this cause for alarm? She briefly considered grabbing Charlie and leaving, but the notion of getting answers from her mother's sister was too alluring.

"Just do it," she told Charlie. "We'll find the others and get out before Sillen notices."

Neither Evie nor Naveena spoke as Charlie worked, drops of sweat beading at his temples despite the chilly air, until, without warning, the alicration fell away. Naveena's energy hit Evie like a wave. It pulled her under, drowning her in familial familiarity for an overwhelming moment until something else broke through — something that gave her pause. The alicrated prison had fallen, but Evie's guard remained up.

In the same moment, Naveena seemed to truly recognize Evie.

"Evangeline," she said, staring at her, eyes gone wide. "I know who you are."

"Adena's daughter," Evie repeated.

"Clement said your name! Once, just once! He had something for you. Something I needed to give to you. 'When the time is right,' he told me." She quieted. "The time must be now. Yes. Follow me."

Naveena stepped over the invisible line that had marked her captivity for so many years, head held high. She paused next to Evie, standing shoulder to shoulder, looking at her out of the corners of her eyes. Half smiling, she said, "Thank you," then marched forward.

"Evie," Charlie whispered, grabbing her arm. "She seems a bit... mad, no?"

"Clearly," Evie said. "But we should find out what she knows." Just like her aunt, she strode onward.

Save the gravel crunching beneath their feet, they moved in silence until they reached the junction Evie and Charlie had originally sought. Naveena walked past it. "Where are you taking us?" Evie whispered. "We have to be careful. Sillen will be around here somewhere."

Naveena stopped to face Evie, glaring. "Sillen lives here," she said. "But it is not his home."

She continued on, past the archives, past the hall Charlie had wanted to take, then paused again. "We climb," she said, and all but disappeared into the wall.

"Naveena!" Evie hissed, but she was gone.

Charlie nudged the orb forward. It illuminated a small alcove. Evie stepped into it, tentatively, and nearly fell flat on her face, having tripped on a stair. "They must go up between the walls of the castle," she said, righting herself.

"Let's go, then," Charlie said, giving her a reluctant nudge.

They climbed in an endless spiral, ascending to nowhere, the orb struggling to illuminate more than a single step before them. Their footsteps echoed but Naveena's, some distance ahead, were silent, as if she'd vanished into the fabric of the castle.

A sliver of light, not from the orb, slashed then widened, making Naveena's slim form visible for a moment before she passed through it. It was a door, cracked ajar. Reaching it, Evie slipped her head through.

The staircase had brought them to the Hall of Portraits, and the door wasn't a door, but the painting of Isabil, swung away from the wall.

Out in the open of the castle, Naveena walked like the confident Arbiter she never was, down the Hall of Portraits, around a corner, and finally, to one more door. She opened it with ownership and started up yet another set of stairs, this one intended for more frequent use, its steps worn and smooth in the centers from years of feet going up and down.

"Go on," Charlie said, glancing around nervously. "Hurry. I'll keep watch for Sillen."

Evie found Naveena standing at the top of the stairs, gazing long-ingly into a room she was never meant to occupy. The velvet blue walls of the Callidora Arbiter's study were faded, their fabric fraying. The fireplace was unlit with cold piles of ash spilling past the grate and onto the floor. The desk in the middle of the room was bare, as were the bookshelves against the walls.

Naveena went to the desk and started pulling drawers open. "Father called me here the night before he died," she said, rummaging around. "He never did that. I thought he had something important for me. Silly to hope for such things, as usual. All he wanted was to give me this," she returned to Evie with an envelope, "so that I could give it to you."

"What is it?" Evie asked, taking it from Naveena. She turned it over. Across the front was her name.

"How would I know? It won't open for me. Yes, I have tried." Her eyes darted hungrily between Evie and the letter.

Evie moved to lift the folded edge, then stopped, hand frozen in midair. Quietly, she asked, "What sins, Naveena?"

Naveena's eyes narrowed.

"When I found you, you thought I was Adena. You asked if I was there to hear your confession. To absolve you of your sins."

Naveena stared at Evie for a long time, her face impassive, unread-able. Evie stared back, behaving as though she had all the time in the world while squirming internally with each passing second.

Finally, squaring her shoulders, Naveena announced, "The man who came for her...I led him to her."

The confession fed the flames of Evie's fire. They licked at her, burning her throat, leaving her stunned, furious, unable to articulate a response.

"You must understand," Naveena continued, her voice low, "I was never wanted. Firstborn, second best. Adena was *everything*." she hissed. "When she met that hollow, I thought I might have a chance. It seemed, for a time, she would run away with him! Father would have had no choice but to name me Arbiter. But no — the hollow ran, without her."

She became serious then, an aunt imparting a life lesson on her niece. "Hope is a dangerous thing, Evangeline. It does not represent what could be. It represents what you are without. You should never hope, not for a moment, if there is the slightest chance you won't get what you want. I hoped that hollow was my path to the Arbitership. He only disappointed."

"Tell me what happened to Adena," Evie said, forcing calm into her words. "Or is this all about you?"

"It was never about me!" Naveena spat. "That's precisely why we're here. Perhaps if Father had included me, had deigned to tell me anything at all, I'd have been less naive. Maybe if Adena had shown me her book when I asked, I would have known better!"

"The book with the golden tree?" Evie said. "Do you know what's in it?"

"She was never without it!" Naveena screeched. "Father was obsessed, too. They locked themselves up here for hours, allowing nobody inside save the local baker with bread. When I asked if I could see it, they made up transparent excuses. It would bore me! It was too complex for me to understand! Or Father's favorite: it wasn't my *place* to know."

She stepped closer to Evie, an unsettling glint in her eyes. "I tried to steal it once. To destroy it. I thought if Adena lost it, Father would be so upset he might revoke her appointment."

"You didn't, though. I have it."

"I couldn't find it."

"Because she'd already taken it," Evie said. "And me, to Rutherford Castle. But a man attacked us! Was it him? You told him where to find us?"

Naveena's eyebrows lifted. "*That* was not me." She was clear, definitive. "I was mad with jealousy, yes, but I never would have sent anyone to kill her." She lowered her voice. "Knowingly."

"Who did you betray my mother to, then?"

Naveena turned abruptly and walked to the window on the other side of the tower. She stood there, gazing outside, saying nothing, for a long time. When she finally answered, her voice was so quiet Evie could barely hear her. "I was vulnerable after Father's death. Impressionable. All I wanted, all my life, was for him to find me useful. When he died, so did my purpose... Then I met him. I was useful to him! I would have done anything."

"Who? What did he want?"

She spun around. "He wanted me," she said, smiling faintly. Her words, perhaps once spoken with girlish pride, sounded heavy with a naivety only realized in hindsight. "One night, after too many Olubil wines, he asked to come here. I obliged. The next morning, he was gone. So was my sister."

"*Who*, Naveena?"

"Adrian Tenebris."

Fear doused the flames of Evie's anger, but only momentarily. An excited thrill, surprising and alluring, reignited them. It was a foreign sensation, a dark desire that should have frightened her, but didn't. It did quite the opposite.

"You've known all along that the Obscures killed her!" She yelled, unable to control herself. "You welcomed them into your castle, invited them into your ranks, allowed them to imprison you, leaving your State vulnerable —"

"This was never my State!" Naveena retorted, flailing her arms. "I wasn't good enough for it back then, why should I take responsibility for it now? Father died, Adena disappeared, and I was expected to fall in line as the last resort, to take on a role I was never prepped to play. Nobody shared with me the Callidora secrets that bonded my sister and father. Nobody bothered to include me in case I would be useful someday, because they never believed I would be! And besides," she softened a fraction, "I don't actually know what happened."

"Surely you saw something. Heard something. Sensed something!"

"When I went to sleep that night, I knew where my sister was. When I woke the next morning, she was gone. There were traces of Alicrat, but they'd been partially masked, rendered indiscernible, both to myself and the dozens of skilled magenu who tried to interpret what had transpired. There was no explanation, no body. As I have always said: she disappeared."

"Because Adrian Tenebris killed her!" Evie said. She exhaled heavily. "I don't understand. What happened to you, then? Why did you give up so easily?"

Naveena huffed. "What makes you think I didn't fight with every bit of strength I had, alicrative and otherwise?"

Evie just stared at her.

"Understand, Evangeline." Naveena tilted her head forward, glaring. "They are cunning. They are ruthless. They act with impunity, doing things most of us wouldn't even dream of on our darkest days, and they do them with *joy*. By the time I understood what was happening — my Mensmen disappearing, Grilt behaving oddly, the arrival of Sillen — it was too late." She turned back to the window, partially, leaving Evie with her profile. "Moon knows how long they tortured me. Horrific obscurities that twisted my insides. Mind manipulations that skewed my sanity. They plucked the will out of me, thread by thread."

"*Get back here, with or without her. Sillen is roaming.*" Charlie's voice, loquered from downstairs, whispered in Evie's ear.

She didn't move. She watched her aunt, searching for an inkling of remorse for the role she'd played in her sister's fate, but there was nothing. Naveena was cold, unfeeling, certainly unhinged, and now, she was unhelpful.

"I'm leaving," Evie announced. Naveena continued to stare out the window. "You're free. Get out of here. Go...I don't know." She paused to reconsider, wondering what her mother would say about this treatment of her sister. But her mother had no say in the matter — she was dead. Naveena had seen to that.

Pocketing Clement's envelope alongside Fontana's note, Evie hurried down the stairs, anxious to get back to Charlie. She was nearly there when a scream, piercingly loud at first, then fainter with distance, pulled her back to the study. She ran to the window where Naveena had stood only moments ago and peered over the ledge. Dozens of stories below lay her aunt, askew on the ground, her body now as broken as her mind.

28

EVIE AND CHARLIE sprinted through the castle, guided by nothing, searching for their friends who likely did not yet know they were in danger.

"If they were looking for Naveena, they'd have been near Clement's tower," Evie said, narrowly dodging a bird that had escaped its cage in one of the exotic halls.

"Shh!" Charlie hissed, yanking her around a corner. He flattened her against the wall with an outstretched arm and put a finger to his lips, eyes wide.

Sillen's nasal voice sounded from somewhere beyond their position. "I don't understand how they could have found her, much less freed her!"

"We should have killed her years ago," came a booming baritone. "I always told him she was useless." And then, "Find them."

"We're not meant to do anything that will raise suspicion," Sillen said. "Not yet. Killing allegedly innocent researchers seems quite the opposite."

"Find them!"

Their voices and footsteps quieted, then disappeared, only to be replaced by more footsteps clipping on marble. These, however, were welcome.

"Thank the sun," said Finneas as he and Oleander approached, having just descended a nearby staircase. "Are you both alright?"

"We're fine," Charlie said, returning Oleander's embrace. "But we need to leave, *now*."

"Naveena is dead," Evie said. "Sillen and Grilt are looking for us."

"Who's Grilt?" Oleander asked. "Naveena? Dead?"

"We'll swap stories once we're safe," Finneas said. "Let's go, then. The foyer is this way." He moved to descend the next set of stairs.

Charlie grabbed Finneas' shoulder, stopping him. "Don't you think they'll assume that's our plan? They'll be on us the minute we even *look* at the front door." He ran a hand through his hair, thinking, and glanced at Evie. "We need another way. A secret passage, like the one Naveena took us through."

His words made something click. "I know how we can get out," Evie whispered, meeting his eyes, noting the flicker of doubt. "Trust me, Charlie."

She didn't give him a chance to argue. With Adena's voice sounding over and over in her head, she led the trio back to the Hall of Portraits.

Surrounded by faces of ancestors past, remember that this one will always outlast.

Once in the hall, she ran up and down its length, muttering. "Christian, Isabil, Erskine... Who is it? Isabil led to the archives, so who leads to safety?"

Finneas grabbed her by the arm, stopping her mid-stride. "Which portrait, Evie? We can look at the plaques and help."

She wrenched away from him. "I'll know it when I see it!" She turned back down the hall, scanning the faces again. "Erskine, Isabil, Christian..."

"Jesus Christ!" Charlie exclaimed. He stood in the middle of the hall, looking so overwhelmed Evie thought he might faint. She hurried to him, coming to a stop, along with Finneas and Oleander, before three portraits.

These portraits were different from the others. Their subjects were contemporary, the colors were vivid, the paint held no cracks from the passage of time. The shiny brass plates beneath them, bearing no scratches, no tarnish, read: *Toddin, Valerian, Sussell*.

The faces seemed normal and well-rendered at first glance. The subjects smiled with the deserved pride of a Mensmen, decked out in the navy dress uniform of Callidora, not unlike the centuries of others scattered around the hall. The eyes in particular were incredibly detailed, with every vein and eyelash — even the sheen of the membrane — visible. It was as if, Evie realized, she was looking at the men in their very real eyes. As she considered this, Toddin's irises darted among the group. Evie glanced at the other portraits. Valerian and Sussell's eyes did the same, meeting hers as if they stood face to face.

"They're in there," Charlie whispered. "Alive. Trapped..."

Finneas got to work immediately, sensing out the obscurity that had woven men into wall. Oleander joined him, and then Charlie, the three of them confused and impressed and horrified with the complexity of the alicration before them, one that would surely take their less advanced Alicrat hours to unweave.

They would have minutes, if that. Entering one end of the Hall of Portraits was an enormous man, substantially taller than any of the three Benclairan men, with a long, Rasputin-like beard. Sillen appeared at the other end, rendering both exits blocked. After one long second during which everyone in the hall stood still, assessing the situation, Sillen flung an arm out with purpose.

Evie barely registered the spear of light flying toward them, so unlike the gentle ribbons of commonplace manipulations that danced through The Fern. And she didn't at all register Oleander's arms crossing in front of the group, weaving some sort of protection that shielded, but did not totally block, Sillen's obscurity. Dull pain struck Evie like a punch to the gut, and she doubled over with her companions.

A conflagration broke out as Grilt and Sillen, Oleander and Charlie, alicrated various means of harm, defense, and distraction while Finneas continued to work on the Mensmen. In the chaos, Evie saw it.

Unbothered by the intensity of the energy around them were white, almost crystalline threads, hovering off a portrait not too far away. Evie sensed threads from the other portraits, too, but they were different;

tightly woven to build frames and paint and plaques. These threads were loose, animated, beckoning. She ran to them.

Find the threads that will keep you safe and follow them through to the secret place.

The portrait they belonged to was smaller than the others, held in an unimpressive wooden frame. There was no plaque. The woman portrayed was petite, with brown eyes, short, white hair, and a placid Mona Lisa smile. Evie tugged gently on her threads. The portrait came away from the wall easily, as if hinged. She swung it wide open, revealing a black hole of nothing behind it. She yelled for the others.

Charlie came sprinting to her first. Halfway there, he cried out and fell forward but stayed upright by grabbing Christian Callidora's ornate frame. He stumbled the last few meters to Evie's position, cradling his left arm with his right hand.

"He tried to break my arm," he managed through gritted teeth. Still, he stood directly in front of Evie, shielding her. "I felt his fingers around my bones."

Down the hall, Toddin was almost fully out of the painting; his head, both arms, torso, and one leg were visible, as three-dimensional as his saviors. Finneas worked furiously to free his last leg while Oleander continued to defend against Sillen's manipulations, which, like the magena in the seraphilles, were cast lazily. Unlike the magena in the seraphilles, Sillen's intentions seemed mild, wanting nothing worse than to throw a punch, break a bone. He thought they were cornered, Evie realized.

Avoiding Toddin's eyes, she yelled at Finneas. "Leave him!"

Sillen looked her way and seemed to notice, for the first time, that there was a hole in the wall. He motioned to Grilt and they started toward Evie and Charlie's position at the same time that Oleander and Finneas bridged the gap. They'd left Toddin dangling, horrifyingly, from the wall.

"This isn't how we intended things to go," Sillen called, stalking down the hall, grinning his slimy grin. "We planned to let you leave. That is no longer an option." He and Grilt both reared back, contorting the energies of the hall into something worse, readying to kill the prey they'd been playing with.

Evie pushed Oleander toward the hole first. He grabbed Finneas' arms on the way, pulling him through with him. She turned to Charlie next. "Go!" she yelled, shoving him.

The Hall of Portraits stilled.

All around Evie and Charlie, threads twisted in slow motion like a protective web. They came from her ancestors' portraits, spiraling from frames and faces toward the end of the hall. They collided with the cruelly manipulated threads of Sillen and Grilt's obscurities in a clash of energy, sending a shockwave through the hall. Portraits shuddered on the walls, clattered to the floor, and Sillen and Grilt were hurtled backward.

Despite the tangle of energy around her, Evie remained fixated on a single thread, thin and silver, hanging between her and Charlie. She stared at it, mesmerized, perceiving everything in one drawn-out millisecond.

Then her perception caught up with reality, and the next things happened fast. Charlie grabbed her wrists, leveraging her attempted shove to spin her into his place, and pushed her through the portrait hole. His face grew smaller and smaller, as though he'd been minuted, before distance blinked him out completely. All that remained was that silver thread, unfurling, unbroken, as Evie fell into an abyss.

Unsure if she'd been knocked out or if she'd just passed out, when she opened her eyes, Evie knew she'd stopped falling. She had no recollection of landing, only the weightless sensation of a free fall as Charlie grew farther away from her, yet she lay on hard, dusty ground.

She rose unsteadily, yelling for him. Her voice echoed, helping her understand that she was in a large, empty space. It was damp, dark, and smelled faintly of earth. She screamed again and Oleander answered. They groped for each other in the darkness until she felt his broad shoulders.

"Where's Charlie? He pushed me but didn't follow! He's still —"

A distant cry cut her off, crescendoing until it sounded like it was right on top of her and Oleander. Charlie's face lit up above them, illuminated by the bit of light he'd had the foresight to pull with him. He came to a halt in midair. Something unseen had slowed, then stopped his fall. Righting himself from that position, he dropped gently to his feet.

"Thank God," Evie said, wrapping her arms around him. "Thank God," she repeated into his chest. "Next time I tell you to jump through a mystery escape route," she said, pulling away to look up at him, "just do it, Charlie." She was smiling. Charlie was not.

"Not without knowing you're safe."

She glanced between them, honing her Alicrat to find that silver thread she'd seen in the Hall of Portraits. Or had she? The thread, like the moment, now felt evanescent.

"Where's Finneas?" Charlie asked, squinting into the dimly lit space.

"Over here," came Finneas' voice. His footsteps sounded until his face entered the radius of the orb. "I was trying to figure out where we are. It seems to be a sizable room, well below the castle, I'd say. I found a narrow passage. It's the only way out, as far as I can tell."

"Where does it lead?" Oleander asked.

"Evie?" Finneas ventured. "This was your move. Any ideas?"

"Wherever it goes, it will be safe," Evie said. "I've been seeing my mother around the castle, as memories. She reminded me of the secret way. The hole in the wall," she added, then repeated, definitively, "It will be safe." She didn't know how else to explain to them what she knew, without a shadow of a doubt, to be true.

"It doesn't appear Sillen and Grilt were able to access the hole," Charlie said, glancing up. "I watched the portrait swing itself shut after I went through. In a way, it's already protecting us."

"And something slowed our falls," Oleander added. "At least, I know I didn't perform my own tardevol. Did any of you?"

Everyone shook their heads.

"It must be a safety measure woven into the escape route," Finneas mused. "Though I've never heard of such a thing."

The passage Finneas had located was dark and narrow, forcing them to walk two by two. As they moved through, Evie updated the others on her and Charlie's success in the archives and their encounter with Naveena.

"She'd gone crazy," she said quietly. "Driven mad by the years of solitude, jealousy her only companion. I didn't realize it at first, but when I left her in the tower, I had no doubt. She was insane. Still, I didn't think she would…"

Charlie's hand found hers in the darkness. "You couldn't have stopped her," he said.

"And now we know," Finneas said. "Adena's murder was more strategic than merely an attempt to steal the Tree Book. It's allowed them to infiltrate slowly, methodically…so unlike their overt takeover of Maliter. They're playing a long game in Callidora."

"To what end?" Charlie said. "And how have the citizens not caught on beyond what we witnessed in town?"

"They have," Oleander said darkly. "We searched every inch of the castle, didn't we, Fin? Totally empty, not a soul in sight. Moreover, every room was locked with a clavis — except one. I don't know if it was left open deliberately for us to find as a warning, or just forgotten, but we were met with a barrage of loquers as soon as we walked in."

"From whom?" Evie asked.

"Not just from whom — *to* whom, as well. Along with decades-old, unanswered messages from Liam and the other Arbiters, we also heard messages that citizens have attempted to send to family or friends outside Callidora. Anything that even *hints* at Obscure activity or Naveena's absence seems to be intercepted before it can get out of the State."

"People are suspicious," Finneas said. "They're just being silenced. It's like — oi!" Finneas and Oleander stopped short, having run into something.

It was a doorknob, which Oleander turned. He strained, pushing against the door, until it gave way unexpectedly and he topped forward, the others on his heels, everyone stumbling into a room. It was small, containing a single window, another door to the street outside, and a stone oven built into one of the whitewashed walls.

Finneas peered through the solitary window into darkness. "Night has fallen. We're still in Callidoralta," he whispered. "But far from the castle, now." There were no shutters and he seemed to realize this latently, crouching and motioning for everyone else to do the same.

"Way ahead of you, mate," Oleander said, already prone on the floor. "See you in the morning."

Evie joined him, exhausted physically, emotionally, and from using so much Alicrat only days after finding it. Recognizing the perceived safety of wherever they'd ended up, her adrenaline fell, and suddenly, she couldn't keep her eyes open.

"Here," Charlie whispered. He pushed something toward her; a shirt and a cloak, resized from his pocket.

She took the shirt and folded it into a pillow, then slid the cloak back. "There's enough for us both. Finneas?"

"In a moment." He was moving around the perimeter of the room, alicrating some semblance of security. "You're sure this place is safe, Evie?"

"Positive."

So certain was she that she drifted off immediately, comforted by Oleander on one side and Charlie on the other, who laid the cloak over her. Right before the world went dark, she caught the scent of freshly baked bread.

29

"*THE DAUGHTER OF LIGHT HAS RETURNED!*"

The cloaked figure stands in the small, whitewashed room. Evie looks for her companions, but they are gone.

"*Why do you always turn up?*" *Evie asks.* "*First the forest, then the field. Now here.*"

"*I told you last time.*" *The figure sighs.* "*I have been looking for you. Leaping from mind to mind for what feels like an eternity, hoping to find you.*"

"*Why?*"

"*So many questions. I liked you better when you were unaware, sprinting through the trees as if your life depended on it. That was more fun. Tell me, where has your mind brought us this time?*"

Evie shrugs. "*If it's my dream, why do you care?*"

"*Have you ever been trapped, Evie? Stuck in a place not of your choosing with only your mistakes as company?*" *The figure moves to the window, not quite walking, not quite floating. It stares outside and Evie strains to see a reflection of its face in the panes of glass. She sees only emptiness beneath the cloak of the hood.*

"*Suffice to say, I have not seen this world in a long time. Not in person, at least. I can only access it through the dreams of others. But I never know*

194

where the dreamer will take me. Am I in this Sfyre? The other? Or the fantasy world of somebody's mind? And so, I ask the question."

"Why are you trapped?"

"I am being punished."

"Why?"

"Because my ideas were considered dangerous."

"Why?"

"I truly do not know." The vulnerable tone surprises Evie.

"How long have you been trapped?"

"Longer than you can imagine." The figure still faces the window, presumably peering outside, trying to understand where it is.

"Why have you been looking for me?"

"Finally, the right question!" The figure spins around. "Tell me, Evie. Do you believe in God?"

"Not exactly."

"Elaborate."

"I believe in God insofar as I believe the concept exists, but the concept is a human construct."

"Go on."

"God is the personification of the existential questions that plague humanity. Instead of admitting we are the imperfect result of a random confluence of events, living lives with little meaning over which we have even less control, the notion of God tells us there is a reason for our existence, that we are on the right path, safe in the hands of a higher, wiser, power."

"So you do not believe there is an actual entity? God exists only in the collective mind of humanity?"

"Those who see God as an actual entity are arrogant and naive. So, too, are those who wholly deny the possibility of a higher power. Humanity does not have enough evidence to support either claim. Really, the only logical view is that there may or may not be something greater than ourselves. But that provides no comfort."

Evie quiets, unsure where her total lack of inhibition on this topic is coming from. Her subconscious, she supposes. She is dreaming, after all.

"I assume you feel the same about the Devil, then," the figure interrogates.

"Every story needs a villain. Good needs evil to necessitate its goodness."

"Oh, how right you are there!" Evie hears the smile in the figure's voice. "But then, the Devil exists only as a foil for God, a way to point to God's goodness? Does the Devil have no identity of its own accord?"

"The Devil is an invention of humankind, just as God is. God satisfies our curiosity. We ask, where did we come from? Where are we going? God gives us those answers. He gives us someone to perform for, someone for whom we want — need — to do good. But other parts of humanity need explaining, too, and those parts craft the Devil. We cannot fathom that evil is inherent to ourselves, and so we claim it has been placed there by the counterpart of good."

The figure laughs, quietly at first, and then in discordant peals. "Is that it? The Devil gets no credit at all? A pity. She did so much for creation, after all. You know, your perspective on this is as naive as the sheep you call humanity. You sit on the fence, refusing to jump to either side. You're afraid."

"Of what?"

The figure moves toward her. "Jump to the left and you must believe the arms of a God you cannot see will catch you. Jump to the right and you gamble whether you can catch yourself. Two leaps of faith, neither of which appeal to you. What if I could offer you a third option?"

Evie tilts her head, intrigued.

"There is no God and there is no Devil, certainly not in the ways they have been portrayed. Certainly not deserving of the fear and respect your cultures have given them. Instead, the creators are as broken and confused as their creation. The flaws in your kind are reflections of those who made you."

The figure is inches from Evie's face now and still, she sees nothing beneath the hood. Wasn't there something there, before?

"That would be easier to believe than the mainstream concept of God," Evie concedes, staying put despite the figure's proximity.

"You agree, then, that perfection is impossible?"

"Of course."

"That good needs evil, as you said? That both must exist to balance the scales?"

"I suppose nobody can be wholly good," Evie says.

"We agree!" the figure exclaims, pleased. "And that is why I have been looking for you, Evie. Because we agree on this, I believe you can help me."

Evie does not immediately reject the notion as she did before. She says nothing.

"You have no idea, do you?" the figure muses. "No idea how ironic it is that you see things my way. After how much she fought, after her attempts to prove an unprovable point, that you would share my sentiments...oh, it delights me!"

"Her? I don't understand."

"You will." The room flashes with sunlight. Evie feels herself slipping away, sees the figure fade before her. "Come see me again soon. We have much to discuss."

30

It was another dark day in the Domus. Magenu — mostly Obscures, but some Eliot-era Mensmen and Maiors who had bought into the doctrine or been frightened into conforming — mingled in the Atrium.

None of them paid attention to Blair as she washed the Atrium's domed ceiling to crystal clarity. Nobody lowered their voice as she whisked dust off the furniture inside meeting rooms. Nobody followed her down to the incinerator, where she emptied waste bins into the flames. And so, nobody realized that she was memorizing the layout of the Domus from her levitated perch as she cleaned the glass. Nobody realized that she committed to memory entire conversations as she dusted. Nobody knew that before tossing garbage into the incinerator, she examined every scrap for confidential information.

Nobody in the Domus paid any attention to Blair. Nobody, except for one person.

It was the end of last year's Fourth when Blair first felt Adrian Tenebris' eyes on her as she crossed the Atrium. At first, she could not discern whether his interest in her was driven by lust or suspicion. Lust, though distasteful, Blair could handle. Exploit, even. Suspicion would kill her. She decided to assume it was lust, then, even if she had to stoke it herself.

The next time she felt his stare, she stifled an involuntary shudder and slowed her gait. She dropped the billowing hood of her cloak and shook her head, letting her raven hair fall around her face in a way she hoped was appealing. She pursed her lips, mimicking the prostitutes she passed in Talus. She felt foolish. She knew nothing of these things. Still, when she risked a glance at Adrian, his eyes were locked on her. That was all it took. He was the most important mageno in Maliter, but he was also a man.

Blair came to know those eyes well — a colorless, but brilliant grey — in the following quarters. So, too, did she come to know his face; its narrow, dangerous edge, but also the playful side that emerged with a genuine laugh or fun-spirited joke aimed at a Mensmen. And then there was Adrian himself.

It puzzled Blair. For all the evil he incited, Adrian Tenebris had an otherwise normal, even enjoyable, personality. Surely, this contributed to the ease with which he had normalized the AO presence in Maliter. She did wonder whether a younger Adrian might be the type she would fall for in the rebellious teenage years she knew some girls had the freedom to experience. But no, she reminded herself. He was the arrogant, heartless leader of a slavishly loyal cult. There was an unmistakable evil about him which, without fail, swooped in to mar any attractive qualities Blair perceived.

Two quarters had passed since they'd shared that gaze and eventually, much more. And still, she hadn't gained anything useful from the relationship. He'd divulged no secrets, discussed no plans. He spoke of the AO as if it were not a forbidden cult that rose from the depths to control the State but rather, as if it was and had been the governing body of Maliter since the beginning of time. He casually mentioned newly developed obscurities as if they were exciting discoveries that would benefit humanity, not contribute to its destruction. He lamented about his Mensmen and deputies who could not control themselves as if they had merely stolen sweets from the kitchen rather than embarked on killing sprees in the countryside to perfect their obscure techniques.

Blair had expected more. She'd started the endeavor with lofty dreams of earning a seat at the table, of gaining insight into the cult's plans for the rest of the Northlands. When she realized this was unlikely to transpire, she hoped instead for a scrap of vulnerability from Adrian; a complaint about an outspoken Mensmen, perhaps, or mention of a burgeoning Norm uprising in some poor, rural town. Anything Blair could exploit to grow her resistance. But after two long quarters, it remained a resistance of one.

Perhaps it was time to kill him, Blair thought. How much longer could she wait to glean something useful in hopes it would bolster a revolt? Maybe his death would be the trigger Maliteran Norms needed. Surely, Blair would be killed too, and surely, another Obscure would rise to take Adrian's place, but there would be a moment of upheaval in which the masses could rally!

But revolutions needed leaders, Blair reminded herself.

She considered all of this as she cleaned the Atrium's floors, ensuring the obsidian coffin trod upon by hundreds of magenu would sparkle, should the nonexistent sun ever shine through the glass ceiling.

"Thank you."

The voice was unfamiliar. Quickly, Blair assessed her own energy, confirming her mask was in place, before turning around.

It was Greer, the previously outspoken Maior of Hayworth and the singular Domus occupant Blair felt *might* be a fellow Norm. True, Greer had voted to approve Adrian's usurpation, but her vote came immediately after another official had refused, which had resulted in Blair cleaning blood off the ceiling and walls. Even Blair would have pledged loyalty under those circumstances, but she also would have made a silent promise to herself to do all she could to resist the new regime. She believed Greer had made such a promise when she smiled and swore allegiance to Adrian.

Blair's Alicrat, keen though it was, didn't tell her this about Greer. Rather, it was an inherent recognition of the same rage Blair held, masked in Greer just as she masked hers. Greer was inconspicuous in the Domus, polite and agreeable, but no matter how effusively she compli-mented the Obscure Mensmen and Maiors, no matter how brightly she laughed at their bigoted jokes, Blair saw the hatred that burned in her eyes when they turned their backs and she believed she was unobserved.

Still, one could never be too sure.

"Excuse me?" Blair said, pretending she hadn't heard.

"Thank you," Greer repeated. "For keeping this place clean." She smiled — rather, the corner of her mouth ticked up in what was considered a smile in Maliter — and walked away.

Excitement roiled in Blair's stomach. She'd heard the emphasis on *place*, the thinly veiled disgust that they had to work in this *place*, the revulsion that this *place* existed to begin with! Was it a sign? An invitation? She'd heard it, hadn't she?

Or was she just desperate for an ally, willing to twist a meaningless tonal change into a sign from the sun itself? This was the problem Blair faced. The window during which Norms could have identified each other safely had passed. Trust was now a luxury, growing more endangered each day. Besides, Blair thought, resuming her work on the floors, even if Greer was a Norm, even if she was willing to risk everything to form a resistance, that brought Blair's paltry one to a measly two. What Blair needed were allies from outside Maliter.

Technically, she had one, but he was proving rather worthless.

It wasn't the rise of the Obscures that had prompted Blair to behave so clandestinely in the Domus. She'd been the same way as an Eliot Castle cleaner, back when things were still considered normal. Her eyes and ears were always open for tidbits she could leverage to improve her position in life — with no pecs in her pocket, information was Blair's currency.

She'd been cleaning the portraits in a grimy corridor of Eliot Castle when she overheard Hamish Eliot's meeting with the Arbiters of Teraur, Iristell, and Benclair. The latter three implored Hamish to *do something* to manage the rise of obscurities in his State. Liam Rutherford had stormed out of the meeting room then, red in the face, running a hand through his hair. Blair averted her eyes immediately, turning back to a particularly disgruntled-looking Eliot ancestor on the wall, but Liam had already noticed her.

"You were listening," he said. A statement, not a question, nor an accusation.

"Yes," Blair said, facing him. Something told her the Benclair Arbiter appreciated candor.

He regarded her for a long minute, eyes narrowed, lips pursed, then asked, "What else have you heard?"

Blair told him everything: that he wasn't the first to try and fail to force Hamish's hand, that obscurities in Maliter were not rising, but rampant, that all the Enforcers were dead or bought off, that on the whole, the situation in her home State was far worse than she suspected he could fathom.

"Maliter is being poisoned from the inside," she finished. She immediately worried that she'd overdramatized things, that she was too influenced by Stin's dire predictions for Maliter's future. In hindsight, she'd been too circumspect — only a quarter later, the corridor in which she'd stood with Liam Rutherford was reduced to ashes along with Hamish and his family.

Days after the burning, a pixie flew straight to Blair's home with a letter from Liam himself, informing her that a Benclair Mensmen was on his way to learn everything she knew about Adrian's rise to power and the Obscures. Just like that, Blair became an informant — albeit, one with little to inform on.

The irritatingly handsome Rutherford had sauntered into Talus as if on holiday. Blair had to push him off the street, dressed as he was in bold, Benclair green, his face shining with the vibrancy of an unburdened life. She redressed him in Stin's quarry clothes. Then, she took him on a tour of Talus.

She started with the Changeling District, where he watched men morph into damaged beasts, competing to see who could conjure the most terrifying form. They continued to the River Dumot, flowing red with blood in the evening, where the Eternals, the smallest, but oldest sect of the AO, liked to convene. Last, Blair forced him through Absent Alley, where the discarded magenu subjected to mind manipulations wandered. They clung to the Benclair visitor with desperate hands, begging to be reminded of their own names, their purposes, who they'd loved and who had loved them.

Blair had forced him to bear witness to the reality of Maliter not because she reveled in his discomfort, but because it was necessary. Liam needed to understand what the State truly faced — surely, living it through his son's eyes would accomplish that. But Liam's son returned home, days turned into quarters, and the Benclair Arbiter did nothing.

The workday at the Domus was over. Blair squatted uncomfortably in the incinerator room, sweat rolling down her back, picking through bins of trash piece by piece. There was nothing of note. There never was. Truly important information was either vanescoed or never written, simply spoken and loquered with careful precision from ear to ear. In either case, the resulting threads were stored in the Domus vaults where only Adrian and Damien, his childhood friend and most trusted lackey, had access.

Blair tossed the remaining scraps into the flames, donned her cloak, and climbed the steps to the ground level. Only Adrian would still be in the Domus, but he would be in his West Wing quarters. Sometimes, after long evenings of talking in the Atrium, he would invite Blair there.

"You cannot go home at this hour," he would say, smirking. "Maliter is a dangerous place." Blair would laugh as if she were on the side that created the danger, not the side that suffered from it.

Even something as intimate as seeing where Adrian lived gave Blair little insight into his secrets. There was one room, though, she hadn't been shown: his office, down the hall from the bedroom and locked with a complicated clavis alicration. There would be something in there, Blair hoped. And she was close to getting in.

Not tonight, though. Tonight, she crossed the dark Atrium quickly, her least favorite part of the day. Despite brushing shoulders with figurative darkness all day, despite the unrelenting grey of Talus, the actual absence of light genuinely frightened Blair. She had a faint memory, her earliest, of being alone in pitch black while the unmistakable sounds of assault rang out. Crossing the Atrium at the end of the day, she sometimes heard whispers of that memory.

"Sleeping alone tonight, hm?"

Blair froze.

The energy she felt was authoritative and brusque, underscored by an unrelenting suspicion. Damien. Blair wasn't sure if it was reserved only for her or if Adrian's right-hand man regarded everyone that way, but she could not recall an instance in which he did not energetically reek of skepticism in her presence.

Damien emerged from the shadows and stood before Blair, arms crossed. Broad to Adrian's narrow, he towered over her. Acutely aware he could crush her even without Alicrat, she smiled sweetly. Appeasement, though her least favorite weapon, always proved powerful against powerful men.

"You should do that more often," Damien said. "Sleep alone, I mean. He's got enough to worry about without an inner wall whore trying to climb the ladder."

Blair dropped her head a fraction. "That's not my intention, Damien. I care for him. But I understand," she continued hurriedly, "that you need to look out for him. He notices, you know. He deeply values your loyalty. He tells me so very often."

Damien lifted his chin. A smile tugged at his lips but never materialized. He took one step closer to Blair. She looked up at him, eyes wide, forcing all the awe and respect she could muster into her gaze. He stared back at her for too long, breathing heavily, eyes swirling with hunger and hatred and that damned suspicion, and then he turned and stalked away.

Blair walked slowly, normally, out of the Domus, continuing to do so for a half mile beyond its gates. Only when she was well within Talus' crumbling walls and back to the derelict streets she called home did she break into a paranoia driven sprint. At her small stone house, she undid Stin's protective alicrations and rewove them twice as strong from inside the safety of the front door. She slid down the wall and collapsed on the floor, legs shaking, chest heaving, completely, uncharacteristically, unsettled.

Stin hobbled out of his bedroom. He was old. Not in years, necessarily — he was only ninety — but from living dozens of lives, all of them dangerous. Blair sensed he was close to death, though she'd been thinking that for years.

His back was prematurely hunched, the result of a few missing vertebrae an Obscure had torn out in the days when the AO were still underground. Stin used to infiltrate their gatherings and sell their secrets to Enforcers for a quick pec until there were no more Enforcers who cared. He had more vertebrae than teeth, though; Blair was certain she remembered a mouthful when she'd been a child. Now there were only nine. His face was a patchwork of scars from knives and alicrations — some received for virtuous, anti-AO deeds, some inflicted as retaliation for his own crimes. Before working in the quarry, he'd been a con man who'd swindled more than his fair share of innocent magenu and hollows out of things they held precious.

Blair suspected that was how he'd come to raise her, though whether he'd coerced someone into giving her up or was saddled with the responsibility of her as punishment, she didn't know. She didn't care. Stin had kept her off the streets, out of the AO's clutches, and in Maliter, a child couldn't ask for more.

He collapsed into a chair. "What in the bloody moon's got you so riled?"

Blair didn't answer. Catching her breath, she alicrated a quick gulp of water. "Anything to eat?"

"Saved you some bread. Obscures are hoarding all the meat lately."

"I heard talk of rations for the general population," she said. "Starting in a few days."

"Bastards. Pixie came."

Sighing, she opened the letter Stin gave her, dated a few days ago.

An Obscure magena was killed in the Silvana Seraphilles. Urgently advise whether the Obscures are aware of the nature of her death.

Blair crumpled the letter into a ball and alicrated it into flames, irritated by the urgency Liam demanded while the urgency she'd been requesting for months went ignored.

"When's that man going to take some action?" Stin grunted, reading her frustration. "You've been risking your life for half a year now. Where are the Benclair forces unraveling the Domus gates, eh?"

"Liam is treading carefully," Blair answered, more in an effort to quell her own anger than to defend the Arbiter.

"Been treading a damn long time." Stin snorted. "I'm sick of it. I've half a mind to partume there tomorrow and bring the entitled bastard down here to show him what we're up against."

Blair laughed. "I doubt he'd take kindly to you showing up. Verstin Mallabrac of Teraur, notorious Northlands con man, lifelong mainstay on the Normalex Scroll of Necessary Captures... Besides," she shook her head, "nobody's going to be partuming in or out of here anymore. They finalized the preventative obscurity at the borders last week, remember? Not to mention all the patrols."

Stin harrumphed. "See if I care. If it takes me finally getting locked up to see some action from that man, I'll march myself into prison."

Blair's laughter faded into a yawn. "I need some sleep, Stin. See you tomorrow. Or not, if you're partuming to Benclair."

In her bedroom, Blair undressed and folded her clothes into a neat pile on the floor. On top of them she placed the tarnished gold bracelet that Stin had given to her when she was a child, claiming it had been her mother's. She put out a fresh set of clothes for the next day — the second in her rotation of three — and climbed into bed. Another day in darkness was over with nothing to show for it.

31

"Hello."

Charlie woke with a jolt, bolting upright, to find a man standing before him. He was old and thin, but perhaps had not always been that way, for his clothes hung off his frame loosely as if they'd been made for someone larger. A grey beard, braided, hung down his chest.

"Easy, there," he said, stepping back and holding up a palm in response to Charlie's lurch. "I'm a friend."

Finneas, Oleander, and Evie stirred behind him, then rose all at once, equally jarred, clustering around Charlie.

The man gasped quietly. "You," he said.

Charlie followed his gaze straight to Evie. "Stay away," he said, moving to stand between her and the stranger. To his dismay, Evie gently nudged him aside.

"Do I know you?" she asked the man, head cocked.

"Brimms," he said. After a pause, he exhaled softly. "I'm sure you don't remember me. You were so young, after all, but we've spent many an hour in this very room, in fact." He tensed suddenly, alert, eyes darting to the window. "Quick!" he said. "Up against the wall!"

Evie moved without question, flattening herself against the far wall where Brimms indicated. Finneas and Oleander followed with obvious trepidation — taking their cue more from Evie than from the man — and stood on either side of her, backs and palms against the wall. Charlie didn't move.

"The wall!" Brimms repeated, and with a flick of his hand, forced Charlie alongside his friends with an alicration.

He continued alicrative movements, twisting and tying across the length of the wall. With each manipulation, an oppressive weight pushed heavier against Charlie's chest. He wriggled instinctively but couldn't move. Unable even to turn his head, he strained to look out the corners of his eyes. He should have seen Oleander, Evie, and Finneas to his right. Instead, he glimpsed the outline of Oleander's profile — part flesh, part whitewashed stone — sink away, leaving only flush wall in its wake.

The front door opened.

"Oho!" Brimms called, now facing the door, his back to the wall. "How does it find you?"

"We're looking for fugitives," a voice said. Someone stood opposite Brimms at the door, but Charlie couldn't make out a face beneath the hood of their crimson cloak. "Escaped from the castle last night. Wanted for murder."

"Oh, my," Brimms said, sounding genuinely shocked. "The murder of whom?"

"Seen anyone?"

"I cannot say I have."

"Four rogue magenu? Three men and a woman?"

Brimms answered with confidence. "I have not seen them."

The visitor stepped into view, peering his head into the room, snarling. "You sure about that? If they're found and their memories reveal they've had help —"

"I would not dream of helping *murderers*," Brimms said pointedly. The visitor stared hard at him, then, motioning to others Charlie couldn't see, left.

Brimms closed the door. "Bloody bullies," he muttered, and rushed straight back to the wall. He stood before the group again, working just as quickly to undo whatever he'd done to hide them.

Charlie was freed from the alicrated protection first and stumbled forward, instinctively gasping for air despite having been able to breathe normally whilst hidden.

"Dissimulo," Brimms said before Charlie could ask. He continued to swipe and untie his way through the air as he moved down the length of the wall.

Finneas appeared next, revealed little by little, until he fell forth as dramatically as Charlie had. "I've never heard of dissimulo before," he said, feeling his body, seeming unconvinced it wasn't still in the wall.

"I invented it," Brimms replied, working on Evie.

"Isn't it on file with the Normalex?" Charlie asked.

"No. It is obscure," Brimms said, just as Evie stepped out of the wall.

"Obscure?" Charlie said. "You can't just —"

"Can't I?" With Oleander partially revealed, Brimms paused his work. "Shall we invite those slogs back inside without the benefit of my dissimulo, then?"

"Did you share this technique with anybody in the castle?" Finneas asked quietly.

"If you mean to ask whether the scum up there forced me to create a way to keep dissenting Mensmen trapped inside paintings, then yes, I did. You'd be amazed what the mind can come up with when the alternative is death." Brimms released Oleander, gave everyone a moment to collect themselves, then addressed the group.

"I'm not your enemy," he said, "and based off that visit we just had, you're going to need my help getting out of Callidora. If you'll come with me, I have a better hiding place than this old bakery where we can come up with a plan."

"This was the bakery?" Charlie said, suspicion momentarily forgotten.

"Was. Been empty for years." Brimms cracked the door open. "Are you coming? Now or never."

Charlie looked at Evie, trying to communicate his uncertainty. After a beat, she joined Brimms and gestured for the others to follow — or not. She was doing that a little too much for Charlie's liking, lately. Always walking off, leading the way, like she didn't need him anymore. Had she ever?

Outside, the sun had barely started its ascent in the sky. The group trailed Brimms down a main street of Callidoralta, dashing through vestiges of the previous night's mist that hung over the pavement. Down an alley that rendered them single file, around a corner, and through one more narrow alley, Brimms finally stopped and pushed open a door.

They followed him into a low-ceilinged room absolutely covered in wax; it dripped down the walls in melted columns, spattered the floor in hardened discs. A table in the center was piled high with candles, some burnt down to nothing, others brand new with pristine, white wicks, and others with no wicks at all, but long, red feathers emitting a glow of their own accord.

"I'm a candlestick maker," Brimms said, as if it weren't obvious. "The only one in Callidora."

"Magenu don't need candles," Oleander remarked.

"Hollows do."

"I didn't think of them," he admitted.

"Few do." Brimms snapped his fingers over the candles on the table, bringing them to life. "I expect you're hungry. I'll rummage something up for you." He left, presumably for the kitchen.

"Everyone alright?" Finneas asked quietly. "That was mildly horrifying."

"Sure was," Oleander agreed. "The whole time, I had the worst itch on my —"

"He just used an obscurity like it was nothing," Charlie hissed. "That's dangerous. That's —"

"Evil?" Evie finished, staring at him, arms crossed. "He did it to protect us."

"Well, who is he, anyway? What makes you trust him? In fact, what's gotten into you at all?" Charlie heard himself, heard his protectiveness and concern bursting out in entirely the wrong way, but he couldn't stop himself. "First, you follow a mad woman through the castle, then you shove us through a hole in the wall, march us through darkness —"

"It's gotten us this far."

"Until it goes *too* far. What makes you trust this man?"

"This man has food for you," Brimms announced. He set the tray he carried, laden with bread, cheese, and meats, on the table. After an awkward beat, everyone dug in gratefully, including an embarrassed Charlie.

"I don't begrudge your suspicions," Brimms said as they ate. "Unusual times, isn't it? One can never be too careful."

"We're just a bit on edge," Finneas said diplomatically. Brushing crumbs off his hand, he stuck it out for Brimms to shake. "I'm Finneas of the Fern, by the way. Thank you for helping us."

"Oleander of Orefo," Oleander said, mouth full, taking Finneas' cue to use their formal Mensmen titles.

"Charlie," Charlie muttered, withholding the Rutherford.

"Benclairans, then. Except you, Evangeline," Brimms said, regarding her again. He smiled. "You've grown."

"How do you know me, Brimms?" Evie asked. "And how did you find us?"

"It's the same answer for both questions. Perdita."

Charlie's mouth hung open, bread and cheese half chewed. Angst forgotten, he turned to Evie, her face a mirror of his.

"I wasn't always a candlestick maker, see," Brimms said, waving his hand back and forth over a flame, oblivious to their shock. "I used to make alicrations instead — ones you'll find on file with the Normalex," he added pointedly. "You may have heard of an affrim? Anyway, Perdita's the reason I started making candles. I wanted to make her life a little easier. She never told me outright, mind you, but I knew she wasn't just baking bread. I knew she was wrapped up in something greater than herself with the Callidoras. And I knew she'd leave me someday because of it." He reflected on this, rolling a bit of wax between his fingers.

Still stunned, Charlie could not form words, let alone one of the dozen questions he had. Neither, it seemed, could Evie. Brimms continued. "Night before she left, she brought me to the bakery and asked me to weave something for her. Something like an affrim that would alert me if anyone came through that door you lot used. It didn't need to be that complicated, really. I affixed the end of one thread to the door and brought the other end here."

He pointed to a lump of wax on the table from which a barely visible thread hung loosely. He picked it up and let it fall again. "This used to be taut, see. I asked Perdita what it was for. 'Just in case,' she told me, cryptic as ever. Just in case of you, I suppose."

"How could she have known?" Evie managed.

"I've no idea how that woman knows half the things she does," Brimms said. "Do you not remember her, Evie? Adena used to bring you to her bakery after hours, sit you up on the counter, and let you stuff yourself with bread and honey." He chuckled lightly. "I understand if you don't remember the bloke delivering candles. But Perdita is simply...unforgettable." His eyes went misty.

"There's a lot I don't remember."

"Anyway," Brimms said, wiping his eyes, "your return isn't the first thing Perdita has predicted that's come to pass. She is worlds beyond us all, that woman."

"You're speaking in the present," Charlie said. "Is she alive?"

"To me, she is."

"Do you know where she is?" Evie asked, and in one breath, rushed through an abridged version of their hunt for a Perdito descendant.

Brimms' face fell. "If I knew where she was, I'd be with her."

"You might still be able to help us," Charlie said. He produced the torn annual page from his pocket and showed it to Brimms. "World's End," he said, pointing. "Does that mean anything to you?"

Brimms leaned closer to the page, squinting, then pulled back, eyes wide. "Why yes, it does. It would mean something to any Callidoran."

"It's the coast, isn't it?" Finneas said.

Brimms nodded. "Beyond the Callidoralta mountains lies a plain, and beyond the plain lies the ragged Callidora Cliffs. Beyond those cliffs lies the sea, and beyond the sea lies land, eventually. Somebody else's land. Long ago, though, Callidorans believed there was nothing beyond the sea. The cliffs marked the World's End."

Charlie's heart fell.

"So Perdita is just *somewhere* on the coast?" Evie cried, verbalizing his thoughts. "She could be anywhere!"

"Maybe not," Brimms said, wagging a finger. He tottered over to a shelf where he pushed things aside, mumbling, and returned to the group with a scroll in hand.

Finneas and Oleander cleared a space on the table for Brimms to

BORN INTO THE NIGHT

unfurl the scroll. It was a map displaying the Northlands — well known to Charlie, Oleander, and Finneas, but no doubt astounding for Evie. To her, the Northlands would look like the fraternal twin of the Other World's Europe, a landmass that may have had the same Pangea beginnings, but had evolved differently. Charlie watched her light up as she recognized familiar coastlines, watched her eyes narrow as she tried to mentally overlay Europe's national borders on those of the Northlands States.

Long, thin Benclair occupied the Other World's Edinburgh down to its Cambridge, England. The Silvana Seraphilles lay over Scotland's Loch Lomond, with a hashed border line drawn to the west of the forest. Callidora comprised the rest of Scotland, all of Wales, and most of England, coursing around Benclair on its north, west, and south. Just below the area Evie would recognize as London began Maliter, sprawling into the Other World's France, Switzerland, and the boot of Italy — frighteningly large. Teraur lay over Ireland and Northern Ireland, and Iristell encompassed Spain and Portugal. A thick line labelled *River Dumot* created the eastern border of Maliter, separating it from the Vastlands, a great expanse of nothing that covered the Other World's Eastern Europe and stretched well into Russia.

"'I am an island of buried treasure,'" Brimms recited. "'I am an island of buried treasure, and there I shall return.' That was her answer every time I asked what she was doing with the Callidoras. Not an answer at all, but now I wonder..." Shaking his head, he assured Evie and Charlie, "Perdita won't be *somewhere* on the coast. She'll be there." He pointed to a minuscule dot in the ocean. "Finimund. The only island off the coast. A tiny little thing, unpopulated and reportedly treacherous to reach. I remember hearing reports of magenu going missing out that way."

"Finimund," Evie repeated. "*Finis mundis.* End of the world. World's End." She turned to Charlie. "What do you think?"

Charlie exhaled slowly. He already knew, just as Evie had to know, what his answer would be. What his answer *had* to be, for his father, for Benclair, for the Northlands. Still, he took his time to think through everything methodically, trying, in the only way he knew how, to regain some semblance of control over a situation that had already fallen

EMILY BISBACH

desperately outside the realm of his control. Sighing deeply, he closed his eyes.

When he opened them, they were fixed on Brimms. "Will you help us to the coast?"

Brimms smiled. "I thought you'd never ask."

32

FIVE LARGE FIREBIRDS, brilliantly colored in shades of red and gold, sat on the ground in Brimms' backyard, long legs folded beneath their lean bodies. Curious black eyes peered over their beaks, regarding the group with wisened calm.

"Allow me to introduce you to my birds," Brimms told the group proudly. "They've been in my family for generations."

"I was going to ask," Finneas said. "Firebirds are quite rare, aren't they?"

"You're looking at the only ones in Callidora, to my knowledge," Brimms said. "Clever creatures, firebirds. Remain focused on your destination and they will carry you there without direction." The birds let out musical caws, nodding cooperatively.

"All the way to the coast?" Oleander asked.

"Certainly. They carry enormous weight with little effort," Brimms said pointedly. "And I daresay, they are your only option at this point. There will be patrols at the borders by now, watching for the folds of a partume. Horses and unicorns are too easily tracked. The firebirds will carry you over the cloud cover. The Obscures won't think to search the skies. Go on, then. Introduce yourselves."

Evie's bird, more golden than red and slightly smaller than the others, gazed at her like they'd already met. She patted its domed head. The delicate plume of feathers that capped it were like velvet between her fingers.

"She's quite young, that one," Brimms told her, tapping the firebird's beak. "Or old, depending on how you see it. Newly reborn from her ashes just three days ago. My grandfather believed her to be immortal, claiming she witnessed the beginning of time."

"The mythology is true, then?" Evie stroked her firebird, her phoenix, wondering how many times it had died and risen from the ashes. Its most recent rebirth, she noted, was the same day she'd found her Alicrat. She smiled and the bird's gold beak parted slightly, seeming to smile back in confirmation of a shared secret.

Charlie joined her, his own firebird trailing him obediently. "'There are three phoenixes in paradise...'" he recited. "'...so, too, there are three baptisms. The first is spiritual, the second is by fire, the third is by water.'"

Evie recognized the lines from the Gnostic texts, though she wasn't familiar with their purpose. Having studied them in the Other World, Charlie fell into a lecture of sorts, doing what Evie knew he loved most: sharing knowledge with her, knowing she was always interested. She listened, but her mind drifted instead to his outburst in Brimms' home, his obvious displeasure at the way she'd taken control in Callidora.

Wasn't that the point of her joining them? She had something the others didn't — Callidora energy — and it hadn't just gotten them through the walls. Her castle had spoken to her, not only through Adena's hazy appearances, but by communing with her Alicrat, giving her direction, protection, instincts. She wouldn't ignore those instincts, Charlie's discomfort be damned.

"Generally speaking," he was saying, still contemplating the Gnostic texts, "Gnosticism offers a mystical, more spiritual approach to creation than the doctrine of the Other World's modern Church."

"The phoenix represents Christ's rebirth, right?" Evie said, turning back to the conversation.

"Not exactly," Charlie said. "Gnosticism holds that the phoenix was created by Sophia, an emanation of an all-powerful entity, along with a malicious counterpart who helped her build the material world.

According to some translations, that counterpart became the source of all evil, so Sophia cast it into an abyss of chaos. The phoenix was her everlasting witness to this act."

Evie looked into her bird's large eyes. They were too soft, too calm, to have witnessed Lucifer's alleged fall from grace. Evie scoffed quietly. Still, to be in the presence of a creature so old...what *had* those eyes seen?

"Get on your birds," Brimms said with sudden authority, just as he'd commanded them to the wall in Perdita's bakery.

Evie whirled around to face him, as did Charlie, Oleander, and Finneas, so urgent was his tone. His eyes were fixed on his house. "On your birds," he repeated, voice low. "Now."

This time, everyone obeyed. Brimms didn't move; he remained facing his home, watching, listening, sensing. Only Oleander was still struggling into position when Brimms spun around, flinging his arms upward, indicating for them to take off.

"Go! They're coming — the Obscures from this morning! Get above the clouds. Hurry!" He rushed the group, prompting the firebirds to heave their wings.

There was still one firebird, sans rider, in the yard. Evie had assumed Brimms would join them in locating Perdita. "Come with us," she implored, keeping her bird grounded despite the other three rising.

Brimms promised he would. "Let me get rid of this lot at my door. I'll be with you right after." He glanced at his home again. "Go, now. Go!"

Evie hesitated, then bent her knees, allowing her firebird to lift off the ground with a flap of its deceptively powerful wings. It rose easily, as if she were no more than another feather on its back.

She joined the others waiting in midair and they ascended in tandem, ten, thirty, fifty meters, until Callidoralta became a patchwork of blue and grey. From the sky, it was a different city, a beautiful place where Evie imagined herself growing up happily, eating Perdita's bread with honey or making candles with Brimms while Adena consulted the Tree Book's secrets, Naveena at her side.

The illusion was ripped away in an instant. From the air, Evie saw a dozen men cluster around the door to Brimms' home, helmed by the red-cloaked Obscure who had interrogated him while she and the others were in the wall. She changed the destination in her mind from the coast back to Brimms' backyard, and her bird immediately responded by tilting into a nosedive. They'd have hurtled back to the ground if Finneas' bird hadn't flown forth, blocking their path.

"Don't, Evie," he shouted over the rush of wings and wind. "They're already at the door. We need to get to the clouds. Brimms said he would handle them."

Evie peered down. The horde of magenu had disappeared into Brimms' home. Small and distant, he still stood outside with the remaining firebird, waiting for the intruders.

Reluctantly, she focused on the coast again, urging her firebird toward the clouds with the others, but something caught her eye as she rose. Smoke billowed from the windows of Brimms' home, all that wax melting, his life's work a puddle on the floor. The Obscures were in the backyard now, encircling him, readying to inflict whatever torture would attempt to discern his role in the group's escape. Before Evie could even think about returning to help, Brimms' bird on the ground took action.

The phoenix beat its wings once, twice, rising just enough to hover over Brimms. It clasped its talons around his head, then twisted grue-somely. Instantly, an alicration killed the bird, but its task was complete. Brimms was dead, his knowledge of Perdita and the existence of Adena Callidora's daughter dead with him.

The red-cloaked Obscure knelt beside the bird, head cocked. Then he rose suddenly, craning his neck to peer into the sky just as urgently as Evie peered down. He was small, and then he was a dot, and then he was gone as the clouds swallowed her.

33

BLAIR HATED to leave the bed's plush, alicrated mattress, its silky sheets. But Adrian's breathing had grown deep and steady, and so she rolled slowly toward the bed's edge. He stirred, groping for her in the darkness, resting his hand on her waist. She froze and waited for him to settle once more. Once upright, she looked at him. His exposed chest rose and fell. A muscle twitched in his cheek. His face seemed softer when he slept, his features relaxing into something callow that almost made him look innocent. Perhaps he was, once. He was somebody's son, after all.

Blair crossed the room with confidence. She knew exactly where to step, having committed the layout of the bedroom to memory. There was the wardrobe filled with black attire, the bed larger than her entire room at Stin's, the full-length mirror for practicing one's sneer, her own discarded clothing on the floor. Nothing important. The office down the hall held something important, though. It had to. Otherwise, Blair had endured the last two quarters for nothing.

It had been a far more challenging ruse than she'd anticipated. She'd understood, quickly, that Adrian did not want to be seduced by yet another fanatic cult member who knelt at his feet, supplicating for his love. What he wanted was to drop the persona of enigmatic leader behind closed doors, to be with someone who allowed him to simply exist. Blair had little experience being that type of soft, sympathetic woman. She had been unprepared for the emotional vulnerability it required, for the moments of genuine connection it forced her to experience. She'd managed, though, mostly by fantasizing about how wonderful it was going to feel to kill Adrian once she got what she needed.

The obsidian stones in the hall were cold beneath her bare feet. There were no windows, and she couldn't see a thing. She toyed with the bracelet on her wrist to calm herself and, ignoring the memories the darkness stirred up, moved forward, counting her paces and reaching the office door in twenty-two precisely measured steps.

Blair did not know exactly how Adrian had woven the clavis that locked the door, but she had observed each time he performed the manipulation in reverse to unlock it, lingering under the pretense of being simply unable to tear herself away from him. She'd memorized each twist of his fingers, mimicked them as she walked home at night, pieced them together as she alicrated the glass ceiling of the Atrium to its crystal clarity.

Now, in the dark hallway, she worked on the real thing. Immediately, threads untangled without resistance and fell away. She moved faster, functioning on instinct more than memory, making sudden changes based on sense alone until a solitary knot remained. She contorted her fingers to pull its strongest loops apart, but they held fast, refusing to yield, as if they knew she had not tied them. That was the thing about threads, though. Some magenu argued the case for energy as a living being, capable of resisting manipulation. Blair believed it operated under a set of laws dictated by nature and could not choose whose fingers to obey or ignore.

The last knot grew slack under her ministrations. The door opened.

The office was as dark as the hallway had been. In all her preparations, Blair hadn't considered the most obvious obstacle — the lack of light. A stupid mistake, given her fear of the dark. She wondered if she could alicrate starlight through the walls and what would surely be a dense layer of Maliter clouds, but she was afraid the manipulation would leave a trace. She cursed silently, shivering. The air in the office was cold. She instinctively moved to a different spot, where the chill subsided. She moved back. There was a draft.

She followed the draft to the wall and nearly cried out with relief when she felt latched, wooden slabs. She swung the shutters open and caught the moon in a rare patch of cloudless sky, bright enough to illuminate Adrian's office.

It was starkly minimal, like the rest of his quarters, its floor and walls the same unrelenting obsidian. Even the desk in the center was just a slab of black stone. Circling it, Blair found no drawers. They existed, she mused, but were likely only accessible by Adrian's touch.

She examined the sparse contents of the shelves behind the desk. A decade of annuals were stacked neatly on one, their edges lined up perfectly. An orb hovered alone on another, rotating slowly. It was a replica of the moon, so precise one would be forgiven for believing it was the real thing snatched from the sky and minuted. Another shelf held a stack of papers, blank save for the top sheet which merely contained a short list of names Blair had never heard of with dates that meant nothing, all hastily scrawled.

> Stonehenge 82nd of the Second?
> Chartres Cathedral 82nd of the Third?
> Triora 82nd of the Fourth?
> Salem 81st of the Second?

She memorized them anyway.

The highest shelf held a book. She did not underestimate Adrian's ability to sense latent alicrations, but a simple venen? Surely not. She recalled the book from the shelf and set it on the desk.

A flurry of leftover emotion struck Blair. Excitement, rage, frustration, curiosity — so much curiosity — and flickers of understanding hit her all at once. Stronger than anything was the overwhelming sensation of confusion: mystified confusion, angry confusion, deeply sad confusion, all hanging over the book like a cloud. Some threads were only days old — Adrian's, no doubt — and some were decades, even centuries, older. The most ancient were frayed down to their last fiber, near silent whispers of the past.

She lifted the cover cautiously. The inner cover bore a symbol: a shield and an open book. Beneath it, a banner read: *LUX ET VERITAS*, and in bold lettering below that, *YALE UNIVERSITY LIBRARY, Gift of HANS P. KRAUS*. Blair had never heard of the city of Yale, nor the Beinecke Library, which was handwritten in the corner.

On the first page of the book were four blocks of text in a language Blair had never seen. The next page contained more strange text and a crudely drawn haricot floren. This continued on the next page, and the next. The book was filled with unreadable words accompanied by stars and charts and florens and other plants, some of which Blair recognized as Maliteran, others, she'd never seen. None of it made sense and she understood the multitude of confusion that emanated from the book. Her own perplexed energy was beginning to latch onto the ancient web. She slammed the book shut, afraid to leave any trace of herself behind.

The office fell into darkness and Blair startled, thinking she'd been discovered. But the room remained as still as ever — the moon had merely abandoned her in favor of the clouds. She returned the book the top shelf and closed the window. Leaving the office in the same state she'd found it, she rewove the clavis and hurried down the hall.

In the bedroom, Adrian's breathing had not changed, nor had his position. He lay on his side, legs splayed and arms outstretched around the absent Blair, who slid back into place carefully. He unconsciously tightened his arms around her, believing just as erroneously in sleep as he did while awake that she was his.

Disappointment plagued Blair the following day. Nothing from Adrian's office furthered her plans. She remained was a spy in a governmental building teeming with secrets she could not find, the sole resistance fighter for a nonexistent movement.

As she trudged down one of the endless Domus halls, halfheartedly flicking alicrations at the floor to keep it polished, she felt Adrian's telltale presence behind her. She immediately snapped into character.

Dressed in all black, as usual, Adrian was the living extension of the obsidian that surrounded him. His polished boots clicked across the stones and the dramatic billow of his cloak swished behind him in step. The top buttons of his shirt were undone, and Blair could see his jugular beating with the annoying pulse of his existence. She envisioned tearing her fingers into it and inviting the Eternals at the River Dumot to lap up his blood.

"Adrian," she said softly, smiling.

"Good morning, Blair." He smiled back, normalcy lighting his features. "How did you sleep?"

"Very well, as I always do next to you." She made herself sick.

He grazed her cheek with a hand. She leaned into his touch, smiling. "I'm glad to hear it," he said quietly. "It's only, I could have sworn you left me in the night."

Blair stiffened, barely, and laughed airily. "You must have been dreaming."

"Perhaps." Adrian said. He regarded her for a long, far too intense moment. She felt him standing on the outskirts of her mind, peering over its walls, trying to see what lay on the other side.

She held his gaze, not permitting herself to flinch, not permitting an iota of discordant energy to sneak past her barriers. "Will I see you tonight?" She took a half step forward, leaving a scant inch between them, and bowed her head, the subtext of submission clear. With a quick glance down the hall to ensure they were alone, she looped an arm around his waist and pulled him against her. He inhaled sharply, any inkling of suspicion pushed aside to allow for the more enjoyable sensation of being wanted. He leaned in, his breath uncomfortably warm on her neck and smelling of semps.

"Perhaps," he whispered. He lingered for a moment, and then he was gone.

Blair resisted the urge to scream after him.

Two quarters she'd wasted in Adrian's bed, thinking she was so very clever for gaining his trust. For fooling him, when really, she was the one who'd been fooled. He presented a curated version of himself to her, just as she did to him, and AO secrets had no place in the exhibit he allowed her to see. She existed only to satisfy his physical needs, to boost his ego. She'd risked everything for nothing and now the scales were on the verge of tipping in the other direction. She'd seen the flicker of doubt that colored his grey eyes.

She *would* see him tonight. She would make sure of it. Tonight, Blair would kill Adrian. And then she would run, and be captured, and be killed, but at least he would be dead. She would find him in what comes next and haunt him for eternity.

Yet, at the end of the day, she still sat in the incinerator room surrounded by bins of Domus trash, unfolding every crumpled paper and piecing together every shred of parchment, looking painstakingly, futilely, for *something* to leverage. Unfolding, tossing, unfolding, tossing, nothing, nothing, nothing.

Blair, he k

Her hands continued the rote movement before she registered that she shouldn't. She reached into the incinerator and grabbed the edge of the paper bearing her name as nearby scraps were licked up. The edges were singed, but the message was clear: *Blair, he knows. Santus Alley. Sundown.*

She burned the scrap, deliberately this time.

Somebody had placed the message in the trash purposefully, knowing she picked through the bins each night. Adrian? A trap? No, he would have killed her in the Atrium as entertainment for his lackeys and a lesson to everybody else. Her heart beat unnervingly quickly. It was a foreign feeling, more intense than the bout of paranoia she'd felt a few nights ago, and it took Blair a moment to comprehend that she was afraid. Still, instinct told her to go to Santus Alley, in the heart of the Changeling District, to meet whomever had penned the warning. She threw the rest of the trash into the flames and ran from the Domus.

The Changeling District teemed with human mutations. One of them, a woman whose face was covered in pustules seeping cloudy yellow liquid, grabbed Blair by the shoulders, shaking her. "*Pecs*," she hissed. "See me decay? I need a medice! Spare some pecsss?" Blair shoved her away. She spat at Blair's feet, her appearance suddenly healthy again.

Santus Alley was empty save the rats scurrying through putrid puddles of water and the pixies, drunk on vocat leaves, buzzing in circles. The figure stepping out of the darkness at the far end was petite.

A woman. She moved closer, her grey hair came into view, and Blair relaxed.

"Thank the sun you found my message," Greer said. "We don't have much time. First, if you don't mind confirming it's you?"

"The Changeling District is a strange place to meet if you question my identity," Blair said.

"We're here for my own protection. If anybody sees me speaking with you, I can feign ignorance and claim I was impersonated. Please, Blair." She alicrated a small fireball and set it hovering between herself and Blair.

Reluctantly, Blair shoved a finger into the flames, recoiling immediately. "Agh!" She stuck the singed finger into her mouth and spoke through it. "Well? I'm not reverting, am I? Your turn."

Greer did the same and barely flinched, but the blisters that rose on her finger were real and she did not revert to another magena's form from the pain. Satisfied, she spoke, her efficiency as a Maior obvious. "Tenebris suspects you. You're lucky you've fooled him as long as you have. I heard him talking to Damien this evening. You'll be in the Osterre by tomorrow."

Blair winced. Screams from the Osterre could be heard throughout Talus every few days before a fresh layer of dirt muffled them. Subsequent prisoners suffered atop the decaying mound of previous victims, yet somehow, the pile never grew high enough to allow escape.

"And your father," Greer continued.

"Stin isn't my father."

"Whoever he is, they're going to take him. You both need to leave. Tonight."

Blair wondered how Adrian had found out. She replayed her actions in the office — was the strange book askew on the shelf? Did traces of her nerves linger? She asked Greer if she'd been aware of her actions.

Greer smiled faintly. "The Domus is thick with wickedness. Genuine evil, hangers-on, and those who are just plain weak. Those are heavy threads to wade through when so few within yourself match."

"My energy was off?"

"No. You have impeccable control."

"Then what?"

"I saw you smile at him. A woman knows that smile."

Blair grimaced. "No need to use it anymore."

"Maybe not, but Blair, we have Gaspare. We meet fortnightly in Pickering. Nobody pays any mind to Pickering, least of all the AO. The population is small, but exclusively Norm. We're trying to…" Greer trailed off, as despondent with the difficulty of forming a resistance as Blair. "We're trying."

"Gaspare?" Blair was surprised to hear the withering Maior of Pickering's name. He was elderly, frail, and seemed likely to blow away with the slightest breeze. Blair had written him off.

"His ancestors were prominent brokers in the treaty that ended the Northlands Wars," Greer explained. "He'd rather die than see Maliter fall to ruin in the grips of the Obscures. Come to Pickering. You'll be safe there."

"Stin will go," Blair said, and decided. "I'm going to Benclair. We can't do this alone, Greer. Surely you've realized that."

"You won't get past the borders."

"I'll figure it out. Contact me at Rutherford Castle."

The alley had grown dark, lit only by the erratic, colorful flashes of light from drunk pixies. The women nodded at each other, then turned in opposite directions, parting ways without another word.

At home, Stin listened impassively as Blair recounted the day's developments. He shrugged in response. "I'm not leaving."

"You damned stubborn bastard!" she cried. "You think you can con your way out of anything, like the old days."

Stin crossed his arms. "Running won't fix anything."

"Neither will being buried alive in the Osterre."

Grunting, Stin heaved his body into a chair. "Never mind me. I know how you can get out of Maliter. Been digging a tunnel from the quarry for the past ten years, haven't we? Me and the hollows. They want out, too. So, we've been digging. Quarry's not far from the Callidora border, after all."

"When will you reach it?"

Stin grinned. "Already did."

"You damned stubborn bastard," Blair said again, in a much different tone. "Promise me you'll go to Pickering."

"I'll think about it." Stin waved a hand her way, then said, "You really didn't find anything in Tenebris' office?"

"Just an old book. Do you know where Yale is?"

Stin stroked his stubbled chin. "Sounds familiar. Might have heard the name, long time ago."

They fell into silence, perhaps their last, Blair knew, and she should have felt saddened. Instead she was burgeoned, realizing she'd gotten what she'd truly needed the last two quarters: confirmation that she wasn't alone. There were others besides herself risking their lives for the cause, and with nothing else to her name, at least she had that.

34

———

THE SEA WAS VISIBLE AHEAD, a dark reflection of the skies that threatened a storm. On the calmer side of those skies, the beat of the firebirds' wings finally slowed. They dipped closer to the blanket of green below, dotted with purple like Scottish heather in a glen, until they touched down softly.

They'd landed on the other side of the Callidoralta mountains. Just as Brimms had said, flatness lay between their position and the coast. It reminded Evie of the Empty Fields, down to the singular tree she saw in the distance.

"Another Eternal Tree?" she asked casually, pretending Charlie hadn't erupted at her, pretending Brimms' head hadn't been violently ripped off by a firebird.

"There's only one Eternal Tree," Oleander said.

Charlie frowned in the way he did when summoning information he'd filed away long ago. "Of course," he finally said. "The Callidora line lives on. Why wouldn't the tree?" He took Evie's hand, seeming, like her, eager to forget the previous hour's events. "You have to see this, Evie!"

They jogged toward the tree, followed by Oleander, followed by the firebirds, people and creatures sprinting across a field and only one of them knowing why.

Though not quite as large as the Eternal Tree, this tree was still enormous thanks to the span of its hundreds of branches. They bore no leaves, making visible the smallest twigs and, most peculiarly, the names that were carved into every offshoot.

"It's a family tree," Charlie said. "The last family tree in the Northlands. There used to be one for each Original, but when the Original lines died, so did their trees. The Callidora tree lives because you do, Evie. Look! Here's your lineage."

Evie squinted to see the names on the span of branches Charlie pointed to. Oleander, on the tips of his toes, helped her. "Celestein. Ingrid," he read.

"I don't know them," Evie said.

"Isabil?"

"Oh!" She exclaimed, pointing. "And there's Erskine, then Clement!"

The names were all carved into old branches, looking so brittle the slightest pressure might crack them in half. But from Clement's branch came a younger, more pliable branch with *Adena* carved into it. From it hung a red apple, bearing Evie's name.

Another apple dangled directly from Clement's branch. It was brown and soft, *Naveena* barely legible on its sunken flesh. The stem broke as Evie gazed at it and the fruit dropped to her feet. It erupted on impact, expelling plump maggots.

"Why wasn't she a branch?" Evie asked.

"The apples represent children," Charlie explained. "Naveena had no children — no reason to become a branch of her own."

A nervousness crept up Evie's back. "Anyone could see this tree," she said, "and know I exist."

Charlie's lips tightened. "I hadn't thought of that." Then, shaking his head, "No. Sillen and Grilt would have made the connection if they had."

"They might not even know it's here," Oleander added. "Family trees are more legend than anything these days, especially in the States where they no longer exist."

Only slightly relieved, Evie circled the rest of the tree, taking in the names of her ancestors. There was Christian again, the sad face from the Hall of Portraits, now an old branch. He had two children — Lucca, a direct ancestor of Evie's whose branch eventually produced Clement — and Christina, one of her many distant ancestors she hadn't the time to note in the Hall of Portraits. Christina's branches were charred, like they'd been burned, but a single, green leaf hung off the last offshoot. Except it wasn't a leaf, Evie realized, looking closer. It was another apple, mostly covered in ash.

"Looks like you've got a long-lost cousin," Oleander said, joining her. He reached up to wipe away the soot on the apple. "Nameless."

"How could that be?"

"Maybe the parents perished before the child could be named," Charlie guessed, circling beneath the apple. He stretched until his fingers grazed the parent branch. "The mother's name was *Arabell*."

Wordlessly, Evie left the mysterious apple to examine the trunk of the tree where *Claire* was carved, the indents worn nearly smooth after centuries of sun and salty air. Claire, the mother of Callidoras, including the nameless apple. Another secret, just one of the many connecting every name on the tree except Evie's. And Naveena's, she reminded herself. Resentment coursed through her. She called to Charlie and Oleander. "Let's go."

Charlie continued to marvel as they left the tree behind. "It's times like this I wish I had a camera," he said.

"What's a camera?" Oleander asked.

"It's a device from the Other World that captures energy from a subject's threads, holding them forever on something called film."

"Impossible." Oleander looked at Charlie like he'd just failed his First Libellum exam. "Threads can't be duplicated like that."

"It's more complicated," Evie said. "The Other World's technology does seem to defy the laws of Alicrat, though. Strange, now that I think about it."

"Or is it Alicrat that's strange?" Charlie asked. "Who's to say which world has the better system?"

"Alicrat is better," Evie said immediately. "It's a natural ability. The Other World's technology is not."

"But look at how innovative the Other World's cultures are without Alicrat to rely on," Charlie argued.

"Magenu innovate. Brimms created the affrim and dissimulo. And you said it yourself, Charlie. Obscurities were innovations, once upon a time. How far could alicrations have advanced if the Normalex hadn't demonized those early attempts?"

Charlie scoffed. "Destruction is never an acceptable price for advancement. Look at your world's atomic bomb. Scientifically innovative, yes. Horrifically devastating for humanity. That's why obscurities must be controlled." He nodded curtly.

Oleander frowned. "Atomic bomb?"

"Not if we want to stand a chance against the AO," Evie said, looking at Charlie pointedly. He avoided her eyes. "What if the Tree Book doesn't help us? What if that war your father is worried about comes and we have no advantage? Worse, what if we're at a disadvantage because everyone is too precious to dabble in darkness?" She paused, considering. "Why does it matter, anyway? Killing is killing."

Oleander inhaled sharply, looking very much like he regretted asking what a camera was. Charlie met Evie's eyes then, visibly shocked. "How can you say that?"

"I mean it. It wouldn't matter if Marcus had killed that magena with an arrow to the heart or an alicration that stopped it from beating."

"It matters, Evie," Charlie said emphatically. "It matters because the arrow does the damage. With obscurities, there is nothing through which your intent is diffused. It's just you. Killing with an alicration requires a degree of malice not needed with a weapon. It's why manual weapons were still developed here, just like in the Other World, despite magenu having the — as you say, *natural* — ability to kill."

They were close to the coast now and the wind had picked up substantially. Evie stared into the distance, hair whipping around her face, sea spray dampening her sweater. She didn't answer for a long time. She scarcely had the words to help herself understand the fire heating her insides, let alone Charlie. It burned not only with rage, but with a painful need for vengeance, and she was only beginning to realize how far she would go to obtain it.

"Everyone has the capacity for evil, Charlie," she said eventually. "I think the reason for accessing that capacity matters. I think the ends can justify the means. If the safety of Benclair was at stake, if your life was at stake, I'd do anything."

Charlie struggled to reply. Oleander piped up instead. "Thanks," he said. "Always nice to be thought of."

It cut the tension — both Evie and Charlie laughed wryly — but Evie was left with the uncomfortable awareness that she and Charlie, always so aligned, were no longer on the same page.

She shouted over the furious crash of waves on the jagged coast. "Where's Finimund?"

Charlie squinted through the sea spray. "Brimms said the firebirds would know where to go. Do you think they can fly in this weather?" The birds let out an insulted caw, each of them hitting a different note to create an offended minor chord.

With no other choice, everyone climbed onto the firebirds once more. Passengers secured, the birds took off with great effort, wings flapping ferociously against the wind. They flew toward nothing, remaining beneath the low clouds, until the dot of an island appeared, growing larger with each strained beat of firebird wings. A ramshackle hut lay in ruins on the island, part of its roof blowing off before Evie's eyes. If anybody had ever occupied the structure, they certainly weren't inside now. But the birds ignored it and instead, swooped low along the sides of the island, close to the water.

From this vantage point, the hexagonal basalt columns that rose from the sea to form Finimund became evident. So unique, Evie thought, until she realized it wasn't. "Fingal's Cave!" she yelled over the wind, delighted. "Did you ever visit, Charlie?"

"No, but I've seen photos. This looks exactly the same."

"Photos?" Oleander shouted.

"Images from a camera, mate."

"Next time," Oleander bellowed, "bring some photos with you."

Evie didn't need a photo to confirm that it was, indeed, this world's version of Fingal's Cave in Scotland's Inner Hebrides, a geographic marvel formed during the Paleocene era. And just as boats of tourists could enter Fingal's Cave, so too did the firebirds swoop into the mouth of Finimund. They slowed inside, their claws skimming the pool of water, the glow of their feathers casting haunting shadows over the basalt formations. They carried on like this, deep into the cave, silent save for discordant whispers of wind and water, until they landed on a rocky shore.

"I guess we walk from here," Evie whispered, clambering off her bird. "I can't see a thing." The phoenix cawed in response, fluttering its wings. A single feather fell. Despite being separated from the bird's body, it maintained its luminescence, providing a bit of light for the journey forward.

They wouldn't need it for long. Another light, soft and white, was visible up ahead. Led by Evie, everyone hurried toward it, tripping and slipping on the uneven rocks, until they reached a tall, smooth stone face. Before the others could discuss, Evie stepped around it.

On the other side lay a remarkable space, hardly what she'd expected of a secret cave dwelling. The stone walls were polished to a shine, reflecting the light of nine orbs. They hovered just above eye level around the perimeter, complimented by a patchwork of the night sky on the ceiling, alicrated to twinkle like the ceilings of the Starsen Inn. In the center of it all stood a very small, white-haired woman, centuries of lines etched into her face. Dark brown eyes met Evie's, just as they had from the portrait in Callidora Castle.

"Evangeline," Perdita said. "At last."

35

"I DON'T KNOW what you know, Evangeline," Perdita said. "There is much to share, and I fear we haven't the time. I suppose what is most important now is for you to understand the path you walk. To understand where it leads. And to understand where your path leads, you must understand where it started."

It started with two sisters.

Born of pure energy from the Ortus, the source of everything, the sisters lived among the threads of existence in the Alterra. For a long time, this sustained them, until they were inexplicably struck by the urge to create. Perhaps it came from the Ortus. Perhaps it came from an even higher power of which we know not, testing the sisters. Or perhaps it was a natural, inevitable shift within the sisters themselves, transforming contentment into insatiable desire. Whatever the reason, the need to create took hold within them both. With the endless threads that spring from the Ortus, they wove The First Sfyre and all that would accompany it: the sun, the moon, the stars, the mountains, the oceans, the grass, the florens, the flowers, the trees. And, of course, the magenu.

The sisters bestowed upon the magenu the Higher Knowledge; a complete comprehension of existence. This meant they understood how their world was woven and participated in its evolution, that they knew from whence they came and where they would go when their bodies died. With such clarity, they had no doubt, no fear, no negative emotions born of unanswered existential questions.

But just as the sisters were struck with the desire to create, the magenu were one day struck with the desire for purpose. No longer satiated by the Higher Knowledge, they sought to enhance their earthly lives. They craved ownership, first over objects, soon over each other. They grew to relish power and longed to expand their territory. They acquired an understanding of wealth and sought to expand that, as well. The narrative of how they came to be was lost in favor of determining for themselves who they could become.

As these cracks formed in the First Sfyre, so too did a crack form between the sisters. Or had it been there all along? The first sister believed they'd made a mistake, miswoven the magenu, for how else could deviances have developed? The second sister speculated such flaws would evolve no matter how diligent the creator. It was natural, she mused. Still, she capitulated to her sister's proposal that they weave a special community of magenu, a cohort with the divine directive to reinstate the originally intended order to the First Sfyre's chaos. Thus, the Originals were created — Claire Callidora, Amos Benclair, Prosperine Iristell, Talbot Teraur and Malek Maliter.

This solution was inherently flawed, for, deeming each other's views of the magenu fundamentally wrong, the sisters had already lost faith in each other. To instill their own beliefs in the magenu, each sister wove an Original entirely her own, one who would share not only her energy, but her values, too. As such, the first sister crafted Claire Callidora with her own delicate threads, while the second sister imbued her chaotic energy into Malek Maliter. Each sister did this believing she was the only one producing an Original entirely her own. Neither knew the other had the same selfish plan to create a reflection of herself.

The Originals established the Normalex and tried to balance the enlightened values of the Higher Knowledge with acceptable deviances, such as competition or the desire for wealth. And yet, despite their efforts, the deepest, most unseemly cracks in humanity remained and worsened. Wrath became violence. Avarice became thievery. Lust became rape. The first sister was distraught! How could the magenu commit such atrocities in the face of law and punishment? The second sister was intrigued. Here, she thought, was proof that these traits were in the nature of their creation.

Perhaps, the first sister thought, having too much power over the world's threads, too much understanding of their existence, caused the magenu's deviance. They had nothing to fear, nothing to keep them on a righteous path. She wanted to start over with a new world and new inhabitants who would not be gifted the Higher Knowledge. The second sister readily agreed. She believed this new sect of humanity would sin, too. She was eager to be proven right.

The Second Sfyre was woven, and its inhabitants, mere humans, did not know they had an inherent ability to manipulate the threads of existence. They did not know where they came from, nor to where they would go after death. All they had were questions about their existence and fear about their future, which would keep them *good*, the first sister hoped. It was not to be so. Just like the magenu, the humans transgressed. All told, the Second Sfyre fared worse than the First.

Despondent after two failed attempts, the first sister decided the problem was *them*. The creators. Clearly, weaving worlds and the lives that inhabited them did not work. They should step back, she thought, and let the whims of fate take over. And so, she created a third world, a lofty realm outside the confines of time and space, to receive the threads from the Ortus, ensuring they fell far from the grasp of her and her sister. She called it the Aevum, and she did not tell her sister of its existence.

The Aevum was populated with weavers whose sole responsibility was to weave the threads from the Ortus exactly as their fall dictated. They could not manipulate, they could not meddle. They had no Alicrat, like the magenu. They had no ability to discover their Alicrat through enlightenment, like the humans. The weavers had nothing. They were hollow.

These weavers — or oracles, or prophets, or whatever your culture may call them — did their duty for years without question, weaving,

weaving, endlessly weaving. But the unexplained impulse that had impelled the sisters to create, the unexplained impulse that had prompted the magenu to sin...that inexplicable need for more struck one of the hollows. Something evolved in the first hollow to bear the name Perdita, a belief that she was meant for more despite everything she knew telling her she was not.

This ancient Perdita grew tired of weaving wretched lives. She grew tired of watching twin souls fall inches from each other, knowing they would never meet. She grew tired of witnessing the slight curve in a thread's descent that meant the difference between a life of plenty and a life of pain. Could she do nothing to change the fates of humanity? She could not, but what about the people whose lives she wove? If they knew what was to come, could their will alter fate?

Many tapestries had been woven before this Perdita came to be and many have been woven since, but Perdita could only access those which she had woven. She looked at them — hundreds, by then — and in the ancient language of the sisters, she wrote all that she saw. They were strange stories that made no sense, but how could they, for they spoke of people and places that would not exist for thousands of years. She recorded them anyway, and with these pages in hand, she left the Aevum through the door that connects the worlds.

This door could have opened anywhere, in any world — such is its nature — but fate sent the ancient Perdita to the Empty Fields of Benclair. From there she walked until she reached the shores of a lake in Callidora, where her weaver's intuition told her to stop. There, began a collaboration that would span generations.

Over the next many years, some weavers followed the ancient Perdita to find purpose in the Sfyres, bringing memories of their tapestries to share with the magenu and humans. Centuries later, the descendants of those rogue weavers still maintain a predictive intuition derived from the unique vibrations of the Aevum. Though, I do not believe any hollow of this world save myself, nor any psychic of the Second Sfyre, has the slightest idea where their gift comes from.

The ancient Perdita knew, of course. Not only did she bring her written tapestries to the First Sfyre, she brought her knowledge of the creation, too. The story of the sisters and the worlds they wove became the Book of Origins, ensuring the Callidoras would never forget their divine beginnings. The pages she'd brought from the Aevum became the Book of Tapestries, intended to guide Callidoras toward a safe and prosperous future. With this book, many terrible things were avoided, though some still came to pass, for they were not addressed in Perdita's Book of Tapestries. She was only one weaver, after all.

We hollows live much longer than humans or magenu, likely due to our connection to the everlasting Aevum. Now in my two hundred and twenty-first year, I have taught the origins and tapestries to Erskine, Clement, and Adena. My grandfather Melcholm lived to be three hundred and fifty-five simply because he refused to go, hounded by Death though he was. And in those three hundred and fifty-five years, Melcholm set in motion the events responsible for the state of things today.

Melcholm was an outspoken hollow with a penchant for the down-trodden. Perhaps this was why he took in an odd visitor without question, allowing him to stay in a room above the bakery. He was a funny little man, Melcholm said, with nervous, intelligent eyes and no Alicrat. He regarded the magenu as "Demons and witches working for Satan," and was relieved by Melcholm's inability to start fires with the snap of a finger. Melcholm never learned who Satan was.

The man was an artist, and not even being lost in a strange land could stifle his creativity. Day in and day out, he stood at his window, drawing and painting. How many paintings of the Callidoralta streets could one produce, Melcholm wondered? But he was not painting Callidoralta at all. He was painting unknown faces and unrecognizable scenes; pastoral fields of gold, odd structures he called churches. It was his home, a place to which, he told Melcholm, he longed to return.

Melcholm impressed upon me as a child that our knowledge was to be shared with no one but the Callidoras. At first, I questioned this, as children do. If it was so important, surely everyone should know? But Melcholm was adamant. "Knowledge is power," he told me. "In the right hands, it does great things. In the wrong hands, it brings destruc-tion." I accepted this and continued studying the complicated language of the sisters while other children played in the streets.

And so, you can imagine my shock when, as Melcholm lay dying, he told me that he had shared our knowledge with the artist. Back then, I felt betrayed. Now, having lived my own long life, having forsaken love in the name of keeping the knowledge contained, I understand. I believe he loved the artist.

His vulnerability was not to be repaid.

The artist disappeared one day, leaving behind nothing but a peculiar painting portraying the worst of humanity. Too stark a reminder of his friend, Melcholm sold it at auction. The artist was not the only thing to disappear at that time, I should add. The Book of Origins was stolen from Isabil Callidora, never to be seen again, though Isabil confided her suspicions to Melcholm that another otherworldly visitor had taken it.

"That is why we keep the knowledge up here, too," Melcholm used to tell me, tapping his head.

I digress.

Where had the artist gone? Beyond the sea? Back to his world? Wherever he ended up, first, he went to Maliter, and in Maliter, he talked. So taken was he with Melcholm's stories of creation, so intrigued — or perhaps, frightened — was he by the man with answers to life's questions, that he repeated all he knew. Maybe he was in a pub, chatting to the barman when an Obscure overheard. Maybe he had unwittingly spoken directly to an Obscure, naively blathering on about the Book of Tapestries penned by an oracle. However it happened, the cult, small and hidden in those days, took interest.

And so, they came for Melcholm.

Torn from his bed with a harsh manipulation against which he had no recourse, Melcholm was taken to Maliter and dumped into what he called "the pit of despair." Words were his only ladder out; it was otherwise inescapable, filled with the bones of those who'd refused to open their mouths.

The Obscures only had one question for Melcholm. What did this mystical Book of Tapestries predict for the fate of their cult?

Now understand, the Book of Tapestries is not as straightforward as you may think. The ancient Perdita translated millions of tangled threads into Alterra Lingua riddles that are confusing even in modern tongues. It is all too easy for one to interpret what they want and not what the Ortus intended. Melcholm used this to his advantage.

"There is a tapestry," he told the Obscures, "that foretells the rise of a great and powerful entity." This much is true. There are many prophecies in the Book of Tapestries referencing powerful, often evil, entities. Spanning thousands of years and two worlds, how could it not? Whether any of them actually referred to the Alicrat Obscura cult is no longer relevant. Melcholm told them that one did, and they believed it to be so.

But believing they were destined to rise was not enough. The Obscures wanted to know what obstacles lay in their path to power. Melcholm tried to evade their questions, but he was tortured with unrelenting obscurities. I know not what was done to him — he never shared the details — but for as long as I knew him, he would wake in the night, begging something unseen to stop, *stop!* We have only the sun to thank that the cult had not yet developed their mind manipulations so oft used today, otherwise, the outcome would have been much different. As it stands, Melcholm acquiesced insofar as revealing another half-truth.

"The prophecy mentions an individual," he divulged, "with the ability to halt your ascent to power. It states no name." Again, this was not a lie, but to the Obscures, it was absolutely nothing! They demanded Melcholm produce the book itself.

Perhaps my grandfather's next words were said deliberately in an effort to protect his descendants and the Callidoras. Or perhaps he was so starved, manipulated, beaten and bloody that his addled mind mixed up the two books, and he thought instead of Isabil's lost Book of Origins. I do not know. All that matters is what he told the Obscures.

"The Book of Tapestries is lost," he said. "Stolen, spirited away to another world."

Thus began the cult's centuries-long quest to find the Book of Tapestries. How they ultimately connected its existence to the Callidoras remains a mystery, even to me. But I know that you sit before me now, Evangeline, because of the artist. Because of Melcholm. Because of the sisters. There is more you must understand, but for now, understand this: your purpose has been written since the beginning of time.

36

FINISHED WITH HER TALE, Perdita stared at one of the nine orbs hovering around her cave dwelling. Evie stared at another. She didn't know what to say. She didn't know what to *feel*. Charlie sat next to her, also quiet. Oleander was not there; he waited on the other side of the stone door. Perdita had asked him to leave, adamant that her knowledge be shared only with a Callidora. Yet when Charlie had made to follow Oleander out, she'd been equally adamant that he remain.

Charlie reached into his pocket now, pulled out two minuted pages, and resized them. Wordlessly, he handed them to Perdita.

"Dear me," she said quietly, holding the images of Bosch's Pedlar in disbelief. "This is Melcholm. Wherever did you find these?"

"They're from the artist," Charlie said. "His name was Hieronymus Bosch. He painted these in the Other World. Er, the Second Sfyre."

"He made it home in the end, then? I always wondered." Perdita returned the pictures of Melcholm to Charlie, smiling slightly.

The cave fell silent again. Evie still stared at the orb; weightless, it spun in place slowly, like a miniature earth on its axis. Was this what the sisters saw when they wove the worlds? A sphere no larger than the fluffy head of a stellan, practically minuscule in their omnipotent hands? The ease with which the thought crossed her mind surprised her, incongruent with her belief system as it was. She'd never humored the idea of a God, let alone Gods.

Feeling Charlie's eyes on her, she pulled her gaze away from the orb. He seemed to be waiting for her to speak. *She* was the Callidora, after all, the descendant of an Original with a creator's energy in her veins. Spun from a creator or not, she certainly didn't feel divine, nor indisputably *good*, as Perdita's tale had made the first sister out to be.

Charlie cleared his throat pointedly. Remembering why they were there — and realizing answers were finally within their reach — Evie faced the old woman. "Do you know the prophecy Melcholm spoke of, Perdita?"

"Of course. I know every word in the Book of Tapestries."

"Do you know who it claims will stop the Obscures?"

Perdita stiffened, considering something. Evie feared she wouldn't say more in front of Charlie, but she relented. Adopting a tone Evie imagined she'd used with Adena, Clement, and Erskine, she said, "It is crucial you understand the prophecy does not claim somebody *will* stop an evil entity, merely that somebody *can*. Though Melcholm did not state it as clearly, the distinctions are rather important. There is a difference between fate and destiny. Even I use them interchangeably at times, but they are not the same." She stared at Evie, brown eyes boring into blue.

"Fate stipulates an unavoidable outcome on which actions have no impact. Destiny requires an alignment of choice, a willingness of the subject. One may decide not to fulfill their destiny." She looked purposefully at Evie, and then Charlie, as if she wanted to ensure the distinction landed with them both.

"When Adena became Arbiter, I began working through the Book of Tapestries with her as I did with all Callidora Arbiters, reviewing its contents to see which, if any, of the ancient riddles might come to pass in her time. That is when I realized only one of them would. At first, I kept this realization to myself. The Book of Tapestries is, as I said, rife with riddles. Quick conclusions lead to rash decisions. I held my interpretation in abeyance for a few years, just to be sure, even as the subject of the prophecy sat in my bakery, legs dangling off the table, eating my bread."

Charlie's hand found Evie's, stilling it. She hadn't realized it had been shaking.

"The prophecy Melcholm told to the Obscures, referencing someone with the ability to stop the rise of an evil entity, speaks of you, Evangeline."

There was a beat of silence, and then, "That's it?" Leaning forward, Evie pulled her hand out from under Charlie's. "I'm our advantage against the Obscures?"

Charlie seemed agitated too, though for different reasons. "Where's the proof? Why Evie?"

"I will divulge no more without the book before me," Perdita replied, tremendous strength in her voice.

Perhaps it was Perdita's refusal to say more, perhaps it was the letdown of what everyone, including herself, had hoped would be a powerfully irrefutable advantage, but something prompted a flare of anger in Evie. "What else have you failed to divulge?" she asked. "My mother's death, perhaps? Did you know she was going to be killed?"

"Not to my knowledge, no."

"What does that mean? The book either said Adena was in danger or it didn't. Which is it?"

Perdita remained calm. "Evangeline, it simply does not work that way. A weaver's tapestries are not straightforward statements pertaining to a person's life or a State's future. The ancient Perdita wrote interpretations of millions of threads in an ancient language requiring translation. Those translations have been further interpreted by her descendants across thousands of years. What's more, not every event in the history and future of time is contained within her book. It would take every weaver holding every tapestry they've woven, standing before us, to even *begin* to fathom the complexity and totality of humanity's story. I am not all-knowing."

Evie started to object, but Perdita continued quietly. "Nothing in the book indicated to me that your mother's thread was fated to fray as it did. If there was, I would have told Clement when Adena was a child. He would have intervened, as he did with you."

"You told Clement to send me away?"

"I urged him to keep you protected. He chose the form that protection took. Though I should add, when I told him I believed the prophecy spoke of you, strangely, he already knew. He already had a plan. I do not know how."

Evie's stomach tightened, an instinctual reaction to the strangeness that even an oracle did not have every piece of her past. "Well, then," she said slowly, returning to the issue at hand, "we need you to return to Benclair with us to read from the book directly. As Melcholm said, knowledge is power. We need to know exactly what the prophecy says."

"Exactly what it says," Charlie emphasized.

"Of course," Perdita said, nodding seriously. Then, in a complete change of tone, she called brightly toward the entrance of her dwelling, summoning Oleander back.

The echo of her voice melted into the same discordant tones that had accompanied their arrival into the cave. This time, the eerie hum grew louder, transforming into a low buzz that caused the orbs of light to vibrate. Evie and Charlie stood, alarmed by the familiarity of it all. It stopped as suddenly as it had started.

"That was close," Perdita said, still seated, unperturbed. "Nothing to worry about, at least not today. It takes a very specific frequency to move the island's vibrations in line with its brother's."

"What are you talking about?" Oleander asked, having just rejoined the group. He looked from Perdita, to Evie, to Charlie. "What happened?"

"You didn't feel that, Ole?" Charlie asked, glancing at Evie. "You must be like Professor Atkinson. Unable to cross. But Perdita, it's not a Sun Day."

She smiled. "It is not. I can predict the Sun Days and ensure I am clear of the radius. The next Estival is in eight days, I believe. One does not need to wait for a Sun Day to make the journey, however. Particular frequencies can nudge the portals into alignment. Sometimes, the wind blows through the cave in such a way that the chords of passage ring clearly, pushing this island closer to its brother."

As if summoned, the wind passed through the cave again, but it was short and sharp this time, nowhere near the sustained rush that had instigated the portal's buzzing moments ago.

"I need not fear accidental passage any longer," Perdita said. "I have remained at this world's end, where the Obscures could not find me, hoping that you would, Evangeline. Hoping that despite the randomness of chance and the chaos of choice, your steps would lead you here. They have. I will pass on what I know, and then, at long last, I will be free of my burden."

"You could have found me in the Other World, as Charlie did," Evie said. "Wouldn't that have been easier than waiting, hoping?"

Perdita smiled in a way that made Evie feel silly for suggesting such a quaintly practical solution to such a cosmically tangled problem. "Your journey cannot be forced by others," Perdita said. "You must make choices for yourself. That is how it must be. This does not come from the Book of Tapestries. It comes from here." She placed a palm against her heart. "My weaver's intuition."

Indicating she wished to rise, she was helped to her feet by Oleander and Charlie. She gathered a few belongings for the journey, demurred when Charlie offered to minute them for transport, and twisted a cloth into a makeshift sack instead. Outside her dwelling, the firebirds waited where they'd been left, dipping their beaks into the fresh water that dripped down the cave walls. Charlie and Evie climbed onto their birds. Oleander took Perdita, who whispered to his bird like they were long lost friends.

The firebirds maneuvered gracefully from the cave. At the mouth, the wind picked up once more, filling Evie's ears with the spectral tones of both worlds as the island of Finimund and an island in the Inner Hebrides of Scotland touched. The low buzz of the portal thrummed so intensely Evie felt it in midair, and as they rose toward the open skies, she could have sworn she heard the echo of a Scottish accent introducing a boatful of tourists to the wonders of Fingal's Cave.

37

THE CREATURE DOVE through the trees, hurrying to get as close to the ground as possible before she disappeared from beneath her magena. She was a firedrake, the miniature, delicate cousin of a dragon with dark blue scales, powerful wings, and a surprisingly gentle disposition, and she had been called forth by Blair.

This was a rare occurrence, as Blair was not often in need of her familiar for comfort or defense. Summoned by fear, the firedrake had found her wandering the vast expanse of south Callidora's blackest night, weak and alone. Together now, they neared Benclair, but their connection was faltering and soon, the firedrake would return to the ether of familiars...

The pit of Blair's stomach dropped unexpectedly, pulling her from the comfort of an empty dream. She struck something wide and solid — a tree branch, she realized latently, which broke her fall. By the time she hit the hard-packed soil, her velocity had slowed and she thought it likely she'd survive, though surely, she would break a bone, perhaps many. Her head struck something unforgiving and she heard, more than felt, a *crack* of pain between her ears. The leaves above her blurred into one as darkness invaded her periphery.

Hours later, she opened her eyes. Her throat ached with each swallow of stale spittle. She'd become too weak to alicrate water miles ago. Or was it days? She no longer knew. Stin's tunnel had spat her out just beyond the Callidora-Maliter border a lifetime ago and she wasn't entirely sure where she was going anymore, nor why. Fractured snippets flashed through her mind. There was the creature, powerful and kind, one she summoned only rarely. It had saved her. Or was she mistaking the firedrake for the wild creatures of south Callidora that called to the night with strange howls, reminding Blair how little she knew of the world? For all the terrible things she saw in Talus, she'd never paused to consider that other States had their own horrors until she was in their midst.

Pain brought her back to the present. Her forearm, mottled blue and swollen, throbbed dully. More agonizing was her right hip, which she could not move. Worst was the sting at the back of her skull. She reached a hand around her head. Her fingers met the sticky thickness of blood. She turned her head slowly, wincing. The gates of a castle lay just ahead.

Or was it the Domus?

Someone lifted her from the ground. The Domus, then. Adrian had found her. She was relieved, in a way. Impending death was a comforting certainty. Had she made it to Benclair, the only thing she was certain of was that she would be a stranger in a strange land with the weight of Maliter's fate upon her shoulders. She would need to convince, rally, inspire others to act. Death would be easier.

It was soft now, the ground upon which she lay. Adrian must have brought her to his room. A sadistic move, convincing her she was safe before demonstrating that she was not. She would enjoy the temporary pleasure anyway. The foreign gentleness of feathers and fabric wrapped around her, coaxing her last bits of conscious thought back to the quiet depths of her mind.

Something prevented her from drifting away, though. A woman with wild hair stood over Blair, turning her head to one side, then the other. Blair winced and the woman winced back apologetically. "I'm sorry," the woman said, "but I must administer the oils now." An attack on the raw flesh at the back of Blair's head ensued. "I'll mend these injuries once the threads are less angry."

"Where am I?" Her voice did not sound like her own.

"Safe. Drink, now. You are severely underwatered." An orb appeared at Blair's lips and she sipped gratefully. "A bit more. How is your arm? Any pain?"

"It's fine," Blair said, surprised that this was the truth.

The woman clapped lightly and smiled. "You can never be too sure when mending bones. The threads are so stiff. Back to sleep, now. You need rest."

Things were clearer the next time Blair woke. She lay in a room larger than the entirety of her home with Stin, its creamy stone walls a soothing contrast to the depressing black rock she was used to. Glancing out a window near her bed, she could just make out the tops of trees and a dimly lit sky. It was either dusk or dawn.

"Good morning."

Dawn, then.

"Don't try to respond. I know you're weak."

A chair scraped across the floor and a man — tall, broad-shouldered, with messy brown hair and a welcoming smile — came into view. "Marcus Rutherford," he said. "Not sure if you remember me, but I —"

"Visited Maliter a quarter ago and failed to convey our dire situation to your father," Blair said. "I remember." The ferocity hurt her throat, but it was worth it.

Marcus held her gaze. "My father is cautious," he said. "He won't take action until —"

"Until Adrian himself is outside your gates?"

"Until he absolutely needs to. We have our own citizens' safety to consider, and Maliter hasn't directly provoked Benclair. Getting sliced in the seraphilles notwithstanding." Marcus pulled the chair alongside Blair's bed and sat, sighing heavily. "There are protocols in place."

Blair struggled to a semi-upright position. She didn't like Marcus hovering over her. "Moon forbid we violate diplomatic protocol," she said cooly, "for a matter so small as the decay of our States." This was not how she'd planned to present her case to the Rutherfords, but something about Liam's son irked her.

"Look," Marcus said. "Now that the AO have infiltrated Callidora, we know something needs to be done." He had more to say, but Blair didn't want to hear it.

"Callidora?" She bolted completely upright. Her head filled with a dense fog. She swayed, boulders pounding against the backs of her eyes. Marcus' hands steadied her and she sank back against the pillows. How ridiculous to have so many pillows, she thought, even if they were the most comfortable thing she'd ever laid upon.

She tried again, more calmly. "What about Callidora?"

"Perhaps we should wait until you're rested."

"How much more resting am I supposed to do?" she snapped.

"Fine," Marcus said. "We've just confirmed Callidora is under Obscure control. It started toward the end of Clement's reign, from the sound of it."

Marcus rose, swiveled his chair backward and sat down again, propping his forearms up against its back as if they were discussing their favorite pastimes. For that alone, Blair hated him. "That's still not enough to convince Liam to act?" she said. "He may not care about the Norms in Maliter, but surely he's concerned about the mighty Callidora in the wrong hands."

"He doesn't need convincing, Blair. He understands," Marcus said, brow knitted. "He understands the AO are not merely outcasts experimenting with obscurities. They're an organized administration that has normalized hate and harm, welcomes anybody bearing those tendencies with open arms, validates their notions of self-importance, and gives them a one way ticket to their own private power trip. And," Marcus leaned closer, "he understands that those tickets have a price. When it comes time for Adrian to collect, he'll have a horde eager to answer his call to arms. He *understands*, Blair."

"Then why," Blair hissed, "hasn't he taken action?"

Marcus said nothing.

"I've risked everything," Blair said. "Things that you, the son of an Arbiter, a *man*, could never even fathom having to risk. Why am I the only one sacrificing, the only one trying? This is not *my* problem. It's not Maliter's problem. It's the Northlands' problem, Rutherford. So tell me what in the bloody moon we plan to do about it!"

She leaned back into the pillows as Marcus mulled it over. She would wait a little longer for him to say something worthwhile, she decided, and then she would summon her nonexistent strength to find and confront Liam.

"Fine," Marcus muttered. "Alright. What if...what if Adena Callidora had a child? What if that child and an ancient book were taken to safety in another land? And what if that child and the book have returned to the Northlands?"

"What if I pull it out of you with an obscurity? This sounds like a children's story. Spit it out."

Marcus laughed. "Fair enough, but everything I just said is true. Adena Callidora had a daughter. She's here, in the Northlands. She has an old book, a family heirloom we think contains something important. Something the Obscures have been trying to find for a very long time."

"Great. What does the book say?"

"We can't read it."

Blair covered her face with a pillow. It did little to mute Marcus.

"We're trying to find an interpreter," he continued. "We have reason to believe it will give us an advantage, ensuring that when we do strike, it will be a deciding blow."

Beneath the pillow, Blair thought of her childhood spent watching Talus crumble as the Obscures rose in power. She thought of Stin, toiling in the quarries with the hollows of Maliter, now forced into hiding. She thought of Adrian in bed, gently running the same fingers across her collarbone that contorted threads into deadly obscurities. Then she thought of Liam Rutherford waiting for someone to translate a book. Blair threw the pillow to the floor.

"It's more complicated," Marcus said lamely, watching her face cloud with anger. "Adena's daughter is important. You'll see."

"I want to talk to Liam."

Marcus stood. "You need to regain your strength first. You'll need it if you plan on telling my father he's wrong." He pushed the chair back to its original position, then returned to Blair's bedside, holding something. "I found this outside where you landed." He handed her a tarnished bracelet. "*Arabell* is inscribed inside. Is it yours?"

Blair snatched the bracelet from Marcus. "It's my mother's name."

"Right," he said, but she could see it meant nothing to him. There was only one mother, one daughter, whom the Rutherfords cared about, and it certainly wasn't Arabell and Blair.

38

BLAIR TOOK A QUICK BATH, eschewing the array of oils and fragrant soaps that had been left for her. She picked through the clothes that were laid out, touching each article suspiciously. Everything looked slightly too large, which a buttoned pair of trousers slipping down her thighs confirmed. She alicrated the waistband to fit and grabbed an enormous sweater that once belonged to a man by the name of John Lewis Medium, according a label stitched inside.

Dressed, she entered a corridor filled with paintings of stuffy-looking Rutherfords. With no one to guide her, she descended a massive staircase that eventually opened to the lower courtyard. Across the way, spotted the familiar scurry of someone with too many things to do and not enough time to do them. A cleaner.

The woman unwittingly led Blair across the courtyard, past an affrim that must have cost hundreds of thousands of pecs, through multiple rooms that seemed to serve no practical purpose whatsoever and finally, into a kitchen.

"Is there anything to eat?" Blair asked. The cleaner startled, letting out a yelp.

"It's all right, Illis. She's our guest." Another woman, stunning and soft, nothing like the harsh beauty of the Obscure women who preened for Adrian, had entered the kitchen behind Blair. "It's Blair, isn't it? I'm so sorry you had to come all this way just to —"

"I had no choice. I must speak with Liam."

"— just to find something to eat," she finished delicately. "Illis would have delivered something to your room. What would you like?"

"Anything," Blair mumbled, plopping onto a bench at the table.

The woman took in a breath. "I'm Juliette Rutherford, by the way." She seemed to expect a reaction.

"Where is Liam?"

Juliette joined her at the table. "Eat first, dear. You are skin and bones."

"We're starving in Maliter. The AO take what they want from our farmers and leave us with whatever rot remains."

"Someone must better train your Enforcers."

"They're all dead. Or worse, corrupt."

Illis placed a plate before Blair. "Cream omelette with fresh peas and some sautéed young seraphille roots," she said. "All harvested from the castle grounds."

Blair stared at the food, not quite believing it was meant for her.

"Surely someone can reinstate order," Juliette said. "What of the new Arbiter?"

"Unfortunately, I had to leave before I could kill him." Blair stabbed half the omelette with her fork and swallowed it nearly whole, followed by the other half. "Illis," she called, "may I have another? And some bread?"

"It's fine," Juliette said faintly, nodding at Illis. Then, turning back to Blair, "It's a thankless role, Arbiter. Liam is often forced to make decisions our citizens do not agree with."

Blair put down her fork. "Are you daft?"

"I beg your pardon?"

"Or just ignorant? Well, you'll find out soon enough if your husband doesn't act." Blair dug into the second omelette, again devouring it, then snatched the half loaf of hot bread she'd been given and ripped off the heel with her teeth. Certain she'd be thrown out of Rutherford Castle in a matter of minutes, she wanted her stomach full.

She'd finished the bread when Juliette finally spoke. Not taking her eyes off Blair, she said, "I'm not ignorant. Certainly not daft."

Blair waited for more. It didn't come. "Well," she said, "I suppose not all of us have the ability to maintain your level of denial."

Juliette scoffed lightly. "Perhaps not all of us have your ability to accept." Blair thought she was making an excuse for Liam, but she added quietly, "I understand what is at stake. Castles, comfort. Normalcy."

Blair started to interrupt, but Juliette cut her off. "My children's lives." She paused. "My entire reason for being."

A prolonged silence followed during which Blair realized, for the first time in her life, how deeply some people were capable of caring. So deeply, it turned out, that they would completely ignore the very thing that threatened to destroy what they loved so much. She wasn't sure if this deserved admiration or pity.

Noise from the courtyard caused Juliette to leap up. Crying out for people named Charlie and Evie, she ran from the kitchen. Blair trailed her to where Marcus and another man circled the affrim, speaking over each other excitedly.

"Is that Charlie?" Juliette said. "Whyever is the on a bird?"

The second man glanced past Juliette, noticing Blair. "You're Blair, aren't you?" Approaching her, he stuck out a hand, which Blair shook briefly. "Finneas of the Fern. I understand you've risked a great deal to come here. I hope we can help each other."

Blair's shoulders lost an iota of their tension. Perhaps there was hope, after all.

Everyone abandoned the affrim for the castle gates — Juliette fluttering and fretting, Marcus straining his neck to catch a glimpse of the firebirds, Finneas observing it all. Liam did not join them. Blair followed, but wondered if now was the time to search the castle, to corner the Arbiter and demand to know what he intended to do about Maliter. Instead, she found herself transfixed by the lush forest outside the castle, the emerald hills surrounding it, the nearby village thriving with commerce and greenery. Though she'd never allowed herself to wonder what the rest of the Northlands might look like, even her wildest dreams would have paled in comparison.

Flashes of red descended as three firebirds landed. Once settled, they bowed before the small gathering, allowing their riders to disembark. Blair recognized one as Charlie Rutherford — he looked so similar to Marcus. Oleander, according to Finneas' greeting, was the one holding up a tottering elderly woman. The last, then, was Evie, the allegedly important Callidora heiress.

She was devastatingly unremarkable. Blair scoffed. No one heard, least of all Marcus, who ran to Evie, grinning unabashedly when she fell into his arms. An embarrassing display from them both, Blair thought. Charlie also seemed dismayed by the performance. He looked away, accidentally meeting Blair's eyes. His narrowed briefly, trying to place her.

"Everyone in my office."

Heads turned toward the bellow. It was not a loquer, but Liam Rutherford himself, standing five stories up and calling to them from an open window.

Charlie leaned toward the old woman. "Are you all right, Perdita? Do you need to rest before translating?"

"I am fine, Charles," the woman said, straightening her hunched posture. "Alterra Lingua is in in my blood." Blair didn't know what Alterra Lingua was, but she knew that the old woman was worth more than all the Rutherfords put together.

She also didn't know if she counted as part of everyone, but she didn't care. She traipsed into the castle with the two Mensmen, the two brothers, the elderly woman, and the delicate princess. Juliette hesitated, seemingly also unsure if she was part of Liam's summation, but she eventually squared her shoulders and hurried after the group.

On the fifth floor, Evie dashed to her room to retrieve a book — *the* book, the one they'd sat around staring at stupidly for months instead of saving Maliter. The others continued, whispering anxiously about the best way to proceed.

At the end of the corridor, Charlie stopped everyone before a set of doors. "We should wait for Evie before we —"

"Go in? No need." Pushing past Charlie, Blair opened the doors and strode inside.

Liam stood beneath a tree, of all things, hands clasped behind his back. If he was surprised to see Blair, he didn't show it. She started to speak but was cut off by the others filing in behind her, greeting Liam in their own telling ways: professionalism from Oleander and Finneas, nervousness from Charlie, and what Blair took to be weary enthusiasm from Marcus.

The group took their seats at a table beneath the tree. A tense silence descended as they waited for Evie and the book. Finneas caught Blair's eye and smiled. Her lip twitched in return. Oleander leaned back in his chair and looked to the ceiling. Marcus pushed away Juliette's hand as she attempted to fix a tousled piece of hair across his forehead. Liam stared straight ahead.

Evie burst into the room then, stopped short at the silence, and said, "Here, Perdita. The Tree Book. The Book of Tapestries." Placing the book before the old woman, she sat down next to her.

Hands to her heart, Perdita blinked back tears. "I wondered if I would ever see this again. It is strange...I have no Alicrat to speak of, yet I can feel every member of my family who has laid their hands upon it." She, too, placed her palms on the book, covering the golden tree and orb that spanned the cover.

Across the table, Blair started to feel something, too. A tangle of complicated threads became visible to her one by one, unknown, yet familiar. They waved in the windless room, curling away from the book and toward her, reaching intrusively. She inched her chair away.

Perdita scanned the room slowly, her eyes lingering on each person. They narrowed over Liam and Juliette, lit up when she considered Evie, and contemplated the brothers with a touch of amusement. A glimmer of something crossed her dark irises when her gaze fell to Blair, brows furrowed in speculation. She shook her head quickly, moving onto the others, musing upon things only she knew and certainly, wouldn't divulge.

Assessment complete, she said, "The secrets are not meant for all. Evangeline, certainly. Charles, you have earned my trust. And you," she pointed a trembling finger at Blair, "you must listen, too."

Blair snorted. "I don't think so. Liam, perhaps we can —"

In a completely different tone not matching her frail appearance, Perdita repeated, "You must listen. The rest of you will leave."

Liam started to object, speaking over Oleander's rushed assurances that the same thing had happened in the cave, that it was simply not the way of things for others to hear! Finneas interjected with something logical, Marcus sighed loudly, Juliette repeated pointless placations. Blair sat back, more annoyed than ever, though understanding, finally, why the State of Benclair failed to accomplish anything useful.

Charlie's voice rose over the others, quieting them. "I understand the importance of containing the knowledge," he told Perdita. "We all need to know what the prophecy says, though. This is not about analyzing the tapestries to determine how Callidora should be governed. This transcends Callidora."

Perdita pulled the book closer. "You may convey my translation to the others when we have finished if you so choose, but I will not recite these hallowed words to unworthy ears."

Seeing no other way forward, everyone else filed out of the study with reluctant reverence except Liam, who slammed the door shut on his way out.

Alone with Charlie, Evie, and Blair, Perdita lifted the cover of the book.

39

The laws were not obeyed
Goodness was not conveyed.
She will send her only son
for he will do what must be done.
Staged betrayal, sacrifice,
none of it will quite suffice.
Later, legend will transform,
word of light will be the norm.

PERDITA PAUSED. Charlie knew she was waiting for him to connect this prophecy to a historical event, as he'd done with every prophecy thus far. Her recitation was nearing two hours because of this. Despite the pit in his stomach as they neared the prophecy in question, this was the highlight of his life, thrilling his historian heart.

Clearly, Evie was not quite as thrilled. "Can't we skip ahead, Perdita?" she asked, not for the first time.

Perdita shook her head. "That is not how one conducts an initial reading of the tapestries."

Blair sighed loudly from across the table.

Charlie wasn't sure why the Maliteran spy was here. Perdita's insistence had surprised him as much as it had seemed to surprise Blair herself. She obviously didn't understand what a privilege it was, or maybe, she just didn't care. She'd contributed nothing of importance, sulking and scoffing instead, and had no reaction to even the most shocking revelations. Earlier, Charlie had connected a prophecy to the events that instigated the Northlands Wars. Evie had at least shown interest in his interpretation. Blair had yawned ostentatiously.

Perdita recited another tapestry.

The snake will be born underground in the dark.
The first to emerge, it will bring changes stark.
Make no mistake, you must kill the snake.
But know that its eager brothers lie in wait.
Bound not by blood, they remain united,
Attached to the head that the great sun has blighted.

"Hm." Charlie slumped back in his chair, running a hand through his hair. "Feuding siblings? Though it does stipulate they are 'bound not by blood.'"

Perdita waited an obligatory moment for Charlie's theory, but this one had him stumped. She continued.

Nature's revolt in promised land,
Lives engulfed by wind and sand.
Labored breaths and wilted grains,
Dust will blow across the plains.
Try to flee for clearer skies,
But heritage has binds that tie.

Charlie puzzled it over. "Promised land? Wilted grains…there was the Terauran famine in 9,234, but I'm not sure about the references to sand and dust…"

"America's Dust Bowl in the 20th century," Evie said, and provided a brief explanation for the benefit of Charlie and Blair.

"Incredible," said Charlie. "To predict the events of not one, but *two* worlds? This makes me reconsider Nostradamus! Evie, do you think he was descended from a weaver?"

Perdita cleared her throat. Charlie thought she might reveal that she and Nostradamus were cousins, but instead, she said, "Evangeline. This is the one."

The energy in the room shifted. Evie leaned closer to Perdita. Charlie rose to stand behind her, examining the page from above. Even Blair took notice, lifting her chin to see across the table.

Longer than the others, the verse in question was one of the few cradled within the gold branches that extended inside from the cover. The Alterra Lingua was no more discernible to Charlie than it had been when he'd first laid eyes upon it as a child, and he felt a rush of habitual frustration before reality sank in. After two decades of obsession, he was about to hear the catalyst for everything that had dictated not only Evie's life, but his own, too.

Perdita straightened in her chair, took a breath, and translated.

> *She is born into the night,*
> *She is a daughter of the light.*
> *Woven with the threads of sin*
> *Of humankind and origins.*
> *Trapped between two Sfyres,*
> *Her truth remains unclear*
> *Until knowledge can convince,*
> *Gentle guidance from a prince.*
> *Choice lead to threads pre-woven,*
> *Justifying all is proven.*
> *She can halt old evil's spread,*
> *She can strike the dragon dead.*
> *Soaked into the Tree Eternal,*
> *Light and dark blood spill at Vernal.*

Perdita sat back against her chair, indicating she was finished.

Charlie nearly drowned in relief. It was a clever rhyme and certainly told the story of someone, but to assume that someone was Evie? He smiled despite himself. It was much too vague.

"The first thing that struck me was the simplest," Perdita said. "'She is born into the night.'"

Charlie glanced at Evie, but she just shrugged.

"Your mother's labor was long and difficult," Perdita told her. "Twenty-four hours, from midnight to midnight. Toward the end, I thought perhaps you would wait and allow dawn to usher you forth, but it was not to be. You were born in the darkest hour of the year, Evangeline. An Invernal child, born into the night."

"And 'daughter of the light?'" Blair asked. She was suddenly curious.

"Ah, you were not present for my history lesson yesterday." Perdita smiled with gentle patience. "The Callidora line began with the purest threads of good from the creator who forsook all evil. All Callidoras are therefore daughters — or sons — of the figurative light. What is your lineage, my dear?"

Blair bristled. "I'm an orphan."

"You still have a lineage."

"These are rather thin connections," Charlie interrupted. "You said it yourself, Perdita. These are interpretations of interpretations."

"That does not mean the correct conclusion cannot be drawn," Perdita said. "Let us consider this line: 'Woven with the threads of sin of humankind and origins.' There are very few people who would fit that description. As I just explained, Evie is descended not only from an Original, but from a creator."

"And the 'sin of humankind?'" Blair asked.

"My father," Evie said immediately, surprising Charlie. Was she eager to connect herself to this nonsense? "He's from the Other World. There's no time to break this to you gently," she said to Blair, "but this world isn't alone. It has a sister."

Blair's eyes darted toward the window as if the Other World might be hanging in the sky like the sun or the moon. "Where is it, then?"

"On another vibrational plane, I guess?" Evie looked to Perdita.

Perdita nodded. "As good an explanation as any."

"Magenu sin here, too," Blair said, either not believing, or not interested, in the existence of a sister world.

"Yes," Evie said, "but many of the Other World's belief systems are built around a notion called original sin. I do think 'sin of humankind' likely refers to the Other World."

"Indeed," Perdita nodded.

"'Trapped between two Sfyres, her truth remains unclear?'" Charlie asked. "What about that one?" His stomach knotted as he said the words out loud. Evie's connection to that particular line was, unfortunately, obvious.

"I've always been trapped between two words," she said, "even if I didn't know it. My past — my truth — hasn't been clear, until now. And you helped me get here, Charlie," she added pointedly. "*Your* knowledge."

"The prince," Perdita said, beaming at him.

"Ha!" Charlie said, triumphant. "I am not a prince. And even if I was slated for Arbiter, wouldn't it say that instead?"

"The Alterra Lingua word used is more akin to *favored son*," Perdita said carefully. "Consider 'prince' a creative choice in my translation."

"Even less likely, then," Charlie muttered to himself.

"'Choices lead to threads pre-woven, justifying all is proven,'" Blair recited. "That could pertain to anyone."

"True," Perdita said. "And by Evangeline making the choices that have led her here, she fulfills that line."

Evie recited the last part. "'She can halt old evil's spread, she can strike the dragon dead. Soaked into the Tree Eternal, light and dark blood spill at Vernal.' I presume the Obscures are the dragon?"

"It's all very vague, Perdita," Charlie said, beginning to pace. "Very vague."

"Not to me," Evie said. Charlie paused mid-stride, staring at her. She avoided his gaze.

"It absolutely is," he pushed. "Admit it, Perdita. You could interpret those words a thousand different ways."

Perdita sighed. "Do not forget my weaver's intuition, Charles. That intuition tells me that when Evangeline's threads fell from the Ortus, they became tangled with those of a great and terrible evil. They intertwined in such a way that, if her choices align, can lead to the end of that evil. So far, her choices have."

"She barely has Alicrat!" Charlie protested.

"She does not need to be the most skilled or ruthless, necessarily. Half the battle is won by choosing to act."

"It makes sense, Charlie," Evie said gently, now meeting his eyes. She looked pained, but continued anyway, "My life *is* tangled with that of a great and terrible evil. Had the Obscures never pursued the Tree Book, Clement wouldn't have sent me away. I would have grown up here, not the Other World. My mother would be alive. The Obscures are directly responsible for the path I walk. Why wouldn't fate give me an opportunity to fight back?"

Charlie ran a hand through his hair, muttering the prophecy to himself again. "'...blood will spill at Vernal,'" he whispered, then, loudly, "At Vernal! The Vernal Sun Day has passed. That was the day we came through the portal."

Blair scowled. "Maybe it means next year. That would be unfortunate. I, for one, won't be waiting around to fulfill the parameters of an old rhyme."

"Vernal does not necessarily mean the Vernal Sun Day," Perdita said. "We are still within the second quarter, are we not? It is still spring. In any case, you have my opinion. The prophecy speaks of Evangeline." She turned to Evie. "What you do with it is your choice."

"That's it?" Charlie said. "I thought the Perditos were meant to help the Callidoras decide how to act on the information revealed."

"We are meant to translate the Alterra Lingua and help interpret its riddles, connecting vague speculations to specific occurrences in the present day, as we just did. Ultimately, what is done with those conclusions is not, and has never been, the responsibility of the Perditos. The Callidora Arbiters have always chosen how to act — or not."

Charlie looked to Evie. Her eyes were downcast, staring at the prophecy. She didn't seem afraid — worse, she didn't seem skeptical. He looked at Blair, who was also staring at the Tree Book, eyes narrow. *She* was skeptical, but clearly, she did not comprehend the gravity of Perdita's assumption.

"There are more prophecies to hear. Would you like me to continue?" Perdita said.

"Yes," Charlie said.

"No," Evie and Blair said at the same time. Evie continued. "We've heard what we need to, for now. Liam and the others will be desperate for an update."

"Agreed," Blair said, standing. "We must confer and plan."

Charlie was about to argue, but Perdita broke into a painful sounding cough. Evie alicrated a sphere of water for her, which she sipped from gratefully. "Dear me," she said when she could speak again. "Another day, then. There is so much to teach you, Evangeline. I must make certain you have the knowledge before it is too late for me. Death has been lurking for quite some time. I do not believe he will accept my protestations any longer."

She moved to lift the book. It proved too heavy. She set it down, looked at Evie beseechingly, and fainted.

40

Evie patiently waited as Charlie recited the prophecy to his father, his brother, Finneas, and Oleander. She remained silent as he outlined Perdita's opinion that it referred to her. She did not interrupt his passionate lecture as to why it did *not* refer to her.

She said nothing because she did not need to. Whether or not Charlie could convince the others that the prophecy wasn't worth acting upon didn't matter, because he wouldn't convince her. She'd believed, from the moment Perdita finished, that it was her life written on that page, cradled by branches from the cover of the Tree Book. Charlie could decide not to believe. Liam could decide not to take action. Evie believed and would act for them all.

"I respect Perdita's view," Charlie concluded, "but it doesn't justify putting Evie in danger." He crossed his arms with finality.

"It could be more explicit, sure," Oleander said, brow furrowed.

"Indeed," Finneas said. "It seems...open to interpretation."

"Marcus?" Charlie prompted.

"It sounds like it fits," Marcus said. He met Evie's eyes, grimacing an apology. She responded with a resigned smile.

Charlie slammed a palm on the table, startling everyone. "It is a riddle, not a decree. It demands nuanced interpretation. Not your strong suit, Marcus."

Liam rose. "Calm yourself," he said, glaring at Charlie. Then, in an unexpectedly reverent tone, he asked Evie, "What do you think?"

All eyes turned to her.

"I came here to find my mother," she started, voice flat. "But I've been forced to accept what all of you knew to be true a long time ago. There's nothing to find."

She paused, her gaze lingering on Charlie. A thousand emotions swirled in the moss of his eyes, none of them good. There was a time this would have given her pause.

"I'm angry," she said. "I'm angry that others thought they could dictate my path for me. Clement, my mother, Professor Atkinson, my father..." She looked away from Charlie. "What good did it do? Everything has led me back here anyway. I don't know how to stop the Obscures, but I believe I have to be the one to try."

Everyone except Blair and Charlie inhaled sharply. Blair remained steely and impassive. Charlie slumped, head in his hands.

"Well, then," Liam said, tilting his head a respectful inch toward Evie. "It seems we had our advantage with us all along. What you are expected to do to fulfill this prophecy, Evie, is another question."

"Let's start with the most obvious concern," Finneas said. "Blair, is it feasible to enter Maliter undetected?"

She nodded. "There's a tunnel from south Callidora to the quarries north of Talus. It's how I escaped. The AO are not aware of it."

"Any weakness you're privy to? A way inside their headquarters?"

"I have a contact inside the Domus," Blair said. "She can help us get in."

"Even then," Liam said, "I do not see how Evie can effectively weaken them, short of killing Tenebris."

"Then she should kill him."

Charlie exhaled audibly. Blair cast him an irritated look and continued. "I know where he sleeps. I know how many vocats he drinks before bed. I know when he wakes and where his office is and how to get inside. If we can get into the Domus, we can get to Adrian." She sat back in her chair, smug.

"Those are some personal details," Oleander said under his breath.

Ignoring him, Blair turned to Evie. "All you'll need to do then, is kill him, Evie." There was something in her expression Evie couldn't place. Distrust? Jealousy?

Charlie stood, reinvigorated by Blair's comment. "We cannot do something so drastic based on something so flimsy! Admit it, Evie. You wouldn't even use this alleged prophecy as a footnote in a thesis. Put your emotions aside and really *think*. You don't believe a word of it, do you?" He shoved the book across the table. It slid into Evie's lap.

"I believe it," she said, eyes on the book.

"You believe it?" he repeated. "Or do you *want* to believe it? There is no proof!"

Still looking down at the book, Evie whispered, "Belief is conviction in the absence of proof." Charlie didn't hear.

"You're the one who claimed this book was important, Charles," Liam said.

"I didn't know it would say *this*!" Charlie took a steadying breath, palms on the table. "The timing isn't right, anyway. It speaks of the Eternal Tree and the Vernal Sun Day. Why is nobody else concerned about that?"

"It just says Vernal," Blair corrected.

"It's referring to the Vernal Sun Day," Charlie said definitively. "If this was supposed to happen now, it would have said 'Estival' instead. The Estival Sun Day is upon us in seven days. And if Evie was meant to kill Adrian in the Domus, it would have mentioned Maliter soil, not the Eternal Tree." He spoke with calm, dispassionate confidence, as if he was debating the taste of vocat versus whisky, not the time and place of an assassination attempt.

"Are there any special trees in Maliter, Blair?" Evie asked. "Anything that could be confused for Benclair's Eternal Tree?"

Blair laughed.

Charlie sat back down, appearing somewhat pleased. "Since when do you place stock in prophecies anyway, Father? Or any of you, for that matter?" He glanced around the room.

"I'm pretty open," Oleander ventured, "what with my Mum's beliefs."

"Aren't you always begging us to consider the past, Charles?" Liam pointed at the Tree Book on Evie's lap. "I do not see a book of forgotten prophecies. I see history, the very thing you have always longed to explore."

"I don't deny what the book is," Charlie said, "nor its importance. I just think we need more evidence to support Evie's role in all this."

"I do wonder," Finneas said diplomatically, "what skills you have, Evie, that would take down Tenebris better than one of us?"

"A valid question," Blair said.

Evie had wondered the same thing, yet her response to Blair was automatic. "I'm descended from an Original," she said. "From a creator." She hastily explained the origins and the sisters' creation of an Original — Claire Callidora and Malek Maliter — all their own, then waited for the discordance she'd felt in the cave, the misalignment of her words and her beliefs. It didn't come.

"A Callidora needs to kill Tenebris, then," Marcus said slowly. "Evie must have something in her blood, in her energy, that will ensure her success."

"Exactly," Evie said, pleased to see Liam, Oleander, and Finneas nodding along thoughtfully.

Exasperated, Charlie said, "Malek Maliter has nothing to do with Adrian Tenebris."

"Adrian is descended from a Maliter," Blair said. All eyes turned to her, stunned by the casual confirmation. Even Evie's mouth hung open.

Blair shrugged. "The Maliters were infamous whores and whoremongers. Everyone in Talus knows that. Adrian brags all the time that the last Maliter Arbiter fathered an illegitimate child who sired the Tenebris line."

"Well, there we have it," Marcus said. "Only a Callidora's energy can combat Tenebris' Maliter energy. Only Evie carries the divine protection that —"

"Have you all gone mad?" Charlie glanced around the room. "Hm? Oleander?"

"Well, my mum —"

"To the moon with your mum! Finneas, really? Divine protection? *That's* what we're going with, here?"

The study fell silent, no one willing to contradict Charlie.

"How will you do it, then?" Blair said loudly, clearly ready to move on. "How will you kill him, Evie?"

Liam answered for her. "She will need to use an obscurity."

Charlie rose so angrily his chair clattered to the floor. He kicked it aside on his way to the door, striking the trunk of the tree and leaving a dent.

"The situation necessitates moral compromises, Charles —"

The slam of the door cut Liam off.

Suddenly, Evie longed to leave the study, to go after Charlie, to go all the way back to Edinburgh, to William Street. But the longing was fleeting, just the last, stubborn vestige of a completely different person.

"Well?" Blair asked again, pretending Charlie hadn't just stormed away.

Again, Liam answered. "Manual methods of killing will not subdue Tenebris. You'll all be dead before she gets the chance to try."

"You'll need to use something quick. Effective," Blair told Evie.

"I've no idea where to begin with obscurities," Evie said.

"I'll teach you."

At this, Evie looked at Blair — truly looked at her — for the first time, and was struck by what she saw. She wore Evie's John Lewis sweater, for one thing. Too big for Evie, it was comically large on Blair. More disconcertingly, her eyes were the same light blue as those that greeted Evie in the moonstone mirror each morning. Blair seemed to notice this in the same moment and they broke their eye contact in unison.

Blair addressed the others. "I've witnessed obscurities my whole life. I've dabbled in them to survive. Obscurities are accessible to everyone. It's simply a matter of diving into a deeper level of Alicrat. I can teach her the basics. Enough to kill Adrian. And if she can't do it," Blair's eyes narrowed, "trust me, I will."

Liam nodded. "Teach her. Use Pembroke's clearing. Evie will show you. The Enforcers won't stumble upon you there."

"Just tell them the truth," Blair said tersely. "Tell them we're working to bring down the AO. Or will the rest of your State be as slow to accept reality as you?"

269

The Mensmen exchanged glances.

Liam reddened. "Excuse me?"

"Sooner or later, you'll have to tell your citizens what's going on. The Northlands has a right to know what's happening. Not to mention, it will take more than the six of us in this room to restore Maliter and Callidora."

"If you're successful, nobody needs to know anything." Liam turned to address Finneas, Marcus, and Oleander. "You three, learn some basic obscurities as well. You will get Blair and Evie to Tenebris at any cost."

He had more orders to bark, but a rap sounded against the curve of the glass behind him. A purple-winged pixie no larger than a hand and bearing an envelope twice its size tapped again, a miniature look of annoyance on its face.

"It must be from Greer!" Blair leapt up and slid the pane of glass open. The pixie buzzed inside and dropped the letter on the table, relieved to be free of its weight.

"*I hope this finds you alive,*" Blair recited casually. "*Your acquaintance made it to the safe house. We await news of your progress in Benclair.*" She skimmed the rest of the letter. "She adds some remarks about your reluctance to act and the lives it has cost," she said, handing the letter to Liam. "I'll let her know we need a way inside the Domus."

Dismissed, everyone filed out of the study. In the corridor, Blair called to Evie, Greer's pixie perched on her shoulder, resting. "We'll start early tomorrow. Be ready." She turned down another hall.

"She's a delight," Evie muttered to Marcus as she walked away.

"She is when she talks to Father." He chuckled, but quickly turned solicitous. Arm draped over Evie's shoulder, walking slowly, deliberately drawing out their time together, he guided Evie to her room.

"Are you worried, Marcus?" she asked as they walked.

"Of course. There's plenty to worry about, from the collapse of the Northlands to the individuals involved. Friends. Family. You."

"You're worried I can't pull it off."

Marcus stopped, pulling Evie so that she faced him. "I believe in you. I know you will do what you need to do. I admire that, though I'll admit, I don't like it one bit."

He took her hand with both of his, brought it to his lips and kissed her palm, then laced his fingers between hers. Pulling her gently, they continued walking.

"If this were merely a question of you and your bravery, I'd be calm. But it's not. There's another aspect, and it's dangerous. So yes, I am worried. For you, not about you."

"I want to do it, Marcus. Prophecy or not, I *want* to kill Tenebris," Evie said. "Is that wrong?"

Marcus didn't answer for a long moment. When he did, his voice was low, as if the portraits of his ancestors might overhear and disapprove. "I wanted to kill that magena in the seraphilles," he said. "She held your life in her hands and would have taken it without a second thought. That type of evil doesn't need to be punished — it needs to be eradicated. Tenebris murdered your mother. You're entitled to want to do something about that, Evie."

Evie's fire raged on, Marcus' words like kindling to the flames. Still, a touch of dissonance emerged, a cloud that threatened to break open and release an extinguishing rain over her desire to kill Tenebris. She did not feel evil, exactly, but evil adjacent, and it was uncomfortable. Then there were Charlie's words from earlier.

You believe it? Or you want *to believe it?*

Perdita claimed the prophecy spelled Evie's destiny, not her fate. She claimed her choices mattered. True, Pembroke would argue that belief was a choice, yet as Evie took stock of her life, all she saw were the choices of others and how every single one had led her here. Taking Tenebris' life wasn't evil, and it wasn't destiny.

It was fate — his to die, hers to kill.

PART III

41

"This is insane." Arms crossed, Evie took a step back.

Blair took a step forward. "This is survival."

Grimacing, Evie regarded the rabbit in the center of the forest clearing where it lay motionless, bound by Blair's alicration. She tried to untangle the threads that confined it, but succeeded only in freeing the rabbit's front legs. It pawed the air as if trying to swim to freedom.

"It's an innocent creature, Blair. Free it."

"No."

"I don't want to do what you're asking."

"Then you will die. Did you forget you're going to face a powerful Obscure in a matter of days?"

"I'll be able to do it then," Evie said. "It's in the prophecy, for God's sake. Besides, Tenebris deserves it. This rabbit..." She gestured, then dropped her arms. "Surely there's a more humane way to teach me. I could pull life from a tree, or shrivel up a flower, or..." She stopped, knowing how ridiculous her argument sounded. In no world would those actions prepare her to kill an Obscure.

"You need a beating heart," Blair said, circling her. "Flowing blood. Pulsing energy. You need to understand what those things *feel* like in the grasp of your Alicrat. You need to learn how to twist and pull and cut so that the heart stops beating, the blood stops flowing, and the nerves feel everything. If you want them to." She looked at the rabbit, impassive as ever. "The threads that weave a life are unlike anything you've encountered. Not that you've encountered much, from the sound of it."

The rabbit continued to run in place with its front legs, trying in vain to escape.

Evie sighed. "Can't you at least knock it out?"

"It won't be the same."

"Just the first one. Please. Whatever I manage won't be quick. I don't want it to be in pain."

Blair looked disgusted with Evie's weakness, but relented. She strode to the rabbit, focused for a few moments, then moved her hands over its body until its lids descended over terrified eyes.

"What did you do?"

"Tied up some consciousness threads. Put it to sleep. I saw an Obscure do it once, to a young woman. A girl." She looked at Evie meaningfully, then moved aside.

The rabbit twitched below Evie, dreaming and oblivious. Reluctantly, she focused her Alicrat until she could sense as far as she'd been able to sense anything. The energy was basic; just cursory threads that told her there was a rabbit. Where were the things Blair mentioned? Its heartbeat, its nerves, its expanding and deflating lungs?

The realization of how plain a picture her baseline Alicrat drew made Evie curious. She would never see deeper, she realized, unless she had a reason to. Pembroke, the Normalex, Charlie...they all suggested that the only reason magenu dipped into obscure levels of Alicrat was to cause harm. Eventually, she would. But now? She was just curious. What did a heartstring look like? What did the energy of a creature's nerves *feel* like?

The shift wasn't immediate, but it was as if this curiosity gave Evie's Alicrat permission to descend the stairs of her mind into a deeper, darker place. The staircase was long, perhaps even unending, but eventually, the blueprint of the rabbit's energy grew more robust. One step more and all at once, its threads multiplied into thousands, millions! They slinked and meandered before Evie, complicated and dense, moving both individually and together like the various parts of a symphonic masterpiece.

Seeing this, existence suddenly was so obvious, Evie could not fathom ever having questioned the workings of anything. But the complexity of what she was witnessing quickly overtook the clarity, knocking her out of her alicrative state just like that evening in the Silvana Seraphilles.

She stumbled backward. "What just happened?"

"I suspect you tapped into a deeper layer of Alicrat, as one must do to perform obscurities," Blair said. "You likely saw a glimpse of —"

"How the universe works, yeah."

"What? I was going to say you saw the energy split into even more threads, separate functions working together, no?"

"I did see that. I guess my mind took it elsewhere."

The moment of pure understanding was already so faded it felt like a dream. Evie refocused and descended the stairs again, bracing herself for another hit of omnipotence, but it didn't come.

"Just take some time to understand how each part feels," Blair instructed. "Find the air that fills the lungs. Trace its journey from the outside, in. Find its blood and feel how it flows, feeding the muscles and organs. Trace the blood back to the heart and focus on the heart's energy — complex in itself. Consider how you might speed up the beats, slow them down, stop them altogether, by manipulating the heartstrings."

Evie fell into a strange autopilot as she felt her way around the insides of the rabbit. She felt its lungs heave with each shallow breath through the threads that expanded and contracted with intakes of air. She felt the steady flow of blood by sensing the relief of oxygenation its threads of muscle experienced. She traced the blood back to the rabbit's heart, which thrummed with a unique energy all its own. The heartstrings spoke their own language, one of physicality and life but also of intangible, seemingly source-less emotion, and Evie found herself surprised that a rabbit's emotional life was so rich.

More surprising was that, for the first time in her life, she saw logical proof of a God — though certainly, not the traditional Christian type. The tapestry of the rabbit's life was like another language Evie knew how to speak, a universally understandable energy that offered answers to questions of existence. Looking at the rabbit, it was obvious, if only for a single, infinitesimal beat of its heart: we are all God, Evie thought.

"Come back, Evie."

The forest as seen through Evie's eyes, not her Alicrat, returned to focus.

"You were in a trance," Blair said. "Don't let that happen. You'll be killed."

"How do you keep from getting lost in it all?"

Blair exhaled heavily. "Lost in what?"

"The meaning..." Evie gestured vaguely, but saw it was no use. She couldn't put into words what she'd felt, and it was fading again, anyway. "Never mind. What now? How do I —"

"Kill it?" Blair shrugged. "However you'd like. Try staunching the flow of blood to its heart."

Deep in her obscure level of Alicrat once more, Evie homed in on the rabbit's blood. Its pulse guided her to the heart where she felt the largest flow; the right and left pulmonary arteries squished uncomfortably between her fingers, though to any bystander, it would have appeared she was pinching air. The force of the heartbeat was stronger than she'd anticipated and the pressure she put on the threads of the artery wasn't enough. The resilient heart continued to force blood through and, unnerved by how much power she'd need to exert to accomplish her goal, she dropped her hands.

Blair's muted voice reached her. "You're thinking too simply. You're not touching the actual thing, remember. Just the energy. Manipulate as you would any threads."

Evie tried again, considering how she performed other alicrations. She cut, tied, wove, untied, stretched, and contracted threads. Any of those actions could be done to the threads of the artery, too. One by one, she plucked individual threads away from the weave of the rabbit's body and collected them in a small loop. Holding the threads like that, she paused, thinking of Pembroke and his two twigs; the majority of magenu, inherently good, and the small, dangerous minority. Was there no third twig for those who harmed not because they wanted to, but because they had to?

"Get on with it," came Blair's voice. "If that rabbit was Adrian, you'd be dead already."

She was right. Evie stepped up to the line that separated mere curiosity and the desire to harm, then crossed it, tearing through the looped threads, her finger like a knife. It was done.

A wave of nausea overcame her. Her Alicrat diminished again. She knelt by the rabbit, now in the throes of death. Crouching next to her, Blair shook her head. "This won't be quick. You could have finished the job if you'd stayed focused. It's a bit of a mess now."

The rabbit's eyelids fluttered, wanting to return to consciousness even as blood filled its insides. Evie closed her eyes. "This is barbaric," she said.

"If you were more aggressive, you could have spared it the misery."

Evie's response was instinctual. "I'm not a killer."

"You're about to be. Look, I get it. I grappled with my morals, too, when I was a child."

"I'm not a child, either."

"I was when I had to learn this," Blair snapped. "Killing isn't palatable, but the alternative we're faced with is worse. I had years to come to terms with that. You have a few days, if you're lucky."

"I told you," Evie said, taking Blair's outstretched hand, allowing her to pull her upright. "I'll have no problem killing Adrian Tenebris. That doesn't mean I harbor a burning desire to mangle innocent rabbits."

"Find the desire. Despite what *you* believe, I see no actual proof you carry divine protection from a creator nobody has heard of before yesterday. This is deadly serious. Maybe you don't understand that, having grown up in your soft, safe world, far from the scum who killed your mother. Did you come here just to meet the same fate by the same man? Do you think it's going to be —"

Evie's fist connected with Blair's cheek, sending a jab of pain through to her elbow. She swore, turning away and cradling her arm.

Blair touched her cheek delicately. "Pathetic."

"Don't you dare talk about my mother," Evie shot. "You have no idea."

"Don't I? My mother was murdered too, you know. And let me tell you something." Blair closed the gap, her smarting face an inch from Evie's. "I'd mangle a thousand rabbits if it meant I could ensure the absolute evisceration of the person who killed her." She lifted her chin a fraction. "But maybe that's just me."

They glared at each other for a long moment before Evie broke the stare, unable to take the coldness of Blair's eyes. Focusing on the trees in the distance instead, she lifted her chin, too, and said, "Get another one."

42

After spending the whole morning learning obscurities with Blair, Evie watched Finneas, Oleander, and Marcus take their turns. None of them were on the verge of joining the cult, but by day's end, everyone had grasped the concept and established a decent ability to delve into their deeper Alicrat.

"Don't overthink it," Blair reminded them as they approached the castle. "Find the internal threads, then just do something with them. Don't dwell on what that something will result in."

"You're speaking like we're actually going to face the AO," Oleander muttered. "I thought we were sneaking in."

Blair stopped in the courtyard, her face illuminated by the green glow of the affrim. "Clearly, you've never had to anticipate danger." Perturbed, she stalked away.

Evie trudged to her room on the fifth floor, ready for a warm bath with the array of oils Illis always left for her. Charlie had other plans, it seemed — the trapdoor to the library was open.

"Finally," he said, waiting with an outstretched hand as soon as Evie's head popped through the floor. "We must talk about the prophecy. Alone."

Evie allowed him to pull her up. Face to face, she was about to speak, but he hurried on, voice trembling. "I am afraid, Evie. It's not my over-protectiveness. It's the prophecy...Tenebris...it doesn't add up."

Glancing over his shoulder, Evie scanned the books he'd pulled from the shelves. Richard Dawkins' *The God Delusion*, the King James Version of the Bible, *Creation Myths* by Marie Louise von Franz, *Finger-prints of the Gods* by Graham Hancock.

Charlie gestured at the books. "I'm trying to find something to fill in the gaps of Perdita's story."

"Gaps? Let's talk to her if you still have questions," Evie urged, taking his hand to pull him down the stairs.

He pulled back. "She's been asleep since she collapsed. She won't wake — Seely gave her something. In the meantime, hear me out. I think there's more to the origin story than what we heard."

Evie nodded. "Perdita said there wasn't enough time to go into all the details."

"We need those details." Charlie dropped her hand and began pacing. "I think they'll prove you're not meant to kill Tenebris."

Evie sighed, louder than she'd meant to. "It fits, Charlie."

"You're right. Reluctant though I was to see it, I agree. It fits with respect to *you*. Not Tenebris."

At this, Evie's brows furrowed.

"Everyone presumes Tenebris is the evil in question because he's who we're faced with right now. But there's no proof the prophecy means him, or even the Obscures at large. And if the Obscures are not the evil cited in the prophecy, destiny will have no say in the outcome if you act."

Charlie stopped pacing and returned to Evie, eyes urgent. He grabbed her by the shoulders. "Pretend for a moment the prophecy has nothing to do with the Obscures. You will deliver yourself to a dangerous man with no moral compunctions and ten times your alicra-tive ability, with nothing protecting you! There is a counterpart you are destined to face, someday. That much I believe. But it's not Tenebris."

Slumping into a chair, Charlie picked up *The God Delusion* with one hand, looking puzzled. "I can't remember why I thought this would help," he muttered, tossing it aside. "We need to know what happened between the sisters. I think it's connected somehow. I've been searching creation myths for hours, hoping that an ancient culture in the Other World told the same story in its own way."

"You've found nothing," Evie said, her own prophecy based on the anxiety in his eyes.

"That's why we need to talk to Perdita." He pushed the other books away from him. The Bible fell to the floor. "Promise me, Evie. You'll wait for me to figure this out."

Sighing again, more softly this time, Evie shook her head, eyes downcast. "Charlie, normally I would be all for caution pending further research." She met his gaze. "But what if you're wrong?"

He didn't answer.

Evie held out her palms like mock scales of justice. "If you're right and I die, one person has been lost." She lowered her left hand an inch. "But if I don't act and you're wrong, the AO carries on, unchecked. Thousands of Northlands citizens die. Including you, maybe. Me. I could die anyway!" She lowered her right hand all the way down.

Charlie shook his head. His eyes were red with exhaustion and, Evie realized with a pang, burgeoning tears. "I am begging you. Do not go until we speak with Perdita."

This time, Evie didn't answer. She was staring, transfixed, at the silver thread hanging between them. In the calm of her library, far from the chaos of the Hall of Portraits, she could see just how unbelievably strong the fiber was. Why, then, did it feel like she and Charlie were fraying?

As the thread faded away from her alicrative perception, she repeated her own words in her head. *Scales of justice. Dead citizens. The AO, unchecked*...they weren't her words. They were a story, a version of the truth she hoped Charlie would buy. She couldn't tell him what she'd told Marcus, after all.

"Let her make her own choices." As if summoned, Marcus stood at the top of the stairs, irritation knitting his brows. "Stop coddling her."

The library was painfully still for a beat, then Charlie rose from his chair and started toward Marcus, who was already striding his way. They met in the middle and stared each other down, their profiles like two sides of a Roman coin.

"You think you have so much control," Marcus said. "That you have the final say in what she thinks, what she does. What gives you that right?"

"I've done nothing but protect her," Charlie said, voice low. "From the moment Mother brought her to the castle, to the moment I found her in the Other World, to right now, I have *protected* her! What have you ever done for her?"

Marcus began to answer, but Charlie's voice rose over his. "You paid little attention to her when we were children. You took no notice when she disappeared. You didn't travel to the Other World to find her. Of course not — that would have jeopardized your position as Father's favorite. You only want her now because you know she's important to me." He pushed Marcus hard in the chest, causing him to stumble back. Charlie braced himself for retaliation, but Marcus made no move.

"This isn't about wanting Evie. It's about letting her go, actually." Marcus paused, the pulse in his temple contradicting his calm tone. "And for the record, little brother, I'm not Father's favorite. He'd have preferred you — the smart one, the serious one, the hard-working one — to be Arbiter. Your choices landed me here. Not mine."

The pain between the brothers was palpable, yet neither reached out to the other; they only stared, green and hazel eyes seeing the other but not understanding him at all, as they had done their whole lives.

Shaking his head, Marcus continued. "I heard you. I know you don't believe the prophecy refers to Tenebris. I know you're looking for more answers in your books. Books aren't going to win this, Charlie. We are. Evie is. We're going to Maliter as soon as Blair's contact accepts the plan we've sent."

Tense, Evie waited for Charlie's rebuttal. It didn't come. Instead, he turned to her. Defeat dulled his face, weighed down his shoulders, as he crossed the library to where she stood. She suddenly had a thousand things to say, to admit, but the words couldn't get past the lump in her throat. They spilled from her eyes instead; silent truths streaming down her cheeks, probably more impossible for Charlie to interpret than Alterra Lingua.

Cradling her face in his hands, Charlie kissed her forehead gently. She squeezed her eyes shut, trying to hone her Alicrat, wanting to sense that silver thread again, to make sure it was still there, but it was no use. She was too emotional, and Charlie was already pulling away.

"I believe in you," he whispered. Without another word, he left.

Only when the trapdoor shut did Marcus approach Evie, uncharacteristically tentative. "Are you okay?" he asked. "I hope you don't think I was out of line, saying what I said."

Evie wiped away her remaining tears. "You two don't understand each other."

"Maybe someday we will."

"You have to try, Marcus. So does Charlie, but one of you has to start. Promise me something? When this madness is over, make amends. If not for yourselves, for me."

Sighing softly, Marcus looked around the library. "All these books," he murmured. "I've never asked him what even one of them is about." He shook his head. "You're right. Once we're back, I'll fix things with Charlie. Something to look forward to, hey?" He held out a hand. "Come. Father needs us."

Outside, a wash of rain pelted the castle as Evie followed Marcus to Liam's study. She crossed her arms over her abdomen, not wanting a single drop of dissonance to quell her fire.

Juliette, carrying a tray of tea and snacks, trailed Evie and Marcus into Liam's study. Smiling broadly, she set the tray on the table. "I thought you might like something to eat," she announced.

Liam glared at her. "Is Illis unwell? Just leave it there."

Nodding, she removed the items from the tray slowly, one by one.

"Thank you, Juliette!" Oleander said, beaming. He, Finneas, and Blair stood beneath the tree. A map of Maliter lay unfurled across the table.

With Evie and Marcus in place, Liam addressed the group. "You will partume to the south Callidora border, here." He pointed. "Blair will take you through the tunnels to the obsidian quarry here, just north of Talus."

Juliette peered over Evie's shoulder, using her as a shield as though she could render her curiosity invisible.

"From the quarry," Blair said, "we'll head to Pickering. It's a desolate place the AO ignores. Gaspare, its Maior, is with us. We'll rest there before going to Talus, where Greer will get us into the Domus. After that, it's up to me to get Evie to Tenebris."

"Blair says you've become adept at tapping into your obscure Alicrat, Evie," Liam said. "You'll be ready?"

"I'd feel better with another day of practice," Evie admitted.

"You may not have that. You'll leave as soon as Greer confirms."

Diplomatic as ever, Finneas said, "I do wonder, Liam, why so soon? Surely it would be prudent to give Evie more time to prepare."

Blair and Liam exchanged glances. "There's no time," Blair said. "Greer's latest message informed that the AO plan to invade Iristell within a matter of days."

"Maribell has been warned," Liam said, "but Iristell has meager defenses. Raising them prematurely will signal to Tenebris that they know he is coming. You'll be ready," Liam repeated. Not a question, this time.

Five pairs of eyes stared at Evie: Finneas and Oleander's, trusting, but anxious; Liam's, stern, but worried; Blair's, unreadable; and Marcus', filled with adrenaline and something else that had nothing to do with the plan, something that made Evie feel like lightning was about to strike. She wondered what Charlie's eyes would say.

The group departed, everyone going their separate ways. Marcus walked with Evie, taking her hand as they turned down her corridor. She squeezed it hard, feeling reckless, thinking that the fog of possibility between them might be a nice place to disappear. Her energy must have conveyed this, because he didn't let go when they reached her door and instead, pulled her to face him, looped his arms around her waist, and leaned in to kiss her.

He was warm and thrilling and for a moment, Evie gave in wholly to the pleasure of a kiss underscored by Alicrat. But he was also foreign, like she could stay awhile, but would never truly belong there. She wondered what it would be like to kiss Charlie instead. More like home, she decided, even as his brother's lips were pressed to hers.

"I've wanted to do that for a while," Marcus whispered as they pulled apart. He pushed an errant curl away from her face and kissed her again, but on the forehead. "Goodnight, Evie." With a classic Marcus wink, he turned to walk away.

Evie's hand hovered over the doorknob. The world on her shoulders — worlds, she corrected herself — weighed heavily. The one person she'd hoped would share the burden wasn't willing. Tears burned her eyes as she internalized this, a disappointment and sadness so different from what her mother's death engendered. That had filled her with rage. This left her empty.

Evie glanced down the hall. Marcus was walking slowly, as if waiting for her to have the very realization that was dawning on her; not only was he willing to share her burden, he wanted to.

She called out. Marcus turned around. She opened her door and tilted her head. Smiling, he followed her inside.

43

"I WAS WONDERING when I would see you again. What an odd place to choose, however. The daughter of light, here in the dark!"

"Where are we?" Evie does not know where her subconscious has dropped her. Into a void, it appears. There is nothing.

"I can give you a better answer to that question than you have ever given me," the figure says. "We are in the Somund, as we always are."

"Why is it so dark?"

"I cannot say. As ever, this is your dream. The Somund is merely a setting for dreamers to build their own worlds, home to millions of sleeping souls and their secrets."

"How was it created?"

"Not by me. And not by her."

"Her?" Instinctively, Evie asks, "Who are you?" There is something nagging, but it lives in her conscious mind, too far away to comprehend."

Light floods what has been pitch black and here, again, is the cratered moon, staring at Evie without eyes, speaking to her without a mouth, reflecting the light of an invisible sun.

"You're the moon?"

"To some. To others, I am a shadow. I am Satan. I am a serpent. I am

the plague. I am to be worshipped. I am to be forsaken. I am so many things to so many people, but at the core of all the parts I play, I am evil."

"Are you, really?"

The moon looks thoughtful. "You have caught me off guard. Nobody has asked if I am truly what they believe me to be. I am afraid I cannot answer. I cannot remember what — who — I once was. I have become what others want me to be. Am I evil?" the moon repeats. "Before, I think not. Now, who is to say?"

The moon begins to crumble. Pieces of rock fall away, pluming dust around the hood. Behind the moon, where the emptiness of space should be, something slowly appears, revealed further with each tumbling rock. It is a face, perfect in its symmetry, feminine and masculine, delicate and strong, chiseled and soft. It is beautiful.

The eyes open and Evie recoils. There is nothing behind the eyes, nothing but a darkness so profound she feels it permeate her soul.

"I am sorry to startle you," the figure says. "It is why I chose to appear to you first as the moon. Something more believable, more benign. The moon does seem to frighten least." The figure laughs, a bright, tinkling sound like shattering glass, so different from the laugh that hounded Evie through the forest in some other corner of the Somund.

"I could have appeared as the Devil, but you don't believe in her, do you?" The perfect mouth smirks. "The moon felt safest. So many cultures do worship me that way. Would you like me to answer your question now? About how the Somund was created?"

Transfixed by the darkness of the eyes, Evie doesn't answer.

"The Somund was created by you, Evie."

She cannot remember doing such a thing.

"Silly girl!" the figure says. "Not you specifically. But you have contributed to its evolution. Each of your dreams strengthens its core so others can find it, too. I do not know who the first dreamer was to use their sleeping mind to build this place, but somebody did. Others joined and the shared subconscious of humanity was born. Very fortunate for me, as I would be incapable of reaching you otherwise. Do not forget, I need your help."

"Why would I ever help you?"

"I would tell you, but you won't remember. Though, something tells me you're getting closer to understanding...out there." The figure smiles. *"I can wait. After all, what's another few days after thousands of years?"*

44

LIGHT DANCED OVER MARCUS' face, boyish in sleep. He squeezed
his eyes tightly, sprawled across half of Evie's bed. She watched him,
vivid images from the last twenty-four hours searing behind her eyelids
each time she blinked. Bloody, mutilated rabbits. Tears in Charlie's eyes.
The moon, crumbling. Twitching paws. Charlie's kiss. Comprehension
of the universe. Marcus' kiss...Marcus' everything.

Next to her, his chest, still scarred from the Silvana Seraphilles, rose
and fell with a vulnerability that did not match his powerful frame. The
night before, Evie had touched the worst scar that ran from his ribs to
his waist and started to apologize. He'd silenced her with a finger to her
lips. Moments later, she'd forgotten all about it.

He stirred. Suddenly unsure, Evie slipped from the bed.

She was getting dressed when she heard a knock on the door. Horrified by the thought it could be Charlie, she tried to sense the energy on
the other side. All she could gather was the age of the wood. She pushed
it open a crack.

"You're awake. Good." Blair shoved her way into the room. "Greer's
response arrived in the night. It's time."

Marcus sat up, rubbing his eyes.

"Oh. Morning Rutherford," Blair said, taking in his shirtless torso with admiration and amusement. "One less stop for me, then. Come. Finneas and Oleander are already in the courtyard."

Leaving Marcus to dress, Evie bolted to Charlie's room, overcome with the need to say goodbye, or beg him to come, or...she wasn't sure. It didn't matter; her knocks on his door went unanswered. She knocked harder, pounded with her palm, jimmied the handle. It was locked, and a quick alicrative assessment told her she didn't have nearly enough time to understand the clavis he'd woven. Calling his name, she grabbed hold of the threads, intending to loquer them.

Instead, she dropped her arms. The threads dissipated. She stood outside Charlie's room for a few more seconds, tears welling. Then she strode away, palms to her eyes, forcing everything back inside where she could confront it later. Or never.

In the courtyard, Finneas, Oleander, Blair, and Marcus stood near the affrim, speaking in low, nervous voices. "You sure you can partume this, Fin?" Oleander asked.

"Blair has explained the destination in great detail," Finneas assured him, focusing hard into the distance. "I've already located the threads."

"There you are," Marcus said quietly as Evie approached. They moved into position next to Blair, his hand landing on the small of her back. "You ran away so quickly."

Evie glanced up at him. Handsome Marcus, charming Marcus, brave, kind, caring Marcus. He was all those things and more, and last night, they had been enough. They would be more than enough for someone, someday. She smiled, then looked away, distracted by someone watching from the fourth floor. It was Juliette in her velvet robe, peering down at them, looking as though she hadn't slept all night. Evie tried to catch her eye, but there was no time.

Blair lifted her leg; Marcus and Evie followed suit. The courtyard stretched and they catapulted forward, small and insignificant inside the tunnel of threads. They struck solid ground a moment later and stumbled forward, catching their breath as Oleander and Finneas materialized next to them.

They'd landed in a vast expanse of wheat-like grass just as the sun was rising, casting its golden sheen over the field. It was beautiful in its familiarity; this part of Callidora reminded Evie of the posters in her middle school classroom with the Pledge of Allegiance plastered across America's beautiful, spacious skies and amber waves of grain. That was all so far away from her now, so unimportant.

"Soak it up while you can," Blair said, watching Evie. "Maliter hasn't seen the sun in years."

The entrance to the tunnel was a few meters ahead, though nobody noticed it but Blair. "It's not obvious," she said scathingly, when Oleander questioned its existence. "Go on. Take a few steps."

Oleander took small, halting steps and fell abruptly into the ground, disappearing as though the earth had swallowed him whole.

"Ole!" Finneas yelled. He moved forward on instinct, then stopped himself. "Very funny, Blair. Can we enter a bit more gracefully?"

She grinned; the first genuine smile Evie had seen from her. "Of course. He's fine, by the way. The initial descent is only two meters. The grass is real," she ran her hands through it, "but it's not rooted into anything. The man who dug the tunnel devised the alicration."

"Anybody could happen upon it," Marcus said, frowning.

"So sorry that we couldn't conjure something more secure for you, Rutherford." Blair took another step and fell into the ground, rolling her eyes as she went.

The others followed, stepping tentatively onto a patch of land that was there, but wasn't, and began their underground trek to Maliter.

―――――

Standing on the precipice of an expansive obsidian pit, heaving and covered in dirt, the group squinted into the clouds as their eyes adjusted. Even without sun, the grey skies of Maliter were comparatively brighter than the tunnel inside which they'd spent the last many hours walking and at times, crawling, through. Below them, a jagged swath cut across the earth, exposing the deepest black. Hollows chained at the ankles raised their pickaxes high, slung them into the stone, and carried armfuls of debris into waiting bins. Magenu, chained at the waist, alicrated larger rocks from the quarry and deposited them directly with a swipe of their arms.

"Can't they see us?" Finneas whispered.

"Not unless they look up," Blair said. "They won't."

She turned her back on the laborers and led the group down the cliffside into a lower, unused portion of the quarries. Dirt and obsidian dust clung to the damp earth on their bodies, rendering them indiscernible from their surroundings save the whites of their eyes. Still, Oleander spun around nervously every few minutes, trying to locate patrols.

"They're only at the entrance, miles from here," Blair said. "The workers' energies are tied to a floccin while they labor. No need for guards everywhere."

Outside the quarry, at the edge of a forest, Blair halted. Everyone stopped short behind her. "The horses should be here," she said. She turned to retrace her steps, but stopped, confident. "They should be here."

"Aye, give me a moment, will you?"

An old man trailed by six haggard horses emerged from the tree line. He smiled when he saw Blair — a wide, nearly toothless grin — and Evie braced herself for Blair's rebuke. Instead, Blair ran to the man and threw her arms around him.

The man held Blair, relief flooding his otherwise hardened features, then pulled away, eying up the group. "I'm Stin. Who are you lot?"

Marcus strode forward, hand outstretched. "Marcus Rutherford."

"A Rutherford. Hmph." Stin ignored Marcus' hand.

"Finneas of the Fern, sir." Finneas gave Stin a respectful nod. Oleander followed his example.

"And the girl?"

"Evie Lennon."

"Lennon," Stin repeated. He stared hard at Evie, averting his eyes only when Blair cleared her throat. "Well," he said. "Who could've thought? In the name of the bloody moon."

"Let's go," Blair said. Ignoring Stin's odd reaction to Evie, she pulled herself onto one of the bony horses.

They rode through the forest until late afternoon, when they reached the eastern boundary of Pickering, a derelict ghost town thick with depressive energy. Homes lay in ruin, seemingly abandoned, until the quick closing of shutters proved otherwise. Except for the emaciated animals scavenging for scraps, the streets were empty — no magenu, no familiars, no shimmering, alicrated threads.

Stin turned his horse into the yard of a wooden home in a state of slightly less disrepair than the others, dismounted, and rushed inside. Blair followed, gesturing for the others to be quick despite the absolute lack of people who might glimpse them. Still, everyone hurried obediently into the house's cramped kitchen where a woman stood, arms crossed. Blair made no move to introduce anyone, and after a beat, the woman pulled a small knife from a drawer. Knife raised, she moved toward Oleander with purpose.

Oleander stepped back, hands up.

Blair sighed, unenthused with the dramatics. "She needs to make sure we're not changelings." She thrust her palm out, allowing the woman to make a small cut on the pad of her thumb.

Warily, Finneas, Marcus, Oleander, and Evie followed suit. Only after each person remained very much themselves did the woman put the knife away, apologizing profusely. "They're infiltrating Norms more and more frequently," she said. "I'd have checked my own mother. Nice to meet you all, then. I'm Greer Laide, Maior of Hayworth. I'm grateful for your help. Though," she frowned slightly, turning to Blair, "they're not exactly what I expected, coming from Benclair."

"I also hoped for more *robust* assistance," Blair said. "They're what was offered on short notice."

"Well, then," Greer said, eyeing their dirty, obsidian laden attire, "get cleaned up, then join us in the other room."

There, a frail man Evie took to be Pickering's Maior, Gaspare, and Stin sat in threadbare armchairs, speaking in hushed tones when the group entered. Stin kept his eyes on Evie, tracing her as she moved to the center of the room and then, slowly, behind Marcus. Even hidden from his direct view, she felt his penetrating stare.

Rising from his chair, Gaspare clapped lightly, welcoming the group. "We thank you for your support," he announced, his voice much stronger than his physical appearance suggested. "Perhaps you can share what you plan to accomplish in the Domus?"

"They're going to kill Tenebris," Greer said.

"Excellent," he said, "for now. Somebody will, inevitably, rise to take his place. We cannot assume the snake will die without its head. It will merely grow a new one. Perhaps less talented, but a head nonetheless." He lowered his voice. "I hope you are not under the impression that this war will be won the night it is started."

Greer agreed. "The AO have taken stabs at the Northlands already, but only by cover of darkness and the ignorance of the other States. If we're successful tonight, it will be the first open attack. Is Benclair ready for that?"

"Benclair is ready," Marcus said in his official tone, though Evie could tell he didn't believe — or didn't want to believe — what Gaspare and Greer were saying.

Greer unfurled a map of the Domus across the floor, motioning for everyone to gather around it. "The Domus is protected with powerful security alicrations," she said. "When an employee arrives at the gates within normal hours, they open. Everybody else triggers a warning and are paralyzed by an obscurity until guards arrive to question them."

Marcus shrugged. "An affrim."

"No. Affrims are primitive compared to what the AO have developed. A few days ago, in fact, another alicration was woven into the gate to sense intentional energy."

Blair groaned.

"It was inspired by your deception," Greer told her. "The alicration now recognizes energy from the magenu's mind. Threads from devout Obscures were used as a baseline. Those not loyal to Tenebris are unable to pass."

"So we'll get in how, exactly?" Oleander asked.

"I'll disable it," Gaspare said proudly. "My ancestors developed the first version of this alicration, centuries ago, when the Original Maliter family was still in power. I've no doubt the Obscures have mutilated the original design, but I've a better shot than anyone at untying their knots."

"From there," Greer said, pushing her finger across the Domus' Atrium, "it's just a matter of getting to Tenebris' quarters."

"He'll be in the West Wing, on the other side of the Domus," Blair said, running her forefinger from the Atrium, up three levels of stairs, and through a labyrinth of halls. "I've never seen any guards in his private quarters."

"There are no guards anywhere in the Domus after hours," Gaspare said. "Adrian brags to the Mensmen and Maiors about not needing personal security. He values his privacy in the West Wing and believes he can handle whatever comes his way."

Marcus smiled. "Until now."

"Until now, the AO had no reason to believe anybody in their right mind would try to break into the Domus," Greer said. Then, with a note of concern, "It feels too simple."

"I thought the same," Finneas said, "but consider the security at Rutherford Castle. A mere affrim. No guards, no patrols. Everybody believes these systems are sufficient. No State has attacked another like this since the Northlands Wars."

"Study the blueprint, you Benclairans," Gaspare said, gathering himself for the journey to Talus. "The Domus in darkness will swallow you whole. I'll see you on the inside."

With that, he left. The room was quiet for a minute, nobody seeming willing to acknowledge that the plan, if they could call it that, was, for better or worse, now in motion.

"You lot, outside," Blair said eventually, pointing at Finneas, Oleander, Marcus, and Evie. "You need more practice with obscurities." She marched into the yard, trailed by the men and Greer.

Evie was moving to follow when Stin grabbed her arm. Before she could protest, he yanked her into a closet and slammed the door, causing dust and dead spiders to rain down. A misshapen orb of light hovered between their chests, casting a glow around Stin's face like he held a flashlight, about to recite a ghost story.

"What the hell?" Evie hissed, yanking her arm out of his grasp.

"Exactly!" Stin pointed a bony finger in her face. "Richard Lennon would have said the *same thing*."

45

LAST NIGHT, as Perdita walked the misty plains of the Somund, Death appeared alongside her. She knew he would.

"Perdita. Your time has come. Are you ready?"

She did not give her usual answer. She surprised him. "Yes. I am ready."

Death cocked his hooded head, grinning a wide, toothy grin. "At last, I can claim the final Perdito. I am honored."

"There is something I must do first, but at the day's end, I will go with you willingly."

"Oh, Perdita," Death cried, shaking his head. "I will not begrudge you this wish, as it is certain to be your last. But I warn you, do not retract your promise. I have acquiesced to you too many times."

Perdita gave Death a stern look. "You have not acquiesced. You have bargained. It is what you do. Do not forget, Acticus, I know you." She knew calling Death by his given name would irritate him. She also knew he could not argue.

For each year Death had allowed Perdita to live beyond fate's original stipulation, for each year she clung to life, waiting for Evangeline, Perdita had traded the name of another soul with frayed threads. And for every extra year those poor souls bargained for, they paid for it *tenfold by keeping Death company in his realm before being allowed to move onto what comes next — if they were allowed to move on at all. All told, Death felt much better in the company of those extra souls than he would have if Perdita had simply died when she was meant to, years ago.*

"One more day," Death said. "And then you will leave this realm. Even I cannot grant eternal life. Even I answer to somebody."

Perdita nodded. She knew. "One day more."

Smiling, Death vanished into the mist.

Perdita opened her eyes for the last time.

Next to Perdita's bed, slumped upon the chair he'd dozed off in the night before, was Charlie. He stirred, waking from a light, anxiety-addled slumber. He'd come to Perdita after leaving Evie in the library, but the old woman still would not wake. She was alive, breathing, but in a sleep so deep even the most rigorous shakes and loudest calls had no effect. And so, Charlie had waited.

He sat upright with a start — Perdita was awake now and staring straight at him. She smiled. "Charles. Evangeline's prince. How fortuitous you would be here. I must speak with you most urgently."

"And I, you," Charlie said, sitting forward. Perdita gave him an imploring look. He sank back. "Er, how can I help?"

She smiled and arranged the pillows around her for optimal comfort, as though she planned to remain in bed for a very long time, then beckoned Charlie to move closer. "There is something about you," she said as he pulled his chair nearer to the bed. "I wonder, do any members of your family have unusual abilities? A whisper of something beyond a typical magenu's Alicrat?"

"My sister, Serena, is an empath."

Perdita nodded. "I feel something similar from you."

"I'm not an empath."

"No, but you are unique. I cannot place it, but it is indeed a remarkable twist that you would be Evangeline's prince. I sensed it the moment you entered Finimund Cave. You have a great and insatiable curiosity.

Something tells me you have the ability to accept the gift I have for you. It is a burden, but you will value it."

She regarded him for a long moment, and then, "I have no children, Charles. I am the last Perdito. Everything — the origin story, Alterra Lingua, the prophecies — will die with me."

Charlie stood. "I'll get Evie."

"We do not need Evangeline."

"She's the Callidora heir! She may well become Arbiter when this madness is over."

"Precisely. The knowledge cannot reside only within her. It is too risky. It is why the Perditos and Callidoras have shared this burden through the ages. I had hoped to do my duty with Evangeline as I had with the others, but I haven't the time. She will learn the rest later. From you."

Charlie fell back into the chair.

"I am dying, Charles. By sundown, I will have moved on to what comes next. As I have no children, I have decided to gift my knowledge to you."

Charlie laughed nervously. "Perdita, you've overestimated me. Yes, I am curious, but I cannot possibly learn everything you know. Not by sundown. Not ever."

Perdita moved her hand slightly. Charlie took it. Her skin was like the tissue paper Professor Atkinson wrapped the Other World's Christmas and birthday gifts in, and he feared the pad of his thumb would rub it right off her bones.

"Minds are labyrinths, Charles," she said. "They take in so much over the course of a lifetime. Then there is the added weight of emotions, which require so much space! Important things are pushed aside, lost to the depths, never to be recalled again." She smiled. "My mind is different. I have lived a solitary life with a solitary purpose. As such, my mind is well organized. Everything is accessible, like that!" She snapped the fingers of her free hand. "You will have no problem finding all that you need."

Charlie understood exactly what Perdita was telling him, but he could not bring himself to believe it.

"I could spend all day reciting to you, and we would barely scratch the surface of what needs to be revealed. Or, you can enter my mind with your Alicrat and take what you need. The origins. The prophecies. Alterra Lingua. As I said, things are organized."

Charlie shook his head. "Delving into someone's mind requires an obscurity."

"Nonsense." Perdita waved her hand. "I have never understood the magenu's inability to differentiate between intentions when it comes to manipulations. There are no evil alicrations, only evil magenu. The so-called natural, legal alicrations you use in your everyday life could hurt another if wielded by a magenu intending to do so, no? Just as many manipulations labelled obscure could have positive uses."

"Yes," Charlie said, "but laws —"

"Were written by the Originals, who were created by the sisters, one of whom feared her progeny so much she spent an eternity trying to suppress their natural evolution. Charles, take it from someone who has witnessed centuries more than you. Manipulating energy for the greater good is *good*. It must be. Don't you agree?"

Charlie nodded, barely, trying to make sense of his own beliefs, which now seemed quite small when compared to a millennia of divine cause and effect.

"That's right," Perdita said, satisfied. "You will understand soon."

Charlie remained unconvinced.

Softening, Perdita said, "You are a gentle soul. Old energy, reborn a dozen times over. I see that. You're not the type to break, or even bend, the rules without a very real need to do so, are you?" She chuckled lightly. "Intent, Charles. That is what it comes down to you. You are not marauding my mind, for I am inviting you in. You shan't trod maliciously, for you are simply incapable."

"I don't even know how I would do this, Perdita."

"If you believe you can, you will. And just think of what you can do as keeper of this knowledge. Think of how you can protect and guide Evangeline. This is how you keep her safe."

And with those words, Charlie knew he would do it. The greater good was one thing. Evie's safety, her future, was quite another. Clever, Charlie thought, of Perdita. He didn't think his feelings were so obvious, but to an oracle, he supposed, nothing was invisible.

He released Perdita's hand and exhaled sharply, considering. He hadn't the slightest idea how to perform a mind manipulation. Perhaps someone could help him. Then again, who? Liam would scoff. Pembroke would refuse. Evie hadn't the experience, Marcus hadn't the patience. Oleander would suggest his mother. Finneas was probably adept, but Charlie was already realizing this wouldn't be a question of technical skill as much as intangible intuition.

To enter a mind safely, even through an open door, would require more goodness than Charlie could fathom. He would have to under-stand the subject but also his own self, lest he become lost in the depths of another psyche. He would need someone to guide and tether, who could help him find the door, but who could also ensure his return.

He ran to the window overlooking The Fern, located the target of his loquer, and shouted for his sister.

"Close the door, quickly," he said when Serena arrived. So caught up in everything was he that he did not notice the redness of his sister's eyes, the streaks of salt on her pale face.

Serena had far less difficulty with the notion of entering a mind than her brother. "I do not know how the Obscures do it," she said, "but sometimes, when I sense the emotions of another and they align with my current state, a doorway emerges through which I could step through, if I wanted to. I never do," she added hastily, "and the doorway disintegrates the moment I distract myself from it. But perhaps that is how to start, Charlie. Align your emotional vibrations. You cannot crossover — peacefully, at least, — if your frequencies are discordant."

Grasping the old woman's hands between his, Charlie focused on her energy. It pulsed weakly around her, the threads of her life thin and breaking before his eyes. Minutes passed. He dipped into a deeper alicra-tive state naturally and allowed himself to let go, trance-like. Serena grew fuzzy alongside him as Perdita sharpened.

Intermittent bursts of emotion from Perdita struck Charlie, pure in their brevity as they shuddered through him. Love. Hope. Trepidation. He could find each of those within himself, too, and easily. He thought of Evie, and love pulsed from him in waves, mingling with the threads of the same emotion from Perdita. When he imagined his loved ones returning from Maliter safely, his hope braided with Perdita's hope. He thought of what he might find in the hollow's mind, of the implications it would have for Evie's fate, and threads of trepidation spilled from him, looping themselves around Perdita's. The threads twined and grew, connecting Charlie to Perdita, but what came next?

"Visualize a door, Charlie." Serena sounded as though she was speaking to him from underwater. "Her mind is open and waiting."

Picturing a literal door, Charlie imagined Perdita swinging it open to welcome him in. His visualization danced into the emotional threads and together they deepened, strengthened. They crawled up and over each other like a climbing vine, building upon each other in this way until a door materialized, sturdy and solid as real wood.

"Go inside, Charlie," Serena said. "But do not forget where the door is. Do not forget how to return to yourself."

Charlie barely heard her. His eyes remained open, green and unblinking, but they did not see his sister, who regarded him intently, nor Perdita, whose own eyes were closed. They saw only the threshold of the door to the hollow's mind and, knowing it was the right thing to do — the only thing to do — he stepped inside.

46

"Verstin?" Evie whispered. "You saved my father's life."

"Did I?" He snorted. "Funny, he used to tell me I'd ruined it. He told you about me, then?"

"Not really, actually."

"That man wasn't forthright about anything. A liar knows a liar, and Richard Lennon lied with each breath. Was anything he said true? Was he from across the sea? Are you?"

"Yes," Evie said, stiffening. "Plem."

"Ha. You're worse than him. Don't want to tell me? I'm too old to care. I just need to know if you've told Blair."

Evie's brows furrowed, questioning.

"Don't give me that. You know what I'm talking about."

"I don't."

His eyes narrowed to slits. "Maybe you don't. Maybe he didn't share *that* with you. Better you don't know, then," he said, apparently deciding. "Better for Blair." He cracked the door open and tried to nudge Evie out.

She slammed it shut, keeping them inside. "I'm sick of secrets," she said. "Tell me what you're talking about."

Verstin sighed, looking resigned not because he'd thought it through, but because it was easier. "Curse the moon," he muttered. "Guess you have a right to know. Breathe a word of this to Blair and I swear I'll kill you myself. That girl has had enough darkness in her life."

"Fair enough," Evie said, certain she would never speak to Blair again after this was all over, anyway.

"I knew he was off from the start, Richard," Stin said. "One minute I'm staring at a field, waiting for some poor bastard to pass so I could relieve him of some pecs. The next, I'm watching someone stumble about, all kinds of dazed. Dressed real funny. I hit him with one of my virdisemp darts — bit of toxin on the end, knocks a person right out. Dragged him to my tent and waited for him to wake up. Turns out he was a bloody hollow. Acted like he'd never seen an alicration in his life! Thought he might be useful, though. Here's a real fool, I thought, a believable fool, for my cons. Before long, we were a productive team. He was a good enough mate at the brothels and pubs, too, or just to share a semp with."

Stin cracked the closet door open and peered outside. "Come on. I'm old. I need to sit."

In the main room, Stin lowered himself into an armchair. Evie took the other. "We conned, drank, and caroused our way through north Maliter, ending up in Talus," he said, grinning. "Those days were fun. We made good money for a while. But our marks were less gullible in Talus, and Richard started talking about leaving Maliter altogether. 'Gives me the creeps,' he used to say. That was the other thing about him — he sure talked strange, using words, mentioning places I'd never heard of. Anyway, 'One more day,' I'd tell him. 'One more con.'"

Through a window, Evie could see Blair and the others in the yard. Oleander focused hard on a small bird which, after a few seconds, managed to fly away. Blair rolled her eyes and glanced at the house, likely wondering where Evie was.

"What did my father do, Verstin?" she pushed.

"We'd had a good day," Verstin said. "Profitable. Had the pecs to spare in a pub. Wrong pub. We were grabbed by a couple of thugs the minute we walked in. They were circled around a girl, a prostitute, doing moon knows what to her. She was crumpled in a heap, bloody, barely moving. Well, they turned their alicrations on us, then. Broke my arm, after a couple attempts." He chuckled darkly. "The cult was still finessing, in those days. Anyway, I don't know what they did to Richard, but you'd have thought he was in the Osterre from the way he screamed."

"That's it?" Evie said. "That's what had him so terrified for the last twenty years?" She didn't question how horrifying the experience must have been, but surely, he could have divulged this information when she'd asked.

Verstin looked at Evie like she was stupid. He lowered his voice. "After the obscurity practice, one of them tells me to kill the girl. Kill or be killed, they said. Commonplace these days, but back then... Well, I tried. I'd dabbled in obscurities. Just curious, you know? But I couldn't do it in the end." He grew serious then, looking like he absolutely needed Evie to believe him. "I'm a lot of things, most of them pretty poor. But I'm not a killer, not like that. I figured I'd be struck dead, but instead —"

"They turned to my father," Evie whispered.

Nodding, Verstin rushed through the rest of the story as if he couldn't bear to keep it inside any longer. "Richard looked at her, looked at her like he *knew* her! She was young and pretty, had those blue eyes like Blair, and she looked back at him and I swear to the sun they knew each other. Swear I heard her whisper his name. She was a prostitute after all, and we'd frequented our fair share of establishments. Anyway, he tells the Obscures he can't kill her. That he's a hollow. Again, I thought we'd be offed."

Verstin peered out the window at Blair. "The things that stick with you, you know? The little details? Well, this boy, maybe twelve, maybe a little older, gets pushed forward from the horde. Soulless grey eyes, even at that age, has a knife in his hands. He gives it to Richard and he...he *smiles*."

Evie didn't need Verstin to tell her the rest, but he was leaning forward, on the very edge of the armchair. "'Don't do it, Richard!' I say. 'Let them kill us. We're degenerates — what do we have to live for?' And your father, he pauses, he thinks, then he says...no, he asks! He asks, 'Maybe there's something?' And he slashes her throat!" Verstin made a crude gesture to accompany this, then sat back, eyes wide, like he could scarcely believe it all these years later.

"Well, the Obscures, they beat us up anyway," he continued quietly. "In the midst of that, Richard ran off, the murdering coward. Left me to die with the girl. Last thing I remember before passing out was her last words. 'My daughter.'"

"Where was she?" Evie asked, glancing again at Blair through the window, seeing her entirely differently than she had a minute ago.

"Hiding in a cupboard beneath the bar, poor thing. Found her hours later. Raised her myself from then on." Verstin rose suddenly, one hand on his hunched back, and hobbled to stand before Evie. He pulled something out of his pocket and threw it on her lap. "Keepsake," he said. "Maybe you can give it back to Richard."

It was a knife — small, with an obsidian handle and a few spots of Blair's mother's blood, rusted over.

"I don't want this, Verstin."

"You think I did for the last twenty-odd years?' Verstin hunched further so that his face was level with Evie's and whispered, "You see him again, give that damned thing back. Let it haunt him from now on. That man deserves no peace."

Blair burst through the door then, trailed by the others, everyone frantic. Evie stood and shoved the knife in her pocket. Marcus made a beeline for her, settling behind her and draping both arms over her shoulders and chest.

"They're coming!" Blair said in a breath. "We spotted them over the fence. Four Obscures, heading this way. We need to go!"

Everyone began speaking at once, making suggestions as to how they should proceed. Verstin bellowed over the chaos. "They're not coming for you lot," he said. "Doubt they know you're here at all. They'll be coming for me. I've been on the run a few days now, haven't I?"

"Don't be ridiculous," Blair said, and started pulling people at random, Finneas' arm, Greer's shoulder. "We'll all leave!"

"If they're that close, they'll track our energy," Verstin said, thinking. "The cellar! We'll put a protective weave over our energies."

He ushered the group toward the cellar stairs and stood at the top, ensuring everyone made it down before following. At the back of the basement, they squeezed into an alcove, a tight, damp space that forced them to squash against each other uncomfortably. Verstin pushed himself in last. Facing the open area of the cellar, he began weaving their protection.

A *thud* sounded from above. Everyone froze, not daring to move, not daring to breathe. Footsteps followed — two, three, four pairs. Verstin resumed his alicrations, very slowly, the way a child might cautiously pad down a creaky hallway to avoid waking their parents.

Alert, Evie's Alicrat thrummed intensely. She was watching Stin's protective weave tighten over the alcove when she sensed it: an investigative energy coming from upstairs. It permeated the floorboards, coiled inquisitively, an alicrative audit on the hunt for a fugitive.

In the same instant, the Obscures upstairs seemed to sense Verstin's manipulations and the group's unmasked nerves. Muffled exclamations joined the footsteps, both growing louder and faster as their owners moved across the home.

Verstin spun around to face Blair. He nodded at her once, smiling, then blinked, pushing a single tear down his cheek. At this, Blair jolted, eyes wide. Oleander held her in place, clamping his hand over her mouth to mute the explosion of protestations that came next. Verstin stepped out of the alcove then, swiftly completed the protective alicration from the other side, and walked to the foot of the stairs.

"Down here!" he called.

More footsteps, then nothing.

Verstin tilted his chin toward his captors at the top of the stairs. Grinning, he opened his arms wide, just like the Obscure in the Silvana Seraphilles. Threads zipped down the stairs and his arms clamped to his sides. He toppled like a plank, his face striking the bottom step, breaking his nose. More threads, taut this time, reeled him up like a fish on a line. Stiff as a board, his body ascended the stairs until he was out of sight, leaving a trail of blood behind.

The entire time, Blair struggled, jostling the others despite the cramped space. Finneas turned to envelop the front of her, encasing her between himself and Oleander. It did little to muffle her yells, but Verstin's protective alicration ensured they were not only invisible, physically and energetically, but silent, too. Blair continued to thrash about after Verstin's body was gone, after the Obscures' footsteps sounded back across the floor. Only when Gaspare's home fell utterly silent did she still, spent.

Nobody spoke when, hours later, Greer untied Verstin's alicration. Nobody spoke as they mounted the horses outside. Nobody spoke as, under the cover of a starless night, they began their journey to Talus, one less soldier among their ranks.

47

IT WAS the most glorious library Charlie had ever seen, filled from the floor to the ceiling with books, every one of them illuminated by ornate orbs that were clustered together like chandeliers. Except there was no floor or ceiling, only an eternity in both directions, and Charlie floated in midair between the unending vertical shelves.

Pushing against a shelf, he sent himself gliding down an aisle of Perdita's mind, passing hundreds of books until, on instinct, he stopped. Grabbing the shelf's edge, he examined the tomes, their titles gleaming in silver cursive on the spines: *The Creation of The First Sfyre; The Magenu's Evil Deeds; The Sisters and the Rogue Mageno; The Originals; The Creation of the Second Sfyre; The Creation of the Underworld; The Deceit of the Aevum; Iluna's Punishment* —

"May I help you?" The voice was tiny, as was its owner, a child with two long, white braids. Dark brown eyes stared up at Charlie. "It's my mind, after all."

Relieved to have a guide in the form of this little Perdita, Charlie asked, "Are any of these your memories?"

"Not many. You'd think I would have plenty, but I didn't do very exciting things. Mostly, this is information. Stories. Facts. There might be some memories, somewhere." She gave him a stern look. "Don't take those. Only take what you need."

"And how do I do that, exactly?"

"You just take it."

Charlie reached for *The Creation of the First Sfyre*. The book felt solid as he pulled it from the shelf, but as soon as it left its position, it disintegrated into a single thread.

"That's for you," Perdita said.

Charlie looked down the aisle at the thousands of books. "Can you help me gather the most important information? There's so much. This will take forever."

Little Perdita pulled a book off the shelf. It remained a real, solid book in her hands. "I suppose I cannot." An orb flickered somewhere nearby. "You don't have forever. I'm dying."

Charlie set about pulling the origin stories from the shelf, leaving their threads hovering to collect on his way back. He pulled and pulled as he made his way down the aisle, grabbing at other titles which, though unrelated to the origins, intrigued him: *Secret Lovers of Isabil Callidora; Clement Callidora's Worst Fear; Christian and Judas; The Door that the Connects the Worlds; Visiting the Aevum.*

Charlie flung books off the shelves and doubled back to gather the threads they left, over and over, again and again. He shoved the threads into his pocket, which had become bottomless and did not fill no matter how much information he stuffed inside. When he was finally satisfied he'd collected all of the origin books and more, he followed little Perdita into another aisle, filled with thousands of identical Tree Books.

"The prophecies. Every single one, memorized." She grinned proudly and watched Charlie repeat the same process with the Tree Books, each individual prophecy its own golden thread.

"Alterra Lingua, now," Charlie said, pocketing the last prophecy.

Perdita's face darkened. She stomped her foot upon the air. "I hate Alterra Lingua. Father made me stay inside all day to study while the other children played! I'll take you there, but I *won't* read anything."

She pulled Charlie down more corridors of books and through a narrow passage containing impossibly high stacks of papers. They slipped between the teetering piles, all seemingly on the verge of, but never quite, toppling. Down another corridor, they passed a thick, wooden door into which a small window was cut near the top. Pausing, Charlie looked inside.

The door concealed a tiny, concrete room. A sliver of light passing through the window brightened a solitary book on the floor. The title read, simply, heartbreakingly, *Brimms*.

"What are you doing?" Perdita stood behind Charlie, arms crossed. "That has nothing to do with Alterra Lingua." She grabbed his sleeve and pulled him along.

His heart fell when he saw the new aisle. It seemed to carry on for miles, shelf after shelf filled with Alterra Lingua. He pulled books, collected threads, faster than before, hundreds down, an eternity remaining.

As he worked, the pressure of Serena's hand upon his own registered somewhere deep in his mind, like a nudge from one's subconscious to wake in the midst of a nightmare. Worried he was in too far, he moved even faster, anxiety knotting his stomach as he envisioned the doorway back to himself slammed shut by death.

"Done," he said, shoving the final Alterra Lingua thread into his pocket. "Is that everything?"

Perdita twirled her braid, considering. "Well, you have the origins, the prophecies, Alterra Lingua... Oh!" Her face brightened. "You'll want a bit of Northlands history. Just for curiosity's sake. You are curious, aren't you?"

She took his arm and pulled him down, down, endlessly down. They passed more books and fluttering pages and a collection of paintings depicting nine spheres hovering in a misty ether. Down and down they went, into what felt to Charlie like a basement, a portion of Perdita's mind she did not often visit. It was colder, dustier, more eerie than the rest of the beautiful library. Some of the shelves were empty, many were rotted. They continued further, now past stretches with no shelves at all, only door after door, old and thick like the one that locked in the memory of Brimms. All the while, Serena's voice stretched toward Charlie like sap dripping down a tree, drawn out and heavy, imploring him to return.

"Why would Northlands history be all the way down here?" Charlie asked Perdita, glancing back up.

"It just is. It's in there." She pointed to an old door, the only one in the row cracked ajar. "Go on. I'll wait here."

The knot in Charlie's stomach tightened as he regarded the child. Her face was round and youthful, eager to please and containing some level of naive wonderment. Yet there was an older quality to it too, as if the loneliness of the old Perdita's life had funneled into this small emanation of herself. A friendless childhood. A loveless life. Her last decades spent in self-decreed exile in a cave, voices from the winds of the Other World her only company. Little Perdita's eyes held something unbecoming behind their dark brown irises, something that Charlie did not like at all.

He backed away. "Take me up."

Perdita opened her mouth to protest but was thwarted by her own mind. The walls shook, the air heaved. Charlie careened into a shelf and the few books it held fell into the abyss. The *thump* of a landing never came.

"What's happening?"

"I told you. I'm dying. Oh, won't you stay?" Perdita cried. "Life was so very lonely. I fear death shall be worse."

Charlie pushed against the shelf and propelled himself up the way they'd come, but Perdita grabbed hold of his foot, trying to yank him back.

"Please! Please stay!" She grasped at him desperately, eyes wild. Charlie shook her off. At the same time, the air trembled again, swinging the door open, revealing an empty room into which Perdita tumbled. Before she could right herself, the door slammed shut.

Charlie forced himself upward. Where was his door?

He made it back to the towers of paper, which were now collapsing. Torrents of pages struck him as he waved his arms to slash a path through, catching glimpses of their contents: *Five loaves to Hansons; 25 to Callidora Castle; Flour delivery on the 42nd; Order more candles.* They were little reminders, millions of them made and filed away over a lifetime.

The library continued to quake. The orbs flickered and dimmed.

Charlie groped along shelves, accidentally pulling books off as he felt his way down the aisles. He collected their ensuing threads with no idea what they contained, desperate both to escape and to leave nothing of value behind.

Around the next corner, there it was. He sped toward the door as orbs shattered like glass and shelves crumbled like sandcastles. Books fell into eternity, striking him along the way. He dodged his way to the door just as the last orb blinked out.

"Charles." It was Perdita's voice, the old Perdita, but Charlie couldn't see her anywhere. "The knowledge is yours now. Keep Evangeline on her path."

Charlie threw himself over the threshold of the door.

Perdita took stock of her mind. The boy had done well. The weaver knowledge that had left the Aevum with the ancient Perdita was gone. The origin stories were gone. The prophecies were gone. She recalled that these things existed, once, but could recall no more. Snippets of her life remained, memories that hadn't the room to come forth for decades. She smiled, recalling her joys, reliving her triumphs.

Next to her bed sat the prince, safe, with his sister. The pair grew fuzzy and bright, then disappeared altogether, overtaken by a soft, white light. A figure emerged from the light; an old man, far more wrinkled than when she had seen him last.

"Perdita," he said. "I have been waiting for you. All my life, and after."

"Do I go now?" Perdita asked. "To what comes next?"

Brimms nodded and took her hand. "We will go together."

48

AT THE SIDE of the bed, Charlie held Serena's hand, with her, but not, as Perdita's knowledge bored into his psyche with persistent force. Each thread imparted a flurry of information, transforming previously blank corners of his mind into chapters of a story spanning infinity, incredible and incomprehensible. Initially, at least. As soon as the final thread wove itself amongst the others, Charlie felt he'd known these things all his life.

He stood with purpose. "Where is Evie?"

"They've gone, Charlie," Serena said, fighting tears. "They left early this morning."

Charlie's disbelief was genuine. "How could they? The border is patrolled. No, it can't be. I must find Evie." He ran from the room, ignoring Serena's protestations and Perdita's lifeless body.

At Evie's room, he forced the door open with an alicration. The room was empty. The library upstairs, too. He made to leave, but something caught his eye. Flung over Evie's bed in a rushed, careless way was his old blue sweater, one that Marcus had borrowed years ago and never returned.

He stopped in his tracks, one singular thought overtaking the thousands imparted by Perdita's knowledge. A second passed, two, three, during which Charlie felt the lance of betrayal deeply, and then he left.

He ran in the opposite direction, to Liam's study, and alicrated his way in there, too, not bothering to knock.

"Where are they?"

Liam was gazing out at The Fern, hands clasped behind his back. He turned, quickly suppressing his surprise. "They left before dawn. Are you just noticing now?"

"How did they get past the border?"

"What difference does that make?"

"I'm going after them."

Liam stared at him for a beat, then shook his head, incredulous. "You're going to Maliter? Just what do you think you can do there?"

"I'm going to stop them."

"You're going to stop them?" The mocking tone was slight, not obvious to others, but Charlie was attuned to it, and it cut in a way that only a knife wielded by family could. "Charles, you've done your part by finding the old woman. Let Marcus handle the rest."

Marcus.

Rage, monumental and personal, overtook a lifetime of deference to his father. Charlie grasped the neck of Liam's shirt and twisted the fabric around the muscles of his throat. Liam sputtered and grunted, his face reddening, but managed to get his hands to Charlie's shoulders to shove him away. Charlie pushed back and at the same moment the study door opened again, distracting Liam and causing him to release his footing. Charlie's force gained traction and he fell forward. The backs of Liam's knees hit the wall, but his upper body struck the glass of the window he was so fond of gazing out of.

The pane broke. Liam, bent at the waist, pitched backward with only his son's hands preventing him from falling out of the window completely. Juliette ran to them, pulled at Charlie's shoulders, begged him to step back, but her cries went unheard. Charlie hovered over his father, green eyes staring into green eyes, neither man betraying any emotion but anger.

"Charlie, please..." Juliette's touch was no longer frantic, but soft as she tugged on his shoulders. He took a few steps back, pulling his father up. Liam grasped at the edges of the broken glass, cutting his hands, and hoisted himself the rest of the way upright.

"What in the name of the sun?" Juliette whispered, looking between husband and son.

"Perdita is dead," Charlie said flatly. He spoke to his mother, not his father. "She allowed me inside her mind before she died to pass on her knowledge. I haven't the time to explain, but they are in danger, Mother. Evie, Marcus, all of them." He turned to his father. "Tell me how they got into Maliter."

Liam touched his throat with a bloodied hand. Charlie thought for a moment he would admit *something* — that he'd misjudged his son, that he'd acted rashly. But Liam Rutherford merely resumed his gruff authority, the Arbiter version of himself that did not require self-examination.

"Prophecy or no prophecy, the ambush will succeed," he said. "I cannot allow —"

"There's a tunnel," Juliette said. Both men turned to her in surprise. "In south Callidora."

Liam tried to quiet his wife, but Juliette's hands whipped up and he stumbled backward again, pushed by the abrupt force of her emotional Alicrat. "No, Liam," she said. "Our children are in danger. What do you expect me to do?"

"They answer to me," Liam said. "I am their Arbiter."

"I am their mother." Squaring her shoulders, Juliette faced Charlie. "They partumed to south Callidora. There's a tunnel to the obsidian quarries outside Talus. They will enter the Domus late tonight. If you think you can stop them, *go*."

Charlie's heart fell. He wouldn't be able to partume to the tunnel in south Callidora. He had no idea where it was, and to turn up in the general region, wandering blindly to find the entrance, would be a fool's errand. Nor would he be able to take a unicorn across the border, given the patrols. He glanced out the broken window at the starry Benclair sky, then lower, where a dim, reddish glow emanated from a window of the stables.

He hugged his mother, nodded curtly at his father, and left the study, ignoring the curses Liam yelled after him. That, Charlie thought, was how it must be. With relief, he released a lifetime of emotions that did not serve him to the basement of his mind. He needed the space for more important information, anyway.

Having understood that Brimms was dead, the firebirds had remained in the Rutherford stables. Nestled together, they raised their heads in unison as Charlie approached, then rose and bowed before he could even voice his request. He climbed onto the same bird he'd ridden from Callidora, and, with the other three in tow, set off to Maliter. As long as the defenses along the border did not extend as high as the birds could fly, he would be able to enter Maliter undetected. And as long as he could reach the Domus, he would be able to figure out the rest. He only hoped he wouldn't be too late.

49

BLAIR FELT NOTHING.

She'd left her emotions — emotions she'd not known herself to be capable of feeling — in that cramped cellar alcove. Maybe Finneas and Oleander had absorbed them. Maybe they were just gone. Regardless, she was empty.

Talus was empty, too. There were no changelings experimenting with disguises, no Obscures tormenting children, no Norms hurrying home, cloaks drawn tightly as if that offered any protection. There was nobody at all to watch the small assemblage of rebels pass, helmed by the otherworldly girl who would save them all, whose purpose was written in the stars.

There were no stars in Maliter's sky, though. Could a prophecy be fulfilled if the heavens were not present to bear witness?

The Domus loomed ahead, its black edges melting into its black surroundings. At the gates, it became immediately clear that Gaspare had been successful. There was no thrum of energy, no tickle of threads reaching out to determine anyone's loyalty. Still, once off their horses, standing before the wrought iron, everyone stayed entirely still, barely willing to breathe. Minutes passed. The surroundings of the Domus remained as deserted as the Talus streets.

Blair pushed against the gate with a single, tentative finger. It gave way.

One by one, they slipped through and treaded lightly up the path to the Domus entrance. At the doors, each alicrated a small orb of light, dreadfully dim from being pulled through the blanket of clouds. Evie's orb was small and patchy. She wrinkled her nose at it, embarrassed, childlike. Blair imagined a crowd of Maliteran Norms standing behind them, cheering them on.

Ladies and gentlemen, she thought wryly, *your savior.*

Inside, the orbs lit only scant meters before them. They moved slowly, as one, to the center of the Atrium, until Finneas held out a hand, halting them. Something was wrong. Everyone tensed, feeling it, and not just with Alicrat. Blair's most basic human instincts screamed that something was amiss.

A shadow flitted across the west wall — the direction they needed to go. There was another. Another. Movement, all around them, impossible to pin down, impossible to escape. They lobbed their orbs to widen the perimeter of light, but they were snuffed out one by one.

Blair's heart beat with such ferocity she was certain the shadows could hear it. Greer's breath was jagged beside her. Evie, Oleander, and Marcus radiated nerves. Only Finneas felt stable, which steadied Blair somewhat. She focused her Alicrat, trying to sense whoever was out there. There were five people, she realized, but she could neither identify them nor detect their intentions.

"You've never liked the dark, have you?" a voice called. "Always rushing through here after nightfall..."

The clouds broke and the moon made a rare appearance, its pale light shining through the Atrium's glass ceiling. Damien stood halfway across the Atrium, grinning next to a bloodied Gaspare, whose hands and feet were bound by an alicration.

"What have you done to him?" Greer cried, bolting forward. A swipe of Damien's hand sent her careening back into Oleander, who managed to remain upright.

"Only what he deserved," Damien said. "What you all deserve."

Through clenched teeth, Blair said, "How did you know?"

Damien looked as though he did not understand the need for the question. "Have you forgotten with whom you've spent the last many months? Adrian knows you." He chuckled lightly. "We've been here, every night since you cowered off, awaiting your return. Because he *knew* you'd return, Blair. And Maior Hayworth!" He cocked his head. "Interesting. I wouldn't have expected you. And you, there — aren't you a Rutherford?"

Blair dug her heel into Marcus' foot before he could respond.

"So, you ran to Benclair for help!" Damien sounded genuinely impressed. "It seems you've been busier than we realized, Blair. Though I must say, this is a disappointing show from the great Liam Rutherford. Of course, I've always thought him a bit of a coward."

"My father is not a coward!" Marcus roared before Blair could stop him.

Damien considered Marcus, looking thoughtful. "Perhaps you're right. Perhaps this is actually quite clever of him, sending a private cohort to do his dirty work rather than stage an all-out attack. That would have been preferable, you see. We would have crushed a Benclairan army. Easily. And with Benclair as an example, the other States would fall in line." He frowned. "I could kill you all right now and I suspect nobody outside these walls would hear of it. Clever indeed, Liam."

As Damien spoke, Gaspare collapsed, clearly having endured an alicrative beating before the group's arrival. Greer ran to him again and this time, Damien allowed it. He stalked around their position on the floor, smiling with sick pleasure as she tended to the wounded Gaspare.

The clouds remained parted during all of this, and Blair's eyes had adjusted in the moonlight. Four other magenu were just visible in the corners of the Atrium, awaiting further instructions from Damien. She glanced at Finneas, catching his eye. He nodded at her, almost imperceptibly.

"I'm sure he hasn't got long," Damien was saying. He was crouched next to Greer now, watching her comfort Gaspare, his back to the group. "He refused to talk, see. We did our best, of course, but he's stronger than he looks." He sighed, poking Gaspare.

Seizing the opportunity, Blair leapt away from the cluster and physically tackled Damien. They slid across the floor, but Blair maintained the upper hand, managing to bind his hands and feet with an alicration.

Pandemonium broke as the others lashed out. Marcus, having stepped in front of Evie, sent an arrow sailing across the Atrium, striking a magena in the chest. Finneas slashed a mageno with the same cutting obscurity that had injured Marcus in the seraphilles. Oleander was focused on the third Obscure and seemed to be trying to break the man's arms, but faltered, achieving only a roughly dislocated shoulder. Greer and Evie went for the last, but neither were focused enough to find any of the Obscure's threads before he hid, much less contort them.

They were weak attempts, the types of things teenagers would try on each other in the streets of Talus, and each Obscure recovered quickly to return the attacks. Confusion and warnings filled the Atrium. Blair ignored it all as she sprinted toward the stairs to the West Wing. She would find Adrian before she was found. She would kill him before she was killed.

Searing pain stopped her in her tracks. An incessant ringing filled her ears, shrill and painful. Her eardrums throbbed until she was certain they would tear apart; no sooner had she thought it than her left ear erupted with a stab. She spun around to find her attacker, but her balance was off. Stumbling as the Atrium whirled around her, she fixed her Alicrat on herself and sensed out the foreign threads. The unrelenting noise in her skull was from an Obscure's shriek, loquered directly into her ears and manipulated to lodge there. She pulled the threads out and the pain reduced to a dull ache.

Oleander came rushing to her side. "You okay?" he asked. His left arm hung limply at his side, having been yanked from its socket in retaliation by the Obscure he'd attacked. "Marcus got him," he said, glancing at his shoulder.

On cue, Marcus cried out. A magena with red hair and an arrow protruding from her chest manipulated something within him; Blair recognized the contortion of a body trying in vain to relieve pain being inflicted from the inside. She located the magena's heartstrings with the intention of crushing them, but there was no need. Evie was focused on the woman, her eyes narrowed in concentration, her hands tracing threads through the air.

"Do it, Evie!" Blair urged, but as quickly as Evie had started her attempted obscurity, she stopped. Disgust clouded her face and she dropped her hands.

The magena regained her composure, whirled around, and squeezed something invisible with both hands. Blair's chest seized up, overcome with a terrible tightness. Evie, too, gasped for air and doubled over, clutching herself. They grasped at each other as their lungs constricted, desperate for contact in what suddenly seemed to be their last moments.

A *whoosh* of air relieved them. The magena stood motionless, then fell forward. When she struck the floor, the arrow in her chest drove through her back where two more protruded, having been shoved in manually by Marcus and Oleander.

Before Blair could assess anything, a gargled cry rang from the farthest corner of the Atrium. There, Greer writhed under the ministrations of the last Obscure. Blair wove an attack as she ran, trailed by the others. Marcus' attempted obscurity hit first, and a ripple of threads struck the Obscure in the back, sending his body into convulsions. Oleander was poised to strike next. He mumbled to himself as he parsed through the endless threads of a human body, squinting in concentration.

"I don't know what I'm doing!" he cried. "What do I do?"

The mageno staggered as Marcus' manipulation faltered and he squared himself again, sneering.

"Anything!" Marcus yelled, trying to regain control of his own Alicrat.

Oleander's hands moved in a practiced route through the air. The Obscure slowed, his limbs stiff and growing stiffer. He appeared annoyed, as if he knew what was happening, and then resigned, as if he knew he could not stop it. He then ceased moving completely, frozen in an uncanny stance with his torso raised three-quarters and his left arm extended. His skin changed color, mottling from a sickly blue pallor into a sparkling white that overtook him like frost creeping across a meadow.

Blair pushed past the others — who looked frozen themselves, horrified — to Greer. She lay prone on the floor, also unmoving, her body sunken and drained of blood, entirely pale save for her bloody face. Her mouth hung slightly ajar, filled to her lips with pooled blood.

"I'm sorry, Blair." Evie was at her side. She was out of breath, covered in blood — from herself, from Marcus, from an Obscure, Blair didn't know. The blood that pooled around Greer's body, the blood the Obscure had pulled from every orifice of her face, soaked into whoever's blood was on Evie's pants.

Blair lowered Greer's eyelids, then stood. "Let's not forget why we came here," she said.

"Wait," Evie said, also rising. She glanced at the frozen Obscure. "He won't...thaw out, will he?" Blair strode to the Obscure, raised a leg in line with his torso, and kicked him over. He hit the floor with a crystalline *ding* that broke his head cleanly off at the neck. It skittered across the floor, hitting Damien, still wriggling on the floor, in the face.

"He's next," Blair said, and marched to Damien's position. She stamped down on his nose with a satisfying *crack*, then reared back, readying an obscurity.

Marcus grabbed her shoulder. "We can use him. Gaspare is right. We started a war tonight. We need to think like we're in one."

"He'll find a way to kill himself before revealing anything."

"We keep him. For now."

Blair nodded reluctantly, dropping her arms. "Fine. Let's go."

"There's still an Obscure somewhere," Marcus pointed out quietly. Finneas, having realized this, was already walking a wide perimeter around the group, scanning the Atrium.

His cry was sudden and urgent. "Oleander! *Down!*"

But Oleander did not get down, not in time, and so Finneas, who had glimpsed the remaining Obscure with a second to spare, leapt before his friend and took the obscurity.

The next things played out in slow motion for Blair.

For an indeterminate moment, the only sounds she heard were her beating heart and her exhalations of breath, both thunderous in her ears. The only things she saw were Evie, Marcus, and Oleander sprinting to their friend and the last Obscure, a slight man with greasy hair and bloody gashes, slipping into the shadows. Her consideration of whether to follow him or the others lasted an eternity as both parties moved in opposite directions. By the time she decided what to do, the Benclairans were at Finneas' side and the Obscure was gone.

Blair had seen many terrible things in Maliter, so many that if some-body asked her what the worst event she'd witnessed was, she would not have been able to answer. They blurred into a series of horrendous occurrences, one indistinguishable from the next, and if given the opportunity to erase one from her memory, she would not know which to single out and destroy.

She considered this as she sprinted to the others.

Oleander and Marcus flanked Finneas. Evie knelt before him, hands clasped around his. He was standing upright and for a moment, Blair believed he was all right. Alive. Still breathing. He was alive, but he was not breathing, for breathing would kill him.

The cruelty lay in its simplicity. The manipulation was not unnat-ural, it was not obscure. It was something used every day, learned by children in their First Libellum. Finneas had shielded Oleander from an aquenum alicration and an orb of water now encased his head. Air bubbles escaped from his nose as he exhaled slowly, fighting the urge to inhale. The look in his eyes startled Blair who, in the brief time she'd known Finneas, had deemed him unshakable. She saw fear, and worse, acceptance.

"It won't obey us," Marcus said. "The threads won't budge." He gestured as if to prove this, moving his hands in a way that normally, an aquenum orb would yield to. The water stayed put, not even a ripple on its surface. He punched the orb with his fist, but it didn't collide. Some-thing invisible surrounded the water, protecting it.

Blair could sense that invisible something but could not discern what it was. All she understood was that it was not only intricate, but resolute. It was as if the Obscure had convinced the threads to obey him and him alone. Impossible, Blair knew, and yet, this seemed to be the case.

Evie pushed her away to stand closer to Finneas. Flanked by Marcus and Oleander, she held his hands to her heaving chest as she cried for Finneas, for Serena, and for their children. Blair fell back obediently, feeling very strongly, very suddenly, that it was not her right to mourn with them, that she had not yet earned her place among their ranks.

She watched them cry for their friend from afar, felt their heart-strings twine with Finneas' to assure him, in his last moments, that he was loved. She watched him smile at his friends, and then she looked away and broke off her Alicrat. She could not watch him take that deadly breath, could not bear to sense his lungs seizing up as they filled with water. She could not add Finneas' kind face to the list of faces she had witnessed bearing pain throughout her life in Maliter.

She looked to Evie and Marcus and Oleander instead and watched a different kind of pain overtake them. It was the pain of loss, it was visceral, and it was, finally, too much. Blair knew then, that of all the things she had seen in Maliter, the faces of Finneas' friends as his body went limp in their arms was the one thing she would choose to erase, if given the chance.

50

EVIE PUSHED, pushed, pushed, then placed her ear against Finneas' chest. Again. His ribcage was rigid. She knew she wasn't strong enough. Still, she pushed. Marcus gripped her shoulders, trying to ease her away. She pulled him closer. He took over the chest compressions, bewildered but pushing repeatedly nonetheless, and Evie tried to breathe life back into Finneas.

Only minutes before, when it was clear Finneas had passed, Marcus and Oleander had lowered him gingerly to the ground until he lay prone. Almost immediately, the orb encasing his head had collapsed, as if it knew it was no longer needed. They'd started alicrations then, fast and urgent, pulling water directly out of Finneas' lungs. Evie had expected him to jolt awake with a sudden inhale, just as people did in the movies. When he didn't, she'd nudged Marcus and Oleander aside to start the compressions, much to everyone's confusion.

Another set of hands found her shoulders as she pushed.

"There's no life left," Blair whispered. "It's no use, Evie. He's gone."

She was right. Finneas was dead, had been dead, for minutes now. Evie slowed, then stopped.

Oleander let out a sob, muffled as he buried his face in Evie's shoulder. Marcus just sat there, silent tears streaming down his cheeks. He took Evie's hand, squeezing it so hard she thought it would break.

"I'm sorry," Blair repeated, as if it were her fault. To Evie's astonishment, she wiped away tears of her own. She watched the others for a while, seemingly allowing them a moment to mourn, before saying, "We must move on. It can't..." She looked at Finneas, then across the Atrium to Greer and Gaspare, then to a staircase at the west end of the Atrium. "It can't be for nothing."

"We can't leave him alone," Oleander said, voice trembling. "I'll stay. You three go on."

No one argued.

Evie rose slowly, not taking her eyes off Finneas' lifeless body. His death was incomprehensible, a twisted fragment of an alternate reality that seemed to have infiltrated her own. She continued to stare, willing a living Finneas to replace the rigid, drenched imposter on the ground.

"Let's go." Marcus' voice, scarcely a whisper, trembled, but his eyes, red-rimmed and wet, were resolute. "Put it aside," he said. "For now."

Breaking her stare, Evie followed Blair and Marcus out of the Atrium.

The stairs they climbed opened into a hallway thick with darkness. The orbs they'd brought from the Atrium's moonlight did little to light the way, but Blair moved down corridors and around corners with confidence. They heard nothing but their own footsteps on the obsidian, saw nothing but the black outlines of each other, until Blair held up a hand, indicating for Evie and Marcus to stop.

"This opens to another hallway," she whispered, hand upon a door. "At the end of the hall is Adrian's office." Marcus moved to open the door, but Blair stopped him. "Not you."

He dropped his arm, incredulous. "You're joking. I'm going where Evie goes."

"Not there," she hissed. "Someone has to keep watch for that last Obscure. You'd only be a distraction in there, anyway." Evie started to protest. Blair cut her off. "Can you really promise that if Marcus was being tortured you wouldn't surrender to Adrian to make it stop?"

Evie couldn't answer. She didn't know.

"By that logic, you shouldn't go in, either," Marcus said to Blair, ignoring Evie's inability to proclaim that she would save him.

"Evie would let me die." She stated it like a fact. "I'd expect her to. Besides, I know Adrian. I need to be in there."

"She's right, Marcus," Evie said softly. "He would use us against each other. We're weaker together."

Marcus stared at her for a long time, not bothering to hide the emotions that flashed across his face: loyalty to Liam and the need to ensure Evie's success; feelings for Evie and the desire to keep her safe; some level of fealty to Charlie, too. None of those things were strong enough against Blair's cold logic, Evie knew. She watched the same realization dawn on Marcus.

He pulled her into an embrace, his arms like an entire house around her, and she considered for a moment how ridiculous it would be to leave them for the alternative that awaited her behind the door. It would be much easier, she thought, to stay small beneath his strength, high on that fog of possibility, chasing lightning. He wasn't Charlie, but he satisfied something else in her. If she tried, she could almost convince herself it was enough.

Neither of them were willing to face reality until Blair wrenched them apart. Turning to her, voice tinged with desperation, Marcus said, "Make sure she comes back."

Something danced over Blair's eyes — a sort of sadness, Evie thought, perhaps because there was nobody trying to make sure *she* came back. She placed a hand on Marcus' forearm. "I'll try, Rutherford."

Evie gave Marcus' hand a final squeeze and dropped it, with it, the impossible alternate reality. With that, she followed Blair through the door and into the blackest throes of the night.

The door shut behind them. Neither of them moved.

"I'm afraid of the dark," Blair said, so quietly, Evie wasn't sure she'd heard the confession. Their hands found each other's instinctually in the pitch black and they started down the hall, Blair counting steps under her breath.

Evie counted, too.

Three. The number of people who had died for her tonight.

Two. The number of Rutherford brothers she'd grown to love.

One. The number of chances she would have to kill Adrian.

Zero. The amount of time left to reconsider her choices.

"What if he's not here?" Evie whispered, paused before the office door. "They knew we were coming. Why would he be up here, waiting for us?"

The door swung open.

51

ADRIAN TENEBRIS' power hit Evie like an obscurity. In the same instant, he smiled, looking almost friendly. "Come inside, won't you?"

Before Evie could begin to fathom the range of threads that built him, let alone find the ones she needed to end his life, she and Blair were yanked into the office. Adrian shoved Blair to the ground and flung Evie to the back of the room. Pain coursed across her skull as her head connected with a stone shelf. She gingerly touched the nape of her neck. Her hand came back with blood, but it couldn't be hers. She was supposed to be protected.

Blair rose shakily. Adrian watched her struggle for a sadistic moment, then began manipulating her with a single hand. Her arms shot out parallel to the ground, so taut it seemed another centimeter would pull them from their sockets, and her legs clamped together, rendering her like Jesus on an invisible cross. He continued his alicration until she finally screamed — a horrifying sound, coming from her.

Dropping his hand, he said, calmly, "Finally. I just wanted to make you hurt a little. After all, you have caused me so much pain, Blair. You might assume I am referring to logistical headaches, what with dispatching Obscures to search for you and fretting over how many secrets you ferried away. Mere administrative duties." He turned incredulous. "No, no. You *hurt* me, Blair. I shared things with you. You, a cleaner, common Talus scum." He spat at her feet, then whirled around to address Evie. "Now, it's not that she left me, mind you. It's that she fooled me. She bested me!"

He reared back and landed a punch across Blair's face. Her cheek smarted and her eyes swam with pain, but she bore no evidence of fear. She stared back at Adrian as blood dripped from her lip, unable to wipe it away, and blinked placidly. This enraged him further and he struck again, then landed a third blow in the pit of her stomach. Clenching her jaw, she continued to stare.

"Never mind." Adrian scoffed, disappointed in her lack of reaction. "I'll deal with you later."

A mangled sound escaped Blair's lips, weak and garbled with blood, but its tone was defiant. Adrian performed one more manipulation and her mouth clenched shut.

Steadying herself against a slab of obsidian, Evie rose. Her head throbbed, the room spun, black dots pulsed in and out of her vision. She could barely stand, let alone tap into the energies of the world, and Adrian was walking toward her. He stopped on the other side of the obsidian desk, facing her, arms crossed.

"And who are you?" He looked her up and down. "Unremarkable. Not unattractive, if you squint. Covered in blood, but not all your own. I've always found that to be the mark of a fighter or a coward. Which are you?"

"Neither," Evie managed.

"Then what are you doing breaking into the Domus? Cowering past my Obscures? Traipsing into my office? Who are you?"

"Evie."

She held her breath, unsure if Grilt or Sillen had discerned who she was in Callidora Castle. If that were true, surely, they would have told Adrian. Yet Adrian did not react. He only asked again, unconcerned, "What are you doing here?"

"I've come to kill you."

He let out a derisive laugh. "Praise the moon! Damien wasn't being dramatic, then. Blair, I expected. But an *assassin*?" He paused, considering Evie. "And you, of all people? Why, you've had a dozen opportunities to kill me and you've merely stood there, wavering on the spot."

As Adrian spoke, Evie's eyes landed on something. A book lay on the slab of obsidian, open to a page displaying Alterra Lingua and a crudely drawn seraphille. It was impossible, unbelievable, and yet, the Voynich Manuscript was not locked away in the Beinecke Library. It lay on Adrian Tenebris' desk in a parallel world.

The black dots retreated from Evie's vision. The thudding in her skull diminished. The world righted around her and the energy of Adrian's office came into focus, thread by thread, starting with the Voynich Manuscript.

The ancient Perdita still lingered in the book's weave after so many years. Evie saw her in her mind's eye, hunched over a desk in Callidora Castle as the story of creation poured out of her. Then there was Christian Callidora, throwing the book across the Arbiter's office in frustration, though Evie could not discern why. Isabil, then, laughing flirtatiously in the archives, smiling at a man. That same man, pulling the book from the shelf, and the flash of an Italian landscape as a portal took him home. Next came centuries of intrigue as the Other World's academics pondered its mysteries, then the Beinecke Library, a black thread for each year the Voynich Manuscript had spent there. Finally, inexplicably, vestiges of Adrian's excitement as he located the book in the Other World, his elation as he lifted the cover, believing he'd found the book of prophecies his ancestors had sought for so long.

All of it — the respect, the curiosity, the frustration, the hatred, the selfishness across thousands of years — imbued Evie. She straightened up a fraction, enough to face Adrian, not enough to let him know she'd found her strength. Quietly, she asked, "What happened to Adena Callidora?"

Adrian's energy shifted palpably. "What does that matter to you?"

She met his eyes. Something more than Alicrat thrummed in her veins, compelling her, directing the scene. Fate? Delusion? It didn't matter now.

"I'm Evangeline Callidora," she said. "Her daughter."

Shock radiated from Adrian in peals, followed by disbelief, anger. The latter was just a blip, the punctuation on a flurry of emotions he quickly suppressed. Eyes narrowing, he regained control. "Well," he said quietly. "You look a bit like her. A poor man's version, at least. I should have known. But then, how could I have? Nobody knew she had a child." His voice deepened. "What are you doing here, Evangeline Callidora?"

"I told you. I'm going to kill you." The same words that had prompted laughter a moment ago appeared to hit differently.

Inhaling sharply, Adrian pushed his lips into a thin line. "Impossible." He shook his head, muttering to himself. "Impossible! Clement did me the favor of dying. Naveena's eagerness to betray her family made her an asset. That left Adena." He glared at Evie. "I was told a Callidora would be my downfall. End Adena, and I would end the great Callidora lineage."

"And yet a Callidora stands before you."

This enraged Adrian. He slammed his palms on the desk and leaned forward. "I did as I was told!"

"As you were told?" Evie's head spun with this new information. "Someone told you to kill Adena? Who?"

Adrian was silent for a beat. Then, quietly, but with obvious pride, "The moon. She came to me. In a dream."

Something screamed from the depths of Evie's unconscious, begging to be freed, but it was drowned out by Adrian.

"Read this!" He slid the Voynich Manuscript toward her. "Melcholm Perdito spoke of this book and all it foretold. Tell me what it says about the Obscures and the Callidoras."

"I can't read it." It was the wrong book, anyway. She smiled involuntarily.

Pain seared through her body; hot, unfathomable pain. Her veins were on fire, her blood boiled, and she was certain she would melt on the spot, draping over the desk like a wilted seraphille, drenching the Voynich Manuscript in liquified skin. It lasted less than a second — an eternity — then stopped, and Evie keeled over the desk, grasping at her body, not believing she was still intact.

"You're a Callidora. You must be able to read this book. So, tell me what the prophecy says," Adrian said softly, "or I will burn you from the inside out."

"The moon already told you," Evie said, catching her breath.

"The moon lied. Read it!" Adrian pushed her head down, his fingers boring into the gash on the back of her head. Worse, Evie felt his other hand, not on her, but in her, as his Alicrat clasped around her heart. She was terribly aware he could stop its beating at any moment. She'd done as much to a dozen rabbits.

"Okay," Evie whispered, thinking frantically. She stole a glance at Blair; her head was lolled to the side and one of her eyes was swollen shut, but she was still conscious, watching Evie with the other eye. "I can read it. I will read it. Just let me ask you something first. Please."

Adrian chuckled softly, his obscurity around Evie's heart loosening a fraction. "What could you possibly want to know?"

Evie chose her words precisely. "What happened in the last hour of my mother's life?"

The corner of his mouth twitched. "I cannot tell you what the last hour of Adena's life entailed." The twitch gave way to a grin. "It just didn't take that long." He watched Evie for a long moment, seeming to expect a reaction she did not give, before his eyes moved to the Voynich Manuscript. His grin became a frown.

"My ancestors sought this book for centuries, you know. 'Lost in another world...' Melcholm had said. Not all of my forebears bought that; some cursed their elders for believing the words of a hollow under duress and focused their hunt in the Northlands, the Iceisles, the Vastlands... Others took Melcholm at his word and spent their lives searching for evidence of this supposed other world, finding only a few scattered legends about vanished townsfolk or bewildered, hollow visitors from another land. Not one Tenebris came close to discovering the book's whereabouts. Until me."

Evie's heart struggled to beat under Adrian's grip. She was weakening. "Until the moon came to you," she said, prompting him.

"She chose me," he said, smiling. "She told me exactly what I needed to know, bypassing the need for the book altogether. 'A Callidora will be your downfall,'" he repeated. "At the time, I took this as validation of my own destiny. Destined to bring the Obscures to power. Destined to destroy anything in our path." He clenched her heart tighter. "Now, I must wonder why she lied to me? Why did she not tell me about you?"

"Maybe she didn't know —" Evie gasped.

"She knows all!" Adrian was angry again, no longer bothering to maintain his composure. "*I* should have known. Something told me it was too easy. Which is why, when I went to kill Adena, I used the opportunity to discover, finally, where the book was. There could be something within, after all, that would tell me how to keep the Obscures in power, how to rise to even greater heights! Or perhaps," he squeezed Evie's heart harder, "something to warn me about *you*."

He pulled her upright using his grip on her heart, creating an unbearable pressure in her chest, until she was at eye level.

"Your mother was not expecting me, of course. I subdued her immediately, and then I entered her mind. Not my greatest skill, in those days, but she wasn't expecting it and rushed to hide certain things. That only made them easier to find. Flashes of various locations in the Northlands that swallowed magenu whole. A young man tangled up in her bedsheets. Her curiosity when the man described where he'd come from."

Evie's heart tightened again — not from Adrian's fingers, but from emotion. She saw her mother crumpled in a corner, arms raised in pointless defense against his obscurities, struggling to hide the Callidora secrets.

"That man proved useful," Adrian said. "I chased him through her mind and found everything she held of him: conversations of another world, of strange contraptions and customs, and plenty more which would help me, years later, when I finally reached his homeland." Adrian considered Evie with sudden interest. "Do you know what I didn't see? You. She protected you. To keep something so important locked away under such duress... Well, take comfort in that."

"And then?" Evie managed.

Adrian lowered his voice, like they were having a private conversation and Blair might overhear. "When I left her mind, I found that parts of her were dissipating before my very eyes, leaving a nearly transparent shade. Her vivacity, the threads that made her *her*, were leaving her body one by one. I'd never seen anything like it." He shrugged. "It was far too easy, in the end. I clasped onto her heart, just as I am doing with yours, Evangeline Callidora, and I *stopped. Its. Beats.*" He squeezed Evie's heart in tandem with his words. "It practically disintegrated between my fingers."

Evie thought she was disintegrating.

"I left her body — what was left of it — on the floor and departed. Quite simple, in the end. Too simple, as I suspected." He frowned. "Alas, it matters not. You delivered yourself to me."

Evie's heart skipped beats, her blood slowed. She raised her hand to strike despite having no target, no single thread to slice or tie or tear. It didn't matter. She caught sight of Blair's face, her one eye wide with disbelief, before her vision blurred. The throbbing in her head returned, excruciatingly slowly, an indication of just how little blood was reaching her brain. She thought she heard a scream from the hallway, pained and visceral, and she thought of Marcus, then Charlie.

Charlie had been right. This was not her destiny, though perhaps, it was fate. Hers to die, Adrian's to kill.

Again.

52

DAMP AND CHILLED, mist clinging to his clothes and the birds' feathers, Charlie and the firebirds descended through the oppressive Maliter cloud cover, unable to see the land below until it appeared without warning. The bird that carried him came to a skidding halt and he tumbled onto the ground at the gates of the Domus.

He clambered to his feet before the enormous building. Moonlight gleamed over the edifice's smooth, black stone, so harsh and unwelcoming compared to Rutherford Castle. The gates were already open and he slipped through, leaving the firebirds to rest. The front doors, too, were ajar. Charlie peered inside. It was a vast, empty space, its floor and walls composed of the same black stone as the exterior with the same disquieting glimmer. He stepped inside cautiously, filled with dread, and saw immediately that his dread was warranted.

Bodies lay scattered across the floor. He rushed to the first and rolled over the rigid corpse. It was an unknown mageno, no older than twenty, with a dislocated shoulder and riddled with arrows. Marcus had killed the young man. Charlie pushed the eyelids closed. Obscure or not, he was somebody's son.

Nearby, blood covered the floor around a woman with no obvious injuries. It cracked across her face like dried mud, pooled thickly inside her mouth, and had been pushed around the floor messily, as if somebody had knelt next her. Somebody had — her eyelids were respectfully closed. The eyes of an elderly man with mottled bruises painting his skin were also closed. Charlie shuddered, certain some grotesque obscurity must have addled his insides.

Further on lay a magena with arrows forcefully pushed through her torso. Marcus, again. More grotesque was a decapitated head in a puddle of water. Droplets fell from its hair, melting from the patch of ice that still covered one eye. Then came the headless body, also partially iced over. Charlie did not dwell on which of his friends could have done such a thing.

Whatever transpired, it seemed the Benclairans had bested the Obscures. Burgeoned by this, Charlie scanned the perimeter of the space, trying to figure out where they would have gone next. He saw, then, one more body. A man in repose, arms folded over his chest peacefully, the way a beloved family member would be laid before their threads were absconded to what comes next. The floor beneath the man was wet, Charlie saw as he grew closer, so wet that the obsidian he lay upon glistened like a precious gemstone. After another few steps, the realization hit like a dull thud.

He sprinted the rest of the way. A mangled noise of disbelief escaped his lips as he collapsed to his knees. He touched his friend, recoiled, then touched him again, warm hands meeting cold, rigid death. Sorrow enveloped him, settled into his bones, and he knew that even if one day he did not feel it so harshly, it would never fully leave him.

He felt an arm wrap around his shoulders, heard Oleander's quiet voice. Charlie turned into his friend's half embrace and wept, worried that Oleander was the only one left, that Evie, Marcus, and even Blair lay elsewhere in the Domus, as cold and unmoving as Finneas.

"We were ambushed," Oleander said. The explanation came fast and garbled. "Obscures...four of them. Everything happened so fast. Finneas...he saved me, he jumped in front of me..." His words dissolved into heavy sobs.

"The others?"

"They went for Tenebris. I couldn't' go, Charlie. I'm a coward. I'm not made for…for this." He waved a hand across the Atrium and its dead bodies.

"Where are they?"

"Up the stairs." Oleander pointed. "Tenebris' quarters. I don't know how to get there."

"The firebirds are outside. Go, Oleander. Take Finneas back —" Charlie's voice caught, "— back home."

Oleander shook his head. "Find them. I'll be here. Besides," he glanced over his shoulder, into the shadows, "we have a prisoner."

A lump against the wall groaned in response.

Leaving Oleander, Charlie sprinted up the Atrium stairs and pushed open the door at the top with far more confidence than he possessed. He stood still on the landing, trying to find Evie with his Alicrat, just like those days in Edinburgh when he'd gone into the city in hopes of catching a mere thread of her. Minutes passed with nothing, during which Charlie was certain she was dead, until, there it was. That silver thread, tethering him to Evie, keeping him connected to her across years and prophecies and worlds and now, across Maliter's Domus.

Marcus stood at the end of the hall, face smeared with blood that matted the rogue lock of hair across his forehead. His eyes went wide, noticing his brother. "What are you doing here?"

Charlie strode to him. "Where is she?"

Marcus met him halfway and shoved him against the wall, holding him there. "Why did you come here?"

Charlie writhed against his brother's grip. "I've come to stop her."

"Leave!"

"I'm not —"

"Leave, before you get hurt, Charlie! Didn't you see Finneas down there?"

Charlie stopped struggling. Slowly, Marcus released him, and the brothers acknowledged their friend's death in painful silence.

"I won't leave," Charlie said, rubbing his shoulder. "Not until I have Evie. This isn't supposed to happen." He tapped his head fervently. "I have it all here, Marcus. All of Perdita's knowledge! Irrefutable proof that Evie is not destined to kill Adrian!" He paused, caught off guard by something he was not used to. Marcus was listening to him.

"We only heard part of the prophecy," he continued. "There's more, but it was broken up throughout the book. When read in its entirety, when considered alongside the full origin story, it points to something completely different. Something bigger than Adrian and the Obscures. Evie has a role to play, but it has *nothing* to do with the man in there!" He pointed to the door at the end of the hall.

Marcus' eyes danced between confused, skeptical, convinced. "What does it say, then?"

"There's no time. We need to get her out of there before she's killed. This is bigger than us. Bigger than Tenebris. Thousands of years in the making, and if Evie is killed, the next thousand years will be disastrous. You need to trust me, Marcus."

Marcus glanced at the door, then back to Charlie. He exhaled, shaking his head, and looked like he was about to step aside when he went rigid, arms pinned to his sides. He looked to Charlie, confused and accusing, but Charlie was trapped in the same way, arms rendered immobile by an alicration.

"You're late, Charles," said a voice from down the hall. "You missed the excitement in the Atrium, and it *was* exciting, wasn't it, Marcus? Your lot put up a good fight. Poorly executed, but that's what made it so interesting!"

The man who stepped into view was bleeding from numerous cuts, which made his familiar, sickly smile look all the more maniacal. Seemingly unaffected by the injuries, Sillen focused that smile, and his gaze, solely on Charlie. "It appears you found what you were looking for in the archives after all."

"What are you talking about?" Charlie whispered.

"Don't play stupid. You were searching for proof that Adrian killed Adena, weren't you? Your attempt to right the scales is two decades late." Then, casually, "Do you really think you stand a chance against someone with divine protection?"

It took Charlie a moment to realize he didn't mean Evie — he meant Adrian. "Divine protection?" he repeated dumbly.

EMILY BISBACH

This excited Sillen. "Oh, you have no idea what you're up against, do you? Adrian is protected, you see, by a prophecy stating the Obscures are destined for power. But also," he stepped closer to Charlie, "by the divine moon herself."

Marcus scoffed. "We know about the prophecy. You've got it all wrong."

"You mean the part claiming someone can halt our ascent?" Sillen waved a hand. "Old news."

"The prophecy isn't about the Obscures," Charlie said, acutely aware they were wasting time. "The power you hold now is coincidental, not fated. And the moon..." He wavered, scanning the shelves in his mind, unsettled that even after the onslaught of Perdita's knowledge, there seemed to be something he didn't know.

"Are you saying the Tenebrises spent centuries searching for that hollow's book for nothing?" Sillen's eyes narrowed. "That Adrian himself discovered how to reach another world, forced both worlds' frequencies to align, dared to make the journey and found the book, for *nothing*?"

"Sillen, we want the same thing, you and I," Charlie tried. "We want everyone in that room to live. Release me, and we can —"

"You seem to know quite a bit about this whole ordeal," Sillen said. "Tell me more."

"I'd sooner die."

Sillen rolled his eyes. "You mustn't be so dramatic. No need to die." He raised his arms before Charlie, concentrating. "I have other ways of obtaining what I seek."

Charlie had barely registered what Sillen intended when Marcus, arms still pinned to his sides, stepped forward to create a physical barrier between his brother and the obscurity Sillen cast.

Immediately, Marcus realized the extent of his sacrifice.

Seeking to siphon knowledge of the prophecy, Sillen's alicration bore into Marcus' mind with parasitic intensity. It took what little he knew, then continued to tunnel in an effort to find more, dislodging and destroying everything in its wake. Foundational threads that made Marcus who he was were torn away. Memories he had not thought of in years disappeared, never to be recalled again. Skills he had honed through decades of practice dissolved in a fraction of the time. The alicration pillaged and Marcus faded; pushed off a cliff, he watched himself diminish on the precipice, smaller and smaller, until there was no longer a self to forget.

Having dissolved a lifetime in a matter of seconds, Sillen quickly refocused on Charlie. But the alicration was now embedding Marcus' stolen threads in its master, and Sillen staggered beneath the sudden onslaught of foreign memories. His other alicrations faltered, freeing the brothers. Marcus collapsed. Charlie tackled Sillen, filled with a vitriol he'd not known himself capable of. He moved to pin Sillen, to strangle him, to kill him with his bare hands in the most wretched manner he could fathom, but Sillen writhed out from beneath him and partumed to safety, vanishing on the spot.

Heaving, Charlie hurried back to Marcus, who was slumped against the wall, staring at nothing. Charlie shook him, slapped his cheek, yelled his name. Nothing. Marcus' eyes, once glinting hazel, had dulled to matte. The charisma that used to dance around his irises like it let its own, joyous life had abandoned its post.

The empty eyes met Charlie's. "Who are you?" Marcus asked timidly.

Gone was the confident timbre that used to irritate Charlie when he heard it ringing through the halls of Rutherford Castle. He collapsed over Marcus, his tears sudden and torrential as their lives together, memories Charlie had not thought of in years, played before him like the old movies he once watched at a theater in Amsterdam, grainy and halting.

"Come on, little brother!" Marcus called. He was seven and already tall. "Let's go to the lake!"

The brothers raced down the hill and away from Juliette's cries that they stay near the shore. They did not stop running until their little legs splashed into the water. Charlie paused, his mother's instructions ringing, but Marcus swam on.

Not wanting to be left out, Charlie took another step forward. His feet sank into sand. He took another step. One more, and his feet did not touch sand, they touched emptiness. His head dipped underwater. He thrashed and broke the surface for one more gasp of air, then sank again. Marcus was there quickly, pulling at Charlie, gesturing for him to swim, but Charlie did not know how.

A creature appeared beneath him, a large, scaly thing that pushed Charlie up. Together, the creature and Marcus brought Charlie back to the shore.

Charlie did not understand how his brother could have done such a thing, luring him out like that when he couldn't swim! He burrowed his face into his mother's chest and cried as his father praised Marcus' heroics.

"It's a watermonk," Liam told Marcus. "Your familiar. You must have felt something very powerful in that moment to summon it."

"Charlie was in danger," Marcus cried. "I thought he was going to die. I couldn't save him!" He turned toward the watermonk, who was panting and wagging its tail, begging for appreciation. "I hope I never see you again."

The watermonk and the lake disappeared, and Marcus was thirteen, standing in the forest, aiming his bow and arrow. He released the arrow, which struck a tree at an odd angle. Disappointed, he yanked it out and broke it in half.

Without looking up from his book, Charlie said, "You just have to practice more."

"What do you know about archery? You're always reading."

"Books are more interesting. I would rather read."

"And I would rather play the piano. But Father said one of us needs to represent him at the Benclair Contests next year. Besides," Marcus reloaded his bow, "this talent will be useful someday. What good are books?"

Then Marcus was taller, broader, sauntering through The Fern with a girl on each arm. "It's true," he told the girls, puffing out his chest. "Father told me that someday, I'll be Arbiter."

Charlie trailed behind them like the second he always was. He didn't care that Father favored Marcus for Arbiter. He cared that Marcus always got what he wanted, and easily, while Charlie had to prove himself at every turn. Flirtatious peals of laughter reached him. He sprinted ahead and shoved Marcus hard, landing him in a muddy ditch.

And then Charlie was in his room on the last night before deciding to run off to the Other World, sulking after being berated by his father for not staying up to date on the political happenings of the Northlands.

Marcus' head poked in. "You okay, little brother?" He sounded awkward. Adulthood had widened the rift between them and neither knew how to speak from their side of the chasm with anything but insults and retorts.

"Come to gloat, have you? As if we didn't already know, it's been made clear tonight. I'm a huge disappointment."

"I've nothing to gloat about." Marcus sighed, joining Charlie on his couch. "Let me worry about Father. He's pleased with my Mensmen training. Finneas wants to join, too. You know he's always seen him as a third son," he joked.

"Must be easy," Charlie muttered.

"What do you want me to say, Charlie? Look, I'm sorry these things don't come naturally to you. I'm sorry Father is tough on you. But the way I see it, you have a real chance."

"I don't want your job, Marcus. I don't want to be Arbiter."

"No, a chance to do your own thing," Marcus said, exasperated. "Go study in Iristell or Teraur. Find that language expert you've been looking for. Just...do what *you* want to do."

It had all sounded so patronizing to Charlie, back then; the jabs about his books, the self-aggrandizing comments about becoming Arbiter. He never truly understood Marcus' sacrifice, never understood that his brother had willingly walked the path laid by their father so that Charlie could forge his own. He only understood now, as Marcus, empty and blank in a dark hall of Maliter's Domus, reached that path's end.

Charlie cried out, a profound, primitive wail that echoed down the hall and surely, throughout the Domus. He did not care. Another sadness settled into his bones next to the one brought on by Finneas' death, and a third unshakable weight nestled itself between the two. Charlie mourned Finneas, mourned Marcus, and mourned himself, for, though he never would have expected it to be so, a substantial part of himself had died with the loss of his brother.

53

STARTLED by the wail from the hallway, Adrian released his grip on Evie's heart. She lunged forward. Too weak for an alicration, let alone an obscurity, she reached into her pocket, grabbed the knife from Verstin, and sliced across Adrian's neck. Blood spilled onto the Voynich Manuscript, drenching the seraphille.

The alicrations over Blair fell away as Adrian lost control. He tripped toward her, one hand over his jugular, the other outstretched as if asking for, or expecting, her help. She yanked the hand off his neck and pushed two fingers into the wound. She pulled down hard, tearing a gruesome hole. The blood flowed free and fast. Adrian crumpled to the ground.

The door to the office opened. Impossibly, Charlie stood there, tear-streaked and trembling. One breath, two, then he rushed forward to envelop Evie, holding her as if she might otherwise disappear. Stiff in Charlie's arms, looking over his shoulder, Evie watched Adrian twitch and sputter, then abruptly lay motionless. He was dead.

Pulling away from Evie, Charlie's eyes landed on the bloodstained Voynich Manuscript. He stared at it, looking as though he wished he had never encountered it in the Other World, then snapped it shut, minuted it, and shoved it in his pocket.

"We need to go," he said.

"How did you get here?" Blair asked.

"Firebirds. Four. Oleander will take Finneas. You need to take Evie so that I can bring Marcus."

Evie heard the defeat in his voice, but it didn't register. Her mind had gone elsewhere; she was detached, in a way that felt profound, perhaps permanent. She'd felt Adrian's blood flow across her palms, warm and sticky between her fingers. She'd watched him sputter and stumble and gasp, watched Blair tear at his flesh with savage satisfaction. She'd seen it all, and yet, she hadn't. She'd floated off to a distant corner of her mind, and she was not sure she would find her way back.

"They took Stin," Blair was saying. "Did you see anyone else? He could be in the Osterre." She ran to the window and peered outside through her good eye.

"There's no time, Blair." Gently, Charlie pulled her from the window. "Dawn is breaking. We need to leave."

Blair under one arm, Evie under the other, Charlie walked them back to where Marcus sat in the hall, leaning against the wall casually like he was waiting for a friend. He was *there*, right in front of Evie, but when she found his eyes, he was not there at all. She fell to her knees, unable to comprehend what had occurred, even as Charlie explained behind her. She reached out — Marcus jerked away, then calmed — and placed her hand on his cheek. His brow furrowed, trying to figure out who she was. Evie whispered her name. His brow furrowed more.

In the Atrium, they found Oleander and the firebirds who, fully rested, had traipsed inside to comfort him. Upon seeing Marcus, he broke again, heaving with fresh despair that not even Blair's tentative arms across his shoulders remedied. Charlie struggled to organize the group, a broken army of the distraught and the grieving, the injured and the dead, and the prisoner, Damien.

Eventually, Oleander pulled himself onto the largest of the firebirds with Finneas' body, rigid and nearly unmovable, balanced over his lap. Charlie arranged Marcus, who was, conversely, quite malleable, and himself upon his bird. An unconscious Damien had already been secured to the third firebird with his arms looped around its neck and a makeshift alicration of Blair's invention keeping him in position.

"I don't know if it will hold," she said, but nobody seemed to care.

She helped Evie onto the last firebird, the same one that had carried Evie from Callidora. It greeted her with a soft tap of its beak and concerned, black eyes. "Hang on tight," Blair told her. When Evie did not react, Blair pulled her arms around her waist and held them there.

The firebirds ran, leaping over the dead bodies in the Atrium, and carried their passengers through the open doors and into the air. The clouds, low and heavy, quickly swallowed the black city below. Once in the safety of the sky, it seemed that nothing had changed. Despite the bodies they'd left in their wake and the bodies they carried back, Evie felt as though she had never been in Maliter at all.

It was a new day in Benclair.

Evie's room was still dark, but she could sense her sleeping companions next to her: Biscuit, wrapped in the crook of her arm, and Blair, breathing steadily on the other side of the bed.

She'd crept into Evie's room in the night to lay next to her. Neither of them had spoken. Evie wasn't sure if Blair had shown up to provide comfort or to receive it, but it didn't matter. She'd been unable to sleep, plagued with images of the dead and the sensation of Adrian's blood on her hands. She suspected Blair had lain awake, too, but once together, their ghosts left them alone.

Evie slid from bed slowly so as not to disturb Blair, dressed in the dark, and stepped into the emptiness of Rutherford Castle, Biscuit padding behind her.

The previous morning, their firebirds had landed at the stables where Liam, Juliette, and Serena waited. Liam and Juliette's relief at the sight of their returning sons was short-lived. Their grief and Liam's self-recrimination over Marcus' condition only increased when, frightened by the strangers reaching for him, Marcus recoiled from his parents and buried his head against Charlie's chest, his arms tight around the person his shell had known the longest.

Serena's reaction had been the worst. Her cry was not the loudest, nor the most anguished, but a quiet cry of confirmation. As the birds approached, she'd sensed Evie's detached stupor, Blair's exhaustion, Oleander's guilt, Charlie's stoicism, and Marcus' emptiness. And although she could see him on the firebird, she could not sense her husband. Only when Oleander laid Finneas' corpse at her feet did she weep, mourning her lost love but also the world she'd built with him, a world she was being torn out of, for it was not a world she could inhabit alone. Now, in the quiet of the castle, Evie still heard her cries as she tiptoed downstairs, across the courtyard, and into the stables.

She settled herself upon Nica, waited for Biscuit to scurry up her leg and into her lap, then they all took off to the west. She'd not told Nica where to go, simply trusting that the unicorn knew what she needed. Hours later, after the familiar Benclair countryside blurred past, Nica crested the hill overlooking the Silvana Seraphilles.

This time it looked inviting, and at the florens' edge, Nica trotted in without hesitation. She took Evie to a different part of the forest, far from the bones of the Obscures, to an area where the seraphilles were young, their carefree energy suggesting they had not seen half of what the other florens had seen in their time. It was comforting, reminding Evie that while things die, others are born.

Sitting on the ground, she leaned against a seraphille stalk and stroked Biscuit, who'd immediately curled into her lap again. She inhaled the forest, exhaled deeply, and the part of herself she'd detached in Adrian's office crept out from its hiding place to face how terribly wrong she'd been.

The fire inside her was gone. Somewhere between Finneas and Adrian's deaths, between realizing how divinely unprotected and how terribly incapable she was, the cloud of dissonance had finally opened and extinguished those delusional flames. Her selfish desire for vengeance had sizzled, away, leaving only guilt, a thick, suffocating smoke that burned her throat.

What had been the point of it all? Perdita, the prophecy, killing Adrian? Evie's head spun with cause and effect, choices and consequences, and she could not make sense of any of it. All she knew for certain was that people were dead and lost because of her blind desire, her blind belief, her self-serving conviction in the absence of proof. She cried, quietly at first, then loud and unrestrained until she had nothing left.

She sensed Charlie approaching before she saw him and Shu. She'd hoped he would follow, but had feared he would not. Joining her on the ground, they sat in silence for a few minutes, watching the blue seraphille petals blow in the breeze. Then, very gently, he said, "Perdita is dead."

Evie didn't think she was capable of any emotion erring on the side of positive, but she exhaled with relief. Perdita had moved on, and whatever came next in this world or the other, at least she would be safe.

"She knew she was dying," Charlie continued. "She had nobody to whom she could pass the Perdito knowledge. She invited me into her mind."

Evie couldn't quite believe what she was hearing. "What was it like?"

"Organized." Charlie smiled. "Incredible. Not without peril, mind you. Between you and me, I think Perdita could have used some therapy."

"So you know everything she knew?"

"The most important things. The origins. Alterra Lingua. Every prophecy, memorized as if I'd studied them my entire life."

"And?" Evie asked.

"I was right."

It was not taunting, not patronizing. If anything, Charlie sounded disappointed. Evie knew why — if he was right, it meant that something bigger than Adrian Tenebris and the Obscures awaited them. She was disappointed, too; she wanted it to be over. But a minuscule part of her, perhaps a single thread, felt hope. If Charlie was right, maybe there was still a chance to make it all mean something.

She straightened up against the tree. "What was missing, then?"

"A great deal." Charlie looked to the sky, frustrated, then down at the ground, running a hand through his hair. "In the cave, Perdita gave us an abridged version of the Second Sfyre's origins. So much more occurred between the sisters after its creation, though. Things which I believe set everything in motion. The sisters have names, by the way. Isolde and Iluna."

"Tell me, please."

"That's exactly what she wanted me to do," Charlie said, taking Evie's hand in his. "Tell you. Teach you. Let's go back to the creation of the Second Sfyre." He cleared his throat.

"Are you going to recite it?"

"Of course." He smiled, just a little. "After all, I worked so hard to memorize it."

54

FROM THEIR MOST high realm of the Alterra, Isolde and Iluna created the Second Sfyre as a sibling of the First — similar, but different. Isolde made the humans of the Second Sfyre dim, scarcely able to understand the world around them, let alone the heavens above them. They had no inherent Higher Knowledge, only questions to which they would spend their lives seeking answers to. With such great mysteries to occupy their time, surely, the humans would not succumb to sin as the magenu had.

Time passed, as it does, and the humans of the Second Sfyre evolved. They split into a myriad of cultures as their respective explanations for the world they inhabited diverged. Some reached enlightenment and found the Higher Knowledge of their own accord, building temples and great stone structures with their self-taught Alicrat. Most did not. Eventually, all would forget, anyway. And inevitably, the humans of the Second Sfyre began to exhibit the same traits that troubled Isolde in The First Sfyre. They fought and stole, raped and pillaged, tortured and killed.

Isolde was distraught that her second attempt at perfection had failed. More distressing was that her own sister, born of the same high energy as herself, did not see the Second Sfyre as a failure. They continued to argue, and when it became clear words would not convince, they began to meddle with their progeny — at first, to prove points, but eventually, just to be petty.

Isolde wove prophets to spread her good word, detangled tapestries she deemed problematic, and revealed herself to the humans who sought enlightenment, promising them everlasting happiness should they follow her doctrine. Iluna created diseases to plague humanity's bodies, demons to plague their minds, and whispered to deviant humans in the night, urging them to commit the atrocities they dreamed of. And when interfering from the Alterra started to occupy Isolde just as wholly as it bored Iluna, Iluna decided to descend.

At first, she went only at night, as she felt more comfortable in darkness, though she assumed a desirable human form that was beautiful to all. Corporeal existence thrilled her; she relished the feeling of solid earth beneath her feet, the warmth of the sun upon her flesh, and of course, her interactions with humans. She fell in love with some, despised others, and manipulated them all, not with her divine abilities, but with tricks of humanity's own creation, which delighted her. She preyed on their weaknesses like pride and greed, lust and envy, but she also admired their strengths — empathy, altruism, sacrifice, courage.

As she moved among the humans and magenu in their respective Sfyres, she became more certain than ever that the very essence of their kind incorporated both good and evil. Most were inherently good, but the capacity for evil existed in them all, whether it was acted upon or not. Moreover, evil as defined by her sister was not so simple, and many of the acts Isolde deemed unforgivable were prompted by the strongest pillars of goodness. Iluna saw this in the men who fought to defend their lovers, in the mothers who stole to feed their children, in the rulers who waged war to protect citizens, in the friends who lied to protect each other's feelings.

This, Iluna thought, would finally convince her sister! The nature of moral scales necessitated evil, but she was convinced that humanity's goodness would always prevail. Their creation was flawed and complex, yes, but then again, so too were they, the creators. She returned to the Alterra emboldened, armed not only with tangible evidence to make her case to Isolde, but with stories of the magenu and humans she'd met whose tapestries did not favor them. She wanted to detangle their misfortunes, to give them a chance at prosperous lives. It was something she and her sister could do together, she thought — something good.

But Iluna could not find the tapestries of those she wanted to save. In fact, she could not find any Ortus threads at all! They were gone, redirected to another realm she had not known existed and could not find, hidden by her sister in the ultimate betrayal.

Iluna raged and Isolde responded in kind. From high above in the Alterra, their anger wreaked havoc on the Sfyres below. Mountains erupted with their fiery fury, seas rose with their torrent of tears, searing heat and deep chills fluctuated as the sisters screamed and shouted from their invisible realm. Civilizations crumbled, buried under the shifting planes of their earths or swallowed whole by floods. Even the paths of threads falling from the Ortus were affected as the sisters fought, for their anger jostled the Aevum. Threads meant for one Sfyre touched the other, gifting those lives with the ability to move between both.

What occurred in the timeless expanse of the Alterra played out over millennia for the humans and magenu, yet they were resilient through these terrible years. True, the magenu forgot the story of the First Sfyre's creation and of the sisters themselves. True, the magnificent cities built by humans of the Second Sfyre were destroyed, reduced to ruins on the ocean floor and legends in a few imaginative minds. Yet both the magenu and humans survived the devastation caused by their creators. They would rise again.

Meanwhile, Isolde finally identified the fatal flaw. It was Iluna.

Her sister was born with a crack, Isolde decided, a defective emanation of the Ortus designed to test her. What other explanation was there? Iluna supported the evil that seeped through the Sfyres, applauding everything atrocious and vile! She opposed the notion of perfection. She ventured to the terrestrial Sfyres to inspire and partake in terrible acts. Isolde could not abide it any longer. She could not fix the problems of the mortals beneath her with an immortal problem at her side.

And so, in secret, Isolde created another world.

This world lay deep beneath the others, somewhere between the depths of the terrestrial Sfyres and the eternal void, impenetrable, accessible only by Isolde's light. And when this strange, obscure world that hovered between solid ground and empty space was complete, Isolde called it the Darkness.

Witnessed by a noble phoenix, Isolde struck Iluna with a deciding blow that sent her hurtling through the Alterra. She fell, a blinding star searing across the night sky, and struck the dual grounds of both Sfyres. This fractured the worlds, creating fissures of energy encircling both Sfyres, perplexing humans and magenu for millennia to come. Iluna continued to descend, into the Underworld and past Acticus, until she reached the Darkness, a place she had not even known existed.

She screamed with rage from her new home but nobody could hear her, least of all Isolde, though the grounds above sometimes trembled with the sound of her voice. Who can say how long she spent in fury before she adapted to her eternal coffin, alone save the roots of the oldest trees? Eventually, she learned to listen to the worlds above her, to find the voices that still spoke of her. She learned how to enter humanity's minds through the Somund, the only realm she could reach, masquerading as the entities that cultures believed her to be. There, she pontificated to those who worshipped her, terrorized those who feared her, and began the long search for someone who could help her.

She may not have started as such, but Iluna became evil incarnate, for only the worst parts of her could survive an eternity in the world her sister created. Certainly, over the next thousands of years, her last threads of goodness flickered out, far from the warmth of the sun as they were.

She remains there, to this day, waiting for Isolde's light to free her."

"Jesus Christ," Evie whispered.

"He's in here, too," Charlie tapped his head, "but we don't have time for Christianity today. You cannot begin to imagine the extent of things, Evie. What I recited still barely scratches the surface, but it fills in what we need to know, for now."

"It really is so much bigger than Adrian," she said. "Terrifyingly so. I...I didn't need to kill him."

"No."

"It won't change anything."

"Probably not."

"And yet..."

Gently, Charlie turned Evie's face toward him. "You can tell me, Evie. Please. From now on, don't be afraid to tell me anything."

"The answers I got were worth risking my life for," she said. It was a relief to admit. "Finneas and the others, though...Marcus..." Tears fell again, fat drops of guilt that never seemed to end.

"Tell me what you learned," Charlie said.

"Adrian didn't kill my mother for the Tree Book. I'd envisioned him demanding to know where it was, her refusing to tell him. It wasn't like that at all. He went there intending to kill her. He was told to do it, Charlie. In a dream. By the moon."

As she said the words out loud, the conscious and unconscious worlds in Evie's mind finally collided. A dark presence, hounding her through a forest. Stalking her across the Empty Fields. A cratered moon where a face should be, and then, a frighteningly beautiful face — the very image of corporeal beauty.

Tell me, Evie, do you believe in God?

I believe in God insofar as I believe the concept exists, but the concept is a human construct.

Evie's blood chilled. She had told a God that its very existence was a figment of human imagination. No...she had told the Devil.

I am a shadow. I am Satan. I am a serpent. I am the plague. I am to be worshipped. I am to be forsaken. I have been so many things to so many people, but at the core of all the parts I play, I am evil.

She had spoken to the moon, just like Adrian. The moon had given him information, false though it was. What did she want with Evie?

You can help me.

I will never help you!

You say that now. There is much you do not yet know.

The dreams spilled out of Evie, one on top of the other. Charlie did not react with the excitement he'd shown when they'd pieced together the meaning of Bosch's Pedlar or found clues to Perdita's whereabouts. Rather, he treated the information like more weight added to the burden he already carried. Evie wanted to shake him, force a reaction, pull the old Charlie out from under the mound of knowledge bestowed by Perdita. But that would be futile, she realized. He had changed.

All he said was, "Iluna has come to you in the Somund. I cannot fathom why. You are prophesied to destroy her."

"She's the evil in the prophecy?"

"Yes. What Perdita read to us was just a fragment. Its other pieces are scattered throughout the Tree Book."

"Why wasn't it all together?"

"Your story has been in the making for thousands of years, Evie. It's comprised of different groups of threads falling at different points in time. The ancient Perdita would have woven them separately, never realizing they were actually patches of the same quilt."

Charlie looked at Evie. His eyes were bright and clear, but pained. Almost regretful, Evie thought. He stared at her for a long moment, as if trying to commit her to memory, as if she was about to disappear before him.

"I'm not going anywhere," she wanted to say, but as soon as she opened her mouth, so did Charlie.

The day steals night away as the sun rises, lest it stay.
Dark is cast to isolation for fear of evil's true creation.
But ignorance breeds fury, pain. Light, too, can be hurt and slain.
Beneath the tree the dragon waits, cast there out of fear and hate.
Silently it coils its tail, counts years before it can prevail.
Snakes protrude from round its head, slither through the land of dead,
make their way to lively realms, to the lands that they can helm.
From below the dragon speaks, doctrine meant to lure the weak.
With a following amassed, re-emergence comes to pass.
Only one can change the path, stop the spread, foil the wrath.
When darkness does emerge, willing death will halt the purge.
Who, then, can assail with sacrifice on such a scale?
She is born into the night, she is a daughter of the light,
woven with the threads of sin of humankind and origins.
Trapped between two Sfyres, her truth remains unclear
Until knowledge can convince, gentle guidance from a prince.
Choices lead to threads prewoven, justifying all is proven.

She can halt old evil's spread, she can strike the dragon dead.
Soaked into the Tree Eternal, light and dark blood spill at Vernal.

Charlie pulled the minuted Tree Book out of his pocket, returned it to size, and opened it to one of the pages Evie had first noticed in Professor Atkinson's library, a sole stanza surrounded by gold branches.

"Here's the part Perdita read that pertains to you. But here's the rest..." He flipped to another solitary stanza within the gold branches, then another, and another.

"They fell into my mind in the proper order. When I found them in the book, I noticed that each part was on a page with branches. It's funny, I remember being perplexed by these particular pages as a child. I theorized they were connected by the branches, somehow." Charlie smiled ruefully, as if his younger self could have prevented everything from happening.

"So the beginning refers to Iluna's banishment?" Evie said. "She's the dragon in the Darkness, coiling her tail around the roots of ancient trees." She thought of Rosslyn Chapel's Apprentice Pillar and the carving she'd once admired, assuming it was nothing more than interesting pagan art. Really, she'd been studying her fated foe. "And the snakes slithering to lively realms?"

"Iluna's evil that seeps into the terrestrial worlds," Charlie explained. "'Doctrine meant to lure the weak' refers to how she's manipulated humanity. Take any great evil in either of the worlds' histories. Iluna has been in their dreams, pulling the strings of their psyches to do her bidding."

"'When darkness does emerge, willing death will halt the purge,'" Evie whispered. "Am I going to die, Charlie?"

Biscuit, who had been listening the entire time, let out a concerned meow.

"I don't know," Charlie said quietly. "It could refer to humanity in general. People need to die for the greater good, as we've learned."

"Or it could refer to me," Evie said. "Light and dark blood. Mine, from Isolde, against whoever is a proxy for Iluna. Maybe Iluna herself. Maybe she's found a way to leave the Darkness."

They sat in contemplative silence, listening to the breeze rustle the seraphille leaves. They really were beautiful, Evie realized, and she began to laugh. Charlie looked at her curiously.

"It's just...the ancient Perdita was a really terrible artist," she said.

Charlie considered the seraphilles, chuckled, but grew serious again. "Speaking of the Voynich Manuscript, did Tenebris tell you how he found it?"

"He saw my mother's memories of Richard describing the Other World. I guess he learned enough to navigate his way and blend in. But I don't know how he got there."

"Sillen mentioned something about Adrian pushing the world's frequencies into alignment," Charlie said.

"Like the wind in Finimund?"

"Maybe." Charlie sighed. "Another mystery for us to figure out. The last thing we need is Obscures forcing their way into the Other World, though more frequent travel would certainly benefit us."

"We're going back to Scotland, aren't we?" Evie asked.

Charlie was quiet for a long time. "There's more to tell you," he said eventually. "More to learn. Professor Atkinson could help us make sense of it all. And it will be safer there. At least until we figure out what to do next."

"What about your family? An Obscure retaliation? What about Marcus?"

Charlie winced at his brother's name. "Everyone needs to heal without me." His voice broke. "I always thought I was the dark moon of the family. If I wasn't back then, I am now. A self-fulfilling prophecy, I suppose."

"You're forgetting that you were right, Charlie. Liam, Marcus, me, we all should have listened to you."

Shaking his head, Charlie straightened up. "Anyway, Blair is keen to work with Father, for real this time, to plan against the AO. He's going to bring everyone in — the other Mensmen, the other States. That's not my place, Evie. It never was. My place is with you."

"We have to come back, though," Evie pushed. She couldn't abandon this world, not after everything she'd done to irrevocably change it.

"We will. With a way to defeat Iluna."

Evie didn't agree, not entirely. She longed to stay in Benclair with Oleander and Serena, Juliette, even Blair. She wanted to help them plan for the inevitable Obscure retaliation. She wanted to liberate Callidora. She wanted to find Marcus' memories. But there were others who could do those things. There were others to fight the war that lay ahead for the Northlands, who could kill the snake that was the Alicrat Obscura cult. There was only one person who could fight the other war, the invisible war, with Iluna. There was only one person who could slay the dragon.

Rather, two people. The daughter of light and her prince.

55

THE RUTHERFORD ESTATE was full again, but not with the carefree joviality engendered by the Northlands Congregation. Dignitaries from Teraur and Iristell, along with what seemed like all of Benclair, had arrived to mourn Finneas. The service was held by the lake, where Liam gave a rushed, official speech, an Arbiter paying respects to a fallen Mensmen. It was Serena's words that left the gathering in tears.

"I know exactly when Finneas died." She began so softly that the already quiet attendees fell into complete stillness. "There was a thread connecting us, invisible to anybody but he and I. One moment it was there. The next it was not. Nothing could disconnect us but death, and I had to admit, I was still very much alive." She smiled faintly.

"Why would I intertwine my life with another, knowing it was possible that sooner than is fair, that life could be torn from me? The better question is: why not? I feared losing Finneas from the moment I met him. Yet, I would love him and lose him all over again if I could. It would be a gift to do so."

Marcus cried as Serena spoke, silently, as were most of the things he did. Evie caught him staring at her sometimes, faint curiosity lining his face as if one thread of himself lingered, wanting to remember. But he could not, and he would inevitably look away, confused. He clung to

Charlie, too, looking to him for approval for minor things. He was not incompetent, but he was not independent. He knew who he was, but for him, that was just a name. The understanding of Marcus went no further.

Nobody was sure exactly what Sillen had managed to siphon and Liam fretted over Benclair secrets in the wrong hands. He enacted a flurry of speculative precautions, but the unfortunate truth was that nobody would know what had been taken until it was too late. Seely had tried her best to heal Marcus and even summoned Pembroke, but he, too, was flummoxed. "A blanket cannot keep you warm with holes," he said sadly. "He is threadbare."

"If we had what was stolen," Seely explained, "perhaps we could put it back. But we cannot mend emptiness. This is something I cannot fix."

Upon hearing this, Juliette hadn't spoken a word, nor had she shed another tear, not even for Finneas, not even as she listened to her daughter accept loss as a cost of love. She stared ahead stoically as Serena spoke. She stepped forward robotically when the congregation lined up to alicrate Finneas' body — Evie had been astounded to learn about the absconding of the deceased, a ritual in which every mourner, one by one, chose a thread and cast it to the wind until the energies of the loved one were returned to the universe. Juliette threw her chosen thread away as quickly as she'd plucked it, turned around, and walked back to the castle alone.

Liam watched her leave, his face a mask of regret. His son-in-law was dead, his favorite son was as good as, and his youngest was abandoning him again for the Other World. Evie caught him glancing at Charlie from time to time, looking like he wanted to say something, but was never able to find the courage. She didn't expect him to.

The congregation dissolved as magenu partumed back to their respective States or walked down to The Fern, where they would pile into pubs and toast Finneas over a glass of vocat. Blair stood next to Evie, watching the sea of people with her cold, blue eyes. Evie was learning to understand them, and lately, they were looking kinder.

"Oleander said you and Charlie are leaving for the Other World," Blair said.

Evie nodded. "On the Sun Day."

"When will you be back?"

"I don't know. When we figure things out, I suppose."

"Don't be long. The Obscures will take time to regroup, but we've started something. We need you."

Evie sighed. "Charlie told you about the rest of the prophecy, then? I —"

"I'm not talking about the damn prophecy. Or that book or that ancient woman. I'm talking about you."

Evie smiled despite herself. "You'll have your work cut out for you with Liam."

Blair downright grinned. "I'm looking forward to it."

There was a pause, and then, not knowing how to explain the need for her next question, Evie blurted, "Was it me or you?"

Blair looked up, squinting at the sun, relishing its warmth on her skin. "I've been wondering the same thing." Then, still staring into the cloudless blue of the Benclair sky, "I don't know, Evie. Does it matter? He's dead."

Oleander joined them. He'd changed, too; he still laughed, he still smiled, he still filled a room with his energy, but it was not the easy, natural Oleander Evie had come to love. He maintained a dulled version of his personality for the sake of the people around him who could not bear one more loss. Behind it, he was broken. Evie heard it in the laugh that no longer came from his belly, saw it in the smile that no longer reached his eyes.

"Ready to go, Blair?" He'd invited her to recuperate in Orefo, and to Evie's surprise, she'd accepted.

She pulled Blair into a hug and held it for a few uncomfortable moments until Blair softened and squeezed her back. When she threw her arms around Oleander, she caught the unmistakable scent of leide-berries, more concentrated and potent than the vocat they'd drank at the Congregation. A lifetime ago. Oleander had found an escape from the pain, it seemed. Evie hoped it would be temporary.

Illis came into Evie's room the following day as she packed for the journey back to the Other World. She, too, had been affected by the losses and moved through the castle like a ghost, performing her duties with considerably less zest than she used to. She handed Evie a wrapped parcel the size of a jewelry box, delivered from The Fern that morning.

"Thank you, Illis. Oh, would you leave this for Blair, please?" She handed her the John Lewis sweater she'd come through the portal in. Illis took the sweater, patted Evie's hand, then pulled her into a hug that rivaled the first she'd given her. She left the room without a word.

Evie tore the wrapping off the parcel, revealing a wooden box bearing a familiar motif — a Green Man — across its lid. Inside, nestled beneath a square of green velvet, was a watch. Its face displayed twenty-four hours surrounded by ninety-three days surrounded by four quarters. Looking closer, Evie saw more numbers, so tiny they were impossible to read. Her fingers grazed a small knob on the watch's side and she turned it, expecting the hands to wind. Instead, the knob pulled out, revealing a miniature magnifying glass with which Evie could examine the outer ring of numbers. They were years — a thousand of them. A tiny hand meant for the ring of years was coiled in the center of the face, like it did not need to be used yet. Turning the watch over, Evie found an inscription.

Time will pass, as it does. From Teller.

It was a curious, inexplicable gift, and it fit Evie's wrist perfectly. As soon as the metal back touched her skin, the hands wound themselves to the current date and time, then began to tick. The year hand remained coiled. It would start working, Evie assumed, at the right time.

She continued packing, folding up various items of clothing from Timpson's Tailors that she wanted take with her. As she considered the trousers she'd worn in Callidora Castle, an envelope fluttered to the floor. Clement's note. She'd forgotten all about it.

My dear Evangeline,

As I write this letter, you are three years old and a curious little thing. So many questions, so many answers neither I nor your mother can provide. I am sorry to say, you will not find answers for the next many years of your life.

It is a strange thing, knowing. Our entire lives, we want to know what comes next. Yet, as that knowledge is gained, it is rarely what we'd hoped for. If you are reading this at the right time, you will understand what I mean all too well, though perhaps, in reverse. You will have been wondering all your life not about your future, but about your past. How can you worry about where you are going if you do not understand how you came to be where you are? I wish I could enlighten you, either in my now or yours.

One day, this will make sense. It is difficult to recognize that truth in times of despair, fear, and grief, but when you close this chapter of existence and move on to what comes next, believe me when I say you will not have regrets. Your last breath, whenever that may be, will be one of complete understanding. You will know that everything happened as it was meant to, and you will be, at last, content.

I will see you soon,

Grandfather

It made no sense, and Evie hadn't the mental capacity to interpret another riddle. She tucked it away with Giovanni Fontana's note to ponder on some sleepless night in Edinburgh. With it, she packed Verstin's knife, now bearing Adrian's dried blood. And, she'd noticed latently, something else of Adrian's. On one side of the handle, carved with the imprecise but careful lettering of a child staking claim to prized possession, was Adrian's full name. Evie felt, inexplicably, that she could not let it go.

She spent her last day in Benclair with Serena, who was struggling to cope, not with the loss of Finneas and her brother, but with the unrelenting onslaught of emotional turmoil around her: her children's confusion, her father's guilt, her mother's grief, and Charlie's pain. His emotion was harder to sense than others, she told Evie. "He's locked it inside a room, deep in his mind," she said. "He thinks he can keep it there forever. You will need to help him."

"I can scarcely process my own emotions," Evie said.

"Yes, you can. You are doing it right now. It is as simple as feeling them. Learning to live with their threads woven into your tapestry. It is how we grow. Charlie is not doing that."

Evie sighed. "I don't know if he'll ever want to, Serena."

"You must force him to. You'll try, won't you?"

Evie told her she would. After all, everything came down to her, in the end. Nobody would have died, lost their minds, had to mourn, if she'd just listened to Charlie that night in the library. She didn't tell

Serena that, of course — she didn't need the burden of another person's regret. Instead, Evie hugged her tightly, kissed Milo and Nim, and promised to bring treats back from the Other World as if everything was normal and nothing was wrong.

Charlie and Evie departed that evening. There was nobody to see them off. Illis had bid them a teary goodbye hours before, forcing multiple parcels of food upon them even though they were partuming this time and would arrive in Ulla immediately. Blair and Oleander were in Orefo. Liam and Juliette had said their farewells the day before. Evie couldn't help but sense their eagerness for Charlie to leave so that Marcus might finally find comfort in them instead.

And so, when Charlie and Evie stood in the courtyard on the evening of their departure, hands clasped, they were alone. The affrim thrummed green — for tonight, the residents of the castle were safe. As Evie took one final look around Rutherford Castle, movement on the fifth floor caught her eye. Marcus stared down at them, timid and bewildered. He lifted his hand as if to wave, then seemed to second guess it. Brushing the shock of hair off his forehead, he walked away.

Nowhere near as skilled as Finneas at partuming, Charlie's attempt landed them dangerously close to Ulla's ancient walls. They went first to the Village Kitchen, redolent with the aroma of earthy stews and filled with residents enjoying their dinners, none the wiser as to what had transpired in Maliter. They nodded their respects to Charlie as he and Evie walked into a back room where Kellan was alicrating water over barrels of barely.

"Charlie, Evie!" He opened his arms wide. "What bring you back to Ulla?" Registering their demeanors, he dropped his arms and his smile.

Without ceremony, Charlie said, "Benclair is in danger, Kellan. The Alicrat Obscura cult has risen beyond comprehension in Maliter and has taken over Callidora. Liam will be working with Teraur and Iristell, but you likely won't hear anything, not for a while."

Kellan straightened up. "What do you need from me?"

"The Eternal Tree." Charlie paused, still unsure how much to reveal to others. "I need to know it will be watched."

"The Eternal Tree is always watched."

"Watch it more closely. It is imperative, Kellan. Dark forces are at work in the Northlands. Keep your eyes open. Be ready."

Kellan nodded slowly. "I'll round up the Old Wares."

"Anything suspicious, send word to the castle, addressed to Blair. Use a pixie, not a loquer."

Kellan looked like he wanted to ask more, but refrained, and they parted ways somberly.

By the time Evie and Charlie crossed the Empty Fields, the sky had filled with a million stars, twinkling down as they had for a million years. In the east, the moon shone with the reflected light of the sun, which still cast a hazy, orange-lavender glow across the western horizon on the longest day of the year. But Evie didn't look to the sky; instead, she stared at the ground as if she could see through it. Iluna was down there somewhere, biding her time, curling her dragon's tail around the roots of the Eternal Tree.

She glanced at her watch from Teller. It was one minute to midnight, and the door between worlds was about to open. Light burst from every branch on the tree, reaching all the way to Ulla and bathing its walls in a brightness that its citizens could not see, but that would transport Evie, Charlie, and the sun only knew how many other worthy travelers with open minds to another world. Hands clasped, they stepped forward together.

56

PROFESSOR ATKINSON, predictably dressed in a sumptuous velvet robe and matching slippers, sat on one of the squashy green couches in the Rosslyn Castle sitting room, reading an old book and drinking from a labeless bottle of what was certainly a very rare scotch.

Tap, tap, tap.

He leapt up, grabbed a fireplace poker, and whirled around. Charlie and Evie waved at him from outside the window.

The two talked over each other as they collapsed in the sitting room, their story tumbling out in fragments. Evie spoke of dragons and unicorns, firebirds and familiars, Charlie recited the history of the AO in one breath, Evie rambled on about Hieronymus Bosch and Melcholm Perdito. They went on like this until, overwhelmed, Professor Atkinson flung a hand to his forehead.

"For the love of God!" he cried. "One at a time, please!"

Charlie took over the narrative from the beginning, speaking for hours, during which Professor Atkinson remained, amazingly, silent. Evie explained what had transpired in Maliter, starting with Verstin's revelations about her father. Charlie jumped back in to reiterate the entirety of the prophecy and the origin story, at which point he pulled

out the minuted Voynich Manuscript from his pocket and returned it to
size.

Professor Atkinson slid from the couch, kneeling before the
Voynich Manuscript. "Dear God," he said. "Is it? *Was* it?"

"Stolen, yes. For the second time," Charlie said, nodding to Evie.
She produced Giovanni Fontana's note and handed it to the bewildered
professor.

"You were right," she said, smiling at his awe. "Fontana stole it from
the Callidora Archives."

"Then Tenebris forced his way here and stole it back from the
Beinecke, believing it to be the book of prophecies his ancestors
sought," Charlie said. "In a way, he did us a favor. I doubt the Beinecke
would have lent it out to a couple academic nobodies like Evie and
myself, but it's ours now. Well, technically," he added, "it's always been
yours, Evie."

Having taken the Voynich Manuscript from Charlie, Professor
Atkinson was now paging through it, mesmerized. "What in the bloody
hell is this?" he cried, reaching the blood-splattered seraphille. Evie shut
her eyes, but the page had already triggered flashes of that night in Adrian's office, his blood on her hands, his recollection of her mother's
death.

Was she dead, though?

Evie turned to Charlie. "Adrian mentioned something about my
mother that doesn't make any sense," she said quietly.

"Tell me."

"He claimed he killed her, but he didn't...eviscerate her. He didn't
use some horrible obscurity that left her mutilated. He didn't vanesco
her body or stage a suicide. He just left her there. Yet Naveena claimed
that the following morning, Adena was gone. Disappeared. No body."

Dipping her head closer to Charlie, Evie lowered her voice. "Adrian
said that when he emerged from her mind, he was startled by how much
she had deteriorated. As if parts of her were dissipating, and the threads
that made her *her* had gone somewhere else."

"What are you getting at, Evie?"

"It makes me think of what Oleander told me about displacement," she said. "That my mother's energy could have been nudged out of this vibrational plane."

Professor Atkinson closed the Voynich Manuscript, leaning toward Evie and Charlie to listen.

"Is there somewhere else, Charlie? Could my mother have saved herself in the most drastic way possible and displaced her energy elsewhere before Adrian could actually kill her?"

"Yes, Charlie," Professor Atkinson whispered. "Could she have?"

Charlie took a sip of whisky, winced at the burn — it wasn't vocat, after all — and looked at Evie. "What you're suggesting isn't impossible."

He took the Voynich Manuscript from Professor Atkinson and flipped to the page that had captivated Evie more than any other since she'd first laid eyes on a photocopied image in Edinburgh University's library: the foldout with nine circles. With the pages expanded, Charlie pointed to the circle in the center.

"This is the Alterra. The sisters' realm. Where, for a long time, the Ortus threads fell." He pointed to a circle above the Alterra, the first of eight surrounding it, and the next, all the way around the page, reciting their names and explaining their purpose.

"The First Sfyre. Our world." He smiled at Evie, then looked at Professor Atkinson. "The Second Sfyre. Your world. The Aevum, where the Ortus threads now fall, where the remaining weavers still weave lives. The Somund, created by humanity's collective subconscious. Then, the Underworld."

"Different from the Darkness?" Evie asked.

"Yes. The Underworld has an origin story all its own, created as part of a deal for a rogue mageno who became Death."

Intrigued, but focused on her mother, Evie pointed to the next orb. "This is the Darkness, then?"

Charlie nodded. "Iluna's realm."

"Hell," Professor Atkinson said.

"And the last two?"

Charlie pointed again. "The Afterlife. The origin story describes it as a precursor to the Alterra. The last stop before the end of the road, before moving on to what comes next. A place where you can stay for as long or as short a time as you like, where you can wait for those you love. When you leave the Afterlife, you must be certain, because once you go, there's no coming back."

"My mother could be there, waiting for me!" Evie said, her voice rising with each word.

"She could be," Charlie said slowly. "But understand, Evie, to be in the Afterlife, one must be dead. It is otherwise unreachable."

"What's the last world, then?" Evie pointed to the final circle.

"The most confounding." Charlie frowned. "In the origin story, the ancient Perdita could only guess at the motivations for its creation, and she wasn't even certain which sister was responsible for it, if either. It's called Abeyance, and it is described as the space that is nowhere and everywhere, never and always. The space with no time and eternity, with neither darkness, nor light, and both. A place to hide, to wait, to forget, and to be forgotten."

"That's incredibly helpful," Evie muttered.

"Adena could be there," Charlie said. "It's not impossible."

Evie flopped back into the couch with a yawn. "It's not impossible."

"This has been an intriguing few hours!" Professor Atkinson said, taking in their exhausted faces. "I can scarcely believe how little I spoke, a true testament to the compelling nature of your tale. I have so many questions, naturally. Why, Evie, this must be what you felt like three months ago in the library. We have come full circle. Delightful, no?"

"What about you, Professor?" Charlie asked, also yawning. "What did you do while we were away?"

The professor raised an eyebrow over the rim of his glasses. "I have continued my research into my family history, which I believed would remain firmly rooted in this world. Of course, I found myself crossing into curious territory once more! It seems I have a mysterious connection to your world that goes back thousands of years. But," he rose, offering Evie a hand, "that is another story for another day. As if we are in Abeyance ourselves, it is both late and early. I dare say you two need some rest. We shall pick up again tomorrow. What do you say?"

Charlie and Evie bid goodnight to Professor Atkinson and trudged upstairs. They walked toward their rooms in an easy silence that felt like the early days of knowing each other, blissfully ignorant of what lay ahead.

"I'm sorry, Evie," Charlie said eventually. "You didn't get the only thing you wanted. The truth about what happened to Adena."

"No," Evie said. "Once again, I'm uncertain she's dead. But the alternative sounds like something I'll never understand."

"What if you could be certain?" Charlie pulled Evie to a stop in the hallway, facing her. A bit of his old self, excited about an impending discovery, glinted bright green in his eyes.

"I have so much more from Perdita's mind," he said, rushed. "More stories, more context, more than I'll ever have time to explain. I must conduct additional research, parse through the information more fully, but...I think we can travel to some of the other worlds, Evie. Not the Afterlife, nor the Alterra, nor the Darkness, given that the requirement for entry is death. But I believe we can reach the Aevum and the Under-world, and travel consciously, together, to the Somund. Moreover, I think we need to. Not just to search for your mother, but to learn about Iluna. We need to understand who she was. Who she became. If we cannot, I don't know..." He raised his arms in desperation.

Evie saw, then, the root of the change in Charlie. It wasn't the burden of Perdita's knowledge, nor the certainty of further, deadlier danger. It was the responsibility of her destiny, the need to ensure she would be successful, at any cost. He'd already paid part of that price by relinquishing control and accepting, just as she would have to, that the rest of it might be paid with her life.

As if he knew what she was thinking, Charlie wrapped his arms around her, resting his cheek on the top of her head. She settled hers against his chest and they stood like that for a long time, not speaking, until her heartbeat matched the steadiness of his. Pressed against him, she couldn't see the silver thread, but for the first time, she could feel it.

It felt like home.

"Letting you go was the hardest thing I've ever done," Charlie whispered.

"Walking forward without you wasn't easy, either," Evie said. "But we both survived. There's nothing to do now but stay the path."

"Together."

"How do we even begin?"

Charlie pulled away and, arms still looped around her waist, smiled very slightly. "Ah, Evie. As Professor Atkinson said, another story for another day. Let's get some sleep first."

Sleep was just what Evie needed. She had to pay somebody a visit, after all.

57

Under a starry sky, Evie runs through the Empty Fields. The Eternal Tree shines ahead, glimmering and gold. The beautiful figure stands beneath it, examining the leaves with a look of wonder, waiting for Evie.

"Ah, look who has come. The daughter of light!"

"And look who is here. The mother of darkness."

The figure does not flinch; her perfect face remains resolute. "Where are we this time?"

"The Eternal Tree."

"You are suddenly forthcoming."

"You already knew."

She smiles. "I am familiar with its roots, of course. I had forgotten just how glorious it is above ground."

"Adrian is dead," Evie says.

The figure's eyes widen. "How disappointing. I would have thought he would join me when his time came." She frowns. "He must be caught up with Acticus. He does like to pilfer my companions. How did he die?"

"I killed him."

The figure claps slowly, deliberately, a terrible clacking sound. Her hands are just bone. "Well done, Evie. I was braced for your failure. Fortunately, you have proven yourself."

"What are you talking about?" *Panic rises in Evie's stomach, urging her to wake up and leave the dream in the Somund, as if it weren't real.*

"You have been so bright with everything else. Why does this truth elude you? Why do you not understand?"

"I understand. You manipulated Adrian, fed him a lie so that he would kill my mother. But the prophecy doesn't speak of Adrian, does it? It speaks of you. It's you who a Callidora is destined to destroy. Adrian failed. You failed, because I had already been born. I already existed with your sister's light coursing through my veins."

"Adrian did not fail. He did exactly what I needed him to do."

Evie is silent.

"He created a mystery for you."

A chill passes through the Empty Fields, an involuntary reaction of Evie's subconscious.

"I knew about you. Born into the night? I am the night!" *The figure spits onto the ground. The grass beneath her spittle wilts and dissolves into the Somund with a hiss.*

"Your grandfather made things difficult by sending you to the Second Sfyre. You would be no good to me in that world. What you need to do, you need to do in the First Sfyre. I had to lure you back somehow — what better way than with the mystery of your mother's death? Certainly, it was a gamble. I could not be sure the information would reach you in the Second Sfyre. I had no guarantee you would not simply live out your mortal life, never questioning your past. And so, I tried to find you myself, to tempt you back as a failsafe. I have been with you your entire life, hunting you across the Somund, glimpsing your world through the landscapes your sleeping mind creates. How thrilled I was to see your dreams taking on settings of the First Sfyre! So, Adrian did succeed, you see. You returned."

The leaves on the Eternal Tree are falling off, one by one. The wind carries them elsewhere in the Somund, to someone else's dream.

"My mother was killed so that I would return to discover why she had been killed?" *Evie manages.*

The figure smiles.

"Then why not have Adrian kill me too, once I was back? He didn't even know who I was. Why didn't you warn him?"

"You are little good to me dead, Evie."

"I am prophesied to end you! Why would you want me alive?"

"First, let us be clear that the prophecy means nothing without your choices. I thought that hollow explained this to you. The prophecy will not come to pass merely by virtue of your existing."

"I am choosing to fulfill it."

"I am counting on it."

Evie cannot find any words.

"Do you know how I came to be in the Darkness?"

"Banished by your sister."

"And what do you think of that?"

"Not entirely fair," Evie concedes. "But you made choices, too. You're not without blame, Iluna."

She recoils at the sound of her ancient name, unspoken for thousands of years. "True. Neither is Isolde. For someone who claims to be so good, so pure, she carried out a terribly evil act against me."

Evie cannot argue with this.

"You will recall, then, that I cannot open the door to my lowly realm. Yes, I can spread my so-called evil through those who act in my name. I can enter the minds of humanity's most susceptible through the Somund, but I cannot leave the Darkness. I cannot open the door."

"But Isolde's energy can." Another gust of wind blows through the Empty Fields. "I can."

Iluna smiles.

"I will never!"

"Ah. Well, therein lies the problem," Iluna says. "What is it your prophecy states? 'When darkness does emerge...' You have already surmised that it speaks not of Adrian, nor his Alicrat Obscura cult. That cult is only one of a million alleged evils that have risen over the years. Kill that snake and another will slither forth. They all come from me, Evie, like Medusa's wild hair. I am their head. I am the darkness in the prophecy."

"I know this, Iluna."

"Once again, the truth eludes you. Kill me. Now."

Evie bursts forward without thinking to wrap her hands around Iluna's neck. They strike air.

"I am not really here." Iluna's voice comes from behind Evie. "You cannot harm me in the Somund, nor I, you." The wind blows harder, seems to blow the stars out of the sky, for they are blinking out, one by one.

"You have decided to fulfill the prophecy, you say. You have decided to destroy the source of all evil. Me. Fair enough. To achieve your goal, we must meet on common, terrestrial ground. To kill me, you must set me free." She smiles at Evie's dismay. "You claim I manipulated Adrian to kill for me. This is true. Who will you be killing for, Evie? My sister has manipulated you through the prophecy and the precedent of goodness she has forced on humanity. At least I had the decency to meet Adrian in his dreams. Tell me, where is Isolde now to help her blessed daughter?"

Iluna waves her skeletal arms over the Empty Fields. Nearly all the stars have deserted Evie, the grass has blackened to ash, and the Eternal Tree is almost bare. A solitary gold leaf clings to a branch.

"You speak of choices. You will need to make a choice after you open the door. Will you kill me because it is right? Because it is written? Or will you let me go? Let the evils in the world carry on, knowing that goodness will balance the scales, as it always does? What do you believe, Evie?"

Iluna walks away, back into the mists of the Somund, to rejoin her essence in the Darkness and to wait, Evie supposes, for her to decide.

"Why me?" she calls out.

Iluna pauses, but does not turn. Her voice reaches Evie on the wind.

"Because you made the choices that led you here. Because it is fated to be you. Who is to say? That, too, is for you to decide for yourself."

She is gone.

Soon, the sun will open Evie's eyes, and it will be summer in the Other World. But for a little longer she remains in the Somund, alone, with far more questions than she started with.

ACKNOWLEDGMENTS

I always knew I would write a book. When I was a child, I could very clearly see my adult self at an antique desk in a European cottage, turning my imagination into words on a page. This future, author Emily was blissfully happy, totally self-actualized, and was getting paid millions to write stories. Obviously.

That is not the person who wrote this book.

I was living in Australia when I started writing *Born Into the Night*, and I'd just been rendered unemployed by COVID-19 layoffs. My relationship at that time was crumbling, along with the dreams and expectations that had directed the last decade of my life. I had no idea who I was and even less of an idea of my place in the world. To escape all of that, I created a new one.

A one-way flight and 300,000 words later, I finished the first draft of *Born Into the Night*. I typed the last sentence from my childhood bedroom at my parent's home with almost nothing in my bank account and even less of an understanding of who I was. Yet, this book couldn't have been written under any other circumstances, and at the risk of sounding dramatic, it saved me.

As I put my life back together, I realized that writing had been the easy part. What followed were four challenging years of feedback, edits, rejection and self-doubt with one thread of confidence holding it all together — though even that often felt like delusion. So, if I have that dark period of my life to thank for getting this story on the page, I have my friends and family to thank for getting this story to you.

Mom and Dad, thank you for your constant support and enthusiasm. For a long time, "It reads like a real book!" was the only thing pushing me forward. Thank you for always being there, not only for this endeavor, but for every chapter of my life that led me here.

Eitan, thank you for supporting my dream, for the constant, positive reinforcement in the form of "You're an author, *daahhling*," and for never making me feel guilty for spending entire weekends at coffee shops.

Judy, thank you for editing my behemoth of a first draft. You taught me exactly what I needed to learn as a first-time author — critical lessons that turned a mere story into a potential book. Your feedback in those early stages meant the world(s) to me.

Becky, thank you for taking that second draft from my trembling hands and for promising to keep my heart and soul safe. You were one of the first people to read what still feels like a deeply personal part of myself, and the care you took did not go unnoticed.

Billy, thank you for your genuine interest in this endeavor (during a job interview with you, no less!) and for reading another early, unpolished draft. Your excitement made me believe I might just have something.

Lauren, thank you for your unwavering enthusiasm, not only about my book, but about my journey. I don't know how you did it, but somehow, you called to motivate me every time I was slumped in a coffee shop, stuck and sick of my characters. You dove headfirst into the First Sfyre with me and stayed there for the next four years. I hope you never leave.

Christa, thank you for bringing your truly exuberant energy to this experience. You made me feel like I was already an author, like you'd just plucked *Born Into the Night* from a shelf and couldn't wait to share it with everyone.

Mollie, thank you for being my therapist throughout this process. You have a gift of helping people see precisely where they need to go, and I'm very grateful to have had you nudging me along when I needed it most.

Allison, thank you for connecting me with the people who would finally bring this story to shelves!

And Josie and Albert, thank you for seeing in my manuscript what I was desperate for the publishing world to see. Josie, you told me exactly what I needed to hear to take *Born Into the Night* over the finish line. Thank you for using your experience and wisdom to help new authors share their imaginations with the world.

Thank you to all of my friends and family who have cheered me on in their own unique and irreplaceable ways: Ben, Ceely, Taylor, Danya, Ashley, Ke, Melissa, Nadia, Bianca, Kristen, Regan, Jacqui, Gio, Becky, Becca, Sam, and Analisa.

Last, but never, ever least: thank you, reader, for taking this book off the shelf and reading it. I hope you loved experiencing the First Sfyre as much as I loved creating it. The idea that a complete stranger has read my words, let alone enjoyed them, is more than I could have ever hoped for when I first sat down to write. Thank you, reader, for making my childhood dream come true.